MEADOWLARKS

A NOVEL

By

Thomas Holladay

I0564025

MEADOWLARKS

First edition. March 26, 2021.

Copyright © 2021 Thomas Holladay.

ISBN: 978-1736914007

Written by Thomas Holladay.

Also by Thomas Holladay

The American Way
Deliberate Justice
Pursuit: The American Way

Standalone
Treasure
The Birthday Box
Meadowlarks
COMES THE CALL: For God and Country

Watch for more at www.thomas-holladay.com.

This book is dedicated to my wife, Wilma, and our daughter Michelle Trixie. Thank you for putting up with me.

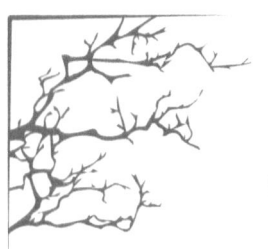

Chapter One

I tried to warn them but they would not listen. *The white man never listens to the Indian anyway.*

Outside my hut, men cried out in the cold night, running for their lives, the glow of their torches and lanterns rushing past, their guns firing from all around. Some of their bullets cracked through the thin walls of my hut, while I sat with my back to the door, afraid to turn and look, crying out to my forefathers for protection, raising my voice against the heavy weight of my fear. It already knew where I was, the dark spirit of that place, protector of the Valley of Wonder, the sacred valley of our ancestors.

Outside, the cries from the miners broke off one by one, some shrill, others in low grunts. Their gunfire tapered with each taking of a life. When the shooting finally stopped, his triumphant scream filled the air. The shrill laugh that followed sent chills across my shoulders and down my back.

A heavy silence fell over the gold camp, a time of breathlessness I could not measure.

The waning flames from my small fire rushed higher. A blast of cold air told me the deerskin cover over my doorway had been pushed aside.

It was there in my hut, standing close behind me. Hot, wet breath touched the back of my neck. It stank of fresh blood. I closed my eyes and continued the ancient chant of our people, even louder maybe.

I did not turn to look.

SOMEWHERE IN HIS NINETIES, not sure exactly, John Crow still remembered his great-grandfather's stories with vivid clarity. He and other children had crowded into his hut on the Washoe County Indian Reservation to listen to stories of the gold rush days in the 1850s. On cold winter nights, they'd turned their backs to the fire, somehow warmer, watching the reflection of the flames flicker in his great-grandfather's eyes, the way they must have looked that night, so long ago.

His great-grandfather's shadow from the open fire would sway and skip across slats on the wall behind him, a magical, fearful dance; a sharp, clear memory.

His great-grandfather had told of how he'd warned the miners not to use explosives to tear up the earth, and not to use acids to purify their raw oar. They were fouling the streams and river in this sacred place of the Paiute.

They had refused to listen to a young Indian hired to provide them with fresh meat.

The morning after the slaughter, the few survivors from outlying camps had looked at him with unjust suspicions. Why had this Indian been spared while so many of their friends lay mutilated and headless, frozen into blood-soaked snow? Everybody, including his great-grandfather, had packed up and left, leaving those frozen bodies for the wolves.

Maybe some had received a decent burial. The church cemetery had some very old, unmarked graves. Willis had never mentioned the old graves.

In fact, nobody ever spoke of what had happened only ten years earlier, that night when terror had again entered this valley.

John climbed onto his front porch, near the giant Douglas fir. On the far side of the valley, shadows crept up the face of the mountain, still some daylight, a good time of day for memories; mostly good.

It had been at the annual mustang roundup down in Reno where he'd first met Jethro and Mary Lou Potter. Jethro had asked John's advice on horses and had purchased all three that John had recommended. They'd hired John on the spot and brought him here to this sacred valley. He had not yet grown to full manhood.

It had taken a few years for John to realize where he was. He could not recall the exact circumstances of his enlightenment.

No matter.

Jethro had purchased the whole valley from the land office down in Sacramento in 1935, not knowing about the gold or about those early miners, the ones from John's great-grandfather's stories. That had been the beginning of the Potter Ranch.

In those early days, Willis Donner had been the only other resident, living up on the Perch, a high granite dome that overlooked the entire valley. The Perch and John Crow's place were separated by a fast-moving stream, impossible to cross from this lofty height.

Around 1940, Jethro and Mary Lou had given Willis clear title to the Perch and about five acres surrounding it, including a small lake and hot spring. Willis had already occupied the Perch since before Jethro and Mary Lou's arrival.

A year later, they'd given John Crow title to one acre, across the stream from Willis. The reason given had been, for services already rendered.

John could see most of the valley from his front porch.

Willis could see the whole valley from the Perch.

John had never felt the fear described by his great-grandfather, not once in all the seasons that had passed, not even after realizing where he was, not until that night ten years past. Since that night, fear fell over the valley with each coming of the full moon.

We must never forget.

John stepped down and walked out from under the overlapping roof planes of his teepee-shaped house. He turned and looked west, over the top of the sheer cliff into which Willis had set long redwood logs supporting the high point of his steeply pitched roof. It looked like a tepee.

Well, half a tepee.

He'd been angry with Willis at the time, thinking Willis was mocking John's Indian heritage.

Not Willis.

He swelled with pride, looking at it. It was a fine house. It perfectly fit the nature of this sacred valley.

Home.

The sun had gone behind the mountain.

Time to prepare.

The family of chipmunks downhill from John's house poked their heads out from their underground homes, saying goodbye to the day, chirping at one another, at the twilight, at John.

A hawk swooped down and they all ducked into hiding. The hawk rose on the breeze, floated over the tall trees near the house, pulled its wings back, and plunged into the forest. The shrill scream of a squirrel announced the hawk's success. He'd found his supper.

The way of nature.

John inhaled deeply of the pungent odor of wolf bane, those night blooming red flowers Willis had scattered about, thicker near John's house. They looked native to the terrain, same as his house.

White smoke hovered above the village, five miles up the valley, rising from the big wood-burning stove in Jacobsen's Emporium, getting ready for the night. The shadow of the mountain had already settled over the village, creeping down the valley toward the Potter Ranch.

Time to prepare.

John climbed back onto his porch, forever amazed by the craftsmanship, the tightly fitted stone and timber of his house, the stone buttress design at the bottom and the way the windows had been so tightly fitted. Willis had a God-given talent, appreciated by everyone but Kidro Potter. Kidro cared only for Kidro.

Getting late.

The full moon rising over the eastern rim stood in stark contrast to the darkening sky, the beginning of a clear night.

Early moonlight on his three-inch thick, solid oak door highlighted the pattern Willis had chiseled into it. The geometric, interconnecting lines resembled a bird in flight, a crow, perhaps, or one of Willis's beloved meadowlarks.

A chill crossed his shoulders, his humbling admiration for such fine craftsmanship. He crossed the threshold, closed his door, and dropped the heavy oak bar into place, a solid barrier against whatever might come. He moved across the upper stone floor and secured the narrow, thick oak shutters over the windows.

Nothing could get inside.

With his fortress secure, John grabbed a match from over his wood-burning stove and lit an oil lamp. He trimmed and carried the lamp down stone steps into his large living space, where he'd spread Navajo rugs over the clean, white-sand floor.

He set the lamp on a table Willis had carved from a fat tree trunk and knelt to light the kindling in his already prepared fireplace. Dry slivers ignited quickly, spread to twigs, leapt from twigs, and crawled up the sides of heavier logs. Heat grew quickly, forcing him to step back.

He fingered the well-worn Bible on the mantle and wondered if this night was from God, or from something else? He'd found no answers from this Bible, not after all these years.

He'd never been able to understand the nature of a night like the one now at hand; not from any sources known to him. His great-grandfather's stories lacked any explanation.

Over these many years, it hadn't come with each full moon. Even after they discovered it would take a young bull calf and leave people alone, it hadn't always come. Maybe it hunted in different places.

Nobody knows.

Why the residents in this valley hadn't left held no mystery for John. This valley was an unnaturally healthy place to live. A Shangri-La.

John knelt in front of the fire, pulled his medicine pouch from around his neck, opened it, and emptied its contents onto the rug. He studied the pile of small sticks, smooth stones, and tiny pieces of bone. After seeing how they lay, he swept up the pile and tossed it into the air, watching the bits and pieces fall again, studying their pattern.

Tonight, it will come.

The hair on his neck stood, with the feeling of an unseen, spiritual force. He threw his head back and lifted his voice in the ancient, melodic chant of his forefathers. Maybe it would help protect him and his lifelong neighbors.

Yes, even Kidro.

KIDRO POTTER SAT AT the dining table Willis Donner had built into the wide bay window that jutted from the side of the Potter kitchen. The wood framed kitchen had been built over the top of the stone-walled carriage house which had become his garage. Being so high up, the kitchen didn't need iron bars or protective shutters. From there, Kidro could see up River Road to the village and all the way around to his lower meadow, where fine, sleek, Black Angus cattle grazed near the brook that wound its way into the tall timber forest at the lower end of his valley.

Down in that forest, the brook took the runoff from the lower hot spring and emptied into the river. Just beyond, the river flowed strong over the falls and down to Pickle Meadow, Leavitt Meadow Recreation Area, and the Marine Corps Mountain Warfare Training Center. The Marines had never ventured into Kidro's valley.

Only a few big trees grew in his lower meadow, those that found deep boulders to hold their roots. The ground was otherwise too soft to support tall trees. Patches of brush hugged portions of the brook and tall grass covered the rest.

His young heifers and steers would be ready for market in another month. The remainder were breeders, sold to canned goods companies when they grew too old.

Every summer he let the Basques drive in herds of sheep to crop grass in both the upper and lower meadows. In return, each year, his family members had received a young lamb and a fine, handmade, sheepskin coat. The trade cost him nothing. The grass needed to be cut. His cattle preferred the feed corn he placed in bins near the brook. Corn produced better beef, anyway.

Yep. Kidro Potter raised some of the finest table beef in California. *In the country. In the world.*

He poured his second glass of Canadian Club rye whiskey, recapped the bottle, and sipped.

He enjoyed this time of day, sipping whiskey. With the sun long gone, the thin clouds over the western rim had turned pink, orange, and gold. Some might call this a beautiful sunset, those who enjoyed such things.

J. J. enjoyed these sunsets; as had his wife, before she got taken.

A little down from the rim and high up the slope, John Crow's house was already shuttered and dark. A thread of white smoke swirled and dissipated into the evergreen trees above the cliff. That stinking Indian had already prepared for the night.

Arrogant squatter.

That stupid, superstitious Indian was his closest neighbor. Kidro didn't have much use for Indians in general, and he'd never liked this one, a real know-it-all when it came to horses.

Across the ravine from Crow's, above the waterfall, lamplight winked through treetops from the Perch, Willis Donner's place. The glass reflected sunlight in the daytime and lamplight at night were constant reminders of Willis's so-called right to be there. Kidro hated that squatter the most.

Kidro's parents had always treated Willis like a favored member of the family, and Kidro had always resented him for it.

Kidro would never be able to get Willis or Crow out. That knowledge gnawed his gut near every night, looking up at their two properties, both properly registered down in Sacramento. He hated himself for hating both of them and doing nothing about it.

He squirmed on the cushioned bench and turned to look up River Road; still no sign of Nason. He drained the last of his whiskey and looked into the adoring stare of Scooter, his Springer Spaniel, sitting on the polished stone floor, patiently waiting.

He knows.

"Nason's always late, isn't he?" Kidro smiled at his dog's sweeping tail, back and forth across the floor.

"You're right." Kidro set the glass next to the whiskey bottle and stood, feeling soreness in his left knee where Gilpin's horse had pinned him against the lower corral rail. At age sixty-eight, Kidro didn't heel as quickly as he once had. He'd probably limp for a month, maybe for the rest of his empty life.

Stupid horse.

Kidro forced himself to walk through the pain to the kitchen door. He lifted his lightweight Levi jacket from a hook and put it on. He made it through the living room with only a slight limp and climbed three stone steps to the entry foyer. He dragged his heavy, black Stetson hat from the deer antler rack Willis had mortared into the stone wall before Kidro could remember. He poked the hat onto his head, opened his new factory-made entry door, and followed Scooter outside.

As long as Kidro lived, Willis Donner would never hang another door. Not on Kidro's property.

Scooter shot down the stone steps and rounded the corner of the garage before Kidro could shut the door.

Pain forced Kidro to use his right leg, limping down the steps, keeping his left knee straight like some kind of cripple. Climbing down steps seemed worse than climbing up. He hated pain any way it came.

That stupid horse cost too much, five hundred bucks and an Angus bull calf.

He wove his way up the rocky path through tall pine and limped out of the woods into his upper meadow, where stubby grass mixed with sagebrush grew in rocky soil. He followed Scooter up the well-worn trail, limping more instead of less.

No stupid canes or crutches for Kidro. He'd work out the stiffness.

"Stupid horse."

Scooter reached that flat stone far ahead of Kidro, chasing those ever-present meadowlarks, howling and baying until the swirling, yellow breasted birds filled the sky. The dog almost never barked, earning Kidro's constant gratitude, but he allowed it for chasing these stupid birds, always singing stupid bird songs.

Kidro had never liked noisy things, especially noisy people like Gilpin. He gritted his teeth, hating Gilpin more with each painful step. That was the one good thing about this sore leg. It gave Kidro another reason to hate Bruce Gilpin.

Always late, Nason's truck sped over the crest in a cloud of dust and slid to a stop near that flat rock.

"What the . . ."

Kidro's Angus bull calf stood in back, the one he'd just traded to Gilpin.

Broad shouldered and fit for forty, Sheriff Phil Nason stepped out of his four door Ford pick-up and walked to the back.

"Gilpin gave you that calf?"

Nason shook his head with a tired dip toward Kidro. "Pounded on his trailer for five minutes." He dropped the tailgate, climbed into the back, and untied the calf. "I know they were around. His truck was parked in front and I could smell refer, like walking into a hippy house in Berkeley." He lifted and carried the small calf to the back of his truck.

Kidro took and set the calf on the ground, gritting against the pain in his leg.

Nason climbed down and picked up the calf. "I found this one in Gilpin's barn, nursing from his milk cow. That idiot's got pot hanging and drying everywhere. I should just arrest his ass. If not for his wife and kid, I would."

"He's probably got a grower's permit. I heard his brother owns one of those marijuana pharmacies down below."

Nason set the calf on the ground, his wry grin admitting the probability of a grower's permit.

"You know how much I hate this?" Kidro followed Nason and the calf onto the wide, flat, blood-stained rock. The surrounding grass stood thick and green, a perfect place for meadowlarks to nest and feed on bloodworms.

Kidro wished Scooter could chase them off for good, knowing Willis Donner loved the stupid things.

Nason tied the lead-rope to the bronze ring he and Embry had installed at the stone's center, maybe five years back. He straightened and stared at Kidro, mystified. "Hate what?"

"Oh, you know what I mean; this monthly ritual. I hate paying any kind of tribute to that son-of-a-bitch, offering up a sacrifice like he's a god or something."

"Kidro, we both know it's not him. If he could, he'd probably kill that thing himself."

"Ah . . ." Deep down, Kidro knew Nason was right, but the hurt from that night, ten years before, seemed like yesterday.

He changed direction, getting to what he really wanted to talk about. "I'm thinking about reopening one of the mines." Not that he needed anybody's permission.

Nason thought about it, obviously searching for words. He turned and looked up the valley toward the village. "You still carrying that torch? You still need to do big things, prove something to your father?" He turned back and stepped closer, making sure to be understood. Hard to see his eyes, getting dark. "He's dead for what, twenty years now?"

"What're you talking about?" Kidro didn't need to prove anything to anybody. He could do whatever he wanted on his land.

"Isn't that what happened ten years ago?"

And there it was, everybody blaming Kidro for what had happened.

Kidro said, "What do you mean? We haven't taken out any ore since Mother and Dad bought those war bonds during World War II. Willis helped in the mine every day."

"Kidro, didn't you have this argument with your mother ten years ago?"

"You saying, I don't have the right?" He leaned closer to Nason and sharp pain gripped his left leg. "Not even Mother told me I didn't have the right. She knew I needed to make my own fortune, ever since Dad died. That's all that bothered her, not that I shouldn't aught to do it." He shook his head, remembering. "She always had everything all worked out." *Never needed me.*

Nason shook his head, disappointed. "Haven't you got enough, Kidro?"

"What good is all my money, if I've got no one to enjoy it with?"

"You never worry about consequences, Kidro. I'm the one has to worry about what might happen."

"You want me to get somebody else?" *I don't want that.*

"You can take it up with the committee if you want. That's how your mom set it up, so you Potters wouldn't have total control over who's the sheriff, or who runs the bank, or who pastor's the church and runs the school." Nason gritted his teeth and clammed up, looking steamed over this.

Not good.

Nason always protected the smaller ranchers but he didn't understand anything. Kidro said, "I'm tired of being alone. I need an heir."

"J. J.'s still around, somewhere. He'll come home. Wait and see."

"That night, when . . ." Kidro staggered backward and planted his stiff left leg, not willing to give another inch, but the words stuck in his throat like a sideways fishbone.

Shake it off.

Kidro said, "That night, after his mother and brother died, J. J. never forgave me. Then, after Mom died, when I fired John and Willis, he said he never wanted to see me again and left."

Nason put a friendly hand on Kidro's shoulder. "Yeah . . . well . . . Kids say a lot of things. I mean, didn't he cash out that trust your mother set up? I think he was out of the Corps by then."

"That was over five years ago and we've heard nothing since. I've been thinking, what if he never does come back? What if he can't come back?"

"What good will opening the mines do?"

"I can get some new faces up here, you know, interview some folks and hire a housekeeper."

"What's wrong with Bee Ralston?"

"You know what I mean. If I can get a nice looking, single gal up here . . ." He looked into Nason. "Maybe get married, have another kid."

"Can't you do that anyway? I mean, why open the mine?"

Kidro had no answer for that one.

Nason said, "I always thought you hated having anybody else around, that you wanted this whole valley to yourself."

Kidro had no answer for that one either.

A blaring horn changed the subject.

Down the slope, Gilpin's pickup truck turned off River Road and churned dust, climbing up the dirt road toward Kidro's upper meadow. All but the dust disappeared in the dip behind the crest.

Kidro said, "I told you he wouldn't like it." He spit at the flat rock. "I hate this stupid ritual." He hated the squatters. Without the Potter Ranch, none of them would survive a single winter. *And maybe that's the answer.* Why should he help them in the first place?

Nason squared his hat, badge in front, getting ready. "Gilpin's not like everybody else, is he?"

Gilpin's truck crossed the crest with a roar. Inside the cab, his round head jerked back, surprised by the nearness of Nason's truck. Gilpin's older Chevy hit the ground in a skid, shuddering to a stop in a swirling cloud of dust, not quite soon enough. He bumped Nason's lowered tailgate and put a crease in the center of the chrome trim.

Not seeming to care about Nason's truck, Bruce Gilpin leapt from his truck and waddled toward Nason, grabbing at his crotch like he had jock-itch or something.

Kidro grinned at the thought.

Gilpin said, "What do you think you're doing?"

"What are you talking about?" Nason pointed at his dented tailgate, angrier than Kidro had ever seen him. "You numb cup of sheep dip, look what you did."

"So, sue me." Gilpin stretched out his leg and scratched his crotch.

Jock-itch for sure.

Nason pulled off his hat and used it like a shield, holding Gilpin at arm's length. "I called you this morning and left a message with Sally. Just now, I banged on your door for five minutes." Gilpin stepped sideways and they circled one another like two Tijuana roosters.

Kidro smiled, hoping feathers would fly. He couldn't help it. Gilpin wouldn't stand a chance.

Bold as can be, Gilpin said, "I was up on my graze getting a calf."

Kidro and Nason looked to the back of Gilpin's empty truck. They both knew he was lying. Kidro said, "Needs to be a bull calf." He looked up at the sky and back at Gilpin "It's already dark."

"Why from me? I never understood that. We don't even live in this valley."

Nason said, "You attended our school. You shop at the emporium. Like it or not, we're neighbors."

"So, I shop at the store. So what? It's a store."

Kidro said, "You use my bank and you drive on my roads."

Gilpin turned on Kidro, eager to tumble in the dust with a much older man. "I just traded you Stoner for that calf. My bull's getting old and impotent. I need that calf."

Stupid. "You should have thought of that before you cut your young bulls." Kidro stepped forward, angry enough to smack Gilpin's fat face.

Gilpin lunged.

Nason deftly slid between them and grabbed Gilpin's arm, blocking his attempted punch at Kidro. "It's getting late." Nason forcibly shoved Gilpin toward his truck.

Gilpin craned over the top of Nason and shouted, "I'm not giving it up! Not to no grizzly, I'm not. I got my rifle in my truck. I'll kill it myself."

"Been tried," said Kidro, thinking about ten years past, thinking about himself and both of his sons shooting it all those times. ". . . by better men than you."

Still controlling Gilpin, Nason said, "The Village Committee will take care of it, Bruce. Get back in your truck and go home."

Gilpin ripped free.

Nason used his hat again, steadily herding Gilpin toward the trucks. After a couple of quick sidesteps, blocking Gilpin, Nason opened the door to Gilpin's truck, ushered him inside, and closed the door.

Gilpin started his truck and slowly backed away, impossible to read his face in the dark. The fool might be planning something stupid.

Kidro didn't care.

"What a pud!" Nason propped his hat on the back of his head and fingered his dented tailgate.

Kidro said, "Yeah, those Gilpins are a brood apart."

Nason chuckled and closed his tailgate with care, no damage to the hinges. He shook his head, pulled off his hat, and climbed into the driver's seat. He started his truck, smiled, turned on his headlights, and slowly backed away.

Kidro turned for home, snapped his fingers, and Scooter followed.

Those stupid birds rose above the treetops. Their swirling blur nearly blocked the light from the rising moon.

GILPIN SMOKED A JOINT and waited on the other side of River Road, backed under the low, wide-spread branches of a giant sequoia, hoping Nason wouldn't see his truck. He couldn't let those two pull this kind of scam on him.

Not today. Not this Gilpin.

Those two wimps were afraid to deal with a dumb animal. He took a hit from the fat, sweet tasting marijuana cigarette and set it in the ashtray.

There.

Nason's headlights moved slowly down the dirt road from Potter's upper meadow. He turned right onto River Road and sped toward the village.

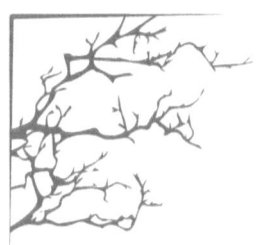

Chapter Two

Barnabas, Jason Potter's American Pit Bull Terrier, lay on the corner of Jason's bed, watching Jason. Except for the brindle patches on his head, Barnabas was pure white.

Jason's ninth birthday would be on November 11, barely more than a month away. Barnabas had been born on November 14. He'd be four. Barnabas and Jason always celebrated their birthdays together.

Sitting at his desk in the corner of his bedroom, Jason had been working on his latest sketch of Barnabas for nearly an hour, the sketchpad propped against his elevated knee where he could study his pencil strokes, feathering and shading. The overall shape of his dog's muscled head and shoulders looked okay, but he needed more detail. The brindle patches around his eyes took time. All those wrinkles changed with his constantly changing expressions. Barnabas had mostly light-blue eyes with tiny spears of dark green, really tricky with a pencil sketch. Jason needed to take his time on the eyes.

Barnabas stared back at him, his un-clipped ears perked, nice and still. Jason squirmed into a more comfortable position, studying the brindle patches around his eyes. He feathered in one of the deep creases over the left eye and darkened the center, a good start.

His mom poked her head into his bedroom and asked, "Did you read tomorrow's chapters yet?" She stepped all the way in and noticed the drawing. "You'd better not let your grandmother see that. You know how she feels about your artwork."

"Uh huh." Jason's grandmother had no use for artists, not since chasing off Jason's grandpa when his mom was still in high school, since long before Jason was born. Jason had to keep all his sketches, drawings, and water colors hidden because of living in grandma's house. He put the sketchpad into a drawer and closed it, bent down, pulled his school binder from his backpack on the floor, and handed it to his mom.

She scanned the printed notes from his desktop computer and Jason turned the computer back on, waiting for her inevitable corrections. She always made him read the material before class, read it again to highlight the important information, go to his computer, and print out notes from his highlights. After all of that, his printed notes went into his binder. That way, Jason could listen to his teacher and only take notes for stuff not found in his books. It was a good system. He could draw in class using his secret sketchpad. Not even his mom knew about that one. He still listened to every word from his teacher, waiting to hear something new so he could write it down in the notebook.

Sometimes he got caught and got into trouble, like once when the teacher threw a whiteboard eraser, hit Jason's head, and asked him about the capital of California. They'd been studying about state government. Jason had told her it was Sacramento. He'd not only learned that from the text book but she'd just finished talking about it.

Ms. Martinez said, "You get up here right now, young man," pointing at the floor in front of the whiteboard. When Jason got there, she'd said, "Draw a circle on the whiteboard."

Jason knew where to draw the circle. He'd been there before.

"Put your nose in it."

Jason stood at the front of the class with his nose stuck to the whiteboard, listening to Ms. Martinez tell the class how stupid he was and how he would never amount to anything, if he didn't stop drawing in class and learn to listen better.

Jason still wondered why she thought he could listen better with his nose stuck to the whiteboard like that.

He got good marks in everything but attentiveness and attitude. How could he get good marks without paying attention? How could he get good marks with a bad attitude?

She's crazy.

He never caused any trouble, not like Jimmy and some of the other kids. They were always cracking off and shooting spit wads at each other.

Mom never discouraged his artwork but she made sure his schoolwork came first. That was most important.

When Mom looked at his third page of printed notes, her eyes shot up and looked all the way through him, scolding the inside of his brain.

How does she do that?

"Jason, there are no letters *i* in Sacramento. Check the textbook spelling, make your correction, and print out the third page again."

"Okay." He took the binder from his mom and pulled the social studies book out of his backpack.

"What about your math?"

"Oh, yeah." He pulled his math workbook from his backpack and handed it to her. While she checked his algebra, he found and corrected his spelling of Sacramento, saved the work, hit the print command, and printed the new sheet on three-hole paper. He tore out the bad sheet and threw it away, clipped the new sheet into his binder, and put the binder into his backpack, next to his secret sketchpad.

"You're very good at math, just like your father." She handed back his work-book. "Supper's on the table."

Hearing her words, knowing that Jason was going into another room, Barnabas bounded off the bed and followed Jason's mom.

Jason turned off his computer and followed his dog into the dining room. The aroma of Chinese food brought a smile. "Oh boy, sweet and sour's my favorite."

"Go wash your hands, first." His mom sat and opened one of the cartons.

Jason turned into the kitchen and found that the footstool had been set in front of the sink, again, a habit his mom couldn't break. Being almost nine, Jason didn't need a stool anymore. He pushed the stool aside with his foot and leaned into the sink to wash up.

He returned to the dining room where his mom had already dished up some beef with broccoli and fried rice for both of them. An empty plate had been set at the head of the table, nearest the kitchen. That was Grandma's place. Jason sat opposite his mom and both bowed their heads. She said, "Thank you, Lord, for Thy wonderful blessings and amazing grace. Bless this house and all who are in it, bless this food that it might nourish us, and bless us that we might better serve Thee."

They both said, "Amen," and Jason waited for his mom to take the first bite. That was one of the things he remembered about his father. After saying grace, he'd always waited for her and Jason to start. She bit into a piece of broccoli and smiled at him. She liked it.

Jason didn't mind broccoli so much, but he liked the beef better. He didn't care for broccoli the way his grandma cooked it, but when it came in Chinese food, it tasted good. "Umm." He sucked the juices off a chunk of beef before choking it down.

"Chew your food, honey. Remember what your father said. You can choke to death if you don't chew your food properly."

Barnabas bolted from under the table and charged into the living room. He bumped and nosed the bottom of the door, spun, and nosed the living-room curtain aside to look out the window.

Headlights flashed on the curtain and Jason's mood slumped. His grandma's car had just turned into the driveway. He sank into his chair and pushed his food around his plate with a fork. His appetite had vanished.

Grandma always changed everybody's mood. His mom smiled that forced smile, winked, and pointed with her fork. He needed to eat while the eating was good.

Too late.

His grandma marched inside and closed the front door.

Barnabas grumbled, wagging and pressing sideways into her legs, saying hello.

Grandma glared down at his dog. "Get this mutt away from me."

Barnabas stepped back, sat, and moaned, demanding her affection. He patiently watched her pull out a pack of Winston cigarettes, her butane lighter, deposit the purse on a side table, take out a cigarette, and light it. After blowing smoke in Barnabas's face, she patted his head. She liked Jason's dog but she hated showing it. She took a couple of puffs, marched into the dining room, and stopped to inspect the food on the table. She glared down at Mom, daring her to say something.

Mom said nothing. Both she and Jason knew what was coming.

"Carolyn, if you insist on poisoning yourself, there's nothing to be done about it. You're thirty-two years old. But, why you insist on poisoning my grandson is beyond all reason."

Mom always sounded like she was whining, fearing she and Jason might be asked to move. She stared at her food and said, "Why do we always have to go through this? You know John and I wanted Jason to eat a balanced diet." Mom's eyes lifted enough to focus on Jason, showing him all that love in there.

Grandma deliberately blew smoke into Mom's face.

Mom wasn't afraid of anybody except Grandma. Everything with Grandma was a struggle. Pasting on a smile and forcing her happy voice, Mom said, "Look, Mom, I got you some Chinese veggies."

Momentarily frustrated but never defeated, Grandma set her pack of cigarettes and lighter on the table and snatched a clean ashtray from the breakfast counter. She set the ashtray on the table, dragged out her chair, plopped into it, and took a long pull from her cigarette. After blowing smoke over the top of Jason's head, she flicked ashes and set her cigarette into the ashtray.

She dished up some fried rice, grabbed her fork, and pushed the rice around her plate, searching for bits of meat that were never there. Satisfied, she opened and examined the carton of Chinese vegetables before spooning some over the top of her rice. She set the carton down, picked up her cigarette, took a puff, blew smoke at Mom, flicked ashes, and returned the half-smoked cigarette to the ashtray.

"Phew!" Jason gagged and waved off smelly smoke before chomping into a piece of broccoli.

"That's right, Jason." Grandma stirred vegetables into her rice, glancing back and forth at Jason. "Eat your broccoli. At least that's good for you." She looked down her long nose at Jason, probably thinking her all knowing eyes were teaching him something words couldn't teach. She was so sure of herself. "Dark green vegetables are the ones that do your brain the most good."

He couldn't count how many times he'd heard that.

She had a way of ruining everything, but she was his grandma. He was supposed to love her.

"Sweet and sour pork is my favorite." Saying that surprised Jason but he didn't know why. After all, it was a simple fact. He held up his empty plate so Mom could dish some up.

She spooned more fried rice onto his plate and opened the carton of sweet and sour pork. It smelled delicious.

"Carolyn! My God!"

"Mom, please." Mom dipped her head and slightly turned away, not wanting to argue with Grandma. She spooned a healthy portion of sweet and sour pork onto Jason's plate. After making sure he had enough, Jason set his plate back down and picked up his fork.

"Umm." Jason chewed on a tender piece of pork, smiling maliciously at Grandma.

She looked sideways at him, puffing angrily on her nearly exhausted cigarette, thinking what to say. With confidence growing in those mean, all knowing eyes, she stumped out the cigarette and lit another. She took a long puff, placed the cigarette in the ashtray, and let smoke flow out with her words. "Pork! My God!"

Mom smiled at Jason, knowing Grandma would pounce when she said, "Mom, even the Bible says we can eat meat."

Grandma slammed her fork down so hard Jason looked to see if she'd broken her plate. She said, "There you go again, with that other poison. If it isn't the meat, it's your superstitious mumbo jumbo. I don't know why you married that man, anyway. What happened to his big endowment? Tell me that. What happened with that big investment he said he made? Tell me that."

"Mom, we've been all through this."

"Oh, right." Grandma's eyes rolled back into her head, then she slammed her stare back into Mom. "He left all that stuff in his office; only Tom Kirby didn't find anything. That's who you should have married. He's a fine young man with a wonderful future. He comes from a good family. I wouldn't need to worry about my own future, if you'd only married him."

Mom's face flushed red and her eyes popped wide open. For once, she turned to face Grandma. "Is that what this is about, Mom, your future?"

Jason wanted to jump up and hug her.

"No!" Grandma stared right back. "We were talking about the poison you're pouring into my grandson. Your husband taught you that religious bunk and look what it got him."

Jason's anger jumped up from the pit of his stomach. He wanted to punch his grandma in her smoke spewing face. "You think my father got killed because he believed in Jesus?"

Grandma grabbed her cigarette, threw him an angry glare, took a long puff, then another, thinking what to say. She relaxed a little and let smoke flood from her nostrils. "I think your father's religion didn't help him when those thieves shot him and took his car." Confidence restored, she took another puff, blew smoke into Jason's face, and thrust her cigarette back into the ashtray. She took a bite of vegetables, raised her eyebrows at him, and asked, "So, what new and exciting things did you learn in school today?" She took another bite of vegetables and waited.

A rush of fear curled Jason's toes. He stared down at his food and squirmed in his chair, feeling her head drop toward him, like a cobra ready to strike. She asked, "They didn't catch you drawing again, did they?"

Jason's mom jumped in, protecting Jason. "Mom, please. Let him eat his dinner."

Grandma took an angry puff, blew smoke into Mom's face, and said, "You need to put a stop to his artistic notions, once and for all. The life of an artist is no life for a young man in this day and age."

"Why, because my father was an artist?" Mom was angry enough for a real fight.

Feeling ashamed and kind of responsible, wanting to do what he could to keep the peace, Jason said, "They showed us how to put a con . . . conde . . ."

Grandma's serpent stare snapped back to Jason. "Condom?"

"Huh." A flow of relief allowed Jason to fork a slice of pineapple into his mouth. It tasted delicious.

"Well?" The serpent's head moved closer and waited.

He swallowed the pineapple whole and coughed a little, clearing his throat. "Oh, yeah. They showed us how to put it on a cucumber."

Grandma grinned with some kind of weird, personal satisfaction and blew smoke toward the ceiling light. "Good for you. Now you won't be getting any girls into trouble."

"Huh?" What could a cucumber do to a girl? How could a condom keep her out of trouble? "What trouble?"

"Mom, he's only eight years old."

Jason said, "Eight and three quarters, going on nine." After all, being nine was important. It meant he'd be half a grown-up, half ready to vote for the president, and half ready to join the Marine Corps, same as his father.

Grandma looked satisfied with herself, blowing smoke into Mom's face. "You're never too young to learn about nature."

KIDRO POTTER LEANED against the hewn stone mantle above his Inglenook fireplace and watched the dance of the flames, letting the heat soak into the marrow of his bones. He'd propped his sore left knee in exactly the right place, getting hot.

Scooter lay at his feet, sleeping in the warmth. At this elevation, even in summer, the High Sierras got cold at night.

He reached up to the mantle, pulled down his tumbler, and sipped rye whiskey, feeling pretty good all over, thinking that Nason might be right. Maybe J. J. would come home. He'd loved it here as a boy, as had Kidro's wife and their other son. Then came that night, ten long years ago.

Strange. Kidro had never appreciated this place. He'd never appreciated his wife and kids. He'd never appreciated his mother and father, not until after their deaths. Even missing his family, he still didn't give a whiff about this place. With his money, he could go anywhere; the French Riviera, Miami Beach, Malibu, Tahiti, anywhere with some decent weather.

That familiar anger welled from deep within, his feeling of being abandoned. A quirk of fate had stolen them all away and this place had become his prison. His thinking never dwelled on how they died, or why. After that night, after they'd been taken, J. J., Kidro's pride and joy, had walked away and had never come back. It had then taken him two whole weeks to recognize his loneliness. Without J. J., Kidro's existence had become an empty hat.

Kidro hated this emptiness. *Well...* For the first time, he realized that hate had replaced the emptiness.

Fine.

The sliver of emptiness that remained reached out for J. J. He must still be alive. He had to be. Otherwise, Kidro would have heard something.

Everybody in this valley had loved J. J., the same way they'd loved Kidro's mother and father. Those same people had never liked Kidro.

Why?

Anger and bitterness had filled Kidro for the past ten years, anger that his only living relative no longer wanted to know him. His favorite person in the world had walked out of his life. His youngest son and only living heir had walked away.

Kidro's bitterness had grown. Bitterness over all of this valley's squatters. His parents had given too much of his valley to others and they had never shown him a lick of gratitude.

Gilpin! That stupid...

"Ah..." He spit into the fire and watched it puff to steam.

Since the death of his mother, all of these squatters had treated Kidro like the outsider. They'd all seen something special in J. J., maybe the way he'd loved everything and everybody. His love for others had never changed. Kidro had to acknowledge that. J. J. had inherited that life-changing love from his grandmother, Kidro's mother.

Funny. When J. J. was with him, they'd all seemed to like Kidro too.

I miss that.

How could J. J. just up and leave?

"Ah!" *Forget about it.*

He tossed back the remaining rye, refilled the tumbler, and noticed that the bottle was half empty.

J. J. would have insisted it was half full, as if it made a difference.

That night, ten long years in his past, when Kidro and Ethan took their shots, when J. J. chopped that thing up with his axe and took off its front leg, it had run off into the thickest part of the forest, down near the river. Kidro thought they'd killed it for sure.

Ethan, Kidro's oldest son, had gotten the closest look. He'd said it was a Sasquatch.

They all thought it had gone off to die someplace.

J. J. had proudly nailed its paw to that big spruce near the barn.

For the first time in a long time, Kidro remembered something awful, something only he had seen, something long hidden in the back pages of his memory. He gulped whiskey and watched the flames dance, trying not to remember.

Can't stop it.

The following day, *ten years ago*, that paw had become a human hand. Kidro had left it there, nailed to that giant spruce. He'd turned and walked into the barn to feed the horses, forcibly pushing the image from his mind.

The following night, that thing had come back to take all of those lives. The morning after, Kidro had gone out to look, but the hand had disappeared.

A chill-cold sweat covered Kidro's body and sheeted his face. He bolted his whiskey, refilled the tumbler, and bolted that down.

His vision blurred briefly and cleared, concentrating on the flames, forcing his old memories to fade.

Scooter stirred at his feet and Kidro bent to gently tug his ears. Scooter liked that.

He straightened, refilled his tumbler, and sipped, refocusing on dancing flames.

Kidro had to admit, this place kept him feeling young, a good reason to stay. He'd never been to a doctor in his life. Up in this high-mountain valley, nobody ever needed a doctor. Everybody figured this valley had some kind of minerals in the water that kept them all feeling young, kept them all so healthy.

He limped into his dark kitchen and stood at the dining table, looking out the bay window at his moonlit lower meadow, where long grass swayed with the breeze, shimmering blue in the brightness of the moon, the moon reflecting off his brook. He saw it as if for the first time.

Magical.

He sipped whiskey, grateful for his sudden appreciation. Why had he never noticed it before?

"They all loved it so." He missed them.

That heavy pit in his stomach pulled downward on his heart, remembering his wife, Heather, remembering his other son, Ethan. Ethan had been named after Heather's father. His youngest, J. J., short for John Jethro, had walked away.

Seeing J. J.'s smiling face through the pages of his memory, Kidro wiped away tears. J. J. laughed in Kidro's inner ear; a voice all but forgotten.

Strange.

All of them danced and laughed through his memory that night, ten long years since he'd last seen them.

My God. His heart felt heavy.

If only we had known. If they had known about the bull calf, if they had used the ritual back then, they might never have had any trouble.

How could we know?

It hadn't come for years, not until that night, *ten long years ago.*

Maybe Nason was right. Maybe it was about the mine. Kidro and his mom had argued about that earlier in the week, *ten long years ago.*

Something struck the bay window hard, right in front of him. He leaned forward and looked up through the window.

Those stupid birds swarmed in the moonlit sky. Some dove and flapped close to the glass. One darted toward him, smacked the glass with its wings, and flew back up to the flock.

"What the . . ." Two yellow breasted meadowlarks hit the window, both looking at him.

Kidro backed into the darkness of his kitchen, spun, and returned to the living room. He refilled his tumbler and wavered, feeling a strange dizziness, not from whiskey. He set the whiskey tumbler on the mantle and watched the hypnotic dance of the flames, somehow seeing the silent flutter of wings.

"Wait." That night, ten years past, the birds had been swarming. He'd forgotten how strange they'd all thought it to be.

Scooter's head bolted up at Kidro's feet, his ears perked, and his hair stood up, sensing something outside, probably those stupid birds. The fire cracked, a log rolled, Scooter jumped up, and Kidro stepped away from the fire.

Then he heard it, a low, animal moan coming from the upper meadow. He'd been expecting that shrill cry, that hyena-like laugh.

Not tonight.

Right then, that would have been a welcome sound.

The pain in his knee and his whiskey buzz had been replaced by a tight knot in his stomach.

Scooter rushed up the steps into the entry, barking frantically, scratching at the bottom of Kidro's new door, the strongest store-bought door he could find.

Sweat slicked Kidro's palms as he crept up three stone steps into his entry and turned into his office. He wiped his palms on his wool shirt and grabbed his Winchester rifle. The steel felt slippery cold. He cranked a round into the chamber, released the safety, held his rifle at the ready, and crept back into the entry foyer to listen.

Scooter's barks and snarls blocked out everything else, his nose pressed to the crack at the bottom of Kidro's new store-bought door. "Quiet, Scooter." Kidro's legs felt like heavy bags of sand, creeping back down the entry steps, crouching near his fireplace, barely breathing. In a flash of clarity, he realized Gilpin had returned to the upper meadow and taken back the bull calf. "Gilpin." A worthless clump of dung.

Scooter's barks grew more shrill, more frantic, scratching at the bottom of the door.

Kidro's mind flashed images of that dark night, *ten long years ago.* He hadn't seen it clearly with the moon behind the clouds, but he remembered the size of that thing, the speed. He and Ethan had shot at it without phasing it. He remembered that ear shattering scream when J. J. had chopped off its front paw. It had stopped Kidro's breathing, just like right then.

He backed closer to the kitchen and knelt where the fireplace blocked his view of the entry. It would not see him there.

The birds flapping and pecking at the bay window behind him diminished. Sounds from the entry grew. He dared not breath.

The pain in his left knee returned, not letting him squat all the way down, not letting him get into a proper position to take his shot. And those birds . . .

His heart thumped loud, mingling with the flutter and clatter of the birds. Sharp pain gripped his left arm and chest, and sweat burned into his eyes.

The front door crashed, sending a spray of splinters across the living room floor.

Scooter snarled and yelped, before his body shot across the living room and smacked into the far wall, a fast, nearly invisible blur. Unnatural, how slowly his dog dropped to the floor, laying there in a twisted heap.

Grief gripped Kidro, increasing the pain in his chest and arm. His last and only friend had been taken.

His rifle slid to the floor, too heavy to hold, and Kidro Potter wept, unable to move.

A large form descended the steps from the entry.

Kidro looked away.

Who . . .

Kidro forced himself to look back. Something seemed familiar.

The huge creature crouched in the living room on all fours, its long, sharp claws clicking noisily at the wood floor, as if to announce its presence. Its eyes glowed red in the dark. It looked into Kidro, holding Kidro's stare as it rose up to stand on its hind legs. It stepped toward Kidro and its angry red eyes faded to a familiar blue.

The pain left Kidro's chest and he stood, no more pain in his knee. He recognized the cheerful glint in those eyes. "J. J., is that you?"

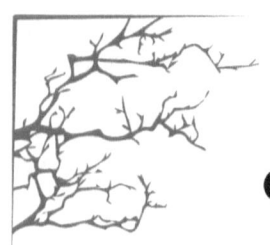

Chapter Three

The next morning, Sheriff Phil Nason woke up early, ill at ease with that unexplainable feeling, a sense that something had gone horribly wrong. He'd had these feelings before, but they'd seldom amounted to anything. This time felt different.

His lady, Dr. Nancy LaRosa, opened her dark eyes. "What is it, Phil? You tossed and turned all night." She always knew if something was bothering him.

"I don't know." He sat up and scratched the whiskers under his chin. "Gilpin stomped through my murky brain all night."

"Why? What's he done now?" Nancy had only lived in the valley for three years, but it had been enough to know Gilpin.

"Nothing, I hope." He got up and went into the bathroom to relieve himself, leaving the door open a crack so they could talk.

"Can I fix you some breakfast?" Her tone said she was getting up. The closet door next to the bathroom opened. Clothes hangers raked across the closet pole. The door closed.

He said, "Coffee would be nice. It'll give me time for a quick shower and shave."

The clinic and classroom were ample, but Nancy's living quarters were a scant couple of rooms off to one side. Her bedroom and full bath were barely adequate. What she called her living room was a nook with two chairs and a lamp table. Someone might read a book in there, nothing more. The tight kitchen housed a small dining table near the window, a nice place to watch the sun come up.

Across the street and half a block away stood the back of Jacobsen's emporium. The Rock Church and school were across the small, no-name creek. Two giant redwood trees between the church and school blocked their view of the mountains. The brick jail, directly across the street, could not be seen from the kitchen window.

Nason stood, gulped the last of his coffee, and Nancy handed him a full travel mug. She turned her face up, inviting.

Nason didn't mind. Her kisses always tasted sweet and soft. She patted his chest and smiled, *Get going.*

Nason pulled on his coat and turned out the kitchen door. Crisp, early morning air slapped his freshly shaved face. He hurried along the wide, covered walkway that ran across the front of the classroom and clinic, not eager to be seen.

The whole valley knew he and Nancy were seeing each other but neither wanted to flaunt it, his reason for leaving his truck parked across the street, in front of the jail.

He hurried across the street, opened his unlocked office door, and went inside. His answering machine showed no messages, bringing a welcome sense of relief. He opened his lower desk drawer, extracted his holstered service revolver, and strapped it on. He closed the lower drawer, opened the upper drawer, pulled out his keys, closed the drawer, and stepped around his desk.

He lifted his official hat from the antler wrack near the door, fitted it onto his head, went outside, took off his hat, and climbed into his truck. He tossed his hat onto the passenger seat, started the truck, backed onto the street, drove past the church, past Jacobsen's, and turned left onto River Road.

Boy, his second cup of coffee tasted good. His taste buds worked better while driving, giving him time to think.

Life had been good, living up here in these mountains, this valley, growing up in this village. He'd learned to ride a horse at age three, when this had still been a horseback community. They'd lived in that little house behind the jail when his father had been sheriff.

Nancy's is nicer.

The schoolhouse had already been built when he started school at age six. Their first teacher hadn't been as good as Vicar Twilby or Nancy, but Nason had a pretty good education, especially by modern standards.

After high school, he'd spent two years studying criminology down at Colombia College in Sonora, where he'd played varsity football. He'd started at middle linebacker, without ever having played in high school.

After college, he'd joined the Coast Guard for four years and had spent the next eight years with the Modesto Police Department. He took a bullet in a gang shootout that broke his hip, leaving him with a stainless-steel femur neck and a painful limp.

The city pensioned him out and he'd had enough of living down below.

His limp had vanished within three months of returning to this valley, and the pain with it.

Maybe it's the water.

Living down below, he'd always missed the clean water and air, and the kind of neighbors who actually knew one another. The pattern of life here didn't require complex, psychological systems of self-defense.

After returning home, he'd helped out around Jacobsen's and helped build the new bank with Kidro's Sonora contractor.

Helfred Jacobsen had hired that contractor to build her new house and Nason had helped with that too.

Ten years earlier, when all that trouble took place, Nason had still been living down below. His father had told him everything he knew about what had happened, and how they'd accidentally discovered this new system, staking out the bull calf in Potter's upper meadow. That system had been working for the past ten years. He hoped it had worked last night.

Since there was never any real crime here, not in the usual sense, his duties as sheriff consisted of maintaining this ritual and helping out with traffic accidents out on Sonora Pass Highway, a rare occurrence on a seldom used mountain road.

When his dad retired six years back, his folks moved down to Grass Valley, where they were getting old fast. He tried talking them into moving back but his dad had seen too much. He was still having restless nights over what had happened ten years earlier.

And that, as they say, was that. It didn't matter that the ritual was working. Dad called it a procedure, said it gave him a bad feeling in his spirit, still keeping him up at night.

Nason already knew what that was like.

Call it a ritual. Call it a procedure. Call it whatever you want. It worked.

He turned up Kidro's driveway and drove over the crest. *No need to bother Kidro.* He rolled downhill toward the house and barn and slowed near the front of the house.

"Oh, no."

Kidro's front door stood wide open, still too cold out for that.

He parked at the bottom of the steps, got out of his truck, and put on his official hat. He stood on the bottom step and looked at the shattered hinge rail of Kidro's new door. "Kidro?" *No, no.* He climbed onto the porch, entered the foyer, and turned.

On the floor, against the far wall, big, green flies swarmed over Scooter's dead carcass.

Nason didn't need to see more, not right then. Anger pushed from inside his gut. He needed to keep hold of that.

Nason reached the Gilpin turnoff at 8:18 a.m. In those three minutes of driving from Kidro's house, his anger had grown to rage, thinking how easily one person could tear it all down, how one person could ruin things for everybody else.

Stupid pud-head.

Sand and gravel road-base churned under new tires on his way to the suspension bridge, a bridge built with Potter money. Kidro hadn't liked it, but, while his mother lived, she'd been head of the family. Out of respect for his mother, Kidro had maintained this stretch of gravel road and the bridge itself, but nothing beyond.

Not anymore.

None of the Gilpins had ever shown a lick of gratitude. Before the bridge, they'd had to ride horses across the shallows, two miles upriver. They hadn't been able to get a truck or car over to their place before the bridge.

Bruce was his father's son, stupid to the bone. His pot addiction didn't help.

Building the suspension bridge had been no small feat. It had taken soils engineers from Sonora more than two years of testing different locations for proper geology before they could even hire the structural engineer. At this location, the foundation rock was solid granite. It was an awesome sight for such a short span. The river gorge ran deep under the bridge, water boiling over rocks thirty feet below.

Sight unseen, Lamar Gilpin, Bruce's grandfather, had filed his homestead claim in Sacramento back around 1960. He'd been as stupid as his brood. He'd never even entered the valley, had never looked at the map, and apparently had not known he needed to cross this river for access.

Back then, even now, they crossed over from unused Potter land. Jethro and Mary Lou had welcomed them, happy to have neighbors for Kidro to grow up with.

"Pud-heads all." Nason chuckled and shook his head. *Growing up with the Gilpins.*

Odd. As much as Kidro liked to complain, Nason had never heard a complaint about the maintenance of the bridge and access road, still maintained by Kidro.

Not anymore.

Why hadn't Kidro simply bought the Gilpin place? Last night might never have happened.

Nason slowed to a crawl and eased off Gilpin's end of the bridge.

The Gilpins didn't even maintain their dirt road, a snarl of large rocks, deep ruts, and muddy puddles. He dropped his truck into first gear and bumped over exposed rocks, his tires dropping into muddy hole after muddy hole. Gilpin's truck should have fallen to pieces long ago.

He rounded the granite outcropping on a rise, still driving uphill, and the larger rocks in the road disappeared, moving farther uphill, farther from the river. He slipped his truck into second gear, drove up the narrow valley to Gilpin's twelve by sixty-foot trailer, and parked next to Gilpin's truck. Before the bridge had been built, the Gilpins had lived in the barn. They had been able to drag materials across the shallows and through the forest, not easy on Lamar Gilpin's horse.

Nason climbed out of his truck and put on his official hat, noticing again how much the place had decayed since that bad storm two winters back, when Nason had called the Pendleton kid out to repair the electric and telephone wires. The wires had been run out here by the Potters when they'd installed the hydroelectric plant at the top of the valley, before Nason was born. The wiring ran underground everywhere but here. Here, the river made underground wiring impossible. They did run them underground from River Road to the river, then up across the bridge, into the trees, and out to Gilpin's trailer. No wires could be seen from River Road.

The Gilpins had never been grateful for any of it, always acting like they were somehow entitled. They'd never even paid an electric bill.

The phone lines came in from Pacific Bell. Everybody paid for those, everybody that had a phone or internet connection.

The Gilpins had both. The phone company billing went through Kidro's bank.

Gilpin's aging bull was penned between the trailer and Gilpin's creek, feeding on a clump of dry alfalfa, not even looking at the moon-eyed cow next to it. Neither one paid any attention to Nason.

The rotten wood steps in front of the trailer had been filled in with small rocks and rubble, an uneven climb to the porch. He took off his hat and knocked, knowing somebody was home. Someone inside was smoking sweet smelling mountain grown marijuana. He smelled it every time he'd come out here.

Nason didn't care about the pot. That was state business, as long as he didn't try to sell locally.

He knocked again and waited.

Nobody answered.

He shouted, "Gilpin," and knocked again. Still no answer. He donned his hat and climbed back down the uneven steps, rounded the front of the trailer, and climbed up the hill toward the barn.

Gilpin's father had built the barn with money borrowed from Mary Lou, probably never repaid.

The barn stood uphill and a hundred feet behind the trailer, sided and roofed with corrugated iron. Tall sagebrush grew over dents and rust at the bottom, needing repair like everything else.

Sweat trickled down his neck and back, already hot from morning sun. The still air in this tight canyon didn't help. He stepped inside the open barn door and waited for his eyes to adjust.

The barn reeked of drying pot, same as it had the previous day, hanging everywhere from joists and rafters, nearly blocking shafts of sunlight shining through two high dormers.

Gilpin sat on a stool near the center of the barn, helping the bull calf take a nipple from his milk cow. His fat belly rested on his legs, nearly reaching his knees.

You fat, dumb . . .

Nason stepped quietly across the barn and snatched Gilpin up by his coat collar.

Gilpin jerked sideways, trying to free himself from Nason's grip. "What do you think you're doing? You got no right." He slapped at Nason's hands, kicked at Nason's legs, and dragged his feet, trying to keep Nason from hauling him outside.

Nason yanked him into daylight and shoved him downhill toward the trailer.

Gilpin spun and slid, tugging up on his worn blue jeans to keep them from falling around his ankles. "You can't do this to me. You got no right."

"Shut up!" Nearing the back of the trailer, Nason shoved Gilpin hard, wanting to punch his ugly, fat face. When a curtain moved at the rear window, he forced himself to calm. "I need to show you something. It won't take long." He grabbed Gilpin's upper arm and dug his fingers into the pressure point against the bone.

Gilpin stiffened from the pain and stopped resisting.

Nason led him toward the parked trucks, knowing he'd leave big black bruises under Gilpin's arm.

They reached the front of the trailer where Sally, Gilpin's wife, stood on the front porch with their five-year-old daughter, Sissy.

Sissy never showed any emotion, tucked tightly between her mother's knees.

Nason said, "Hi, Sally. I need to borrow your husband for a few minutes. He'll be right back." He leaned close to Gilpin, put pressure on his underarm, and spoke softly. "Don't make me hurt you in front of your wife and kid."

He deposited Gilpin in the passenger side of his truck, closed the door, walked around the truck, took off and tipped his hat at Sally, climbed in behind the wheel, and tossed his official hat into the backseat. He started the truck and put it into 2nd gear. He took a wide turn, back toward the river, drove to the granite outcropping, dropped it into 1st gear, and drove slowly downhill over boulders and ruts.

Gilpin grinned, probably at the beating Nason's truck was taking.

Nason decided to let the fat pud-head walk back from Kidro's.

Driving across the bridge, Nason said, "Was Mary Lou Potter who built this bridge. Without it, your father and grandfather had to ford the river on horseback two miles up, still on Potter land. Before that, you couldn't even get a trailer in here.

"When you were snowbound all winter, it was the Potters who found a way to help. Without their benevolence, there'd be no Gilpins in this valley."

"So?"

Nason cleared the bridge and churned over graded gravel toward River Road, thinking this moron probably didn't even know what the word benevolence meant. He'd almost never shown up for school as a boy.

Nason said, "When you fell and broke your arm, wasn't it Kidro Potter who took you into Carson City? Wasn't it Kidro who paid the hospital bills? Back then, we had no doctor."

"So?" Gilpin poked his chin out, defiant. "They got more money than God."

Nason turned onto River Road, driving toward Potter's house. "Wasn't it Mary Lou who loaned your grandfather the money to build that barn? Did she ever ask for a penny back? Did you Gilpins ever offer to repay?"

"So what? We still can't afford a barn like Potter's got."

Useless.

Nason drove the short distance and turned up the cobblestone drive toward the Potter house and barn. "Didn't Kidro pay you five hundred dollars for Stoner, on top of that Angus calf?"

"So? What's your point?"

Nason parked in front of the house and turned in his seat, facing Gilpin. "The point is this: I've never seen any sign of gratitude, not from any of you Gilpins."

"Gratitude for what?" Gilpin was still defiant. "What business is that of yours?"

"So, you think the Potters owe you because they have more than you?"

"Sure. Why not? We've always been good neighbors, ain't we?"

"That's it! Get out!"

Gilpin just sat there with his fat belly slumped over his fat legs.

"You numb . . ." Nason jumped out without his hat and rushed around his truck. He threw open the passenger door and Gilpin sprawled across the center consol, hiding behind his out-stretched hands. "What for? I don't want to see that greedy old skinflint."

Nason slapped Gilpin's hands aside, grabbed him by his collar, and yanked him from the truck. Keeping Gilpin in front of him, Nason shoved hard, and Gilpin crabbed up the steps backward onto the porch.

Eyes wide, mouth open, arms outstretched, Gilpin kicked back against the stone wall near the entry, waving his hands defensively. "Do I have to go in there? Can't he come out?"

You stupid, whining . . . "NO!" Nason yanked Gilpin to his feet, spun him, and shoved him past the shattered door into Kidro's entry.

The stench of stale blood and feces forced Nason to hold his breath. He didn't want to go in there either, but he needed to finish this.

Gilpin's feet dragged across every carefully fitted stone, being half carried down into the living room.

Gilpin saw the dead carcass of Scooter laying in a heap on the floor against the far wall and pushed back toward the entry.

"Quit it." Nason pushed Gilpin toward the center of the living room and Gilpin's hands flew to his mouth.

Nason viewed the room in flashes, like snapshots from a coroner's report.

Kidro's twisted body lay on the wood floor near the couch, chest torn wide open, heart and head both missing.

Gilpin choked back vomit at the sight of it.

Large green flies swarmed in Kidro's open chest cavity, thick as a shag carpet and buzzing louder than any swarm of bees.

Sucking foul air, Nason turned toward the fireplace.

Kidro's severed head sat up on the stone mantle between a glass tumbler and a near empty bottle of whiskey. His half open, glassy eyes stared back at them, barely visible through swarming, bright green flies.

"Mmpff." Gilpin tore away from Nason and lunged toward the entry, with green flies swarming over him, diving at his ears, nose, and eyes. He swatted at the flies and spewed vomit on his way out the door.

He turned back from the front porch, looked at Nason with wide, pleading eyes, until large, bright-green flies covered his face. He shrieked, threw his hands over his mouth and spewed vomit between his fat fingers.

Blinded by flies, he spun, slipped, and sat down hard in his own vomit.

He scrambled to his feet and his jeans dropped around his ankles.

Large, green flies swarmed over his dirty underwear and into the hairy, fat crack of his butt.

He gasped air and crabbed down the front steps sideways, on all fours, hopelessly swatting at flies as he went. He reached the bottom quickly and collapsed onto the cobbled driveway, chucking vomit where he lay.

Nason watched from the high front porch, being careful where he stepped.

Flies swarmed thick over Gilpin, buzzing loudly in their frenzy. *Bizarre.* Nason chuckled.

Gilpin gasped, jumped to his feet, snatched up his pants, and scurried past Nason's truck. He scampered up the driveway to the top of the rise, still swatting at flies, and disappeared over the crown of the driveway.

"What a pud." *Maybe he learned something.*

Probably not. Nason would surely have trouble taking that calf to the upper meadow. He needed to beat Gilpin to his barn and grab the calf. Hopefully, that thing wouldn't come again. Unfortunately, Gilpin would then get his calf back.

What would happen next? The ritual had just become a small consideration. Kidro would never have set up a trust for the valley in case something happened to him. Not Kidro. Without Potter support for the clinic, the church and school, the bank, the hydroelectric plant, the roads, what would happen to the rest of the people in this valley?

That pud-head had taken it all down.

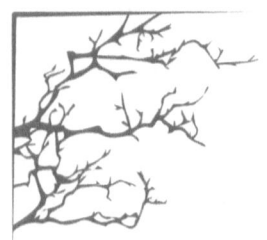

Chapter Four

Tom Kirby's two staff editors had been nagging him all week and most of that morning to make a decision on which stories to use in the next editions of their two children's magazines. After a fifth memo, losing patience late in the day, not really caring anyway, Kirby called them both into his office, sat them down, and asked, "What is your problem?"

Bob Hendricks, the moron he'd hired to replace John Potter, said, "We've got a stack of good stuff. We'd like a little input from our publisher."

Kirby didn't like that, a shot aimed right between his eyes. "Your job is to make these decisions." He looked from Hendricks to Tim Thornby, the company's long-time line editor. Thornby's dead eyes stared back, like a man who sleeps with his eyes open. He looked at Hendricks. "Should I find somebody else?" *Idiot!* Kirby never should have asked that question.

Hendricks said, "That's up to you, Mr. Kirby. You're the publisher." Hendricks could go wherever he wanted. He was a top copy editor, just afraid to make that final decision.

Kirby said, "Look, John Potter had no problem making these decisions. I told you when I hired you, that's your job now."

"The first two times I did that, you told me I was stupid. You did it in such a voice that your whole staff now questions my authority."

"Yeah, yeah." Kirby smiled and shook his head. "Those just weren't the kind of choices Potter would have made." Kirby had no idea if that comment was true or where it came from. *No big deal.* He'd push it through. That had always worked in the past.

Both his editors sat, stone faced, waiting for Kirby to make a decision.

Kirby said, "What's the layout? What are my options?"

Hendricks said, "*After School* has a kind of nursery rhyme theme. I think Carolyn Potter's fiction piece about a little boy's imaginary dog is good. It has a lot of cute rhymes."

"Okay." Kirby spread his arms and leaned over his desk. "What's the problem?"

Hendricks said, "We've also got a nice word game. If that sounds okay with you, we can close out *After School*."

"Fine. What about *Teen Dreams*?"

"We've got another piece by Carolyn Potter, a story about a girl's swim team and an honor student, about her bad family life and her need to earn a college scholarship."

Kirby said, "If we give Carolyn too much, the others might think I'm playing favorites."

Hendricks said, "She's becoming a very good writer."

Kirby shook his head, *No good.*

Hendricks asked, "Have you read any of the material?"

"I don't have time for that. That's why we hired you."

Hendricks spread his arms and leaned closer, obviously mocking Kirby's earlier gesture, a deliberate insult.

Kirby didn't dare fire the prick, reminding himself of why he'd hired him in the first place. Hendricks had delivered some very large school textbook accounts, vastly increasing the value of Kirby Publications. He needed to sign Hendricks to a long-term contract and give him more authority.

Kirby forced himself to be nice. "Flip a coin, Bob. Make a decision. Do whatever you think best."

For whatever reason, Thornby woke up. "John Potter never flipped a coin in his life. He made decisions."

Small wonder Hendricks didn't like Thornby. Soon, as a show of good faith, Kirby would allow Hendricks to hire his own line editor. Ignoring Thornby, Kirby said, "Come on, Bob. Get it done. I promise not to squawk, even if you run with both of Carolyn's pieces." He couldn't afford to give her a raise.

Hendricks smiled a little, slapped Thornby's shoulder, and they left.

The mere mention of John Potter prompted Kirby to find the key and open his private drawer. That folder with the papers nobody could ever see was under his 10mm Colt Delta Elite, a very similar weapon to his Marine Corps issued sidearm. He set the weapon on top of his desk and pulled out the file. Potter's one page deal memo was on top, no need to touch the sheet. He needed to keep it looking new. He might need to deny ever having seen it, but he did need to keep it.

His parents had been gone for a little more than four years. Flying their single engine Cessna over the Sierra's at night had been stupid. Their bodies had never been recovered, though searchers did find the crash site. After seven years, his parents could be legally declared dead. If there was an audit, he might need to show where that hundred-thousand-dollars had come from.

One of the last two things his father did as publisher was to purchase six children's magazines, dumping all but two to reduce competition and streamline distribution. Most of their advertisers had come over to these remaining two.

Before that purchase, Kirby Publications had published one magazine, a variety of coloring and picture books, and a limited number of educational texts.

They'd done well enough to own the house in the Palisades and the cabin in Utah, where they'd intended to spend that Christmas skiing, but they never made it.

Shortly after buying up the magazines, his father had been temporarily short of cash for printers and payroll. He hadn't enough time to mortgage a property and he'd wanted to keep total ownership of the firm, so he'd borrowed a hundred-thousand from John Potter.

Kirby had seen that pass book in boot camp, the one thing that looked out of place during inspections, resting there in the top tray of his foot locker. It had been left to him by his grandmother and he had never touched it, not until Kirby's father needed it.

The deal memo gave his father thirty days to pay Potter back with a flat ten percent interest. After thirty days, if the loan was not repaid, Potter would receive twenty-five percent of the profits from these two children's magazines, for life.

Over my dead body.

Kirby's father had planned on repaying the loan when they returned from Utah. He'd only needed about a week to secure a loan from their bank. Either way, it had been a good deal for John Potter.

Too good.

At the time of purchase, the advertising revenues for these two magazines had amounted to just over fifty thousand dollars a month, all profit, with a small profit from distribution. Three years later, those two magazines brought in more than three times that amount in advertising alone, and distribution was way up.

Six months after his parents went missing, the forestry service suspended search operations in the Sierras and Potter started asking questions about his share in the magazines. He'd even shown Kirby his notarized copy of the deal memo.

Fool.

That same night, Kirby broke into Potter's desk, retrieved his copy, and shredded it.

It all happened on a Friday night, shredding Potter's copy and his meeting with Lester, Kirby's bookie. They held their meeting in a booth in the V.I.P. room of the Cabo Cantina, Kirby's favorite sports bar.

Kirby remembered every word. He'd said, "Listen, Lester, you're always telling me how you know certain people."

"I know lots of people." Lester had given a nod toward Omar and Lummis, his two constant companions. They'd been standing at the bar, muscles bulging through their sports jackets.

Kirby said, "I mean, what if I had a friend who wants someone to disappear?"

"Disappear, or die?" Lester never liked misdirection.

"My friend says the guy has a really nice car. A new C-class Mercedes, the kind of car people get killed for." It had been leased by Kirby Publications, no problem.

"He a politician or a cop?"

"No. He's just a guy. His name's John Potter. I can find out his schedule, when and where he'll be alone."

"It'll cost your friend ten grand." Lester's eyes narrowed to chilling slits, his voice remained matter-of-fact.

"What? What about the car? It's worth thirty, easy."

"I gotta get something." Lester issued a casual shrug. "I'm taking a big risk."

"Well, so am I, and I'm not getting anything."

"He's your friend, not mine. He can take it or leave it." Lester had that look, knowing Kirby didn't have many friends.

Banks were open Saturdays. Kirby had withdrawn the money and had met Lester again for breakfast, a waffle shop way over on Adams. Kirby had given him the money and the address of their printer in Culver City.

Potter would be there Sunday night for final layout approval of one of their magazines. Kirby couldn't remember which one.

Carolyn Potter had worked at Kirby Publications before Kirby enlisted in the Marine Corps, and he had barely noticed her. Her and

John met at a party thrown by Kirby's parents, their first weekend liberty. *Love at first sight.* Potter had worn his dress blues, and they'd gotten married two months later. Maybe she'd already been pregnant.

Potter volunteered for Recon Battalion, did two weeks training at the Marine Corps Mountain Warfare Training Center, and his company had deployed to Afghanistan, where he'd been awarded the Bronze Star for Valor and had come back without a scratch.

Carolyn had quit working for the magazine when she had the kid and had come back a month after John's death. In all that time, she'd only asked once about this stupid deal memo. Kirby had denied any knowledge. *Of course.*

If an audit occurred, Kirby would deny ever having seen the memo.

No problem.

She'd probably jump at a hundred grand with market interest plus ten percent.

Stupid broad. She did have a pretty face and a nice body, getting a little flat in the butt from too much sitting. She was still too good for Potter.

CAROLYN POTTER FINISHED writing the rough draft of a new story about a relationship between a kitten and a puppy, her new piece for *After School*, their magazine aimed at pre-teens. She glanced at the clock on her computer monitor, 2:44 p.m. If she left right away, she could be in front of rush-hour traffic, plenty of time to pick up Jason and Jimmy. She turned off her monitor and grabbed her purse.

"Sorry, Carolyn," said Allison, Mr. Kirby's private secretary. "He wants to see you before you leave."

Carolyn stood. "It's my day to pick up the boys. He knows that."

"Sorry." Allison had always been polite, a long-time employee. She'd been the senior Kirby's secretary when Carolyn had first started working for Kirby Publications. The junior Kirby, Tom, had been in the Marine Corps, as had John.

The door to Mr. Kirby's outer office remained open. Allison followed Carolyn in and sat at her desk. She nodded toward the half open door to Mr. Kirby's private office. "Just go on in." She rolled her eyes, saying she knew how unfair Tom Kirby could be.

Tom Kirby sat behind his father's big, impressive, antique desk, with a nice city view through the picture window behind him.

She walked all the way in and swung the door wide open.

He motioned toward a chair and said, "Close the door."

She closed the door and sat, clutching her purse over her tightly closed legs. "It's my day to pick up the boys. You know that."

"This will only take a minute." He stared at her bare knees, being obvious about it. He glanced at her face and looked back at her knees. "Hendricks picked your story for this week's edition of *After School*. He's impressed with your writing."

Some might think Mr. Kirby handsome, always well groomed, always well dressed. His beady, wide-spread eyes gave her the creeps, always undressing her and staring at her boobs.

"Thank you."

"He wanted to run your swim team story in *Teen Dreams* but I didn't want our other writers to think I was playing favorites with you."

"Oh, I like that story."

He stared into her eyes, licking his lips like a big lizard.

Yuk.

"Yeah, we got into an argument over it and I finally gave in. What I wound up telling him was that we can't afford any raises right now. Sorry."

"Is that all, Mr. Kirby. I need to . . ."

"Are you doing okay? I mean, I think about you, you know, since John . . ."

"Mr. Kirby . . ." *Don't go there, please.* "It's Jason's birthday."

"Oh, yeah. I nearly forgot. What should I get for him?"

Give his mother a raise. She bit down on the thought.

JASON POTTER AND JIMMY O'Connell waited outside their school in Echo Park. They both lived up the hill from Sunset but on the other side of Echo Park Lake and Alvarado Blvd.

Both of their moms wanted them to be picked up after school because crossing Alvarado was too dangerous.

Jimmy had been Jason's best friend for more than two years, always riding to and from school in one of their mom's cars. Both of their moms were usually a little bit late picking them up, but, on Jason's birthday, Jason's mom was later than ever. They had to wait outside the schoolyard because the gates had to be locked.

Clouds had piled up against the mountains and Jason had started shivering from the cold. Most kids didn't wear jackets to school. That was too un-cool.

When cold drops of rain hit Jason's head and neck, he stopped caring about being cool. He wanted his coat, he wanted to be warm, and he wanted to be safely tucked into the backseat of his mom's car. "It's getting cold, Jimmy. You got anything in your locker?" They could climb over the gate if Jimmy had a sweatshirt or something in his locker. Jason's locker only had books that he didn't need to take home. If Jimmy had a sweatshirt, at least he could be warm. Maybe he had a sweat-shirt and a coat. Then they'd both be warm.

"Na. We're okay." Jimmy's hands were in his pockets, toughing it out. He was a pretty tough kid anyway, always getting into fights during recess and after school. He took karate classes on Saturdays and his dad practiced with him early every morning.

Must be nice to have a dad.

Jimmy looked at his watch. "It's quarter to five already. Where's your mom?"

"I hope she didn't have an accident." Neither of their moms had ever been this late.

Jimmy said, "Maybe we should walk."

The sky had grown dark, Jason's shirt was getting wet, and she'd never before been so late. "Do you know the way?"

"Sure. We can go across the park where my mom goes to feed the ducks." Jimmy motioned with his head and started walking toward the freeway, keeping his hands in his pockets to stay warm.

Jason thrust his hands into his pockets and followed Jimmy downhill toward the park.

Down near the bottom of the hill, three bigger boys turned and started climbing uphill toward them. They all wore matching black t-shirts and camouflage cargo pants, slung low so their underwear showed. They were toughing the cold rain too. They stopped a block downhill, talking to each other, looking up at Jason and Jimmy, maybe planning something bad. They all looked much older, at least in high school, and they all had those tattoo bracelets around their wrists with those red and blue flames shooting up their arms. They all had real short hair, like those Marine Corps pictures of his dad.

Jason said, "Maybe we should go back and wait for my mom."

Jimmy said, "It's already too late." He pulled his hands out of his pockets and kept walking downhill.

Jason did the same. He wasn't scared, not really. Jimmy could lick anybody. Only, his teeth were chattering because of the cold.

"WHY YOU ALWAYS MAKE me call?" Lester sounded angry, chirping over Kirby's office phone in his high pitched, South Central speak, right now doubting Kirby's integrity, *the little sleaze*. If not for Omar and Lummis, Kirby would go down there and slap the little jerk sideways.

Kirby said, "You're not supposed to call me here. You know the deal."

"The deal is, you lose, you pay. It ain't complicated."

"No, the deal is, I have a salary in my father's company. I get paid once a month. That's why, when I lose, I always pay you at the beginning of the following month." Kirby leaned back in his chair, having fun for the first time all week. Sitting behind his father's big desk made him feel stronger, safer. Nobody pushed him around in his office. "You're not supposed to call my office." That was the deal they'd made after taking care of John Potter. Until that day, it had been honored.

"No-no." The little jerk was grinding his teeth again. "You win, you come down and get paid. You lose, you supposed to come down and pay. That's the way it's supposed to be."

Allison knocked softly and poked her head in. "Someone's here to see you about John Potter."

Kirby held his breath and cocked an ear in her direction, waiting.

"He came all the way from Reno."

Kirby motioned for her to send him in and returned to Lester, "Look, are we on for Sunday's games?"

"When we gonna get paid?"

"If I lose, you'll collect on the first of the month, like always."

"You been layin' off a lot o' bread this month. More than usual." Lester clicked his tongue into the phone, what he did whenever he was thinking about it. That was better than grinding his teeth. "You better be good for it. I don't wanna send Omar and Lummis on no visit."

Allison ushered a short, slouchy man into his office and Kirby finished with Lester. "Look, I've got to go. Are we on?"

"You better be good for it." Lester hung up.

Kirby hung up and stood to take this puffy faced guy's business card: "Richard (Dick) Wharton, Confidential Inquiries."

The guy was over fifty and not doing well. He sneered sideways and yanked out a plaid handkerchief, barely having time to sneeze into it. He carefully unfolded the soggy looking handkerchief, searched for a clean spot, made his decision, and blew his nose into it. He gave it three sputtering blows before opening the soggy rag to look at a disgusting glob of muck. He shook his head and looked at Kirby through watery eyes. "You'll have to forgive me." He shook his head apologetically and reexamined the fresh load in his handkerchief. "I get these things twice a year, spring and fall, every year."

Kirby said, "I hope it's not contagious."

"No, no." He shook his head, carefully folded the soggy mess into the outside pocket of his wool tweed jacket, and offered his right hand. "I get this twice a year, spring and fall."

Kirby thought not. He sat behind his desk and motioned to the chair in the far corner.

Before sitting down, Dick's left hand went up, his red face wrinkled, and he reached for his handkerchief. Too late. The disgusting little slob sneezed a nasty glob onto Kirby's handmade, tribal Persian rug.

Kirby tossed him a box of Kleenex, too slow again. The Kleenex hit sneeze-face in the shoulder and landed on the floor.

"Thank you." He bent down and snagged several tissues, trying to clean the rug. His nose wrinkled, he grabbed several additional tissues, filled them with muck, and carefully examined the sticky looking sludge. No telling what this guy thought he might find in there.

Kirby took decisive action. He stood, thrust his hands into his pockets, and carefully guided his waste basket around his desk with his foot. Having safely delivered his hazardous-waste disposal unit, Kirby backed around his desk and both men sat. Kirby absently wiped his hands on his silk vest, wanting to toss this little sneezer out the window.

NO! Don't touch him. "What's this all about?"

Wheezing and stuffed up, Dick said, "I've been retained to locate John Jethro Potter." His nose wrinkled, getting ready to blow, but the threatened explosion subsided. "California State tax records show he was working here, just a few years ago." He bared his teeth, yanked out another clump of tissue, closed his eyes, and sneezed into it. He folded the wad carefully, blew more muck into it, spread it to examine it, and finally dropped the mess into Kirby's abruptly infectious disposal unit.

"How did you get access to his tax records?"

Sneezer's eyes watered, his nose wrinkled, he blinked tears, and asked, "Does that really matter?" One hand shot to his sneering, wrinkled face while the other reached for the Kleenex. The sneeze subsided and his watery eyes waited for an answer.

Without warning, he sneezed another glob of milky looking muck onto Kirby's handmade, tribal Persian rug. His bare hand caught a second sneeze, the slimy muck dripping through his fingers. He grabbed several tissues, cleaned his hands and wiped his face.

He searched the wad of tissues for evidence. After a brief but thorough examination, the disgusting fellow grabbed more tissues and bent to clean the glob from Kirby's carpet. He tossed the mess into the disposal unit and pulled more tissues, blew his nose, examined it, and tossed it in with the rest.

He pulled more tissues and cleaned the carpet a second time. "I'm awfully sorry about this. I get these twice a year." He smiled apologetically, slid back into the chair, and asked, "You do know John Potter, do you not?"

"Why?"

"His father has passed away." He looked like another sneeze. It passed. "I've been retained by his bank to locate his only heir, John Jethro Potter. Kidro Potter, his father, left a quite substantial estate."

CAROLYN DIDN'T REACH Jason's school until after dark and everybody had gone. She'd left her phone at the office or she'd have called Jimmy's mother to pick them up, having been stuck in traffic on the Santa Monica Freeway. Maybe Jimmy had a cell phone. Maybe he'd called his mother to pick them up.

I hope so.

Jimmy's mother did online surveys in her home office so she had plenty of time. Carolyn couldn't remember if Jimmy had gotten a new iPhone last Christmas. It might have been one of Jason's other friends.

When Jason had asked for one, she told him she didn't want him playing games and watching Tik Tok all day. She hadn't wanted to admit that they couldn't afford it. That kind of news would have spread like cancer, the way kids talk.

It only took ten minutes to get home from the school but Jason wasn't there. She put the Carvel cake into the freezer and called Jimmy's house.

The phone rang twice and a man answered, "O'Connell residence." It wasn't Jimmy's father.

"Is Janine in?"

"Who's calling?"

"This is Carolyn."

"One moment." People were in the room talking, muffled voices Carolyn couldn't make out.

Janine screamed, "Where were you?" After scuffling noises and more muffled voices, that same man said, "Please, Mrs. O'Connell, let me handle this." He wasn't talking into the phone but his voice sounded clear. When things got quiet, he asked, "Are you Carolyn Potter?"

"Yes." She sat on the arm of the couch, trembling. Something had happened.

IN A HURRY, TOM KIRBY drove up Melrose toward Beverly Center to buy Carolyn's kid a Swiss Army watch. Carolyn had said she couldn't afford it, that it was probably too much for the kid's age, but Kirby didn't care. He needed to impress her, show her that he really cared. After all, he was John Potter's kid.

He put on his headset and dialed Lester.

"What you want?"

"Don't call me on my office phone anymore. Call me on my cell."

"Who you talking to, boy?"

"Knock off the crap, Lester. We've been doing business too long for that."

Lester didn't say anything.

Kirby said, "I need to lay down more on the Dolphin-Jets game."

"How much?"

"Ten."

"Thousand?"

"Yeah, ten thousand on the Jets."

"How you gonna pay that if you gonna lose?"

"Pay? Ha! There's no way the Dolphins can beat that spread. Not in New York. The Jets are too strong and Miami's got no quarterback."

"You lose, how you gonna pay?"

"Vegas messed up this time." Kirby knew how rarely that happened. It was his time to cash in. After about ten seconds of silence from Lester, Kirby said, "Look, I just had a huge windfall. I'm going to marry into a huge fortune, could be bigger than my father's whole company."

"Yeah? Who's the unlucky lady?"

"Thanks, you piece of . . ." He thought better of it. "Listen, you don't know her." Kirby knew she liked him. He could tell. She was just holding back because of the kid. What difference would a kid make on lonely nights? "She's loaded and doesn't even know it yet."

"You talkin' crazy. I don't take no long shots without you pay on time. You're in too deep already." Lester sounded resolute. He probably knew it was a sure win for Kirby. He'd probably laid a bundle down for himself and he didn't want to change the spread.

"Look, in less than two years, my parents will be legally dead. This whole publishing business will be mine, along with the house in the Palisades, the ski lodge in Utah, the trust fund, and whatever else there is. Are we on?"

"You still talkin' crazy. You know the kind of interest builds over a year?"

"You know my Mercedes?" Kirby was just desperate enough for that. "You've seen it."

Lester clicked his tongue, thinking, the little snake.

"Come on, Lester. I feel a win here. It's my time."

"That's what losers always say."

"This car's worth at least fifty."

"Don't that belong to your old man?"

"No. It's mine. He's got a Rolls Bentley in the garage. It belongs to the company, and Mom had a Beemer."

"You owe money on it?"

"No. I paid cash. I have a car allowance. Check with a dealer. It was new last year." *Stupid little . . .* "Look, Lester, I like you. We go way back. Don't make me find a new book." Knowing his cell phone would lose signal in the underground parking at Beverly Center, Kirby pulled over to the right and double parked on Melrose, listening to Lester's clicking tongue.

"How I gonna get paid, wait for your daddy to get officially dead, wait to you marry a millionaire? All that interest gonna give everything to me."

"Hold the pink on my car." *You little sleaze.*

"You crazy. You know that?"

"Yeah, crazy to be working with you. You're a pain in my butt. Are we on?"

"I just wrote it in my book. Where can we meet?"

"I'm just pulling into Beverly Center. I need to buy her kid a birthday present. I'll meet you at the Cabo Cantina, say, ten o'clock?"

"I gonna send Otis. Bring the slip."

"Of course." As soon as Kirby hung up, his phone rang. He pressed the phone icon. "Hello, Allison. Glad you called. Get somebody into my office to clean the carpet and disinfect the whole place. That guy left a nasty virus. Call the CDC. Tell them to wear their hazard suits."

"Mr. Kirby, something's happened. Carolyn Potter's little boy is in the hospital. She called about the insurance."

"Tell me he's covered."

"No, sir. You changed our group coverage in June. We only cover employees now. You wanted to see if the governor would expand public healthcare."

"What did you tell her?"

"I told her I'd check into it and get back."

"Good. Is it serious?"

"He's in intensive care. He's been unconscious for more than two hours."

"What?"

"He's got a head injury."

"That's a long time."

"Yes, it is, especially for someone his age. Kids usually bounce right up, even when they're bleeding."

"Was he bleeding?" It'd be a real stroke of good luck if the kid died. Kirby would hate looking at John's kid all the time.

Allison stayed silent. Why wasn't she answering?

"Well?"

"Sorry." Allison sounded unstrung, probably because she didn't like deception, being evasive with Carolyn. Allison was loyal, though. As long as she stayed loyal, she could like or dislike whatever she wanted. She finally said, "The other line's blinking, probably her again. She didn't mention any bleeding. What should I tell her?"

"Tell her I'm on my way," *right after I get her kid his stupid watch.* "Don't say anything about the insurance. Tell her you're still checking or something. Where is she?"

CAROLYN SAT IN THE darkened hospital room. The nurse had told her they always did that with head injuries because his eyes would be sensitive to light. Carolyn felt like she'd been there for days, waiting and hoping for any kind of movement from Jason.

The curtain had been drawn between Jason and another patient, a little girl from a car accident. Her constant moaning irritated Carolyn. With Jason in what might be a coma, someone should keep that little girl quiet. Her injuries would completely heal, a broken collar bone and a few stitches on her chin. Nothing serious. She'd be going home the following day.

Why won't she stop? Jason needed for her to be quiet.

Carolyn wiped her eyes for what seemed the millionth time but her tears kept flowing.

"Oh, Lord," barely a whisper, a start to a prayer not yet formed in Carolyn's mind. Where were those prayers that had the power to help her son? "Lord." This city had taken her husband and now it was trying to take her son.

A soft groan came from deep inside her, crying out to God. The words were not there, not on her tongue and not in her mind, only in her heart. Her mind stayed focused on that memory, the first time Jason had looked up at his daddy, the way he'd reached out when John picked him up and said, "My boy." John had just returned from Afghanistan.

Her tears flowed.

Even at age eight, no, nine years old today, Jason looked tiny in that big hospital bed. He looked like a Frankenstein doll with his shaved head and seventeen stitches, all swollen and purple. The whole side of his face had swollen with purple bruises. The doctor told her there'd be a scar over his left temple, even though a reconstructive plastic surgeon had done the stitching.

Seventeen stitches. "Lord." They told her that the scar would be hidden by his hair and rarely seen. Their concern was weather or not

Jason would quickly regain consciousness. They had warned her of possible brain damage, or worse.

Worse? God, what does that mean? Did they think he might die?

Tears flowed and she searched for words that might get God's attention. None came.

Carolyn's mom looked in from the corridor. "There's someone here to speak with you." She helped Carolyn to her feet, led her to the door, and pushed her into the corridor. *Mom can stay with Jason.*

A man in an unbuttoned, tan sports jacket and pressed blue jeans waited with a clipboard. His colorful Hawaiian shirt was open at the collar. His carefully styled brown hair showed some gray at the temples and at his neck. A gold badge was clipped to his belt. "Mrs. Potter?"

She stepped into the corridor and closed the door. "Yes?"

"Is Jason Potter your son?"

"Yes."

He opened his hinged metal clipboard, took out his pen, and scribbled some notes. "I need to ask you a few questions about what happened this afternoon." He looked directly at Carolyn, making sure she paid attention. "Does your son own a pocket knife or carry any kind of knife?"

The question surprised her. "No, of course not."

"How can you be sure?" The man sounded arrogant, self impressed. That offended her, but he was a police officer. These days, they were so well groomed and oh, so polite. "Who are you? What's this all about?"

"Oh, sorry." He pulled out a folded leather carrier and flipped it open, showing his L.A.P.D. identification. "My name's Art Latanzio, L.A.P.D." He put his identification away and waited for an answer; to what, she couldn't remember.

He recognized her bewilderment. "How can you be sure your son doesn't carry a knife?"

"I'm his mother!" She folded her arms and stood in front of the door, instinctively protecting her son.

"Yes, ma'am." He sounded so polite, so well groomed, so arrogant. "We're aware of that, but we hear that all the time. Most parents don't have a clue what their kids are up to."

Her hand went to her throat, sensing something bad. "Why are you asking me that? What happened?"

"Our preliminary investigation shows evidence of some kind of struggle, like your son and the other boy were having some kind of a fight."

"Jason? Fighting? That's impossible. He and Jimmy are best friends." Her hands dropped to her sides. Both of her fists balled around the cotton flannel fabric of her blouse. "Why? What happened?"

"I guess you haven't heard yet," so polite, so well groomed, smelling of cologne. He lowered his clipboard and stepped closer, watching her, ready to grab her. "I'm the one who answered the phone at the O'Connell residence. We were just on our way here when you called. I thought it best to keep his parents away from you. She's very upset."

"Why? What happened to Jimmy?"

"Jimmy O'Connell was pronounced dead on arrival, in the emergency room."

Carolyn bumped back against the door, her knees buckled, and she slid, sitting on the floor. Tears dripped off of her chin and she couldn't stop them.

"Carolyn?" The man's voice sounded familiar, close. She tried to look through the blur of her tears. She wiped away tears and found Latanzio's pressed jeans, his polished shoes, and his white socks.

Out of nowhere, Mr. Kirby knelt by her side and slid his arm around her shoulder.

It made her feel creepy. She pulled away and stood, buried her face in her hands, and leaned her shoulder into the wall. She couldn't bear to look at him. Jason might die, because of him. He'd kept her late, looking her up and down with his wide set, beady eyes.

"Sir," Latanzio's tone stayed in the polite range. "You'll have to step back. We're conduction a criminal investigation."

"Who's we?" Mr. Kirby sounded angry. "Who in blazes are you?"

"Detective Lieutenant Arturo Latanzio, L.A.P.D."

"You have identification?"

"Yes, sir." Latanzio pulled and flipped open his identification, shoving it under Mr. Kirby's nose, not so polite anymore. "Are you this woman's husband?"

"No." Mr. Kirby poked his chin over the top of Latanzio's clipboard, ready to pounce.

"Then, sir . . ." Detective Lataznio lowered and slapped the flap down over his identification. "You'll have to step back. I have more questions for Mrs. Potter."

"You think so?" Mr. Kirby put his hands on his hips and leaned close to Detective Latanzio's face. "I heard what you just told her and I saw her reaction. Do you really think she had anything to do with what happened?"

Not looking so cocky, not so sure of himself, Detective Latanzio took a step back. "That's what we're here to find out, isn't it?"

"Who in blue blazes is we?" Mr. Kirby looked up and down the corridor, over Detective Latanzio's shoulder, down at Latanzio's clipboard, and waited for an answer.

"Are you her attorney?"

"No, but I can make a phone call and have my attorneys all over your badge." Kirby pulled out his Android, opened it, and started scrolling his directory.

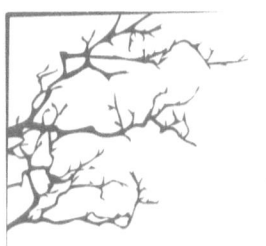

Chapter Five

Paintings of God and Jesus, and of a woman holding a baby adorned the awesomely high ceiling in Jimmy's church. Though Jason had never been in a Catholic church before, he figured that's what all of these paintings must be, pictures of God, of the man Jesus, and of Baby Jesus with his mom. The whole ceiling had been painted with blue sky and billowing white clouds, and some winged baby angels flying around. Seeing God and Jesus and baby angels and stuff made Jason feel better.

He sat between Mom and Mr. Kirby near the center of the church. Lots of people sat in front of them. The benches behind were mostly empty.

Mr. Kirby never looked directly at Jason, even when he looked sideways. His eyes were so far apart he didn't even need to turn his head. Jason could never guess what he was thinking.

Who wants to?

He always knew what his mom was thinking. Her eyes said everything. Right then, she wasn't feeling very good.

At the front of the church, Jason couldn't see him, a man said, "At times like this, we all tend to ask ourselves why. Why was Jimmy O'Connell taken at such an early age? Why have they not found those responsible for this hateful act? Why, Holy Savior, has another child been taken from us? Why, in this City of Angels, has one of your own been so brutally destroyed before his time? Why have his . . ." The words droned into a meaningless murmur, as Jason's mind drifted into memories of Jimmy, their days together, like that time Jimmy had taken a roofing nail to school and they'd put it under Ms.

Martinez's back tire in the school parking lot. Neither of them had ever liked their home room teacher.

They'd hidden behind a van and watched her get into her car. When the backup lights came on, Jimmy had said that the back tire would explode. It hadn't. The car had backed over the nail but nothing had happened. After she'd left, they'd gone to look and the nail had been gone. Jimmy had said that her tires must be made from solid rubber.

Wish he was here.

Ms. Martinez and a lot of other teachers attended Jimmy's funeral, mostly sitting near the front because they were more important. A lot of other kids were there too, mostly with their parents.

Jimmy had lots of friends.

None of the teachers told Jason hello. Neither did any of the other kids. Jason expected that. After all, this was his fault. His mom had been late picking them up.

Jason scratched his head, itching like crazy.

His mom pulled his hand down and softly slapped it, reminding him not to scratch his stitches.

He sat on his hands and watched his feet swing back and forth under the bench, not quite long enough to reach the floor.

Jason felt Mr. Kirby's beady eyes, looking at him. Jason looked, but Mr. Kirby had already turned back to the front. He'd probably been looking sideways again.

It had been Mr. Kirby's yelling outside his hospital room that had awakened Jason. Waking up to see Grandma sitting there hadn't been much fun, but Jason had gone home the following day, two days before Jimmy's funeral.

Mom and others stood and knelt on the padded rail in front of them. Jason followed them down. Voices all around him softly said, "Hail Mary, full of grace, the Lord is with Thee. Blessed art thou among women, and blessed is the fruit of thy womb, Jesus." Not knowing the words, Jason stayed quiet. Mom and Mr. Kirby stayed quiet too.

Everybody stood to sing another song he'd never heard before, mostly the choir. The pretty song folded into his memories, thinking about Jimmy again. That night when Mom had been late was supposed to be Jason's birthday party. Jimmy had been his only invited guest, him and Barnabas. Grandma didn't like having a bunch of kids in her house.

Wish Jimmy was here.

People stood, moved sideways between the benches, and stepped into the center aisle. Jason stood and followed Mom with Mr. Kirby to the end of a long line of people, all moving slowly toward the front of the church.

Mr. Kirby stood aside and pushed Jason in front of him, holding his shoulders, pushing him close behind Mom.

People in front took turns looking into a fancy white coffin with polished brass handles and trim. Behind the coffin was a big statue that looked like a giant version of Jimmy's necklace of Jesus on the cross. Jesus looked sad.

Jason followed his mom up two steps, where she looked inside the open coffin. She moaned softly, looked at Jimmy's parents, and lowered her head. She wasn't feeling very good.

Jimmy's parents looked sad too, dressed in black.

The priest next to them wore a white robe and a gold-colored scarf. He looked sad too.

Mr. Kirby pushed Jason toward the coffin, his turn to look.

Jason yanked free and turned away. "No." He didn't want to see Jimmy in there. He jumped back down the steps past Mr. Kirby and ran toward sunlight, shining through the open front doors. Jimmy ran right there with him, laughing and racing, always in the lead. The sun felt good.

JASON SAT IN THE BACKSEAT of Mr. Kirby's car, travelling across town in a long line of other cars. Mr. Kirby drove slowly but they never stopped.

Uniformed cops sped past on motorcycles and stopped at cross streets to block other cars so they wouldn't need to stop.

Mr. Kirby finally turned into a big, grassy yard and parked in a long line of other cars.

Mom said, "We're at the cemetery, honey. Do you want to give him a flower and say goodbye?"

"Okay."

Mr. Kirby opened the back door and Jason got out. He tried to grab Jason's hand but Jason turned away and grabbed his mom's hand instead. They all walked across a huge lawn to gather around Jimmy's closed coffin, resting on canvas straps over a big hole in the ground. Some kind of box filled the bottom of the hole.

Jason nodded at Mary Lou Anderson and Jaime Ortiz, two other kids from their school. They both lived across the street from Jimmy.

Ms. Martinez stood next to Ms. Wilkerson. They both nodded at Jason. Their frowning faces told Jason how they blamed him.

Everybody blamed Jason.

Jimmy's parents stood on the other side of the coffin with Dot, Jimmy's four-year-old sister. Dot was small for four. Jimmy's father held her in the crook of his arm.

Jason hadn't seen her in church. She smiled and waved her flowers at Jason, as if nothing was wrong. Jason waved back. At least she wasn't blaming him.

The priest moved his right hand in that funny motion and kissed his fingers. Everybody stayed quiet and watched the white canvas straps slowly unwind from fat, polished brass pipes. The coffin slowly sank into the hole and the box at the bottom. The priest tossed dirt onto the coffin and said, "Ashes to ashes, dust to dust. From it we came, and to it we must return."

Everybody said, "Amen."

The priest said, "Dear Lord, accept young James into Thy tender embrace. Strengthen his family to store their love forever in Thee, ever looking for the day when they might again be united in Thy heavenly kingdom."

Everybody said, "Amen."

Several baskets of flowers had been arranged around the open grave. More flowers stood on fancy wire fences sticking into the grass. People started picking flowers and tossing them onto Jimmy's coffin.

Jason backed away. Why were they killing flowers and giving them to Jimmy?

Mom tossed some flowers into the grave. Maybe she knew why. He'd ask her later.

MR. KIRBY PARKED ACROSS the street from Jimmy's house and Jason let himself out of the backseat. He knew Jimmy's house, having been there so many times. He looked both ways, ran across the street, climbed the front steps, and squeezed onto the crowded front porch, where a lot of grownups talked softly. They gave him those sad frowns. They knew this was Jason's fault.

The front door was open so Jason went inside.

A lot more people stood in the dining room eating stuff with their fingers. Jason didn't feel like eating anything. He looked up the stairs toward Jimmy's bedroom.

Dot sat halfway up in her white dress, still holding her flowers. She'd bent or broken some of the stems. She stood and climbed down the stairs, one slow step at a time, holding the rail to keep from falling. She dropped some of her flowers and stopped. She wanted to pick them up, so she looked at Jason.

Jason climbed up quickly and helped her with her flowers.

She hugged her flowers and smiled.

Jason helped her climb down to the bottom of the stairs.

Jason's mom and Mr. Kirby stood near the dining room table with Jimmy's dad. Jason couldn't see Jimmy's mom anywhere. He took Dot's hand and led her across the room to stand near his mom.

She held hands with Jimmy's dad, like a handshake but not shaking.

"Thank you for coming." Jimmy's dad looked tired.

"I'm so sorry." Mom wasn't doing very well, like she might start crying again.

Mr. Kirby stood behind Mom and grabbed her waist in both hands, talking to Jimmy's dad. "It's my fault, Mr. O'Connell. I needed to talk with her before she left my office. She might otherwise have been there on time. If there's anything I can do, please let me know." He let go of Mom, reached into his vest pocket, and handed Jimmy's dad a card.

Jimmy's dad glanced at the card, set it on the dining table, grinned thinly, and shook his head. "It's not your fault, Mr. Kirby. It's this city." He looked out the front window and fanned toward the street. "It's the traffic. It's this world we live in, all this illegal immigration, this sanctuary business." He took off his glasses, wiped his eyes, and pinched the bridge of his nose where his glasses left marks. His voice wavered, maybe not wanting to say it. "Everything's turned upside down. Nobody cares about truth or justice anymore. It's all about perceptions."

Ms. Martinez turned and looked at the back of Mr. O'Connell's head, a strange look.

Mom wasn't talking right then so Jason tugged the back of her dress.

She turned to look.

Jason said, "Me and Dot are going out back."

"Okay, honey." She smiled and raked Jason's hair to the side, looking into him with all that love.

She turned away and Jason led Dot out the back door and down the steps into Jimmy's fenced backyard. Dot ran to the big tree with the swing Jimmy had never let her use. The swing had been for boys only, Jason and Jimmy.

Jason put her in the swing and gave it a shove. "Lean back when I push and stick your legs out."

She did, not changing position when the swing rushed back, her legs still sticking straight out.

Jimmy's right. Swings are for boys.

Stupid girls.

Jason kept pushing and Dot kept leaning backward, holding her legs straight out. He pushed her for a long time.

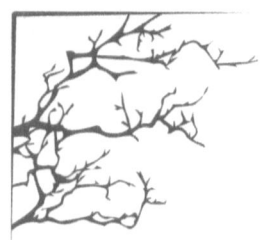

Chapter Six

A week after Jimmy's funeral, Mr. Kirby came over to pick Jason and his mom up at Grandma's house. He started his car and turned back, making sure Jason had buckled his seatbelt. "Don't do anything funny back there. These are leather seats." He pulled away from the curb, turned downhill to Alvarado, and turned right. He drove under the freeway, turned left, and took the freeway toward downtown. After a short distance, they got off the freeway at Temple. Jason liked reading the signs.

He rubbed the side of his head, itching like crazy. Rubbing worked okay. Mom had already told him not to scratch, maybe a thousand times. The stitches had been removed a couple of days earlier but sometimes it still itched like crazy.

Mr. Kirby turned into an alley, rolled down his window, and stopped to take a slip of paper from a machine. He rolled up his window, a yellow gate went up, and he drove under a big building into an underground parking garage.

He drove past a lot of other cars under the building until Jason's mom said, "Look, there's a space." Mr. Kirby drove into the space and parked. Mom turned to look at Jason but he couldn't see her face. Underground was too dark. She said, "Okay, honey, we're here." Jason unbuckled his seat belt and everybody got out.

Mom tried to take his hand but Jason pulled away. He was too old for that stuff. He was nine.

They walked down a wide aisle between cars and joined several other grownups, all waiting for an elevator.

The elevator door opened, nobody in there, and the grownups rushed to see who could get inside first. Mr. Kirby held the door open while Jason and his mom pushed their way into the large elevator, squeezing between people toward the back, where there was plenty of room. Everybody else wanted to be in front. Mr. Kirby stepped in last, pressed one of the buttons, and the door closed.

The elevator started moving and Mr. Kirby pushed through the people to be closer to Mom. He asked Jason, "You ever been in an elevator?" He didn't really care. He had dead eyes. Too dead to really care.

Jason said, "Of course. They've got one at the school administration building and one at the hospital. We're going up to the fifth floor. I watched you push the button. I'm not stupid, you know."

Mom rubbed Jason's shoulder and smiled, asking him to calm down.

Some of the other grownups smiled at Jason and shook their heads, grinning like they knew Mr. Kirby was a poophead.

At least Mr. Kirby was not his dad. Jason felt grateful for that.

The elevator stopped at the third floor and chimed. The door opened and three of the grownups got out. A lady with a stack of brown folders stepped in and looked at the lighted numbers on the wall panel. She didn't push anything. The door closed and the elevator moved again. They stopped at the fifth floor, it chimed, the door opened, and Mr. Kirby said, "Excuse, please."

Jason pushed out first and waited in a wide corridor.

Mr. Kirby held Mom's waist from behind and pushed her out into the corridor. They walked side-by-side, plenty of room.

The poophead took them to where a whitehaired man in a light gray suit waited.

Jason wore his new dark blue suit.

Mr. Kirby shook the man's hand. "Thanks for coming, Walt." He let go of the man's hand and fanned toward Mom. "This is Carolyn Potter, one of our authors."

The man didn't smile at Mr. Kirby, but he did smile at Mom. He shook her hand. "I'm Walter Emerick, Emerick, Bessel and Waters. We specialize in corporate law but I know the judge. We sponsored her into law school at U.S.C." He held Mom's hand, leaned closer, and smiled a private kind of smile. "Don't let on I told you that." He winked, let Mom's hand go, and looked at Jason, more serious than he'd been with Mom. "You must be Jason. I've heard quite a lot about you."

"Like what?"

"Oh, that you're a good student, that you don't get into fights, and that you're really good at math and art. Stuff like that." He turned to Mr. Kirby and said, "We need to talk about that other thing."

"Yeah, I know." Mr. Kirby looked mad about something. "I'll get with you guys right after the first of the month."

Mr. Emerick stepped around Mom to look into Mr. Kirby's eyes. "We're climbing into some serious numbers, here. If not for your father . . ."

"Okay, Walt! Right after the first." They stood close, looking into each other like they wanted to start a fight. Mr. Emerick stepped back, shook his head, and opened the glass door. The painted sign read, "JUVENILE JUSTICE." Mr. Emerick led them down another corridor to an office. The raised brass letters on the dark wood door read, "JUANITA SANCHEZ."

Inside, they all stood in front of a desk where a woman wrote some notes into a long book. After she finished a line, she looked up and smiled. "Hi, Mr. Emerick. How nice to see you again. The judge is expecting you." She stood and led them through another door and into a bigger office with windows.

Dressed in a black suit with pants but no tie, another woman stood from behind a large desk and smiled, taking and shaking Mr. Emerick's hand. "Hi, Walter. I'm so glad to see you. It's been a long time."

"You've come a long way, your honor. We're still waiting for that promised Mexican dinner."

Her hand rushed to her face, her mouth and eyes wide open. "Oh, my goodness. I completely forgot. How about Saturday night. I've heard good things about Gracias Madre. They've got vegan, if you want."

Mr. Emerick said, "Do they have real food?"

She said, "I'm sure they do." She laughed a little.

He said, "Sounds good."

"How many?"

"Just myself and Ellen."

She said, "I'll make reservations and call you later."

"I'm looking forward to it. We can get caught up."

They were good friends. Anybody could see that.

"We'll be video recording this session." She glanced at Jason and Mom. She looked back at Mr. Emerick. "Is that okay?"

After glancing at Mr. Kirby and Mom, Mr. Emerick nodded, *okay*.

By then the other woman had gone and the door had been closed. The lady in black looked at Jason and motioned to a chair by her desk. "You must be Jason. I'm Juvenile Justice Juanita Sanchez. Do you know what that means?"

Her suit fascinated Jason more than her name. All three buttons had been fastened, stretching the fabric so tight, it looked like it might tear. Her boobs and belly pushed out and formed folds that ran all the way to her back. She bent close to his face and raised her eyebrows, getting his attention, waiting for an answer.

"Course." Jason sat in a big wooden chair. "That means you're a judge for bad kids."

She smiled, satisfied. "Not all of them are bad. Are you bad?"

"Gosh." Jason shrugged. "I don't know."

She sat. "Well, that's what we're here to find out." She pointed to a video camera mounted in the corner behind her desk. "This will be recording our conversation. Is that okay?"

"Sure." Jason smiled at the camera. The red light was on.

Mr. Emerick leaned on the front of the lady's desk and dipped his head toward Mom. "This is young Jason's mother, Carolyn Potter, and this is Tom Kirby, her employer. He's one of our corporate clients."

Mom and Mr. Kirby leaned across her desk, shook her hand, and sat in chairs against the wall.

The judge quietly read from an open folder on her desk then closed it. She stared at the closed folder for a long time before looking at Jason. "Do you understand why you're here, Jason?"

"Sort of."

"Well, we're all here to find out what happened on November eleventh."

"That was my birthday. I'm nine."

"Well, you're getting to be a great big man now, aren't you?"

"No, ma'am." Right then, he didn't feel very big. "I only just turned."

"I see. So, tell me, Jason, what happened right after school on your birthday?"

"My mom was late picking us up." *Yikes.* He hadn't wanted to say that. He turned to look.

Darn. Mom was crying again. She dug into her purse and found a handkerchief.

"I see," said the judge.

Jason turned back and faced her.

Her dark-brown eyes leaned closer. "Can you tell me anything else?"

Jason's chair felt sticky and he squirmed, trying to get more comfortable. His collar felt tight, probably because of his tie. He pulled at the knot then remembered it was one of those clip-on types. He folded his hands in his lap and watched his thumbs wrestle with each other. "Me and Jimmy waited and Jimmy asked where she was." He looked at the judge. "It was cold and rainy." Jason's voice sounded funny to his inner ears, like someone sitting behind him, someone he couldn't see.

"I see." The Judge opened the file and read some stuff. "What happened next?"

"It was getting dark so Jimmy decided to walk home."

"Okay. Then what happened?"

"I followed him, of course."

She waited for more.

"Some bigger boys walked up the hill and stopped us. It was already dark out. That's all I know."

She looked straight at him for a long time, not smiling. "Can't you remember how many boys there were?"

Jason took a deep breath, watching those images trudge through his memory. "Of course. Three. Anybody could remember that."

She made a note. "What happened next?"

Jason didn't want to remember any more but she looked right into him and waited. "Jimmy knows karate and he's teaching me how."

"I see. So, did Jimmy start a fight?"

"No. Course not. Me and Jimmy tried to get away but it was uphill and we had our packs full of books and stuff."

"Stuff?"

"Yeah, pencils and paper and stuff."

"Did you or Jimmy have a knife or anything?"

"Of course not. Our moms won't let us do that."

"Okay." She made a note in the file. "What happened next?"

He turned and touched his ribs, showing her where. "One of them slugged me in my side and pushed me down." That unseen voice from somewhere behind Jason sounded like he was whining. Jason hated that.

"I see." She leaned close, being a friend. "And, what about Jimmy?"

"Jimmy's my best friend. He could lick anybody."

"I see. So, what did he do?"

"They pushed him down, too. He could beat 'em, but they were too big. There were too many . . ." He shook his head.

She made more notes in the file. "Tell me, Jason, what happened next?"

"One of them, the littlest one, he told us to give them our money, or else."

"Or else what?"

Jason shrugged. "Or else."

"I see. And, what did you do?"

"I only had two dollars and I was on the ground."

"What about Jimmy?"

"Jimmy told the littlest one, I think he was their leader, he told him we knew who he was. That was when the biggest one slugged Jimmy real hard. I could hear it even."

"I see. So, what did Jimmy do?"

Tears flowed down Jason's cheeks and dripped onto his clenched fists. "He kicked at the biggest one, but the other one had a knife. He cut Jimmy three times and Jimmy stopped kicking." Jason could see Jimmy's eyes like he was right there. "Jimmy tried to tell me something but he was bleeding all over." Jason grabbed the arms of the chair and slid forward to touch the floor with his toes. Maybe he could run.

"Okay, Jason. Can you remember what happened next?"

"Let's give him a minute." Mr. Emerick stepped between Jason and the judge and sat on the corner of her desk. He smiled at Jason and asked, "Are you okay, son?" He leaned forward and held Jason's shoulder like he really cared, but he wanted an answer.

"Jimmy was my best friend." Tears ran down Jason's cheeks.

"You miss him, don't you?"

"Yes, sir." Jason wiped his face and took a deep breath.

"Well, I think we're almost done here." Mr. Emerick stood and looked at the lady judge.

She smiled and nodded.

Mr. Emerick returned to his chair.

"Okay, Jason." The judge smiled, being friendly. "After Jimmy got hurt, what happened next?"

Jason looked down at his wrestling thumbs. "Jimmy whispered he was sorry. I couldn't hear but I could see his lips."

"Sorry for what, Jason?"

"I don't know." Jimmy's last comment had haunted Jason. He'd dreamed about it, seeing it over and over in his sleep. "It was my fault. It was my mom who was late." Jason looked.

Mom had buried her face in her handkerchief. Her shoulders shook.

Jason said, "I'm sorry, Mommy."

She moaned and shook all the more.

Mr. Kirby reached over and rubbed her back.

Jason hated him for that, for touching his mom. He turned back into the judge's friendly dark eyes, her smiling red lips. He said, "Maybe because his karate never showed up."

"I see." The judge smiled until her big white teeth showed. She flashed her eyes at Mr. Emerick. She looked back at Jason, not smiling anymore. "Okay, Jason, can you remember what happened next?"

"One of them kicked me here." He touched the left side of his head where they had just taken out the stitches. "I never saw it coming. I only had two dollars, anyway. I remember looking at Jimmy, then I got kicked. I can't remember after that. Okay?" He stood up close to her desk, feeling sticky all over, trying to breath the way he should.

Maybe I can get away.

"Okay, Jason." She touched his hand, trying to calm him. "You're doing a very good job. It's all over now. You can relax."

Jason backed toward his mom and leaned into her chair, pushing into that safe place between her knees.

She folded her arms around him and pulled him in, nice and snug.

The judge hadn't finished, still looking at Jason. "Can you tell me what these boys looked like?"

"They were bigger. I already said." Seeing this wasn't enough, he went on to describe their different sizes, their clothing, their tattoos and haircuts, all he could remember.

The judge wrote a bunch of notes in her open folder then looked at Jason for a long time. "Can you tell me if they were white, or oriental, or African American, or what?"

"Oh, yeah, Jimmy said they were illegals."

"Illegal what?"

"Mexicans, of course."

BY THE TIME MR. KIRBY drove them home, Jason felt tired all over. He had finally come to terms with one fact; his best friend had gone away. He'd never see him again, not until Heaven.

Mr. Kirby had been talking to Jason's mom all the way home but Jason hadn't been listening, not until Mr. Kirby got off the freeway. He said, "I wish you'd think about it. I know John would have wanted you to remarry. His son needs a good father figure."

Good grief. Jason's mom would never marry a poophead like him. Whenever Mom wasn't looking, Mr. Kirby would stare at her boobs and at her lap, licking his lips like a big, beady-eyed lizard.

What a creepy creep.

"Not right now, Tom." She didn't look at him. She looked out the window instead. "I'm sorry."

"What is it?" Mr. Kirby sounded mad again. "Am I too ugly, or what?"

"It's not you." She sounded sincere. "It's . . ." She poked her thumb toward Jason and shook her head, searching for words like she did with Grandma. "There's just too much happening right now to even think about something like that."

"You know how I feel about you." The creepy creep flinched toward the backseat. "You and the kid, that is. Besides, it's been a long time since . . . Well, you know."

"Tom, I'm grateful for all you've done. Without your help, I just don't know what we would have done. Please, tell Mr. Emerick to send me the bill."

"Nonsense. What are friends for?" Mr. Kirby turned right onto Waterloo Drive and stopped at Grandma's house.

Finally.

Jason unbuckled his seat belt, opened his door, jumped out, and slammed the door, letting Mom know they were home.

Barnabas waited at the gate, prancing and moaning, always happy to see Jason. Jason opened the gate and got licked all over his face, until Mom followed him into the yard and closed the gate. Barnabas jumped up, saying hello to her, too.

She asked, "How are you feeling, honey?"

"Jimmy's gone, isn't he?" He took a deep breath and let it out. "I can't see him until we get to Heaven." *Jimmy and Mom. Not that poophead.*

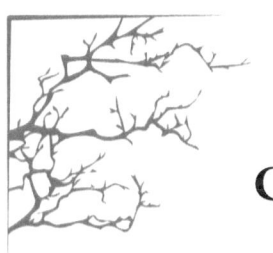

Chapter Seven

For what must have been the tenth time, Carolyn's mother said, "Why do you need to move all the way up there?" Carolyn didn't know whether she was hurt or angry, hard to tell with her. She always made everything difficult.

"Mom, please. I don't want to forget anything. Please . . ." *Stop distracting me.*

Mom said, "Why can't you buy a nice place near here? This is your home." She scowled, her usual expression, standing in the doorway and fanning her cigarette like a wand, telling Carolyn to put her stuff away and stop all this nonsense. It seemed absurd, after she'd threatened to throw Caroln, Jason, and Barnabas out a hundred times.

Carolyn placed the last of her books into a cardboard box and shifted them around, making sure she could close the flaps. She could. She forced a friendly smile and turned to face her mother. "Mom, we've talked and talked about this. A better neighborhood might be safer than Echo Park, but this whole city is changing and you know it. There isn't anywhere that seems to be safe these days."

Mom took a puff from her cigarette and narrowed her angry stare.

Good grief.

Carolyn picked up the roll of packing tape, closed the cardboard flaps, and taped the box shut. "Look at that woman in Beverly Hills, that literary agent. She got shot to death just driving home, and the police don't have a clue why that guy did it. He committed suicide and didn't even leave a note." She finished taping and faced her mom. "That's just crazy."

She fanned her mother's smoke out of her face. "And Jimmy . . . For all we know, it was some gang initiation that killed him. The police still don't have any suspects. They're too busy with sensitivity training and going to barber shops." Carolyn stepped closer, needing for this to sink in. "It could just as easily have been Jason's funeral."

Mom said, "You're even turning my own grandson against me."

"What are you talking about?"

Mom's comment had absolutely nothing to do with the conversation to this point, nothing but meanness. Carolyn picked up the heavy box of books in both arms and moved toward the door, ready to use the box as a battering ram.

Her mom dropped a long cigarette ash into her cupped hand and stood aside. "You can't wait to get out of here, can you?" Mom was hurting but she was right.

Carolyn couldn't wait to get out. She was suddenly and unexpectedly wealthy, and she already loved the independence that offered. It made her stronger. Maybe in her own house, with Mom as her guest, getting along wouldn't be so difficult. "Mom, I've invited you to come with us. What more can I do?" Gratefully, her mother had declined.

Carolyn pushed the heavy box in front of her and squeezed through the doorway.

Mom followed close behind, puffing out a fresh cloud of smoke. "You know I can't do that. Without me, that office would be lost."

Carolyn turned and pushed the security screen door open with her back, looking into her mother's desperation. "You're always complaining that no one in that office appreciates you." Carolyn stopped on the front porch. "They gave that other girl your raise, didn't they?"

Mom followed her onto the porch. "She's young and pretty, that's all." Carolyn turned and walked toward the street.

Jason and Barnabas waited at the front gate.

"Hurry up, Mom." Jason opened the gate. "Barnabas is ready to go already. He pooped and everything."

From the porch, Mom said, "I hope you cleaned it up."

Jason smiled. "Course."

The dog sat on the sidewalk, looking at Carolyn, shaking all over like he might be left behind. Carolyn carried the box to the back of a small U-Haul trailer, set it on the floor, and pushed it tight against the other boxes of books. After making sure she had the key, she closed and locked the cargo door. She had planned to tie everything into place but she didn't have time. All of her carefully packed boxes would shift and tumble into a big pile of stuff, but she didn't care. She'd deal with it later. Right then, they needed to get out of there.

"This is your home." Mom stood inside the gate, teeth clenched and tears welling. She flipped her cigarette into the street and dusted off her hands, as if wiping both Carolyn and Jason out of her life, forever. There would be no goodbye hugs.

"I'll call you as soon as we get there. Okay? After Jason gets through his first school year, who knows?" She shook her head and looked toward the San Gabriel Mountains. *Freedom.* She looked at her mom. "We might not like it there. We might decide to move back." Ventura or Santa Barbara might be far enough away from her mom.

THEY REACHED THE GRAPEVINE at 10:15 a.m. Carolyn took Highway 14 through Palmdale and Lancaster before stopping for lunch and gas in Mojave. From there, she drove north on 395

through Red Rock Canyon, up the east side of the Sierras, and stopped for the night in Bishop.

Early the next morning was her first taste of fresh mountain air, crisp with a scent of pine. It smelled of freedom.

PREDAWN LIGHT WAS WILLIS Donner's wakeup call. The Perch had ample windows facing east. The first wink of sun from over the mountain peaks at the eastern rim of the valley lit his whole interior, good light for cleaning up after breakfast.

Morning and night, ever since he could remember, he'd bathed in the hot spring near his west facing doorway, before swimming in the near freezing water of his small lake.

Water from his hot spring and lake fed into the nearby stream and flowed over the waterfall into Potter's upper meadow. He'd long since built a trail, a series of short switchbacks that followed the stream down the steep face of the Perch.

Judging from the angle of the sun, it was near 9:00 a.m., when he stepped out from under the trees at the top of Potter's upper meadow.

Whatever had happened the night before, there would be work today.

Being the son of a Southern Baptist preacher, Willis had never touched tobacco or alcohol; much less these modern drugs. He kept himself fit, busy with stone masonry, carpentry, and the like. The only thing that wore him down was not knowing what lay ahead.

"A worrisome nature brings a wrinkled brow," his father had often preached. For his many adult years, Willis had never learned not to worry after a full moon.

It wasn't so bad after this new ritual, the worrying part. A dead calf was a blessing.

Before the ritual, what he had sometimes found brought misery, for him, and for others. That kind of pain couldn't be buried with hard work. It lingered in his soul.

Thank you, God. The severed head and carcass of another bull calf lay on that sacrificial rock, chest ripped open, heart gone. The ritual had been working for several years. Nobody suffered from that. The beast of this place had been satisfied. He wouldn't come back before the next full moon. Maybe not even then.

Nesting meadowlarks fed on bloodworms at the edges of the rock, ignoring Willis, singing their heavenly songs, maybe even comforted by his presence. Heat from this rock kept these birds here year-round. Like the Perch, this rock ran deep into the belly of the earth, warmed by geothermal energy.

He freed the tie from under the calf's jaw, grabbed an ear, and carried the heavy head seventy yards to a dark pool in the slow-moving brook, a quarter mile below the waterfall. The pool went deep, down where large fish and blue crawdads could feed on it for a month.

Willis unsheathed his hunting knife and walked back down to that flat rock, to the calf's carcass. Starting at the open chest cavity, he slit the hide in an ample arc around the genitals and cut them free, cleaned out the entrails, and carried it all back to that deep hole. He tossed the genitals and entrails into the pool and watched them sink, much slower than the heavy head.

Small fish darted out from under the bog in a feeding frenzy, slowly disappearing into the deep.

He knelt, cleaned the knife in the stream, snapped it into the sheath at the small of his back, and washed his hands. He returned to the carcass, hefted it over his shoulders, and followed the dirt road uphill to an opening in the fence, where he crossed onto Jim Embry's place, moving steadily uphill toward the mine.

He stopped at the rock-debris field below the mine and adjusted the weight, looking up the well travelled path. He carried the carcass up the rubble mound quickly. His feet knew the way. He topped the rise and walked across the flat of rubble to the boarded-up entrance of the mine, near a giant Douglas fir and a huge boulder. A long-used chain hung from one of the tree's fat limbs.

Willis climbed onto the boulder and laid the carcass on top. He opened a small work shed near the boarded-up mine, pulled out a length of hemp rope, and tied it to the rear hooves of the dead calf. He looped the other end of the rope through a ring on the chain and hoisted the calf into the air. *Good.* Blood still drained from the calf's open neck.

The sun felt hot. He removed his jacket, draped it over a small branch, and jumped down from the boulder. He walked to the far edge of the debris field, to a place near the cascading waterfall. The mist cooled him. He grabbed a tree root and leaned out into the flow, taking several mouthfuls of cold, fresh tasting water.

The water washed his face and drenched his shirt, nice and cold. He returned to the top of the boulder, stepped into the shed, grabbed a wooden bucket, walked back to the waterfall, and filled the bucket.

He washed blood off the rock and refilled the bucket to wash the area down again. Clean rocks kept the flies and mosquitoes away. He quickly skinned the calf, picked the hide clean, and nailed it to the closed door over the mine. This spot had a southern exposure to the sun, an ideal spot for tanning.

He spread tanning oil over the hide and put the oil into the shed.

Using a hatchet, he split the calf down the center of the spine and washed away jelled blood, inside and out. He returned the tools to the shed and took down half of the calf. John Crow would pick up the other half later.

Something in the air grabbed his senses and he looked toward the village.

They're here.

JOHN CROW HAD BECOME used to Helfred Jacobsen's ire. It didn't bother him much, considering what she'd lost. Still, placing some of the blame on him didn't seem right.

He'd had a feeling they'd be coming that day, but he'd hoped to avoid Helfred. Though used to it, he still didn't like her glares and her scolding tongue, which was why he'd waited until after lunch to set up his Indian crafts at the far end of her porch. From there, he could see up River Road toward Sonora Pass.

He always hoped she wouldn't see him, but she always did.

With Olen's prodding, she allowed John to set up on weekends for that occasional tourist who might accidentally take the turnoff and drive down from the highway. It was a beautiful drive. They always stopped for directions, sometimes buying John's crafts.

Olen would remind her how good it was for business. When they saw a tall Indian selling stuff from Olen's stone window ledge, they always went into the store. That day being a weekday, John hoped she wouldn't chase him off.

Maybe these new Potters would put him back to work. The Ralstons, the Pendletons, and some of the others still hired John whenever they got a new horse. Even Jim Embry did that. None of them liked breaking horses. Breaking horses had always been easy for John. They nearly never bucked.

The Gilpins had never hired John. They'd always broken their horses the hard way, using steel bits that sometimes hurt the animal's mouth. The Gilpins didn't care. John doubted if they ever gave it a thought.

After Kidro's death, Jim Embry had taken the Potter horses over to his place. Otherwise, Gilpin would have snuck in there and taken Stoner. He would have left the barn door open to claim that he'd found Stoner running wild. He'd claim that a wild horse belonged to whoever caught it. Range law.

Lot of thieving nonsense.

John's neck itched from Helfred's eyes, burning through the storefront window at his back. He didn't need to look.

Why did she hate John, anyway? She'd been blaming him for ten years for something he had no control over.

John had been here longer than most, *sure*. He knew the way of this place. They all knew the essence of John's knowledge. Maybe that was why she hated him. Or, maybe it was where he lived, up near the Perch. Maybe she thought he could have done something to stop it.

Like what?

Feeling her walk onto the porch, he pulled his hat low over his eyes and pretended not to notice.

A car.

MOM SAID, "LOOK, HERE'S Jacobsen's Emporium."

Jason woke up, sitting in the front seat.

Barnabas leaned forward from the backseat, licking Jason's face, excited.

"Cool." He pushed Barnabas into the back and wiped dog slobber from his face.

"Isn't it beautiful?" Mom parked in front of an awesome looking store, built with stone masonry and heavy timbers, the kind of architecture Jason's dad had always liked. Mom said, "This is where they said to get directions."

"Huh." Jason opened his car door and Barnabas scrambled over the top of him, getting out, too fast and strong for Jason to stop.

Barnabas rushed up the stone steps under a deep overhang from a second floor and charged a tall man standing back in the shadows, near a window.

Jason ran after his dog, hoping he wouldn't hurt anybody. The dog wouldn't bite but he was very big and strong, and he liked jumping on people to say hello.

Barnabas stood on his hind legs with his front paws propped against a man's stomach, getting his head and neck scratched.

The man was tall and lean, wearing a brightly colored shirt neatly tucked into worn blue jeans. His jeans were held up by a wide belt with a polished silver buckle. His long, white ponytail flowed over his shoulders from under a wide rimmed, black cowboy hat with a colorfully beaded hatband. A feather poked up from the hatband, taller than the hat.

Indian jewelry, beaded shirts, wood carvings, and other beaded leather goods were displayed along the window ledge behind him.

"Wow! Are you a real Indian?" Jason had never met a real Indian before.

"Yes, I guess I am." He had a friendly smile and a face like leather. "This your dog?"

Barnabas leaned into the man with his tail wagging like they were best friends, smiling his dog smile like that, tongue hanging out the side of his face.

"Yes, sir. His name's Barnabas. He's an American Pit Bull Terrier."

"Jason." Mom sounded worried about something, standing right behind Jason. "Keep your dog under control." She smiled her apologetic smile at the Indian. "I'm sorry. That dog's too strong for a leash. He drags us wherever he wants to go." She clapped her hands but Barnabas ignored her, getting his ears scratched like that.

"It's okay, ma'am." The Indian lifted Barnabas's front paws off his belt and dropped him to the porch. "Me and animals get along fine." He leaned down and rubbed Barnabas's shoulders. Barnabas liked it. "I'm John Crow." He smiled and tipped his hat toward Mom.

"I'm Jason and this is my mom."

"Yes, we've been expecting you."

"Nice to meet you." Mom shook his hand, then he shook hands with Jason. His long fingers completely wrapped Jason's hand. His skin felt tough as an old canvas tarp. He let go, leaving Jason with a good feeling.

"Come on, Jason." Mom shoved him down the porch and through a double doorway into the store.

Tall, free-standing, wooden shelves left narrow corridors throughout the large interior. All of the shelving carried all kinds of cans, rags, and boxes, mostly food and stuff. Wooden chairs, light fixtures, ceiling fans, farming tools, and even toilet seats hung from the beamed ceiling above the shelves.

A woman and a man stood behind a glass-front counter near the back. Both looked older than grandma. Both threw their arms out, waving around at different times, maybe arguing about something. Jason couldn't hear about what. They hadn't yet seen Jason or Mom

Jason and Mom approached a glass-front counter, getting close enough to hear.

The woman said, "I don't want him out there during the week. Weekends are bad enough."

The man said, "He doesn't hurt anybody." He sounded calm. His back was turned toward the counter. Both had funny sounding accents.

"I don't care." She wagged her finger in the man's face. "He's got no business selling his junk in front of my store."

"You know why he's here."

"I don't care! He's . . ." She stopped talking, finally seeing Jason and Mom. She smiled and elbowed the man, turning him around.

He smiled.

She said, "Hallo! You must be them Potters, from down below." She seemed friendly enough.

The man's smile looked friendly too. "We been expecting you, couple o' days now." He looked down at Jason, taking his time, studying Jason's face. "Look, Momma, his bright blue eyes. Don't he look just like his papa?"

"He sure does, by golly." She grabbed a glass cookie jar and strutted around the end of the counter, spun off the bright red metal lid, and held the open jar toward Jason. "Your papa always liked these." She shoved it closer, insisting.

They were chocolate chip. Jason could smell them. He looked at his mom for permission.

She smiled. "Just take one."

He reached in, took a big one, turned, and walked toward the porch. He needed to talk to that Indian.

"Young man!" Mom's voice stopped him in the doorway. He turned back.

Her eyes scolded. "What do we say?"

Jason smiled at the woman and said, "Thank you."

"You're very welcome." The old woman smiled and spun the red cap back onto the jar.

Jason went outside.

Barnabas leaned sideways into the Indian's legs, still getting his back rubbed.

"Umm." The cookie was the best ever, sweet and moist. "I never saw a real Indian before. What kind are you?"

"I'm Paiute. My people have lived up here in these mountains for hundreds of years. We're mostly working for ranchers now, like down in Owens River Valley, or over in Walker and Carson. I used to work for your great grandfather." He slid a couple of hatbands to one side and sat on the window ledge, still rubbing Barnabas's head and shoulders. He patted Barnabas's side, pushed with his knee, and Barnabas plopped down in front of him, looking back-and-forth between the Indian and Jason.

Jason picked up a cool looking beaded-leather pouch the size of Grandma's coin purse. "Wow! What's this?" It had been looped and stitched around a braided leather necklace, cinched tight. He squeezed it. Stuff was inside.

"We call this a medicine bag." John took and opened the bag in such a way that Jason downed his cookie and instinctively cupped his hands. John poured out a collection of small bones, polished stones, feathers, and small, smooth pieces of wood. Some of the polished stones were clear like glass. Others were gray, green, blue, or black. John spread the open pouch toward Jason and Jason carefully poured the stuff back inside. Jason asked, "What's it for?"

"You're supposed to wear it." John cinched the pouch and dropped the braided necklace over Jason's head.

It hung around Jason's neck to the center of his chest, *too cool*.

"Your father wore one just like it." John showed him a similar pouch hanging around his own neck. It looked much older. "I wear one too."

"What's it for?"

"Only us Indians are supposed to know that." He bent down to Jason and spoke softly. "I'll tell you the secret. Wear it so the spirits know who you are. They'll protect you."

"Wow, how much?" He needed to ask Mom.

"Oh, you can't buy one of these. It has to be a gift or it has no power." He smiled, matter-of-fact.

Barnabas stood up and wagged.

"Come on, Jason." Mom carried two grocery bags down the steps. The old man followed with two more.

Jason followed Barnabas down the steps and Mom handed him one of the bags so she could open the trunk. "Oh, dear." She set one bag between two suitcases and moved other stuff to make room for the other. She studied the load and closed the trunk.

The old man put his two bags into the backseat, left the front seat leaning forward, and stepped away.

Jason snapped his fingers and Barnabas climbed into the back. Jason pushed the front seat back, sat in front, and closed the door.

Mom climbed in behind the steering wheel, closed her door, and pointed down the road, speaking to the old man. "So, we just follow this all the way to the end and turn left."

"Yes, ma'am. You can't miss it. You'll see."

"How do we pay for supplies again?"

The old man pointed across the street at a city-looking building. The sign said, "Potter Bank and Trust." High windows, up near the roof, ran across the front. The old man said, "Just go in there when you get a chance. They'll have you sign some paperwork and set up your account with us. Then we can submit the monthly billings directly to your bank. They'll send you a copy, of course." He started to turn away and stopped. "Everybody will be in church on the second Sunday of next month, just before school starts. They're all anxious to meet the new Potters from down below."

"Where is it? How do we get there?"

"Right behind the store, here. It's called the Rock. You can't miss it. Service starts at ten o'clock sharp."

"Well, we can't thank you enough." Mom started the car, and they both waved to the old couple, already at the top of the steps.

They both waved back, both wearing big smiles.

The Indian had already gone, trinkets and all.

Wow. Jason hadn't seen him leave.

"This is called River Road." Mom drove them down a grassy valley with tall mountains on both sides, sounding like she'd been there before. "The road goes all the way to our new home where it ends, so we can't miss it."

"Huh." Jason listened, looking out the window to the right, where tall trees steadily drew closer to the road, blocking out his view of the mountains. A lot of grass grew on Mom's side, with some cows all scattered out behind a wire fence. "Look, Mom." The trees on her side looked way far away, growing up the side of the mountain, too far to walk. "Are those our cows?"

"I don't know, honey. Look, here it is." The paved road ended at a big pile of rocks. Those dense trees on the right side cut across behind the rocks and continued way past. A large boulder on the left had been neatly engraved with fancy letters that read, "POTTER RANCH."

Mom turned up a wide driveway paved with rounded stones that made their tires sound funny. The driveway curved up a hill to the right and Mom stopped.

A broad-shouldered man carrying a wooden box and wearing tools around his waste walked to her side of the car.

She rolled down the window.

The man looked lean and strong, just like Jason's dad. "Ma'am?" He shifted his toolbox and tipped his straw cowboy hat. "Name's Willis Donner. I live just above." He nodded toward the more distant mountains on the left. "Just been checking on the temporary door I hung to your house. I'll stick around to help you unpack."

GOOD GRIEF. Barnabas followed Willis everywhere, ignoring Jason again. First that Indian, and now Willis Donner. Barnabas had taken to both of them right off, Willis maybe even more than the Indian, like he'd known them both his whole life.

Willis carried another box from the back of the trailer and Jason ran up the front steps in front of him.

Mom waited in the open doorway to her new office. "That box goes in here, Willis." She led him through the office with a desk and into her new bedroom. She liked Willis, too, maybe because her stuff got unloaded first.

All of the boxes stacked in the entry and living room belonged to Jason, not as many as Mom's. Jason had already carried the smaller boxes upstairs by himself. His new bedroom was in back, over the kitchen.

Willis finally grabbed a box from the entry to help Jason, one big box at a time.

Jason and Barnabas followed Willis upstairs and down, box after box, then Jason finally stayed in his new bedroom and let Barnabas follow Willis.

Jason's new bedroom was gigantic. There were two double beds and two large dressers with a wide table under a window between the beds. From this window, Jason could see through trees, so close he could almost touch them, to what Willis called their upper meadow. A cool looking waterfall was up past the meadow. If he climbed onto the table with his knees and got really close to the glass, he could see the U-Haul trailer in front of the house, but not the car.

Willis took a wardrobe box into the large bathroom and Jason followed. Willis opened the door to a long closet and set the box inside. He gave Jason a curious look. "Want me to unpack it?"

"No thank you, Mr. Donner. Me and Barnabas can do that."

"Call me Willis. Everybody else does."

"Okay." Jason liked Willis a lot. He was open, not like Mr. Kirby. Willis's eyes were clear and looked right into Jason, not in his general direction like Mr. Kirby. Mr. Kirby would never say to call him Tom, like he always did with Mom. Mr. Kirby wasn't friendly like Willis Donner, or like . . . "Say, what's that Indian's name again?"

"You mean, John Crow?"

"Oh, yeah. That's it."

Jason's new bathroom was bigger than anything, with a long, high window and everything. It even had two sinks. They were different than bathroom sinks Jason had seen before.

Willis said, "Those are called pedestal sinks, made from Italian marble. Faucets are solid brass." Willis crossed the bathroom and opened the opposite door. "You seen in here?"

Jason followed Willis into another large room with a big window. Book shelves and books filled the walls between the bathroom door, another door, and the window. Everywhere, finely crafted stone and polished woodwork explained why his father had appreciated the houses whenever they drove through good neighborhoods on weekends.

Two desks stood under the long window that overlooked a gigantic, grassy meadow, with black cows near a stream. It was beautiful, way downhill, surrounded by tall trees and mountains.

Both desks had comfortable looking chairs and there was even a phone on one of the desks. Jason could put his computer there. The reality hit him. "Wow, is this a library?"

"That's exactly what it is." Willis looked around and touched a couple of shelves where wood had been chipped. He looked closer, like he might want to fix it. "This is where your father and your Uncle Ethan learned their lessons from your great grandmother. She used to allow for me to come in here and read. Light from the window's real good during the day." Willis had a far-off look, maybe remembering something special.

"You can come and read whenever you want, Willis. Don't worry, I'll tell Mom."

Willis smiled like he would. "When your father was ten, Mary Lou, that's your great grandmother, she started me building on the church and school. That's where your father and uncle graduated high school. That's where you'll be going to school."

"I'd rather study here." Jason had no fond memories of his school in L.A.

"You'll like this school just fine." Willis crossed to the far corner and waited. A round stair railing between book cases led down. He nodded and pointed behind Jason, to the other door. "That door goes into the hallway, across from your grandparents' old bedroom. After your grandma was taken and after Mary Lou died, your grandpa, Kidro, slept downstairs in your mother's bedroom."

Willis pointed down. "This goes down to the pantry." He started down.

Jason and Barnabas followed.

At the bottom was a hallway with three doors and high windows. Willis pointed at one of the doors with his thumb. "Through there's your mother's bathroom and bedroom." He pointed to another door. "Over here goes down to the meat locker and garage. There's a heavy door down there with a crossbar for protection. It keeps the critters out. Make sure it's secured good and proper at night. I'll show you after I finish with your front door." With a dip of his head, Willis opened the third door. "Through here's the pantry, like I said."

The pantry had a washer and dryer, a big wash sink, high windows, a lot of shelves with canned goods, bags of sugar and flour, boxes of cereal, liquor, soap and stuff, and two more doors.

"Why did Mom buy groceries?"

Willis ignored the question. He opened one of the doors to another bathroom. This bathroom was more like Grandma's house in

Echo Park, a tub with a shower curtain, a toilet, and a sink. Unlike grandma's, this bathroom had a high window.

Willis opened the other door and Jason followed him into the huge kitchen. They turned through the double swinging kitchen door, crossed the living room, and climbed three steps into the entry, where Willis had previously hung a sheet of plywood across the front door opening. He'd used a thick, long piece of leather as a hinge. It had a gate latch to keep it closed.

"Oh, there you are." Mom sat behind the desk in her new office, using her new computer already. She grabbed her purse and walked into the entry. Speaking to Willis, she said, "How much do we owe you?"

Willis stuck up his hand and shook his head, *no*. He pulled his straw hat from a hat rack made from animal horns and slowly turned it between his fingers, nervous, not looking straight at Mom. "I gave a list of materials for your new front door to Olen. Give him a call and he'll have the stuff up here the next day. Only take me a day to get it made up."

"How much will that cost?"

Willis shrugged and looked at her. "Olen can give you the sales slip. He runs open accounts with all the suppliers from down below."

"I mean, for you."

"Things work different here. My home was technically built on Potter land, so I kind of take care of this place. John Crow comes around to tend the livestock. He lives on Potter land, too. Mary Lou, the boy's great grandmother, she used to pay us but not no more. Not since they give us titles to our properties." He twirled his hat between his fingers. "She and Jethro paid when I built the store, the church, the school, and such." He looked at Mom. "Not no more. Not Kidro."

"Willis . . ." She looked at him with those eyes, holding her purse open like that. "I don't mean to be rude. This house is the finest workmanship I've ever seen, but maybe we should just order a nice custom door somewhere and have you install it."

Willis stopped spinning his hat and stared at her. "Kidro had a factory door. It wasn't . . ." He looked out the open door toward River Road. "I mean, we got things up here. A factory door won't hold up. Tell you what, if you don't like my workmanship, I'll buy whatever door you want and install that instead."

Mom gave up and closed her purse. "Okay. Do you have a phone?"

"No, ma'am."

"How can I get ahold of you, you know, when the truck comes?"

"I live up on the Perch."

"The Perch?"

"Yes, ma'am." Willis fanned his hat toward the kitchen. "Up on top of that granite dome, near the waterfall. You can see it from the kitchen or from upstairs. I'll see the truck coming. He always stops at Olen's for Helfred's cookies and coffee."

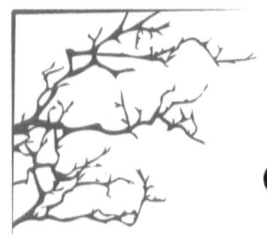

Chapter Eight

Sheriff Phil Nason turned left off of River Road onto the gravel road onto Jim Embry's place.

Early rays of sunlight touched the western rim of the mountains, reflecting from windows up on the Perch, not a cloud in the sky. Even though an early morning chill still bit, Nason knew they had a hot day ahead. Not so much at the Potter house, on the eastern edge of the valley, surrounded by mature pine trees. Sun wouldn't reach their house before 10:00 a.m.

He drove in a wide circle in front of Embry's stone and timber ranch house and rolled downhill toward Jim's wood sided barn. Embry's single-story house had been built on a natural knoll above the gentle slope leading down to River Road. The whole long valley sloped downhill, west to east, toward the river.

Embry's barn sat a hundred yards down slope from his house. When their heavy oak shutters were open, as they were on that morning, they could see over the barn's high-pitched roof, all the way down to River Road. Embry's house was typical Willis Donner, impenetrable stone and heavy timber, exquisitely detailed, and well planned.

Nason had grown up in Potter's Valley but had no idea what Willis thought of him or of his family. The little brick house behind the jail had been their only home, not built by Willis. The house and jail had been built during the gold rush days and had been renovated by Nason's father, with help from Jeff Ralston and Olen Jacobsen.

Willis hadn't built very much in the village, only the store and the church. Jethro and Mary Lou Potter had paid for those.

The jail might be safe, with brick walls and iron bars, but not as safe as Willis-built homes. Twenty grizzly bears on methamphetamines couldn't breach Embry's house, or the Potter place, or Olen's store.

Jim Embry liked everybody and everybody liked him. The Embrys had always been a likable brood, crazy as drunken racoons, but harmless. Phil and Jim had been close friends since 1st grade.

They had enlisted in the Coast Guard together and Jim had gotten married to a girl he met in Frisco on their first liberty. He had served his four years in the Coast Guard and had moved back up to Potter Valley, wife, twin baby boys, and a big fat cat.

Willis built this place for Embry's parents more than twenty years earlier. It looked as fine today as it had back then.

Nason parked in front of the barn and climbed out. Embry had left the barndoor open a crack.

Jim opened the door wide from insider. He must have heard Nason' truck. He motioned for Nason to turn around and back up to his two-horse trailer, into which Kidro Potter's two horses had already been loaded.

Nason got back into his truck and followed Jim's hand signals, backing up until Embry slapped the back of his truck, signaling Nason to stop.

Nason put his truck into park, climbed out, and helped Embry hook up the trailer.

Embry made sure Nason saw the thing. His old truck had been backed into one of the stalls with the hood up and a tarp thrown over one of the fenders. Just for show. Embry's truck ran fine. He'd forgotten to plant any mechanic's tools.

They climbed into Nason's truck and Jim said, "You meet them new Potters yet?"

Driving slowly, Nason said, "Jim, they just got in yesterday afternoon." He made a wide turn in front of the house and Embry's wife waved from the porch. Nason waved back. "Why did you need for me to come out here?"

"I told you, my truck's on the fritz." Nason knew better. Jim knew he knew better. "I didn't want to go over there by myself. I never met these Potters before."

"Neither have I." Nason drove downhill, keeping drag on the loaded trailer. "You had no problem picking these horses up after Kidro got taken."

"Ah, I didn't want Gilpin sneaking over there to grab the stallion." Jim got right back on subject. "So, have you heard anything about them?"

"Not yet." Nason changed the subject. "How's the old man?"

Early sunshine on Embry's slope highlighted small patches of green grass, mixed with purple blooming sagebrush and scattered dandelion.

"Same-o, same-o." Embry settled back for the short ride. "Pops complains all day about never going anywhere." He smiled and shook his head. "You couldn't drag him out of that house with this truck and both of them horses." Embry couldn't help himself, getting back to it. "Wonder what these new Potters are like. The twins been asking all morning."

"Gosh, Jim, your boys aren't asking stupid questions, are they? I wonder where they'd get that from."

"Bite my jumbo."

Nason turned onto River Road and accelerated toward the Potter place.

"Think they'll be up yet?"

"Don't know, Jim."

"Think they'll reopen the mine?"

"I hope not. I can't help thinking that's why Kidro was taken."

"I thought you blamed Gilpin."

"That, too." Nason slowed near the end of River Road and turned up the cobblestone driveway onto Potter Ranch.

BARNABAS GROWLED AND jumped off the bed, stirring Jason, barely awake. When his dog scrambled onto the table between the beds, Jason sat up. Barnabas growled again, propped his front paws on the window sill, and opened the curtain with his nose. He put his head against the glass and craned his neck, looking toward the driveway.

"What's up?" Jason climbed onto the table and looked toward the driveway. He couldn't see anything to growl at.

Barnabas whined and grumbled, shaking all over, looking at Jason like that.

"Okay." Jason dressed quickly and followed Barnabas downstairs.

Barnabas waited at the plywood door, quivering and whimpering, telling Jason to hurry.

Jason unlatched and opened the door.

Barnabas bolted out, rushed down the front steps, and charged toward the barn.

Cold air bit into Jason's face, he grabbed his jacket from the rack, pulled it on, and hurried after his dog.

Down near the barn, a stocky man stood behind a pickup truck and a round-topped trailer.

A skinnier man backed a horse down a ramp from the trailer.

Neither man saw Barnabas, charging straight at them. When the dog growled and barked, charging in and out, the horse bolted sideways from the ramp, jumped onto the cobblestone paving, and reared.

The man holding the horse let go of the reigns and disappeared into the trailer.

The other man pulled a gun and swung it around, trying to aim at Barnabas.

Barnabas charged back and forth, lunging in and out, growling and barking at the horse's feet, too fast to get shot.

"Barnabas, *NO!*"

Barnabas stopped under the horse and crouched, ears and tail up, looking at Jason.

Jason ran as fast as he could, but not fast enough.

The horse flooded steaming green pee all over his dog's head and back.

Barnabas bolted backward and barked like crazy, but he'd stopped charging.

The stocky man pointed his gun at Barnabas.

Jason shouted, "Don't shoot him, mister. He won't bite."

The man grinned and lowered the gun, letting it hang at arm's length. He lowered the hammer with his thumb.

The skinny man inside the trailer poked his head out, watching Jason approach.

The bigger man said, "Crap your pants, Embry?"

The man in the trailer laughed a little, relieved.

"You must be Jason Potter." The heavier man holstered his gun and fastened a safety strap. He wore a small badge on his pistol belt and a larger badge on the front of his tan cowboy hat.

"Yes, sir."

"I'm Sheriff Phil Nason, and this here's Jim Embry." The sheriff smiled at the skinnier man.

Mr. Embry watched Barnabas.

Barnabas leaned into Jason's legs, wafting a strong odor of pee.

Mr. Embry said, "Just come to bring your horses." He took off his hat and held it out with both hands, like a shield between himself and Barnabas.

Jason said, "We have horses?"

Mr. Embry said, "This here's Stoner." He put on his hat, grabbed the horse's reigns, and jumped to the ground. "He's got some thoroughbred." He led the large, mostly black horse toward the barn. He looked back at Jason, nodding toward the trailer. "Other one's Dandy."

A smaller, brown and white horse stood in the trailer, rump facing Jason.

Mr. Embry said, "She's a pinto mare. I've been looking after them since . . ."

"Yeah," the sheriff interrupted. He put his hat on and stared at his friend. His look said to shut up. He looked at Jason, "When we heard you'd arrived, we thought we'd bring them over. Hope it's not too early."

"What's going on?" Jason's mom had come down from the house, wearing new blue jeans and a long-sleeved shirt, her arms folded against the chill.

"Hi, Mom." Jason extended his hand toward the two men. "This is the sheriff and his friend, Mr. Embry. They brought our horses."

"Horses?" She shook her head apologetically and put a hand on top of Jason's head. "We don't know anything about horses. But I do know, they're a huge responsibility."

"John Crow used to take care of Potter stock." The sheriff reached up and pulled a skeleton key from a small opening in the stone wall of the barn. He unlocked the door and pulled it wide open, big enough to back his truck inside. He smiled at Mom and took off his hat. "You must be Carolyn Potter."

Mr. Embry led Stoner into the barn.

Mom said, "Yes. I'm sorry, your name was . . ."

"Phil Nason, ma'am. That's Jim Embry." He motioned toward the open barn door and put his hat back on. "I'm the local deputy sheriff; not that we much need a sheriff up here." He smiled, looking past Jason and his mom. "Ah, here comes Crow now."

John Crow rounded the corner of the garage and walked toward the barn.

"Just in time," said Mr. Embry, already backing the other horse down the ramp.

Jason asked, "What's his name? I forgot."

Mr. Embry said, "Her name's Dandy. She's a real gentle eight-year-old. Anybody can ride her." He led Dandy into the barn.

"Morning, John." Sheriff Nason tipped his hat.

John smiled hello to the sheriff and spoke to Jason. "Good morning." He took off his black hat with the feather to speak to Mom. "Morning, Mrs. Potter."

"Please, call me Carolyn." She shook John's hand and smiled. "Good morning." She shook hands with Sheriff Nason and Jim Embry. "Anybody want breakfast?"

AFTER BREAKFAST, AFTER Mr. Embry and Sheriff Nason left, John helped Jason give Barnabas a bath, then Jason followed John into the barn.

The horses stood way in back with nothing keeping them in their stalls but a length of rope hooked across an opening. The sand floor had footprints everywhere, both horse and human. High windows above a loft gave them plenty of light to see spiderwebs everywhere.

John opened a door near the front of the barn and Jason followed him into a room the size of Jason's bedroom. Two lower windows had thick iron bars fitted into the heavy stonework. John said, "This is the tack room." Saddles on wood stands, folded blankets on wooden shelves, and open burlap bags filled with different kinds of grain took up most of the wooden floorspace. Rope and leather stuff hung from wood beams overhead. The wood floor had been littered with empty peanut bags and an empty whiskey bottle. Spiders lived in here, too.

John swept a spider web away with the back of his hand and shook his head. He didn't like the mess. "There's hay for fodder and more feed up on the loft." He grabbed a bundle of fancy looking, interconnected leather straps and a short piece of rope from a sloppy pile of stuff on the floor. He handed those to Jason and slung a blanket and a piece of lamb's wool over his shoulder, grabbed a saddle, and led Jason across the barn. He hoisted the saddle onto a rail fence near Stoner, spread the blanket and wool over the rail next to the saddle, and looked into the horse's eyes. "I don't know what kind of horse this'll be. It came over from Gilpin's just before . . ." He looked at Jason. "Should we find out?"

The big black horse looked at Jason, waiting for an answer.

Jason shook his head and said, "Okay." He hated being afraid. Jimmy had never been afraid of anything. He pointed to the lamb's wool. "What's that for?"

"Fleece?" John looked at Jason, making sure that's what he meant. "Fleece is used to cushion the saddle. These days, most saddles come with fleece sewn into the underside, but not these. Willis made all the Potter saddles the old way. By hand."

John's hands had a mind of their own, the way he took the short piece of rope from Jason, quickly tied a knot and looped rope back through it. He unhooked the rope gate from the stall opening and walked slowly up to the horse, looking into his eyes.

Stoner's head bobbed up and down, acting nervous.

John slipped the loop over Stoner's head with perfect timing and led him out. "I hope this horse hasn't been ruined. He's been with the Gilpins for the past two years, since he was just a colt."

Barnabas sat over by the tack room, a safe distance from Stoner's pee.

John led the horse to a big wood post at the center of the barn and looked inside a small wooden barrel set on top of a stump.

Jason looked but the barrel was empty.

John said, "We usually keep green apples or carrots in there, but it's been a while. Horses like apples and carrots. Jacobsen can deliver some out. Ask your mother to tell him it's for the horses. He'll bring out a full basket of whichever's in season."

"Did you know my father?" *Stupid.* John had already said that he did.

John smiled. "Your father was good with horses, good with all animals, really. Maybe he gave some of that to you."

Jason hooked the post with one hand and walked slowly around it, getting nearer to the horse.

Stoner wore a white patch on his head and another one on his chest. He was black everywhere else, except for white socks above his front hooves.

Jason asked, "Who are the Gilpins?"

"Some of your neighbors. They have a small place in Blind Creek Canyon, just across the river."

Jason inched closer to Stoner.

John said, "Careful."

When the horse lowered his head and pressed it into Jason's chest, Jason instinctively reached up and rubbed both sides of the horse's massive neck.

"Never seen anything like that." John shook his head and tied the leader rope to an iron ring in the post. He walked to another door at the side of the stone walled barn, not as big as the open front door, lifted down a heavy looking wooden bar, and leaned it against the wall. He pulled the thick wooden door inward and bright morning sunlight flooded the barn. He moved slowly up to Stoner, untied the horse, and led him out into a large corral where pine needles lay on windswept sand.

Dense trees beyond the corral sloped steeply downhill into mist. The sound of water crashing over rocks pushed back up through the trees, a sound he had not noticed from the front of the barn. Morning sun had created a rainbow in the mist above the trees. The air smelled clean and crisp. *Totally awesome.*

The rumble of a diesel engine turned Jason back into the barn.

Willis Donner entered the tack room. Before Jason could get across the barn to ask, Willis carried a pair of stacked sawhorses out. He dipped his head, saying hello.

Jason had to move fast to keep up, following Willis across the driveway to where a flatbed delivery truck was backing toward the front steps of the house.

John laid a hand on Jason's shoulder, stopping him. He said, "That's the material for your new front door. You'll be in the way."

Barnabas kept going, happy as anything to see Willis.

John said, "Come on, let's get you fitted out."

John led Jason across the barn, grabbed the saddle and fleece, and strolled into the corral. He tossed the saddle over the top rail of the fence, looped the harness, and pulled it tight. He measured Jason with his eyes and said, "Willis makes doors and shutters out of three-inch-thick white oak. It always comes up ready milled to Willis's specifications and measurements."

"Did Willis make our house and this barn?"

"He did." John adjusted the stirrups, shortening them, looking back and forth at Jason's legs. "He built the store and the church in the village, he built my house, Jim Embry's house, and the houses of a few others farther up the valley. He's a fine craftsman and a good planner. Most important, he has a real sense of how to fit a man's inner self."

"Our house is awesome. So's this barn."

"My house, too."

Jason followed John back into the tack room where John found a two-step wooden stool. They went back out to the corral and John put the stool close to a stirrup. "Climb up here."

Jason climbed to the top step.

"Grab the saddle horn with both hands." He touched a round handle at the front of the saddle. "Then put your left foot into the stirrup." He pointed.

Jason could barely reach the saddle horn and his foot couldn't find the stirrup.

John grabbed his foot and put it in there. "Now, stand up and throw your right leg over the top of the saddle. Then sit down."

That part came easy. Finding the other stirrup did not.

"Take your time. Get used to it and let me know how it feels."

Jason's right foot finally found the stirrup and he stood up, barely above the saddle seat.

John said, "Building doors and shutters, Willis uses tongue-and-groove oak with hot glue and brass brads. The doors never sag and never seep any cold air. You drop that oak bar into place at night, and nothing can get inside."

Mom stood in the open doorway, arms crossed, not happy about something.

Jason climbed down.

Mom said, "Time for lunch."

"Already?" Jason wanted to stay with Stoner and John.

She said, "It's twelve-thirty. Come on."

Jason jumped off the stool and walked toward her.

She said, "You coming, John?"

"Thank you, no. I need to get some work done."

Neither John nor Willis broke for lunch, so Jason and Mom ate alone.

After lunch, when Jason returned, John had cleaned and raked the barn floor and corral, and Jason couldn't see any spiderwebs.

"Wow." The saddle had been placed on Stoner's back. Jason wasn't sure he could reach. Though Stoner's back was no higher than the fence, his thickness put the stirrups higher off the ground. Even standing on the stool, Jason couldn't see the saddle horn.

John said, "Maybe we should try Dandy first. She's smaller and easier to handle."

"No! Stoner's my horse. He and I both know it."

"Maybe we should ask your mother." He looked at Jason man-to-man, very serious.

"Awe, what does she know? She's afraid of everything."

John turned back into the barn like he didn't even hear.

"Come on, John. We don't need her."

John returned to the corral. "You'll need this bridle." He carried the bridle toward Stoner, making sure the horse saw him coming before putting it on. "Horses like to see a man. Looking into a man's eyes tells the horse what kind of person he is. I think they can look right into your soul." He led Stoner in a wide circle and stood him in front of Jason, eye-to-eye.

The horse looked into Jason and lowered his head, nudging Jason's chest and snorting.

"Never saw the like. Not even with your father."

"I told you, he's my horse. And we both know it, Stoner and me." *Even if Mom and John don't know it.*

John smiled and moved to Stoner's side to cinch the saddle tighter. "Always let the horse breath out a few minutes then cinch it up a second time." John led the horse around again and positioned his left side near the stool, close to Jason. "You need to mount and dismount from the left side."

"Why? I'm righthanded, you know."

"Horses are trained from the left. They sometimes get nervous if you try from the right."

"Okay." Jason stretched up, grabbed the saddle apron with both hands, and jumped into the left stirrup. He stood up in the stirrup, gripped the saddle horn with both hands, kicked out with his right leg, and settled into the seat.

Stoner moved under him, and Jason realized how big and powerful the animal was, like Jason wasn't even there.

"Okay." John ducked under Stoner's head and handed Jason the reins. "Let's let him walk around the corral a little." John held the lead rope, pulling the horse. "This here's called a hackamore rein. It doesn't have a steel bit. Steel bits can hurt the horse's mouth. I can see from the marks that Gilpin used a steel bit, so we'll need to retrain your horse." Walking in a wide circle, John pulled straight down on the lead rope, keeping the horse's head down.

After two turns around the corral, John stopped and looked at Jason. "Only pull tight on those reins when you want him to slow down or stop. If you want him to go, give a soft kick with both legs. If you want him to turn left, give a firm kick or two with your right leg, not too hard. If you want him to go right, give a kick or two with your left. Got it?"

Jason nodded, more eager than anything to start running.

John turned Stoner's head toward the center of the corral and unhooked the leader.

Jason held the reins in both hands, still holding the saddle horn, just in case. Instinctively swinging his feet front to back, he said, "Come on, Stoner."

The horse didn't budge.

John said, "Not like that, Jason. Just lift both legs straight out and let them fall."

Jason followed John's instruction.

Stoner lurched forward with awesome power and trotted around the corral.

Jason's legs went stiff and he froze, still holding onto the saddle horn.

The horse's back rose as Jason's rump dropped and he landed hard against the seat. His feet left the stirrups and Jason slid sideways. The ground rushed toward him, he held out both hands, and he crunched headfirst into soft sand. "What happened?" He sat up and brushed sand from his face. He jumped up and Stoner was right there in front of him, looking into him. He wondered what had happened, too.

"You okay?" John brushed Jason's back.

"Course I am."

"Well, get back up there." John climbed up and sat on the corral fence. No more help from him.

Jason led Stoner back to his stepstool.

BY LATE AFTERNOON, Jason figured he'd learned everything there was to know about riding and caring for horses. John had even shown him how to brush Stoner down. Tomorrow, they'd clean the loft and tack room and give both horses baths. There'd probably be a lot more spiders up in that loft.

John took a final look around the corral and barn and closed the side door. He strained under the weight of the heavy bar and dropped it into stone cradles on both sides, solidly securing the door. "Be sure you secure this place. We've got some pretty wild things, up here in the mountains. We don't want anything getting in here after your horses."

They walked outside and John closed the main door. He locked it and set the key in the high cubbyhole, way too high for Jason or his mom. Jason said, "John, how can me or Mom reach that?"

"I'll find something to put here by the door."

Jason followed John toward the house. The sun had dropped low over the western rim of the valley.

Willis was still at work, chiseling on the face of their new door, with Barnabas right there watching. He'd built and hung the door before lunch.

Willis waited for Jason to climb onto the porch before saying, "If you can find your mother, I can show you how this works."

"Wow." Willis had spent the whole afternoon chiseling an elaborate, geometric pattern into their new front door, not sure what, maybe some flying birds. "That's so cool." He turned to thank John and say goodnight, but John had already gone.

Jason rushed inside and found his mom in the kitchen. It was an awfully nice kitchen and it smelled good. "Hurry up, Mom. Willis needs to show us something." She finished basting a roast, closed the oven door, followed Jason back across the living room, and up three steps to the entry.

Willis turned the polished brass knob and opened the door. "This here's a special-order Baldwin latch. The door's three inches thick. It's mortised in at the mill shop, so it's good and solid. I set angle iron into the top and bottom of the door for overall strength, and these hinge straps help keep it from sagging. Plus, I set some brass brads into the hot-glued, vertical tongue and groove joints."

The door hung on four long straps of steel, each supported by old looking steel hinge pins previously cemented into the granite stonework. He opened and closed the door a couple of times, showing how easily it worked, and how snuggly it fit into the jamb. "No weather can seep in."

He picked up a heavy looking wood bar and dropped the ends into stone cradles on both sides, just like the side door in the barn. "This here bar will block any intruder. There's a big prowler up here likes to hunt by moonlight." Willis looked at Jason. "Had your grandpa, Kidro, done this, he'd still be alive today. It took more than sixty years for the old door to give up to termites. He should have let me install another. Wish he had." Willis lifted the bar down and leaned it into a corner near the door.

Mom said, "That looks very heavy, Willis. I think that Baldwin lock should be sufficient." She turned the knob and opened the door.

"No, ma'am!" Willis seemed angry, the way he looked at Mom. "No Baldwin latch will be enough up here. When the moon's up and bright, you lift that bar into place at night." He looked from Mom to Jason and back. "Olen delivers a lunar calendar every month. Be sure to mark it." His stare pushed a chill across Jason's back.

Willis said, "You and the boy lift it, if you can't lift it alone." He poked his thumb toward the wooden bar. His stare made it an order, not a request.

Mom looked at the outside surface of the door, the chiseled birds. "Willis, this is beautiful." She ran her fingers over the carving and looked more closely. "Are these birds?"

"Yes, ma'am." Willis looked down at the floor, shifting his weight from one foot to the other. "It's nice of you to notice. They're meadowlarks."

"Yes." She said it kind of absent, still looking at the door like she wanted to say more. "You need to let us pay you. You've worked here for two whole days and never even had lunch."

"No, ma'am." Willis shook his head and held up his hand, not a chance. He smiled at Mom. "Tell you what." He looked at Jason. "You ever been trout fishing?"

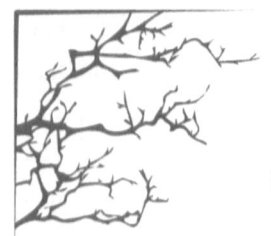

Chapter Nine

J ason tossed and turned all night, wondering what fishing with Willis might be like. Thinking it must be morning, he opened the curtain to a crescent moon and starry sky. He switched on his lamp and opened his night table drawer. His Swiss Army watch said it was already 4:22 a.m.

Barnabas dropped his head onto Jason's shoulder with a grumble, wondering what Jason was up to. He followed Jason into his bathroom and watched Jason use the toilet, wash his hands and face, and brush his teeth. He hurried getting dressed in sneakers, jeans, and a sweatshirt.

His mom opened his bedroom door, wearing her bathrobe, surprised to find Jason up and dressed. "Did you brush your teeth?"

"Course." He pushed past her, hurried downstairs, and turned on the front porch light. That heavy bar rested in the corner. Mom never put the thing up, probably too heavy. He unlocked the door latch and let Barnabas out into the cold and dark.

Mom asked, "You want something to eat?"

"No. Willis said we could eat after."

"Well, I poured you some orange juice. At least come in and drink that."

He followed her into the kitchen and gulped down his juice.

She came in and watched him rinse the glass and put it into the dishwasher. She opened the pantry door and grabbed a heavy-looking sheepskin coat, slightly dirty around the cuffs.

"This might have been your father's. There's a newer one the same size. We'll keep that one for church and school."

"Thanks, Mom." Jason pulled it on and rushed out to the front porch, but Barnabas had not returned and Willis hadn't shown up. He stepped down two steps and looked toward the barn.

"Yes!" Light shown through the open barndoor. In the quiet of early morning, the faint sound of water crashing over rocks from the river gorge reached him. *Awesome.*

Jason ran down the front steps and light from inside the barn went out. He stopped, unable to see anything past the glow from the front porch light. High above the barn, a dark blue sky outlined the shape of the mountain. Day was coming.

Barnabas's claws raked the cobblestone driveway, coming up fast. Jason braced.

His dog's front paws plowed into Jason's chest, nearly knocking him down.

From the darkness, Willis said, "The dog needs to stay here. He'll scare the fish." Willis walked into the light carrying only one fishing pole.

"Don't I get to catch any?"

"Have to ask the fish." Hard to tell if Willis was joking. He never smiled very much.

Jason put Barnabas inside the house and followed Willis around the corner of the garage, under the kitchen light, up a slight hill to a flat that ran across the back of the house, then down a trail that led them into the lower meadow.

Willis asked, "You bar that new door last night?"

"No. I think it was too heavy for Mom."

Willis stopped and looked at Jason, enough daylight then to see how serious he was. "You need to help her. You're the man of the house."

Jason nodded. "Okay. I will."

They followed a dirt road to a barn made of logs, less than half the size of their main barn. It had a low, flat roof. Willis struck a match and lit a lantern, trimmed it, and hung it near a flatbed truck. Stacks of hay jammed one side of the truck and sacks of corn feed had been stacked against the opposite wall, leaving just enough room to get in and out of the truck. "Is this our truck?"

"Yes. Your grandfather bought it to feed your cattle after he let John and me go." Willis grabbed a wicker satchel from the back of the truck, blew out the lantern, and led Jason back outside.

Daylight had grown enough to see sleek, fat, black cows feeding from bins near the creek. Willis said, "Me and John have been taking care of your stock since your grandpa got taken." He spun Jason and looked into him, serious as anything. "You need to bar them doors."

"Okay, Willis. I promise."

Willis kept looking at Jason, like he wanted more.

"How much do we owe you?" That's what Mom would ask. "You and John Crow, for feeding our cows?"

Willis looked surprised, like he didn't know how to figure it out. "John did most of it. Talk to him."

Jason followed Willis farther down the dirt road and asked, "Where does it go, Willis?" The dirt road disappeared into tall trees at the bottom of the meadow.

"There's a hot spring down there with a small house. I built the house for your great grandparents. They liked staying overnight and using the spring. It's nice year-round. They liked it most in midwinter." Way down the road, a family of deer saw them and moved slowly into the trees.

"Are those your trees, Willis?"

"All the trees in this valley belong to you, all the way to the top of the ridgeline; you, not your mother."

"And Barnabas and Stoner?"

"That's up to you."

"Awesome."

They followed the road for what seemed an hour but Jason knew it really wasn't. The sun still hid behind the mountain. Sun had reached the mountain on the far side of the stream, the mountain where John and Willis lived. It had not yet reached the valley floor.

Jason never wore the watch that jerk had given him for his birthday. It was way too big and heavy. He might wear it on special days. It did look cool.

About halfway down the long meadow, Willis said, "Let's cut across here." He led Jason closer to the creek.

The water looked deep. At the bottom, the force of water pushed long grass flat, swaying back and forth in a swift current.

Willis took a Styrofoam cup from the wicker satchel and knelt near the stream, deliberately pushing the tall grass flat with his knee. He dug into the black earth with his fingers and found some big, fat worms. He put them into the cup with some dirt, put a lid on the cup, and put the cup back into the satchel.

"What's that, Willis?" Jason pointed at the satchel.

"That's a creel. That's where we keep the fish we catch until we cook and eat them." Willis found another worm in the ground and showed Jason how to put it on a hook. The worm didn't like it, wiggling like crazy. "These fish are wild, so you need to sneak up on them. If you walk too close, you can push water from the wet ground into the stream and they'll feel it, or they might see you or your shadow. Either way, they won't bite." Willis stood and looked over his shoulder.

The sun still hid behind the eastern mountain.

On the other side of the valley, reflected sunlight blinked through the trees. "Is that the Perch?"

Without looking, Willis said, "That's John Crow's place. Hard to find the Perch from here. It's on this side of the falls, behind them tall trees. You can see it from your house but not from way down here." Willis looked up there and smiled. He could see it. Jason could tell.

Jason looked up the dirt road at their new house and realized how far they'd walked. Their house stood way uphill from them, and was nearly surrounded by trees. The overlapping rooflines played into each other, climbing ever higher until they met at the stone chimney. "Our new house is awesome. Thank you, Willis."

"Thank your great grandparents."

"My dad always took us to look at nice houses on Sundays, after church. This house is the coolest ever." Maybe this was why his father had grown up wanting to be an architect. "Now it's ours, huh, me and my mom, and Barnabas?"

Willis smiled and touched Jason's shoulder. He nodded toward the stream.

Jason said, "Huh." He could hardly wait to catch some fish.

Willis picked up the pole and pulled out three arm lengths of fishing line. He ducked and crept closer to the stream. He stopped and looked back. "You want to try first?" He offered Jason the pole, not teasing.

Jason stepped back and shook his head. *Not yet.*

Willis pulled out another arm's length of fishing line and laid it carefully over grass where it wouldn't tangle. He looked back at Jason, making sure he was paying attention, and tossed the worm-baited hook high into the air. The loose line played out quickly, tightened, and the worm dropped into the water, upstream. It only traveled about a foot downstream before the line jerked tight, the pole bent sharply, and Willis stood.

Jason's chest pounded with excitement, watching the taught line run up and down the stream, with the pole nearly bent double.

Willis held the fat end of the pole upright, close to his chest, and walked to the edge of the stream.

Jason stayed close, looking down into deep, fast-moving water. Deep down, barely visible, a big fish darted under the grassy bank they both stood on.

"Careful, here. We're standing on bog." Willis stuck the tip of the pole into the water where the line went under the bank. "He gets tangled in roots down there, we'll never get him out." He cranked on the handle and the reel clicked like crazy.

"What's that noise? Is it busted?"

"That's the drag. If it's set too tight, a big fish can break the line."

After another minute of reeling in and clicking back out, Willis pulled a flopping, foot long fish onto the grassy bank and dropped his knee between the fish and the water. He grabbed the fish with his left hand and stuck a finger down its throat, twisted it a couple of times, and pulled out the bare hook. He put the twitching fish into his creel and pulled a clump of long, green grass. He dipped the grass into the stream, placed it into his creel, and positioned the fish on top of it. He yanked more grass, got it wet, and put that on top of the fish. "Wet grass keeps the fish from drying out." Willis stood, reeled in line, and hooked the biggest ring on the fishing pole. He cranked the reel just enough to bend the pole a little, keeping the line tight.

"Are we finished, Willis?"

"We're all finished here. Fish won't bite here for the rest of the day." Willis carried the pole back out to the road and walked toward the house. "Nothing will bite for a quarter mile downstream, neither."

Willis led Jason past some cows eating grain from a bin and turned back toward the stream. When they got close enough, they both ducked. Willis pulled out line and baited the hook. He pulled out more line, handed the baited hook to Jason, and nodded toward the stream.

Jason threw the worm as hard as he could. It landed in a thicket of brush on the other side of the stream. He yanked the line back and the hook snagged.

Willis tried to free it but the line broke and he had to put on a new hook. He gave Jason the worm this time and quietly coached with his hands.

Jason poked and slid the squirmy thing up the hook and poked it through again.

Willis nodded. "Good job."

Bright sunlight had reached them and it was already getting hot.

Jason handed Willis the pole, took off his heavy coat, and tied the sleeves around his waist. He followed Willis to another location upstream.

Jason tossed the worm again, grabbed the pole, and the line went tight. The fish pulling so hard that Jason nearly lost the pole. He tightened his grip and cranked the reel. The drag clicked as the fish darted upstream and down. The fish finally got tired and Jason lifted it onto the shoreline.

Willis unhooked it and put it into the creel.

They moved to three more locations and Jason caught two more fish, then Willis led him to a wide bend with shallower water. He showed Jason how to clean and scrape the fish and to toss all the guts into the water. Willis said the crawdads would eat it. Cleaning the last fish, Willis said, "Nice golden trout. Real nice."

"Our teacher told us these are endangered. Shouldn't we throw it back?"

"Hooked too deep. It'll die. He swallowed the hook all the way down and tore up his gut." He packed the cleaned fish into the creel with more wet grass.

Jason said, "Won't we get a big fine?"

"This is your property, son. You can do whatever you want. State fish and game don't come in here; or anyone else, for that matter. This meadow hasn't been fished since before your dad went away." Willis shook his head, remembering something. "Near forgot." He reached to his back pocket and pulled out a brand-new hunting knife in a handmade, leather scabbard. It looked like the one he was using to clean fish. He said, "A mountain man needs a good knife." He unbuckled Jason's belt, pulled half of it out, and fed the scabbard onto it.

Jason refastened his belt and reached behind for the knife. It was over his right-side, back pocket, just like Willis's. "Awesome." Jason pulled the knife and ran his thumb down the length of the blade, testing for sharpness. "Ouch." He'd cut his thumb. He looked at the cut but couldn't see any blood.

Willis grabbed his hand and spread the cut, looking for how deep it was.

Seeing only a thin, red line, Jason said, "Awe, it's only a scratch, Willis. It's not even sore anymore. Not really."

Willis pulled Jason down to the water and washed his hand, kind of angry. He said, "A knife ain't no toy. Never run your thumb down the blade like that. You want to check the sharpness, drag your thumb across the blade, like this." He took the knife and showed Jason, making sure he understood.

Jason took the knife and dragged his other thumb across the blade. He understood. This knife was sharp, but going across the blade it wouldn't cut. Jason put the knife away and washed his hands again.

Something down in the rocks under shallow water caught Jason's eye, something round and golden, about the size of his new Swiss Army watch. He untied his heavy coat, laid it on a rock, and waded into knee deep water, a little deeper than it looked. The fast-moving water tugged at his pants, so cold.

"Careful." Willis climbed onto the rock where he could see better.

Jason rolled up his shirtsleeves and reached into the water, clear as the sky. He picked up the rock and stood to look at it, wading back toward Willis. He held the beautiful, frosty white rock up to the sun, with a gold-colored rock stuck in the middle. "Gosh, this is heavy." He climbed back to shore and showed it to Willis. "Look what I found."

"That's a gold nugget, Jason. Break off the quartz, it's near pure. This valley's full of the stuff."

"And it's ours, me and my mom?"

"Yep. You own the mineral and timber rights to this whole valley, ridgeline to ridgeline, like I already said." Willis's head darted in three directions, as if touching the high peaks above the valley with his nose. He looked at the gold nugget, then studied Jason, head to foot, waiting for something.

Jason said, "And, we can go prospecting for it?"

"That's right. This valley was a mining camp, a hundred-and-sixty years back."

"Why'd they leave, if there's so much gold here?"

"Most died over two bad winter nights. The rest left, less than a week after. Then, several years later, your great grandfather came here with Mary Lou. They reopened one of the mines but did it slow. Didn't tear up the place or burn the soil with chemicals. That's it up there by the falls." He nodded toward the waterfall and a large mound of small rocks. "After they figured they had enough money, they shut it down. They respected the natural wonder of this place."

Jason looked at the heavy gold nugget and looked across the stream, toward the waterfall. A big bird circled above the falls. "What's that?"

"Bald eagle." The bird folded his wings back and dove into the trees.

Jason looked down the valley at his tall stand of trees, his forest, and at those deer grazing near his cattle. They'd come out from under the trees. He tossed the nugget back into the creek. "We don't need to tell Mom or Barnabas."

MOM MUST HAVE BEEN watching for them from the bay window in the kitchen, watching them hike back up the dirt road through the meadow. As soon as they walked into the kitchen, she pulled a platter of fried potatoes from the oven and set it on the table with some salads.

Willis handed her the creel and said, "You might want to put the biggest one in the freezer. It's a good baking size." He hung Jason's coat on the back of the kitchen door and turned into the pantry.

Jason followed him through the pantry and into the laundry room where they both washed up. The sink was plenty big for both of them.

Willis didn't use salad dressing so Jason didn't either. Whatever Willis did was good enough for Jason. Anyway, it tasted good without.

Mom had already seasoned and was frying the fish in butter, glancing at a recipe book she'd found in the pantry. By the time they finished their salads, three fried fish were on the table, one for each of them.

Willis said, "Mighty tasty fixin's, ma'am. Never tasted better." He licked his fingers, set his plates in the sink, rinsed his hands, and slapped them on his jeans to dry them.

Jason washed his hands at the kitchen sink, too.

Mom grabbed his hand to look at his cut thumb. "What happened?" She seemed plenty upset.

"Awe, it's nothing." Jason pulled his hand away. "Willis already washed it and showed me how to do it right." Jason pulled his new knife and dragged his other thumb across the blade, showing her how.

"Where did you get that?" Her shrill voice sounded like when he'd fallen off grandma's back porch and she'd thought he got a broken leg.

"Willis gave it to me. A mountain man needs a good knife. Isn't that right, Willis?" Jason turned, looking for support, but Willis had already gone.

She spun him back, mad as anything. "You listen to me, young man. You don't take gifts from strangers. You already know that."

"Willis isn't a stranger." Jason sank, searching for words that might work, not looking right at her. "He's Willis."

"We've only known him for four days. We don't know anything about him, other than he's a good handyman."

"Handyman? Mom!" Jason spread both arms wide, turned slowly, and fanned their surroundings.

"I don't think Willis built this house." She folded her arms and stared at him, the way only she could stare, those eyes of hers. "It's been here too long. Besides, you know what I mean. We don't know anything about him." She took the knife and set it on the table. "You don't take something as dangerous as this knife without talking to me first. I don't care who wants to give it to you." She softened and smiled a little, just a little, looking out the window. "And, I don't like that Indian teaching you to ride a horse without asking me first."

"Mom." That frustrated Jason. "John's the best horse teacher in the whole world."

She turned back, those eyes smiling now, forcing her mouth to frown.

Jason said, "Can I have my knife now, please? A mountain man needs a good knife, you know, like a rancher needs a good horse. Come on, who's going to clean the fish when I take you fishing? Don't you know anything?"

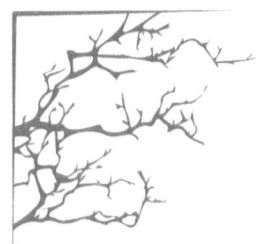

Chapter Ten

On Sunday morning, by the time Mom drove them up River Road, it was already past 10:00, and Jason hated being late. Everybody would look at them like they were morons.

Mom always took so long getting ready. She reached over and touched the front of his hair for the millionth time, making sure it looked okay. "You need a haircut."

"Mom, we don't even know if they have a barbershop up here. John and Willis both have long hair. I don't mind."

She said, "Remind me to check on that today." They rounded a curve and those two giant trees showed up, not much farther. She said, "You've been getting up very early. What's going on?"

"We've got horses to feed and take care of." Jason always got into the barn by first light. He couldn't wait to see Stoner and Dandy. Besides, by the time he finished in the barn and got cleaned up, breakfast was ready. His system worked great.

The following day would be a school day. His system would need to be adjusted, just when he'd gotten it running smoothly. "I need to get up earlier. School starts tomorrow."

"Isn't John Crow taking care of the horses?"

"He feeds the cattle first thing in the morning, then comes up to clean the barn and make sure we've got the right amount of feed and stuff."

"He's not letting you ride outside, is he?"

"Just around the corral, like you said. Stoner needs to get out and run. When are you going to learn how to ride? Then we can ride together."

She looked at Jason sideways. She didn't want to answer.

"It's okay, Mom. John's the best teacher, ever. You'll see."

She turned off River Road near the store.

Jason dreaded what he knew was coming. "People always stare at us, whenever you're late."

"I'm sorry, Honey."

"We don't even know any of them. Can't we go to church next Sunday instead?" Maybe she could be on time.

"We're here now, Jason." She drove past those two giant trees with a long, log building in back. The small, steep-roofed church had been built against a tall, skinny rock, probably why they called it the Rock Church. She turned into a small parking lot and parked. "Don't you want to meet our new neighbors? I'm looking forward to it."

They rolled up the windows, got out, and locked the car. She tried to take Jason's hand but he pulled away and ran in front. He'd gotten too big for holding her hand. He slowed to a walk and looked at the church. The eaves of the high pitched, green metal roof came down close to the parking lot. The deep overhang nearly hid the stone walls behind, tightly fitted, like their house and barn.

A flock of yellow breasted birds fluttered around and sat on the roof ridge, all looking at Jason. *Creepy.* He rounded the corner and waited for Mom under the deep overhang of the gable roof, protecting a wall of wood and glass. Maltese crosses had been chiseled into the faces of two front doors. It all looked like Willis's workmanship.

Inside was crowded, everybody dressed in black. The men and boys wore wide rimmed black hats. The women and girls wore black bonnets tied under their chins, all seated on high-backed wooden benches, all looking down and reading from their Bibles.

Mom hadn't brought their Bible.

A tall, skinny man stood up on the altar without a hat, probably the pastor. His long, gray hair looked like he just got out of bed. He read from a big, gold edged Bible.

The front door closed with a thump and the pastor looked up. "Aha." He jumped from the altar and rushed toward them. "You must be the new Potters, from down below." Everybody turned to look at them. Some of them even stood. *Good Grief!*

Jason felt stupid in his new tan suit, especially with Mom wearing her new summer dress.

Everybody else wore black.

The pastor said, "I'm Marcus Twilby, vicar here at the Rock Church, and the head schoolmaster." He grabbed Mom's hand with both of his and shook it like crazy. "We've been expecting you all morning. Glad you could come." He shook Jason's hand and smiled. His hands felt clammy. Jason let go.

Mom said, "I'm sorry we're late." Her usual apologetic tone.

Everybody stared at Jason's light-colored suit.

He turned back toward the door, seeking escape. He stopped.

John Crow stood in the back corner, below the low edge of the steeply pitched ceiling. He smiled, saying hello.

Being late felt okay, seeing John. Even his summer suit no longer bothered Jason.

He looked around but couldn't find Willis.

Vicar Twilby ushered them to the front, where Sheriff Nason and Mr. Embry made room for them to sit. What must be Mr. Embry's wife and his two boys sat next to him. Both boys had red hair, green eyes, and lots of freckles. They had to be twins. Nobody could tell them apart. They smiled and nudged each other, both looking at Jason, probably making fun of Jason's new suit.

Jimmy O'Connell was like that, having fun all the time. *Wish he was here.*

Everybody sat and returned to reading their Bibles.

The vicar returned to the pulpit and said, "We'll all get a chance to meet with the Potters after." He looked down at Mom and said, "We're reading from Acts of the Apostles, Chapter Twelve, where King Herod is attacking members of Christ's early church." The congregation fell silent and read from their Bibles.

Sheriff Nason gave Mom his Bible and turned to share with the woman sitting on the other side of him. Maybe his wife.

Jason looked over his mom's elbow, pretending to read. He'd rather be fishing with Willis.

The vicar officiously cleared his throat, everybody closed their Bibles, and Vicar said, "This chapter reminds us of how God sometimes allows his people to be burdened by terrors beyond their control. It reminds us of how all things fall under the authority of God's infinite purpose. Remember, Lucifer was created by God and cast down to earth with his rebellious horde, in a time before history began.

"Over the summer, after the death of Kidro, we studied the Book of Job. We learned that Lucifer may not touch one of God's own without permission. We also learned how hopeless are our efforts to fathom God's divine purpose. Thus, we pray for his protection and strive to guide our lives toward His righteousness.

"Since before my arrival, you have followed a ritual path that bore fruit, perhaps a path inspired by God. When this ritual was interrupted, disaster followed. Whether our protection came from faith in this ritual, or from some complex quirk of nature, does not matter. In the end, all things great or small come from our creator. By practicing this ritual, we do not seek in any way to question His divine purpose." The vicar thrust out his chin and looked at the congregation, expecting some kind of response.

They all stood.

Mom and Jason stood too.

"Let us pray." Vicar's voice grew loud and sounded practiced. "Oh, glorious Lord, our beloved Savior, protect us through this dark night, when the moon is full and bright. Keep us safe within and without, and forgive us our transgressions. Though ritual might abide, let us not thrust Thee aside." Everybody said, "Amen."

Jason and Mom said it late and soft.

Led by the vicar's booming voice, the congregation sang, *Leaning on Jesus.* Even with no piano or organ, their singing sounded harmonious and beautiful. When they finished singing, everybody turned and filed through a side door, whispering back and forth, glancing at Jason and his mom, probably talking about how funny they were dressed.

Jason looked.

John Crow had already gone.

Jason and his mom followed the others outside, walked along a footpath, and crossed a small field of uncut grass, where chipmunks poked their heads out of holes to watch. Everybody filed into the long, log building, where four fat, wood posts held up the center of the roof. Three long tables had been fitted end to end near the center with platters of food and plates and stuff.

Some of the women removed aluminum foil and cling-wrap, uncovering fried chicken, fish, beef, corn, salads, and a lot of deserts. The congregation formed a line and picked up plates.

Having already eaten breakfast, Mom led Jason back outside. She pulled Jason along the front porch to where the vicar was talking to a small group of women. Seeing their approach, the other women went inside.

Mom said, "I'm curious to learn more about your school."

Vicar smiled and pointed with his head. "We're standing in front of the main building. On average, our pupils post the highest test scores in the state."

"Who would I speak with about Jason?"

"That would be me. As I said in church, I am the schoolmaster. I earned my PHD in theology and church history at the University of Aberdeen in Scotland. I earned my master's in education at Oxford. I am a Rhodes Scholar, madam." He thrust his chin up, folded his hands behind his back, and rocked up and down on the balls of his feet.

"How many teachers are on your staff?"

"Myself and Dr. La Rosa. She teaches math and science across the street, at her clinic. She also serves as our community doctor and works for the county coroner's office." He pointed past the church and trees to a one-story brick and glass building across the street. "I teach the three Rs, reading, rhetoric and religion. Tomorrow being the first day of the new school year, we will give Jason a series of tests to evaluate his status."

"Jason's a good student. He's always had very high marks. He's going into the fifth grade."

The vicar threw Jason a doubting glance. "We shall see, madam. We shall see."

"What about sports, or art, or music?"

"We do have an archery team and some of the older children belong to Four-H. We're much too small for team sports, like basketball, baseball, and the like."

That was all Jason needed to hear. His attention switch turned off and he walked off the porch into the yard.

Those birds still fluttered at the top of the church and all around the dome of that tall rock, still looking at Jason. He shook off a chill.

Some of the kids had gathered around that pair of giant trees near the road, sitting above the ground on lofty roots, eating lunch.

The grown-ups stood around in small groups eating and talking, not paying much attention to their kids.

Mom stayed on the porch, still talking with Vicar.

Jason unbuttoned his jacket and strolled across the yard toward the trees, toward the other kids. The Embry twins saw him coming and started shoving one another, still having fun, still talking about Jason's tan suit. He was sure of it.

The other kids slowly moved away from the twins.

"Hi. I'm Jason Potter. I'm nine."

"I'm Jake," said one of the twins, shoving his brother. "This is my brother, Peter, 'cause he's a big peter."

"Am not." Peter shoved back. They both had big front teeth and plenty of freckles.

Jason couldn't see any differences.

"Call me Pete." His big front teeth smiled at Jason. "We're eleven." He gave Jake another shove, back and forth. He reached into his pocket and pulled out a pocket knife. "Jake bet me you couldn't do this. I bet you could."

"Do what?"

"Jake bet you can't carve your name in this Sequoia. The bark's too tough." He opened his pocket knife and offered it to Jason.

"Awe, I got my own." Jason reached behind, pulled out his new hunting knife, and proudly displayed it to the twins. "Willis Donner gave it to me."

The twins stared at the knife and at Jason, maybe thinking he was lying.

Jason climbed onto the high ridge of a giant tree root, examining the vertical ridges and deep valleys in the tree's bark, looking for a good spot. He cut into the bark and found it soft, easy to carve. It took only a minute to carve a clean looking "J," already starting on an "A."

"What do you think you're doing, young man?" The vicar grabbed Jason's wrist and lifted him away from the tree. "Give me that." He took Jason's knife and stared at it for a long time, like a poisonous snake or something. "These trees do not belong to us, and we do not go around damaging what doesn't belong to us. Not in this valley, we don't."

The twins and all of the other kids had magically disappeared.

"Oh, Jason." Mom sounded apologetic again, looking like she might start crying or something. "How could you?"

Good grief. Speaking to the vicar, Jason said, "I know these trees don't belong to you. They belong to me, me and my mom."

The vicar blinked like his brain had shut down. After a moment, he grinned and said, "Yes, well, I guess they do at that." He let go of Jason's wrist and returned the knife. He shook his head, frowned, and spun away. He stopped to look across the field at the twins.

They stood close to their parents, looking down at their shifting feet.

Jim Embry shrugged nervously and smiled at Jason.

The sheriff looked up at the sky, where afternoon sunlight blinked through trees at the western ridgeline. He pulled Jim Embry's arm and both men walked toward the parking lot.

Embry's wife and twins followed close behind.

JOHN CROW NEVER STAYED for their monthly pot-luck. Some of them treated him like an unwanted outsider. He didn't much care for the white man's culture anyway. On nice days like that Sunday, he liked the walk into the village and back, following one of the many deer trails through the forest, keeping in shape, staying limber. It was faster before his horse up and died, his only real friend since that night ten years back, since J. J. went away, since Mary Lou died, since Kidro fired him.

John Crow had grown accustomed to his solitary life, no trouble at all. The white man's culture was filled with gossiping women and scheming men, nothing of interest to John Crow.

These new Potters seemed different than the rest. The woman was much like Mary Lou, maybe why J. J. married her. The boy was very much like his father. John appreciated the way the boy had smiled at him in church. His life had purpose again, working for these new Potters. Maybe he'd live another fifty years.

This time of year, deer were coming down. He could see the signs. A taste of deer meat would be welcome. Kidro had been the only man in the valley to ever shoot deer with a rifle. Everybody else used bows and arrows, only shooting them with a rifle if they'd been wounded. Most folks hit their mark with the first arrow.

The Ralstons used a military crossbow, but the others, those who hunted deer, they all used longbows and arrows made my Willis Donner. Olen Jacobsen brought the lemonwood all the way up from Oxnard. John Crow sure liked his Willis Donner bow, made to fit his size. The others probably liked theirs too.

Local kids learned to use a bow and arrow in school, first learning which eye was dominant. Willis made them different, right-handed or left. This local team went to the state archery finals every year, the only real competitive sport they had.

Four H was outside the school and more individual. This valley's ranchers always showed well at the county fair, livestock or on horseback. John and Willis would have young Jason in those competitions by next year, maybe. The year after for sure.

It was already late when John left the deer trail and followed his own well-worn path toward home, only a couple-of-hundred yards.

"Mm." The smell of rabbit stew filled his senses.

He'd left his door open for air and that raccoon had gone inside again. He kicked at it, chasing it out, set his Bible on a window ledge, and dished up supper, rabbit stew over two slices of sourdough bread. He sat on his front steps to eat, watching late sunlight climb up the eastern wall of the valley, soon to disappear into late afternoon.

A nice buck stood down in the trees near the stream. It watched John, unafraid.

Time to prepare.

He finished eating, went inside to clean up, and it was already getting dark. He closed and barred his heavy oak door, closed and barred the window shutters, and lit the lamp. He picked up his Bible and turned down onto the carpeted sand floor of his main room. He set the Bible on the mantle, grabbed the box of wooden matches, and knelt to light the fire.

The sky had been clear all day. It would be a cold night. He pulled the Bible down from the mantle, knelt before his fireplace, and let the book fall open. Fate fell on the Gospel of John, Chapter 3. He'd read it so many times, it nearly always opened to that page. He read it again, trying to understand. He'd always loved the light, always tried to do what was right, so who could explain the coming of this night? Who could explain his need to prepare, his need to call out to Jesus.

His spirit cried out to all the lesser gods of this planet in his need for protection against the dark. Who could explain that? Not John Crow.

Why did this thing stay here, anyway? Why didn't it move on to the next valley? *Of course.* John knew the why of it. This valley belonged to this thing, not to the Potters.

Why had John not been taken?

Maybe it was the strength of his barred door and shutters after all. Maybe it was the chiseled etching on the door. Why had Kidro not replaced his door with a proper door, a door made by Willis? Would their Willis-made door protect these new Potters? Who could know?

He returned the Bible to the mantle and dropped back to his knees. He pulled the medicine bag from around his neck, opened it, and tossed the contents onto the rug. He gave them a glance, swept them up, and tossed them into the air, watching them fall and scatter, examining the pattern of stone and bone.

It will come.

A familiar chill rushed across his shoulders and down his spine. He closed his eyes, lifted his voice, and filled his home with the ancient words and phrases of his people, hoping his chant would protect him through this night.

"DID YOU ASK HIM ABOUT television?"

Mom was supposed to ask someone after church. Now it was already bedtime and Jason had forgotten to ask about it earlier.

She adjusted his blanket, making sure he was covered.

Barnabas sat on the floor, waiting for her to finish, waiting for Jason to let him climb onto the bed.

She said, "The cable companies won't come up here. He said it took an act of the California Legislature to get phones up here. Your grandmother paid for the run into the valley from the highway."

"Who said?"

"Mr. Jacobsen." She kissed Jason's cheek and stood clear.

Jason nodded at Barnabas.

His dog jumped onto the foot of the bed, clawing, turning, and scraping, making it comfortable before he laid down.

"What about satellite TV?"

"The mountains are too high. They block the signal."

"Gosh, I'm sure glad we've got the internet." Jason's computer was already online in the library.

Mom said, "Reading is better anyway. Forming mental images is good exercise for the brain. That's what . . ."

"I know. That's what my dad always said. He never saw a television before he joined the Marine Corps." She'd told him that a million times, why she'd never let him watch grandma's TV.

She smiled, went into the hallway, and poked her head back in. "Goodnight, honey." She turned out the light and left the bedroom door open a crack, just like at Grandma's.

Jason pulled the covers up to his chin, pressed his feet against his dog, so snug and warm, and thought about those Embry twins. He couldn't let anybody make him look stupid like that. Even if they beat him up, they wouldn't mess with him again. Jimmy had taught him that. He didn't know which one to go after first. They both tried to make him look stupid. He'd just ask them both, who wants to fight. They'd probably fight each other making up their minds. Jason smiled. He could hardly wait for his first day of school.

He sat up and opened the curtain. The moon was all the way up and big. Maybe it looked bigger because of how high in the mountains they were. Under a clear sky, he could actually see shapes on the face of the moon. He didn't know why they called it the man in the moon. He couldn't see anything that looked like a man, but it was sure bright. He could probably read under that moon.

Barnabas growled and rushed to Jason's side, ducked under the curtain and bumped the glass with his nose. His muscles tightened, shaking his whole body, like he wanted to go outside.

"What is it, Barnabas?"

His dog placed his front paws on the window ledge and stretched upward. He wanted to see the upper meadow.

"Silly dog. You can't see past all those trees." Maybe there was something in the trees. Jason got to his knees and ducked under the curtain with Barnabas. Maybe they could see better like this, with both of them looking.

Barnabas licked Jason's cheek and whimpered, bumping Jason's face with his nose and growling, saying something. Then Jason heard it, a moaning, screaming kind of sound that might come from a cow or a sheep, or maybe even a deer. Someone was in trouble. The screams grew louder, more frantic, and Barnabas turned and bumped the window so hard that Jason feared the glass might break.

He wrapped both arms around his dog's neck and dragged him away from the glass.

The sounds from outside stopped, and Barnabas sat still, looking at the window and listening. Whatever had been out there must have gone, but Barnabas kept listening.

Jason laid back and tried to pull Barnabas with him. His dog remained stiff, shaking all over.

A shrill, eerie scream came from outside and Barnabas stood over the top of Jason, protecting him, still looking out the window.

A strange kind of laugh followed, loud, echoing, like a hyena's laugh. Barnabas barked back at it twice, warning it to keep away.

Quiet followed.

"Barnabas, did Mom bar the front door?" He wanted to go down and check but his muscles wouldn't move. He couldn't remember her barring the door since that first night, almost two weeks before. She'd said she could barely lift the bar and that she was sure the Baldwin hardware was strong enough. Besides, Jason needed to go out early to feed the horses and he couldn't take it down by himself. He wasn't big enough. Not yet.

He pulled the covers up, grabbed Barnabas, and held him close until the dog's breathing slowed. Barnabas finally plopped down next to Jason, lowered his head onto Jason's chest, took a deep breath, and closed his eyes for the night.

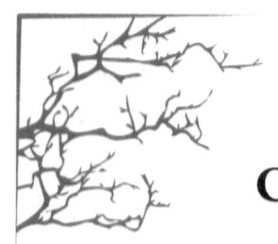

Chapter Eleven

S trange sounds had Carolyn tossing and turning all night, imagining all things that go bump in the night. She wondered if these night noises were a regular occurrence. Her husband had never said anything about noises in the night. He'd never mentioned his childhood at all.

The way Tom Kirby used to kid him about being a hick, she assumed he'd grown up in a small town with a normal childhood, nothing unusual. She'd found just the opposite. Unusual defined their new home.

Why here? She and Jason could afford to live anywhere. This house and barn were beautiful, yes, but this ranch required more knowledge than Carolyn could learn in three lifetimes.

Willis and John seemed happy to take care of things but something felt out of place. Maybe Carolyn's mom was right. Maybe they'd be better off living down on the coast, somewhere with good schools and safe streets.

She rolled out of bed, dressed quickly, and went upstairs to wake Jason.

Jason and Barnabas had already gone out to the barn.

She hurried downstairs, opened their new front door, stepped out into the cold, and stepped down two steps so she could see the barn. The Milky Way above the mountain ridge beyond the barn announced another clear day.

By the time she prepared fresh fruit, hot oatmeal, toast, and a glass of milk, the clock on the large Wolf range read 7:30.

Barnabas rushed into the kitchen and slid into her legs, waiting for his morning greeting.

She bent to scratch his ears and Jason came in. He took off his sheepskin coat and disappeared into the pantry to wash up for breakfast.

She poured herself a cup of coffee and sat at the dining nook, watching morning sun creep down the face of the mountain to the west. The waterfall sparkled in brilliant contrast to the surrounding greenery.

Jason sat on the bench opposite and peeled a banana. From where he sat, he could see up River Road, all the way into the village. "The horses are both happy to see me now." He took a bite of banana and chopped the rest into his oatmeal.

"You're the one who's feeding them." She smiled and sipped coffee, thinking how at home she felt in this kitchen.

Jason said, "No, it's more than that. We're good friends. John says horses make friends for life, like me and Jimmy." He hurried, eating his oatmeal.

"Chew your food, Jason."

"I am." He wasn't. "There's the bus already."

Carolyn stood and stepped around the table, behind Jason.

A yellow school bus sped almost straight toward them, the only vehicle on River Road.

Carolyn did not miss city traffic. She said, "Are you ready for your first day at school?"

"Yes! I need to talk to those Embry twins."

"I'm glad you're eager to make new friends."

Jason didn't look very friendly. He jumped up and set dishes near the sink.

"I'll get those, Honey. Go get your jacket."

Carolyn followed Jason into the entry, with Barnabas right behind. Jason tugged on his lightweight jacket and opened their new door.

Barnabas pushed out past them, charged down the steps, and disappeared around the corner of the garage.

They walked onto the front porch and Jason started down the steps. He stopped halfway down the steps and turned back. "Gosh, where's Barnabas? He should be here to say goodbye."

"I don't know. He ran around the corner of the garage when you were putting on your jacket."

Jason said, "There's a breeze. Maybe he smelled something."

"He's probably exploring. I'm sure he'll be waiting for you when you get home." *Home.* She liked the sound of that.

The small school bus rushed over the top of the rise and slowed. The female driver waved on her way toward the barn. She made a wide turn and drove up to the house. She stopped at the bottom of the steps and opened the door.

Jason trotted down the steps and turned back. "Don't forget to let Barnabas into the house. Okay?"

"I'll watch for him." On such a cold morning, she'd watch from the bay window in the kitchen. He'd probably bark, anyway.

Jason climbed onto the bus and sat in the first seat on the right side. The door closed, the heavy-set woman waved, and the bus drove back over the crest of the driveway.

Carolyn couldn't remember the bus driver's name. They'd met after Church. She served as the community barber, cutting hair on odd numbered Saturday afternoons at Jacobsen's Emporium.

Carolyn turned back toward their new, beautiful front door, and Barnabas strutted around the corner of the garage, carrying something large in his mouth. He dropped it in front of the steps and sniffed it.

"Lord!" Barnabas sniffed at the front leg of some animal.

Carolyn rushed into her bathroom, found an old towel, put on a jacket, and went back outside.

Barnabas licked the bloody end of the leg, ready to start chewing.

"Barnabas! No!" Barnabas stopped licking and looked up at her, ears perked, asking why.

She hurried down the steps, wrapped the leg in the towel, walked around the corner of the garage, and followed Barnabas up a trail through evergreen trees. He knew the way. She walked out of the trees onto a rocky flat with tall grass and scattered sagebrush.

Farther up the gentle slope, a man knelt, working on something.

Barnabas rushed toward him and Carolyn followed. When she got close enough, she recognized Willis Donner.

He stood and carried what looked like some animal's severed head toward green shrubbery, maybe a stream from the waterfall. Willis disappeared, probably going downhill to the stream.

Barnabas stopped where Willis had been working to sniff at something bigger. "Lord" He sniffed at the mangled, headless carcass of a small cow.

Large, green flies filled the cow's open chest cavity.

Yellow breasted birds circled overhead.

"Yuk!" Barnabas licked blood from the large, flat rock under their feet. "Barnabas, leave that alone." She clapped her hands and the birds swirled higher into the morning sky. Barnabas didn't listen. He kept licking blood.

She shoved him with her knee, keeping him away from the blood, the flies, and the dead cow. The rock felt warm under her sneakers. *Odd*. Morning sun had not yet reached her upper meadow.

The birds fluttered and settled into clumps of tall grass near the rock. Some poked their beaks into dark soil, bringing up fat, red worms for breakfast. Barnabas didn't bother with the birds and the birds weren't bothered by him.

Sensing something, she turned.

Standing a few feet away, Willis tipped his hat and said, "Morning, ma'am. Sorry you had to see this." Barnabas lunged at Willis, moaning and nibbling Willis's hand.

Carolyn unfurled the towel and dropped the leg next to the carcass. "Willis, just what is going on here?"

Willis removed his hat and looked into it, turning it slowly between his fingers, thinking what to say. "Did you put that bar into place last night, like I showed you?"

How dare . . . "That's none of your business. Answer my question." Willis seemed way too bossy to be an employee.

"Like I told you before, we got something wild up here."

"Was that one of my cows?"

"No, ma'am. This here calf belonged to Jeff Ralston. Sheriff Nason carried it up here yesterday." Willis looked bewildered, obviously not used to being questioned. "I always clean things up, being Potter land and all."

She relaxed a little and turned, looking up the valley at Jacobsen's Emporium, so beautiful. She said, "You can see the whole village from up here." The surrounding mountains and trees, the river gorge, the waterfall, and the stream running into the lower meadow. Even the tall trees below that. The waterfall cascaded between two giant boulders, stunningly beautiful.

Home. She liked it, more than before.

The flock of birds sang, looking at Willis.

She said, "What a beautiful sound. What kind of birds are these?"

"Meadowlarks, ma'am. The warmth of this rock keeps them here all year. That, and the food, of course, the bloodworms." Willis positioned the hind legs of the carcass, preparing to lift and carry it.

The song of the meadowlarks soothed Carolyn and her mood softened even more. Still, Willis needed to be told. "You don't know how much Jason has been through. He lost his father a few years ago, and, more recently, he lost his best friend, both to violence. Had he seen this . . ." She snapped her towel in the direction of the slaughtered calf.

The birds fluttered into the air and quickly resettled, resuming their singing. She said, "Well, I don't know what I would have done."

Barnabas bolted toward the waterfall, the birds flew into the air, and Willis turned.

John Crow walked quietly toward them, not ten feet away.

Barnabas jumped up and down at his side, snapping playfully at his hand, saying hello to another friend.

John said, "Morning, Mrs. Potter. You ready to meet up with Dandy?"

"Good grief." She had completely forgotten about her appointment with John, her first riding lesson. The panic attack made her dizzy.

I promised Jason.

BY 3:00 P.M., CAROLYN had suffered quite enough of John Crow and Dandy. "Stand up in the stirrups," he'd kept saying. *Good grief,* the bones in her butt felt like they needed to be in a cast.

Lord, why didn't they make saddles with butt cushions?

The throbbing complaints from the bones in her butt were interrupted only by the yelping pain from the insides of her thighs and knees, raw hamburger on a hot griddle. On top of all the other complaints and yelps from inside her legs and her butt, her shaking thigh muscles couldn't walk another inch. Not that she'd thought much about it since her husband's murder, but she didn't see how sex could ever be possible again. *Ever!* Whoever dreamed up horseback riding should be shot.

What about men with their eggs? Good grief. She could only imagine.

Lord! The coffee tasted wonderful.

Having finally made it into her kitchen with a soft pillow from the living room, sitting on that pillow over this cushioned bench filled her with . . . *Well,* there were no words. If she didn't move a muscle, she could almost forget the pain in all of those different parts of her lower body. Then, she might only feel the stiffness in her lower back and tummy.

Yippy.

Oh, no. The school bus rounded the curve on River Road and slowed near their driveway. She couldn't allow Jason to see her like this. He'd never stop laughing about it. He'd be just like his father.

John, her husband, had nurtured a sick humor when women suffered for trying to do things men were naturally good at. *The fiend.* At least she hadn't fallen off the way Jason had.

Using both hands, she gingerly slid from the dining nook and slowly stood. Her stiff legged walk to the sink not only hurt, it had to look terrible, like walking with leg braces. She rinsed her cup and bent to put it into the dishwasher. Not so bad. Standing straight brought sharp pain to her lower back and she grabbed the edge of the countertop for support.

Barnabas scrambled from under the table and charged into the living room. His best friend was home.

Jason entered through their new front door before she could waddle to the kitchen doorway.

"Hi Barnabas." He laughed the way he always did when being licked all over his face.

She could see it so clearly in her mind. No need to walk one inch to see it again. If she could stay here in the kitchen doorway, maybe he wouldn't notice her condition.

He carried an armload of new schoolbooks down the entry steps and across the living room.

Barnabas rubbed against his leg with every stride.

Jason's left eye had been bruised purple and his shirt collar had been torn.

"What happened?"

"What do you mean?" He sounded so innocent.

"You know very well, young man. What happened to your face? Why is your shirt torn?"

"Awe, it's nothing, Mom." Jason brushed past her, marched proudly into the kitchen, and deposited his books on the dining table. "Me and those Embry twins made friends, that's all."

"Some friends." She crossed her arms and tried to look stern. She wanted to turn him over her knee and remind him of what happened to him and Jimmy, but she couldn't, not today, maybe never again. Her body just couldn't.

"Huh." He actually agreed with her, pretending not to understand her sarcasm. *The little fiend.* "They want to come over and meet Barnabas." He proudly rubbed his panting dog's oversized head. "I said it was okay."

"Okay?" She smiled, walking as normally as she could to the refrigerator, hoping he wouldn't notice her stiffness, or her uncontrollable winces of pain.

He noticed. "What happened? Did Dandy throw you off?"

"No!" She pulled out a bottle of fresh milk and closed the door. "What makes you think that?" Moving slowly, she poured him a glass of milk and set it on the table.

"You're walking all funny, like you fell down or something." Jason took a drink of milk and licked his upper lip. He gulped down the full glass and held it out for more.

She poured another half glass. "Isn't that fresh? Mr. Jacobsen brought it by this morning. He delivers groceries twice a week. All we need to do is make a list and give it to him when he comes, then he brings it the next time. Come on, let me show you something." She led Jason into the pantry, where Mr. Jacobsen had filled the lower shelves with large cans of Science Diet dog food. A 25-pound bag of their dry dog food sat on the floor beneath.

"Awesome."

She pointed at the stair doorway. "There's a new Range Rover down in the garage. It belonged to your grandfather."

"I know, Mom. Willis already showed me."

"Good grief. We've been here nearly a month and I didn't even know. Nobody ever tells me anything. Did he show you the natural refrigerator and freezer down there? I love the way it's cut into all that icy rock. It's so cold in there. I can't believe we don't need to buy a freezer."

"Of course not." Jason sounded so matter of fact, *the little monster.*

She loved him more than she could have ever imagined.

He took off his jacket and hung it on the back of the pantry door. His shirt had gotten bloody too.

"Whose blood is that?" *Lord.* He'd fed his new knife onto the back of his belt. "I thought I told you to leave that knife at home."

"Awe, Mom, all us guys have knifes. Most of the kids only have pocket knifes, so this one's special. They all know it's from Willis because he makes the scabbards."

"Special, my foot." *Ouch.* Sharp pain shot up her back from stomping her foot. "You leave that at home from now on."

"Awe, Mom."

"Whose blood is that?" She spun him and marched him into the light near the bay window.

His dog growled at her anger.

She said, "You shut up."

He growled again.

Jason always said that his dog needed to be in charge.

"Awe, Mom, don't worry. It's not mine."

"Whose is it? Did you cut somebody?"

"No, Mom. Jake Embry got a bloody nose, that's all. He's okay, though. Vicar made us shake hands."

"What if you were to pull your knife and cut somebody? What if somebody else pulled a knife? Have you forgotten what happened to Jimmy?" She knew she shouldn't have said that. He needed to forget.

"Awe, Mom."

"You want me to take it away from you?" She held out her hand.

"No." He took a step back, looking dejected. The overacting little creep had made her the bad guy, again.

He reluctantly unbuckled his belt, slowly slid the knife off, and set it on the table.

"Did you see the front of the house?" Some gardening had been done near the entry steps.

"You mean the flowers Willis planted?"

"Yes. He must have planted them while I was in the corral with John and Dandy." While she was sitting on that brick John Crow called a saddle.

"He did that yesterday when we went to church." Jason looked at her legs, figuring out her stiffness, *the fiend.*

"Funny, he didn't say anything to me about it." How could they just do whatever they wanted? Why didn't they ask permission?

Jason said, "Why didn't you notice yesterday?"

She said, "Don't you think he should ask someone before he goes and plants a garden?"

"Awe, he told me all about it on Saturday. I forgot to tell you. They bloom at night in the moonlight, even in winter; especially if you plant them where the sun can keep the soil from freezing so hard. Willis says the flowers are real pretty red with a yellow center."

At least he'd asked somebody. "What are they called?"

"Wolf Bane."

Chapter Twelve

On Thanksgiving Eve, Carolyn sat in the dark of the Rock Church with other parents, all waiting for the curtain to rise for Act III of *Pocahontas and the Captain*. It had been their school project for the past two weeks, making props, rehearsing, and finally setting stage on the church altar. The first two acts had been wonderful.

They'd been in this valley for more than two months and Carolyn loved it. This had become their home, and it had happened quickly. Her earlier jitters had nearly been forgotten. With the horses, the fishing, and his new friends, Jason acted like he'd been born here and had never left.

Time passed quickly in the mountains. It had only taken a couple of days for John to teach her to ride and another week for the soreness to pass. Daily exercise was necessary for horses and good for riders. She already felt stronger, especially in her lower body. She liked it.

After getting Jason off to school, she'd spend the rest of her mornings on her computer, writing articles for the magazines and submitting them online.

Tom Kirby praised her efforts, saying how much he appreciated her hard work. That felt good, too.

John Crow and Willis Donner made ranching easy. They took care of their cows in the lower meadow and Allen Brothers came up twice a year to buy prime beef. After their chores in the lower meadow, John cleaned the barn, chopped and stacked firewood, and kept the barn supplies fully stocked. Willis regularly checked the coal oil drums and propane tank, and kept both gravity furnaces clean. Carolyn had insisted, and the bank paid their wages from the ranch operating fund, and Olen delivered groceries.

Without fighting L.A. traffic every day, Carolyn had ample time to explore the handwritten recipe books from the pantry and to teach herself how to cook. That might take a while, learning to cook, but the recipes were easy to follow and the results almost always tasted wonderful. The following day would be the first time she'd ever even thought about cooking a turkey dinner.

Olen would deliver a fresh turkey early in the morning, Thanksgiving Day, along with all of the necessary ingredients and appropriate side dishes, including two pumpkin pies and fresh whipping cream. She could already taste the pumpkin pie.

Her and Jason had gone riding almost every afternoon, as soon as Jason got home from school. Jason insisted on it, rain or shine. John always had the horses saddled and ready by the time the bus arrived. They rode for about an hour and gave the horses their heads coming home. Jason always won. Stoner was bigger, younger, and stronger.

About a month earlier, after Jason left for school, Carolyn had saddled Dandy and gone riding alone. Those awful noises had come from their upper meadow the night before, and she and Barnabas had gone to investigate. When they arrived at that flat rock, Willis had already carried the head and guts off someplace and looked ready to carry the carcass. She'd asked him whose cow had been killed. It had been one of Jim Embry's bull calves. That was when Willis had corrected her. They called them cattle, not cows. Carolyn didn't understand why that mattered. It didn't.

What mattered was that she wanted this business off of their property. It was too gruesome for Jason to see, *ever*. That it happened at all was an outrage. These people, nice as they seemed to be, had some very strange customs.

The simple truth, as she saw things, was that she and Jason were outsiders. These people were slow to trust them, which was why she could never get a straight answer about this horrible ritual.

Helfred Jacobsen had called it a ritual. Olen had given her a strange look at the time, appearing to warn her to be careful about what she said.

Still, they all acted friendly and seemed honest. She'd even started leaving her car unlocked with the keys in the ignition.

She might learn to live with this ritual, if she had to. Her fear was centered on Jason. She couldn't allow Jason to see that carnage in their upper meadow. Not ever. They needed to do this business somewhere else. She needed to make time and talk to their banker about this. He would tell her everything he knew. After all, it was her bank now, hers and Jason's.

The vicar stepped out from behind the curtain and the small church grew quiet. He said, "Now, with the completion of Act Two, we've seen thanks offered up to our Creator. Let us be grateful, today and tomorrow, for the special blessings from our Lord, and for the abundant generosity of Jethro and Mary Lou Potter." He smiled at Carolyn, making sure she was listening. "Their trust fund keeps this school free from government funding and, thus, free from the secular teachings of the public-school curriculum.

"Down below, in our public schools, they now teach that the pilgrims gave thanks to the Indians for teaching them how to farm and plant corn. What gibberish, as if Europeans never hitched a plow to an ox and never knew how to plant or harvest corn. My friends, corn is mentioned many times in the Old Testament and in the New.

He opened his Bible to a tabbed page and said, "I read from the Gospel of John, Chapter Twelve, Verse One: 'Once about that time, Jesus went through the cornfields on a Sabbath; and his disciples, feeling hungry, began to pluck some ears of corn and rub them in their hands.'" He turned to another tabbed page. "Again, from the

Gospel of Luke, Chapter Six, Verse one: 'One Sabbath he was going through the cornfields, and his disciples plucking the ears of corn, rubbing them in their hands, and eating them.'"

He closed his Bible with a loud thump and looked out at the congregation. "We use the New English Bible from the Oxford University Press. Some of the more modern versions of the Bible have changed the word corn to grain. This modern effort to kill Christianity in America will not enter this valley, thanks to the benevolent leadership of the Potters." He smiled a Carolyn, as did many of the other parents.

Good grief. Carolyn sank down in her seat and looked at her clasped hands.

Vicar Twilby said, "Now, it's time for Act Three, Breaking Bread."

The curtain went up, the vicar stepped down and took his seat, and Carolyn swelled with pride.

Jason had been chosen to play Captain John Smith, the leading role.

Sissy Gilpin played Pocahontas, cute as can be.

The stage lights came up and Carolyn joined in the applause.

The altar had been dressed to look like a small clearing in the forest with the students costumed as Indians and pilgrims, all facing the audience in a wide half-circle.

Dressed as Indians, the Embry twins held a large, live turkey across a large wood stump at center stage. One held the head and the other held the feet. The large bird flapped and struggled to get free but the boys held him fast, both having a good time.

Jason approached from behind the stump.

Carolyn clutched her throat, hard to breath, unable to move.

Holding something shiny, Jason lifted his hands over his head.

Lord! He held a hatchet.

Jason swung down with the hatchet, and a loud thump onto the stump followed.

One of the twins stood and dropped the turkey's severed head. The other twin let go of the feet, and a flurry of feathers rushed toward Carolyn. Hot blood flew into Carolyn's face and the large, flapping bird landed in her lap. The bird's wings slapped her face, while the neck sprayed hot blood.

"Eeeyoo!" She threw the heavy bird into the aisle.

Olen Jacobsen grabbed its feet, wings still flapping, and rushed out the door with it.

The small church erupted with applause, cheers, and laughter.

Carolyn shook with bewilderment and rage.

The twins laughed, pointing at Carolyn and Jason.

Carolyn wiped hot blood from her face, grabbed Jason, and rushed out the door. She threw Jason into the passenger side of their car, climbed in behind the wheel, and started the engine. "Buckle up."

"What's wrong, Mom? Didn't I do it right?"

She knew she needed to drive carefully. Cold rain had been coming down all day and had turned to ice. She stepped on the gas, rushed backward, and her car slid on the ice. She stomped on the brake but the car kept sliding, until her tires slid up the slight hill onto dry pavement and stopped.

The congregation poured out of the church, all looking at her, all looking concerned, not laughing anymore.

She threw her car into drive and stomped on the accelerator. Seeing the gas pumps behind Jacobsen's Emporium, she lifted her foot off of the gas pedal, cleared the parking lot, turned left, and her car went into a spin. Their weightlessness seemed to take forever, until her car stopped with a loud, jarring crunch.

Stunned, she looked out the shattered windshield at one of the giant redwood trees.

Jason said, "Don't worry, Mom. These trees belong to us."

His words faded and Carolyn Potter swirled into a very dark, cold place.

SIPPING COFFEE AT THEIR dining nook, Carolyn's mood fit the dark-gray morning, remembering the night before, all of those gawking faces.

She'd awakened with a bright light shining in her eyes and a woman telling her to look to the right, then back to the left. Dr. Nancy LaRosa had been examining her after she plowed her car into the tree. She'd said, "No sign of concussion or trauma." The doctor had actually been cheery, speaking to everybody standing around the car. "I think she just fainted."

They'd all laughed softly, so embarrassing.

It had been snowing when they'd put her and Jason into the backseat of Sheriff Nason's truck. He and his girlfriend, the doctor, had brought them home.

Home. Good grief. She was no longer sure if she liked it.

Carolyn had never driven in snow or ice before and she knew she should be grateful. Nobody had been hurt.

She didn't feel grateful. She'd wrecked her car.

I know, I know. Her opinion of this place went up and down like a yoyo. At that moment, it was decidedly down. Way down.

How could these people force Jason to do something so vile as to chop off the head of a live animal and not ask her first? How could John Crow put Jason on a horse without asking? How could they kill these poor baby cows on her land without her permission? She'd get to the bottom of that one. After all, the banker worked for her.

"Oh, great." Outside, hard snowfall completely blocked her view of their lower meadow. She loved that view. Fate had just taken that away.

A loud knock at the door interrupted her sullen mood.

She got up from the table and put her coffee cup on the kitchen counter. Walking across the spacious living room reminded her of the wonderful warmth in this house, even with it snowing outside. She stepped up into the entry and opened the door, so beautifully carved.

Olen Jacobsen stood on the front porch with two bags of groceries. Barnabas wagged into his leg, tongue hanging out, smiling, licking cold air.

At the bottom of the steps, Jason worked on his first snowman.

Why am I not helping him?

"Happy Thanksgiving." Olen smiled like nothing had happened the night before.

She wanted to fly into him the way that headless turkey had flown into her, tell him that she and Jason were leaving, that they were all the sickest bunch of ghouls she could ever imagine. She said, "Happy Thanksgiving, Olen." It hadn't been his fault. She opened the door wide.

Olen carried the groceries into the kitchen and set them on the counter. He turned and looked at her like the father she'd never known. "How you feeling this morning?"

"I'm fine. Want some coffee?"

"I shouldn't. I got plenty stops to make today." He hesitated by the sink, needing a nudge.

She pulled a cup from the cupboard and filled it.

"Smells good, by golly. Be right back." He marched through the living room and went outside.

She set his coffee on the table, refilled her cup, and set it across from his. She started taking groceries from the bags and he returned with a large turkey. The sealed-plastic covering wore a picture of his store and a 'Jacobsen's Emporium' label. The packaging looked as commercial as a supermarket *Butterball.*

"Olen, that's a big bird."

"Ya, ya. That's the one from last night, fresh as can be."

"What?" Carolyn backed up and sat on a dining bench, feeling lightheaded.

Olen sat across from her and watched her hands.

"Good grief!" She was strangling a stock of celery.

Olen said, "Up here, people usually kill what they eat; fish from the streams, deer from the forest, cattle, sheep, chickens, or turkeys. They got to learn. The annual school play is part of that learning." He'd sensed that was what was bothering her? He sipped coffee. "Gosh, that's good coffee."

"I found some coffee beans and a grinder."

"Ya, Kidro's custom blend. You want me to get the same for you?" His eyes searched hers, asking so much more.

She smiled and nodded, *yes.* He should bring more coffee and, *yes,* she felt fine. This old Swedish man was humble, cautious, and thoughtful. Maybe she could trust him not to spread this around. "Jason had a bad experience before we left L.A. His best friend was . . ." She looked into her coffee and took a sip.

"Ya, we heard about this. Sheriff Nason told us about it, couple weeks before you came. Was at the Rock, a Wednesday night Bible study, as I remember."

"He told everybody? Who told him he could do that? Who do you people think you are?"

The soft smile in his eyes quieted her. The palm of his hand rose toward her, calming her. "Up here, we try and help one another out. If someone's got a problem, they take it to the Rock. After Kidro got taken, your bank sent an investigator to find your husband. Was him who found you. Sheriff got his information from the investigator.

Guess the investigator got it from your boss, Mr. Kirby. Sheriff gave us a complete report so's we'd all know who was coming. Please believe me, no harm was intended."

"Complete report? What else did he tell you?"

"He told us about what happened to J. J., how he got shot."

"And?"

"Told us you worked for Kirby Publications on some kind of children's magazine."

"Anything else?"

"Let's see . . ." he took a sip of coffee, thinking, not looking nervous in the least. "You lived with your mother down below, and that Jason has a dog. I think that's about it."

"I'm surprised he didn't give you my dress size."

"Mrs. Potter, nobody means you any harm. We don't get many new people here. We see the same faces day in and day out. So, when we heard you and the boy might be coming, we had a lot of questions." He shrugged. "Natural curiosity." His sincerity made her feel ashamed.

Her reaction to the previous night had transformed into something she might have expected from her mother. She didn't want to be like that, flying off the handle without a thought for others, and never backing down.

She relaxed and looked at the turkey. "Well, that's certainly a big bird. How long will it take to cook?" By her being conversational, maybe Olen would understand. She and Jason were both fine.

"Ah, Helfred wrote out a recipe card. She uses a butter sauce with lemon and curry and other seasonings for basting. Makes it real moist and tender. I got it out in the van with those fresh pumpkin pies."

She nodded, smiled, and changed the subject. "Olen, did somebody check my car? How bad is it?"

IT SNOWED HARD ALL morning on Thanksgiving Day, and Jason welcomed it. He needed it.

Willis and John showed up around noon, said hello to Jason and Barnabas, and went inside to get warm. That was okay, too. Sgt. Snowman was Jason's soldier anyway. He didn't need help getting him into shape, except for Capt. Barnabas, of course. He'd curled up on the porch, out of the snow, keeping dry.

Neither Jason nor Barnabas had ever seen snow before, so Barnabas didn't trust the stuff. He hadn't set foot off the porch yet, not even when Jason went to the woodpile behind the barn to find Sgt. Snowman's arms. They were still green and Jason left the pine needles near the ends. They made good hands.

Jason had already piled snow behind Sgt. Snowman. He piled on more snow, rounded it, and packed it tight, a good size for Sgt. Snowman's head. Jason picked up the heavy ball of snow and slammed it down on Sgt. Snowman's shoulders. It looked bigger than Capt. Barnabas's head. He stuck the branches into both sides and walked around to the front to take a look. His sergeant still needed a face. Jason needed to go inside for that stuff.

Speaking to Barnabas, he said, "Sgt. Snowman can stand guard at night. That means you get to stand guard in the day." Barnabas didn't need to answer. He'd always been a good soldier.

Mom opened the front door and Barnabas jammed past her, going inside to get warm. "Come on, honey. It's time to eat."

"Did you find him some eyes and a mouth?"

Mom nodded and said, "I found him a hat and a nose, too."

"Can't I put them on now?"

"Come on. Everybody's waiting."

He went inside.

She closed the door behind him and helped him off with his heavy sheepskin coat. It was plenty warm inside.

She hung the coat by the door.

Jason pulled his half-frozen mittens off with his teeth. He set the mittens on the hearth near Barnabas, laying there on a big dog pillow, almost asleep already.

Jason marched into the kitchen. "Gosh, that smells good."

Mom said, "I hope it came out okay."

A huge, dark brown turkey sat on a platter in the center of the kitchen table.

John and Willis stood near the bench, waiting.

"Awe, you guys can sit down."

They smiled but ignored his invitation.

Mom said, "Wash your hands, honey."

"Mom, they're already clean from the snow." He showed them to her, all wrinkled and pink.

"Come on." She opened the pantry door and waved toward the sink.

He washed up then took his place at the head of the table, the only chair.

Willis and John still stood, waiting.

"You guys need to sit first, because Mom gets up and down all the time."

They sat opposite each other on the padded benches and slid toward the window.

Mom sat next to John, looked at Jason, and everybody lowered their heads. Being head of the family now, it had become Jason's job to say the blessing. "Thank you, Lord, for this our home, and for all our new friends, especially for John and Willis, and thank you for this snow. It's so cool. Bless this food that it might nourish us, and bless us that we might better serve Thee. Amen."

"Willis?" Mom handed him the carving knife.

Willis slid back out so he could stand and carve the turkey. He cut the tie string from the legs, set the knife down, and filled a bowl with stuffing. It smelled awesome. He picked up the long fork and knife, removed the drumsticks, and set one of them on Jason's plate. He sliced the breast next and piled the platter with white meat.

Mom put some green beans, dressing, and gravy on Jason's plate and he helped himself to a buttered roll and some cranberry sauce.

Everybody dished up except Willis. He didn't seem to have much of an appetite. He ate a little dressing, a small slice of turkey, and some vegetables. No roll or cranberry sauce.

Mom noticed and asked, "Is something wrong?"

"No, ma'am." Willis barely glanced in her direction. "Mighty tasty victuals. My appetite must have stayed to home. I apologize."

That was enough explanation for Jason and it seemed to satisfy Mom. They ate the rest of their Thanksgiving dinner in silence.

Jason said, "That was better than grandma's restaurant," choking down the last of his dinner roll and cranberry sauce. "Can I be excused now?" He'd only eaten half of his giant drumstick, while eating all of his vegetables and dressing.

"You want your pumpkin pie later?"

"Huh." Jason sprang from the table, ran all the way through the living room and up into the entry. He pulled on his sheepskin coat and Barnabas joined him, grumbling at the front door, eager to go outside. He hadn't left the porch all day, so he probably needed to pee really bad.

"Here, you forgot these." Mom handed him his mittens, warm from the fire but still wet. "Is your sergeant a cavalry man?"

"The best."

"Good. Wait here." She turned into her office and came back with a black cowboy hat. Inside were two big buttons, a short fat carrot, and a long-stemmed pipe. "I think this hat and pipe were your grandfather's." She handed the upside-down hat and stuff to Jason. "Let us know if you need anything else."

"Thanks, Mom." Jason shoved the mittens into his coat pocket and opened the door. "You coming, Barnabas?"

Barnabas rushed onto the porch and stopped. He had forgotten about the snow.

Mom closed the door and Jason started down the front steps, being careful on freshly packed snow. He slapped his leg and looked back at his dog. "Come on. You don't need to lay down in it."

Barnabas slowly followed him down, looking and sniffing wherever he stepped. Once down, he followed Willis's and John's tracks around the corner of the garage and disappeared.

Jason climbed the mound of snow behind his snowman and put the hat on top of Sgt. Snowman's head. He pulled it down until it fit perfect. He held onto Sgt. Snowman's body and leaned around it to put the eyes in place, then the nose and the pipe, back and forth, making adjustments until his sentry looked ready.

Barnabas barked, already back from his business, bounding back and forth in chest deep, white powder, biting into it, playing with it. Good soldiers like Barnabas always learned fast.

The door opened and John followed Willis onto the porch, both already wearing their coats and hats.

"Are you guys leaving already?"

"Getting late," said John, and they started down the steps.

When they got to the bottom, Willis looked up at the sky and said, "There's more snow coming."

How did he know that? Jason only saw gray clouds, same as all day.

Both men plowed through knee deep snow toward the corner of the garage then turned back, looking at Mom on the porch.

She didn't want them to leave yet either.

Jason asked, "What about pumpkin pie?" They couldn't have eaten it already.

John rubbed a round tummy and puffed his cheeks out, too full to eat more.

Willis said, "Maybe next time." His mouth turned downward and his powder blue eyes pierced into Jason, like he was mad about something. "There's a moon tonight." He poked his thumb toward the front door. "Remember to drop that bar."

"MM. ISN'T THIS GOOD?" Mom took another bite of pumpkin pie and licked whipped cream from her upper lip.

"Best ever." The whipped cream tasted better than the canned stuff grandma sprayed on everything." He took another bite and talked around it. "Too bad John and Willis didn't get any."

"Don't talk with your mouth full."

He smiled and forked in another mouthful.

This kitchen table and bay window were way cool for looking outside. It had stopped snowing and it was getting dark, but still with some daylight. The air was clear and clean, watching lights come on in the village, uphill from their home.

Sheriff Nason's truck rounded the curve on River Road and his headlights came on. His truck turned off River Road and slammed into deep snow, plowing toward their upper meadow.

"This has got to stop." Mom stood and left their plates on the table. She opened the pantry door, lifted down her sheepskin coat, and put it on. Jason joined her and she helped him into his coat. They hurried through the living room into the entry and followed Barnabas outside.

"Careful," she said, going down the snow-packed front steps. "Burr. It's cold out."

Barnabas knew where they were going. He followed the tracks of John and Willis around the corner of the garage ahead of them.

He and Mom rounded the corner of the garage and found Barnabas waiting at the tree line.

Seeing them, Barnabas plunged through snow, leading them up the trail through the trees.

Mom said, "Don't let him get too far in front of us."

"Barnabas!" Jason clapped his hands and his dog stopped. They reached the tree line at the bottom of the upper meadow and Jason held his dog's collar, waiting for Mom to catch up.

Jason could barely see over the top of deep snow, maybe even deeper in the middle of the meadow.

The sheriff took a black calf from the back of his truck and handed it down to Mr. Embry. The sheriff jumped down and both men led the calf to that steaming rock.

The meadowlarks flew into the darkening sky.

Mom placed a hand on Jason's shoulder and he said, "Don't we need to go and make them stop?"

Mom backed him into her legs and hugged his chest, her way of saying, no.

Barnabas shook like crazy, wanting like anything to make them stop.

"Barnabas smells them." Jason knew his dog couldn't see over the snow.

"We won't need to wait long." Mom reached over Jason and scratched Barnabas's head.

Sheriff Nason and Jim Embry returned to their truck, the truck backed away from that steaming rock, and they started back down toward River Road.

Mom let go of Jason, Jason let go of Barnabas, and Barnabas plowed in front of them, jumping over snow that reached Jason's thighs.

Jason's feet and legs had gotten wet, making him shiver from the cold. He could barely see the calf's head from where they were, but Barnabas had already reached it, barking like crazy.

The birds swirled into the sky and swarmed overhead.

"Barnabas, *NO!*"

Barnabas stopped and looked at him, ears up, asking if Jason was crazy.

Steam rose from all around the flat rock, dry in the middle.

Jason walked onto the rock, nice and warm under the bottoms of his shoes.

The flock of birds circled overhead and Jason said, "What are they waiting for?"

Standing next to Jason, Mom said, "Willis told me that they stay close to the warmth of this rock. Feel it?"

"Huh."

Barnabas sniffed at the calf, probably being cautious after Stoner peed all over him.

The calf didn't like it much, crying out in a high-pitched voice, scared of Barnabas.

Mom untied the calf and pulled it off the warmth of the rock, leading it downhill along their previously plowed path.

Barnabas followed close behind the calf, sniffing its butt and legs.

Jason said, "Too weird." Mom turned and Jason pointed.

The birds swirled directly overhead, following them, getting hard to see in the growing darkness.

Scant moonlight pierced through dense clouds, giving Mom barley enough light to find the key and open the barn door. "Here, Jason." She handed him the leader rope, shivering as much as Jason.

The door opened outward without a problem. Snow had not reached under the deep overhang of the roof. She turned on a light inside.

Jason led the calf into an empty stall while Mom half-filled a bucket with water. Jason forked hay into the stall while Barnabas waited by the door.

After checking to be sure everything had been done, Mom said, "Let's get back into the house. I'm freezing."

John Crow had already lit the potbellied stove, keeping the barn much warmer than outside, but not as warm as in the house.

TWO HOURS LATER, HAVING put Jason to bed, Carolyn sat behind the big antique desk in her downstairs office, again feeling out-of-place. She hadn't yet mentally claimed this office or the master bedroom as her own. These rooms felt like someone else was watching her. Not that she believed in ghosts. She didn't. Still, a strange presence seemed to occupy these two rooms.

On that Thanksgiving night, the presence felt stronger, like an angry person looking over her shoulder, making it hard for her to concentrate on her work. She'd been working on a post-Christmas, back-to-school article about a boy, his dog, and his snowman.

Having some wild animal killing helpless baby cows on their property didn't help. At least she'd taken care of that problem, for now. She needed to go in and speak to the sheriff and her banker to end it forever.

The phone rang and it startled her, that loud ring she'd only heard in old movies. Who could be calling on Thanksgiving night? Maybe her mom. It rang again, so loud. She might never get used to it. She picked it up. "Hello."

"Your Christmas article is fun." Tom Kirby's voice was welcome, for once. If nothing else, he was rational.

She pushed back in the comfortable leather chair and listened, surprised at being happy to hear his voice.

He sounded more excited than usual. "I can't wait to get up there and have that guy . . . what's his name?" He seemed to be scrolling down, scanning the article. ". . . John Crow! I can't wait to get on a horse and have that guy teach me how to ride. We opened the magazine with your article on page three, right past the content page. That picture of your kid on that great big horse is perfect."

"You mean Jason?"

"Yeah. Sorry. I always do that, don't I?"

"It's still nice to hear. Thank you. It's the first time, you know."

"First time?"

"You've never opened with one of my articles before. It feels good."

"Well, get back down here and we'll do a lot more of that. Your writing has improved every week, which reminds me . . . Say, listen, we want you to rework that book you submitted back when father first hired you. We want you down here so we can work on it together."

"Oh, I don't know. Jason likes the school up here very much. He's already made some new friends and the school is really very traditional, not like what's happening in public schools."

"What does that mean?"

"It feels like Tom Sawyer and Huck Finn up here. You know what I mean."

"You mean, they don't follow the state curriculum? How can they get away with that?"

"They operate on a trust fund from John's family estate. They don't take any state funds at all."

"What about college?"

"Kids from here score very well on the S.A.T. You know the level of education John had."

Tom's hesitation meant he was thinking about it, maybe remembering some of John's intellectual discussions with his father. "Yeah, John was a smart guy. No arguments there. Still, if you're going to mix in today's culture, you need a good, liberal education. If you want to get ahead."

"You mean like teaching third graders how to put condoms on cucumbers? Or celebrating Cinco de Mayo instead of the Fourth of July? Good grief."

"Okay, okay. Take it easy. I just want what's best for the kid. I hope you know that."

"You mean, Jason?" She was already sorry she'd answered the phone.

"Yeah. Sorry. I need to work on that. What I was talking about . . . I mean, what's so different about what they teach?"

"For instance, the three Rs here are reading, rhetoric and religion."

"What about math and science?"

"Math and science are taught by the local physician. Nobody ever gets sick up here, so teaching keeps her busy."

"Nobody gets sick?"

"Let's just say, it's a very healthy lifestyle and I don't need to worry about Mexican gangsters stabbing Jason because I'm late picking him up."

"Okay, okay." Another hesitation meant he was organizing his thoughts. "You sound different. It's just that, well . . . I know this makes you feel uncomfortable, but you're missed, and not just by me. The rest of the staff asks about you all the time."

"Tell them I said hello, and Merry Christmas."

"Come down for a visit and tell them yourself."

"I don't know when that could happen. We're getting into a rhythm up here. Maybe that's why my writing is flowing so much better. This place feels like home, especially for Jason. His family roots are here. We both feel that." She pushed that sense of hot breath on the back of her neck aside. At least it wasn't her mother's hot breath. Or Mr. Kirby's. She turned to look. Nobody there.

"Okay, okay. So, what about your book?"

"Can't we work on-line?"

"If you insist, and it sounds like you do."

"I do." No more bugeyes from across his desk.

"That sounded final."

"We have responsibilities up here, a whole community of them."

"Yeah, I bet. Running a ranch must be a full-time job. I'm surprised you can find time to write at all. Why should you care about your readers or this magazine?"

"That's not fair." She no longer needed a job, no need to be careful about speaking out. His snotty attitude would have frightened her before. Not anymore. With her new freedom, it insulted her.

"Okay, okay. Sorry."

She said, "This ranch practically runs itself. We have help for that. It's the community I'm talking about. Our responsibilities here go back four generations."

"Maybe we should run an article about that." He still sounded sarcastic. "You know, your kid riding his horse into town to save the townsfolk; real John Wayne stuff."

"You mean Jason growing up in a situation where he can actually do good for others?" Tom Kirby was such a jerk.

"Sorry." He sounded like he meant it, so she throttled back on her growing anger and listened. "So, what do you think? Should we run an article about sudden responsibilities, or something along those lines; you know, growing up and adjusting?"

"I'll think about it." That calf in the barn and what was happening in her upper meadow slammed into the front of her brain. "But, listen, since you called, I'd like to talk to you about something else."

"Us, I hope."

Yuk. "Tom, please." *What a jerk.*

"Okay, okay. Give it to me."

"Well, there's something going on up here. It's happening on my land and I'm not comfortable with it, especially not with Jason; you know, after what happened in L.A."

"These gangs are springing up everywhere. You can't escape it."

"They're not springing up here."

A heavy thump against the entry door brought Carolyn to her feet and she dropped the phone.

Barnabas slammed into the base of the door and raked the stone floor, wanting desperately to get outside.

Something on the porch wanted to get in.

Barnabas frantically raked, snarled, and barked.

"Lord!" She'd forgotten the oak bar, again. It leaned against the corner.

Another heavy thump at the door stopped her breathing.

The second thump sent Barnabas into a furious frenzy, somehow dragging her feet from her office into the entry, where she leaned on the door to try and keep it closed.

Jason leaped from the bottom stairstep and lurched into the door with both hands, helping her keep it closed. His face twisted and his mouth turned down. His eyes flooded with tears.

Clawing and snarling, Barnabas wanted desperately to protect his Jason.

The Baldwin doorknob popped off the door and skittered down the steps into the living room.

Something heavy pressed the door inward.

Short, rapid vapors puffed through the open crack like something laughing, something toying with them.

The power of this thing overwhelmed Carolyn. It could come in any time it wanted.

Her tears flowed and she whined in fear, unable to even slow this thing.

"Mommy, it's too big." Jason's face stiffened with determination at the sight of his mother's tears. He pushed back with his arms and knees.

Near the base of the door, a large, furry paw braced its long claws against the stone jamb and slowly leveraged the door inward.

Barnabas snarled, pounced, grabbed the foreleg between his powerful jaws, and yanked.

The beast outside the door howled in pain and lifted Barnabas off the floor, slamming and bumping him, trying to pull free.

The dog braced his front feet against the jamb, his back feet against the door, horizontal to the floor. His powerful jaws held tight, his muscles bulging, his massive head jerking and twisting.

A crunch of bone, a twist of Barnabas's head, and the door slammed shut.

The creature outside howled in agony.

Carolyn lifted the heavy bar into place, not bothered by the weight. She pulled Jason into herself and both backed away from the door.

That thing outside scratched and clawed, still trying to get inside. Its deep-throated snarl told them of its anger.

Willis had been right. With that heavy bar in place, it could never get inside.

Barnabas growled, pawed, and nose bumped at something furry near the base of the door.

"Barnabas, *NO!*" Jason grabbed his dog's collar and pulled him back.

"Lord!" Carolyn froze at the sight of the bloody, severed paw, still alive. Its long, sharp claws raked at the stone floor, blindly searching for something to grab. She tossed the entry rug over it, rolled it up, picked it up, and looked for a place to put it.

"Dear God." It moved under the rug with power, trying to get at her. She rushed down the steps into the living room and put it up on the mantle, out of reach. She backed away and raked her hands on her jeans, trying to rub away that feeling of something moving, something powerful.

"God! Are we safe here?" Could they ever be safe here?

She suddenly felt very tired and needed to get some sleep. She'd think about it in the morning.

Jason tugged her elbow and asked, "Mommy, what about the garage? Did you remember to bar the door down there?"

Chapter Thirteen

Early the next morning, after a quick breakfast of juice and cereal, Jason and his mom pulled on their sheepskin coats and took Barnabas outside.

Sgt. Snowman had been trampled and peed on. Patches of yellow and red ice had replaced white snow and had entrapped the cowboy hat, pipe, and carrot. Jason couldn't see the buttons.

"What the heck?" Barnabas peed on it too.

Mom said, "Well, let's go find it." The trail of blood and tracks led around the corner of the garage and disappeared into the trees leading to the upper meadow.

They turned back toward the barn and Jason said, "Are you sure it's dead?"

"Dead or alive, I'm sure the horses can outrun it."

Mom climbed onto the stump near the barn door, grabbed the key, and opened the door.

Jason followed her into the warmth.

She said, "Anyway, it's got to be in a weakened condition."

Jason helped saddle and bridle the horses and gave the calf some corn feed and fresh water. It liked the corn feed.

They climbed into their saddles inside the barn and rode the horses out, leaving the barn door open. Jason said. "Last night was the scariest ever, but I'm still glad we saved that baby cow."

"Me too, honey. We should have listened to Willis and barred the door."

Barnabas lifted his leg near the corner of the garage, peeing on frozen blood.

Mom said, "Thank God for Barnabas. Your dog saved our lives."

"Huh."

"He sure was mad at that thing."

Jason said, "Barnabas isn't afraid of anything." They followed the dog up the trail through the woods. He slowed down in the upper meadow, sniffing at frozen blood, not so much of it anymore.

The bloody trail didn't lead to that flat rock. It led straight toward the waterfall, the path Willis always used. They followed the bloody trail to a large pond at the bottom of the waterfall. Jason had never before gone this far up the mountain. He figured Mom hadn't either.

Mom said, "This is beautiful." Freezing mist from the waterfall had created icicles on the surrounding trees and rocks. She smiled at Jason and turned back to the pond. "I wonder where it went."

Jason said, "Do you think it can swim?"

Large boulders blocked enough water to create the deep, dark pond. Jason could walk around the pond to the other side, but probably not Stoner. He might stumble on the icy boulders and get hurt.

Dandy and Stoner lowered their heads to take a drink and Mom said, "I can't see where it came out."

"There's too much ice. Why didn't it go around instead of getting wet? It must be awfully cold?"

"I don't have any idea."

"I hope it drowned." Jason couldn't see deep enough to know.

"How dare they lure that thing onto our property? That sheriff is going to get a big piece of my mind. I'll call him as soon as we get back."

Jason turned Stoner toward their house. "Race you home."

SHERIFF PHIL NASON had been awakened by a call from the California Highway Patrol at 2:22 a.m., Friday morning, the day after Thanksgiving. There'd been an accident out on Sonora Pass Highway. A truck driver had called it in.

Deep snow had forced Nason to roust Jake Pendleton and his equipment to clear the road out of the valley and down the highway to the scene of the accident. Jake had a backhoe and small dump truck.

Jake always bolted an adjustable snowblade onto the front of his truck after the first snow, which had been the day before, on Thanksgiving Day. It had taken him an hour to get the blade hitched and get to Nancy's. It had taken another hour to get to the scene of the accident.

What a mess.

A lumber truck had jackknifed coming down the east side of the pass and had dropped his load onto a passenger car, a family returning to Sanora after a gathering over in Hawthorne, Nevada.

Nobody had advance notice that a storm would hit, one of those seasonal things that happens in the High Sierras, so they'd failed to close the pass in time.

The front of the car had been crushed, killing the driver and his wife instantly. The 6-year-old boy in back would be okay, only a broken arm and hypothermia. The baby had been nearly frozen to death, but they expected her to live, with possible brain damage.

The truck driver's Peterbilt truck had been hanging over a cliff with more than a one-hundred-foot drop to sliding granite rubble. He'd been scared witless.

Nason hoped he wouldn't blame himself for what had happened to the family. The freak storm had nothing to do with him.

What a mess.

By the time the snowplow from Sonora reached them, followed by the plow and tow trucks from Bridgeport, the sun was up in a clear sky.

The highway patrol took the truck driver back down to Sonora, a rescue helicopter took the kids and dead parents, and Nason headed back to his office, arriving at 3:17p.m.

The potbellied stove was on slow drip and his office was toasty. He peeled off his sheepskin coat, put it on a hanger, and hung it on the back of the door. He hooked his hat over the coat and used his hands to walk around his desk, exhausted. He eased into the cushioned comfort of his armchair, laced his fingers behind his neck, and leaned back, squirming into that comfort spot.

The flashing red light on his answering machine wouldn't allow his eyes to close. The never used machine had six messages, barely readable through his tired, burning eyes. He leaned forward, propped both arms on his desk, and pressed the message button. He dropped his weary head onto his left arm and listened to six beeps, then the electronic voice said, "No messages." He pressed the erase button and settled back into his chair. "Thank you."

He pushed away from his desk, laced his fingers behind his neck, and propped his boots onto the top of his desk to get comfortable. He closed his eyes, squirmed into that comfort spot, and darkness swarmed over his thoughtless mind.

"There you are!" Carolyn Potter's harsh tone forced Nason's unwilling eyes to open. He had no idea whether or not he had slept, or if he had, for how long.

His heavy boots thudded to the floor and he sat upright, struggling to unlace his fingers. He mustered all of his strength, leaned forward, spread his fingers onto his desk, and focused on his hands. *Yes*, he had 8 fingers and two thumbs. His vision returned and he looked up into her big, dark blue peepers.

She looked like she could see the inside of his dull mind. *Gorgeous.* She waved a rolled piece of rug at him and marched up to his desk, angry about something. "I've been calling you all day."

"Why didn't you leave a message?" He scrubbed his face with both hands, chasing cobwebs. He needed a shave.

"I didn't know what to say." She waved that piece of rug like she wanted to throw it at him. "I'm still not sure if I know what to say. I called to see if you were here so I could come over."

"I've been out on the highway all night. There was a bad accident, due to the storm. I just got back and I'm tired." He stood to stretch out his kinks, suppressing a much-needed yawn. He took a couple of deep breaths, unable to stop his muscles from shuddering. "What's this about?"

"We had an incident last night." She waved that rug one last time and set it on his desk. "Something tried to get into our house."

Dazed from lack of sleep, Nason absently stared at the rolled rug and cocked an ear in her direction, waiting for more.

More came in a rush. "How dare you stake out that poor baby cow on my property? No telling what kind of dangerous animals it could attract."

"What?" Trepidation slammed up from the bottom of Nason's tired feet and prickled the hairs at the back of his aching neck. "Are you talking about the bull calf?"

"If that's what it was, yes. You tied it to a rock in our upper meadow. Who told you, you could do that?"

"The Village Committee has an easement." Nason was more tired right then than at any time in his life. "Kidro set it up after . . ." She didn't need to know the rest of it. Not yet.

"An easement to do what?"

"Actually," A rush of relief flooded over him. ". . . you'll have to speak with Bill Whatling about that. He should still be over at the bank. He can give you the actual language. He'll probably give you a copy of the deed. Though, I know Kidro had a copy." He looked down at the rolled rug. "Why? What happened?"

She leaned closer, more intense. "Some kind of animal tried to get into the house last night. If it hadn't been for Barnabas . . ."

"What happened to the calf?"

"We managed to save this one. It's in our barn."

"What? How . . . Lady, you have no idea. Didn't you bar your door?"

"Not at first, no. Then, after, we put the bar into place and it went away."

"After what?"

"Barnabas got a hold of its front leg." She pointed with pride at the rolled-up piece of rug.

A cold chill spread across Nason's shoulders. He hesitated before lifting the top flap of the rug, not enough to see what was inside. He took a deep breath and unrolled the rug across his desk. "Why . . . NO!" A human hand had been chewed off above the wrist.

Carolyn gasped and backed up to the door. Her eyes went blank and she turned to stare at the door, like some switch had been turned off in her brain. She glanced back and Nason and nodded toward the door. "I'm just going over to speak with Mr. Whatling."

IN THE WORKINGS OF Carolyn Potter's subconscious mind, there were things that happened and, well, things that just did not happen. By the time she crossed the road and climbed the steps at the bank, the image of the severed human hand had been completely washed from her conscious memory. It had never happened. How could it? When she passed through the vestibule and entered the bank, the wall clock read, 4:22.

"Hi, Carolyn." Bell Whatling's always friendly voice rang like a musical chime. "What can we do for you?"

Carolyn was in no mood for musical chimes. "I need to speak with your husband."

Bell jumped to her feet, probably sensing Carolyn's mood. "Sure. He's been wanting to go over the estate since before you arrived." She led Carolyn into a deep, stone framed doorway behind her desk. She smiled sheepishly at Carolyn, knocked softly, opened the door a crack, and said, "Mrs. Potter needs to speak with you."

"Bring her in." Bill Whatling's voice boomed with the same sham cheeriness as his dopey wife.

Bell swung the door wide open and ushered Carolyn into a large stone and oak paneled office with expensive looking antique furnishings. Leather bound books lined the shelves on both sides of the door, a nice office.

Bill turned off his computer monitor and jumped to his feet. He adjusted and tugged at his wrinkled suit and rounded his desk. His eyes narrowed into slits that matched his thin-lipped smile.

Carolyn shook his clammy hand and he pressed her backward into one of two leather armchairs facing his desk. "Thank you for coming in. I've been wanting to go over your accounts."

The door closed behind her, leaving her and Bill alone.

She said, "I need to speak with you. Do you have a few minutes?"

He circled back behind his desk and sat. He looked at her and smiled. "Of course. All the time you need. After all, we work for you, me and Bell, that is. You all but own this bank. Or, actually, your son owns this bank." He leaned back in his chair and relaxed. "Whatever you need, we're here to help. Whatever it is."

A flash of light crossed the high windows, causing her to turn, probably sun reflecting from a passing car. She sat, forcing herself to calm. "I need some answers."

"Whatever it is, I'm here to help. Can we get you some coffee or something?" His fat hand hovered over his intercom, eager for an affirmative answer.

"No, thank you." She took a moment to read the man but his expression went flat. *Oh well.* "Mr. Whatling, there are people taking liberties on our property. I was told you would explain all of this."

"Sure." His head sank between his shoulders. He spread his hands. He forced a smile under his nervously blinking eyes.

She leaned forward, ready to jump into his face if he dared any kind of evasion. "Sheriff Nason tells me there's an easement of some kind allowing him access to my upper meadow."

His forced smile disappeared. His eyes stopped blinking. He leaned back in his chair. He looked over the top of her head. His eyes shifted, like reading a sign on the wall behind her. "Actually, it's an irrevocable trust deed." He looked at her and his forced smile returned.

Carolyn said, "That's stupid. Who would do that? How can they have the right to put poor, defenseless animals out there as bait to attract wild beasts? Why would anyone allow their property to be used like that? It's just stupid."

Whatling laced his fingers over his round belly, again looking over her head at the bookshelves behind her, eyes moving like he was reading another sign. "Yes, well, it actually gives the Village Committee, or their appointees, the use of a small portion of your land." He looked at her again, all business, no nonsense. "It's like a small flag lot, the gravel road being the flag pole, you see." He nodded and smiled, obviously thinking he'd answered her questions.

"Don't you dare give me this runaround. Answer my questions." She didn't believe his lying lips for an instant. "Who would do such a thing and why would they do it?"

"Oh." He actually looked relieved. "That would be Kidro Potter." He leaned forward, propped his elbows on his desk, smiled, and spread his hands. "Anything else, Mrs. Potter?"

"He gave you permission to brutally murder innocent cows?"

"Whatever the committee deems necessary, until such a time as they deem it to no longer be necessary."

"Committee? What committee?"

"Ah, yes. Well, Mary Lou Potter, your son's great grandmother, set up a committee to govern local affairs, like the school, the clinic, maintenance of our roads, and of the hydroelectric plant at the top of the valley. They left a substantial endowment to take care of the needs of this valley." He pasted that smile back on.

Frustrated by all of the doubletalk, Carolyn jumped to her feet and leaned across his desk. "This committee can do whatever they want on our property? Does that include cruelty to animals, Mr. Whatling?"

He folded his fat hands onto the edge of his desk and looked at his twiddling thumbs, thinking about it. He looked up at her. "With regard to that, you'll need to speak with Sheriff Nason."

"I'll need to speak with my lawyer."

He stood and faced her head-on, confident but polite. "That would be fine. I'll be happy to recommend a good one."

"No thank you. I have a very good lawyer. Perhaps you've heard of them; Emerick, Bessel, and Waters."

"No, ma'am. But I'll be happy to provide them with a copy of the trust deed and whatever else you might direct us to submit."

WHEN SHERIFF PHIL NASON got to Jim Embry's place the sun had already gone behind the mountain. They only had about an hour of daylight to get this done.

Plowing through snow, going uphill on Jim Embry's gravel road, proved tricky. He should be wearing chains on at least the back tires but he didn't have time to put them on. He'd certainly need chains to drive up to the waterfall. Embry could put them on in front of Potter's barn.

The Perch. Nason hated even to think about that.

Embry would probably drop a load in his shorts.

Jim waited on his deep front porch, watching Nason plow snow in a wide turnaround. When the truck got close, Embry waded into knee deep snow and timed it just right.

Nason stopped and rolled down the passenger window. He said, "It might be easier to climb in through the window."

"Bite my jumbo, Nason." Embry had always been stubborn, always doing things his way. He yanked the door until it opened wide enough to squeeze his lanky frame inside. While Embry still had one foot on the ground, Nason rolled the truck slowly forward, forcing Embry to hurry, using snow to push the door closed. "Dang it, Phil! You trying to break my leg?"

"We need to hurry. We don't have much time."

"Hurry for what?"

Nason followed his own plowed path back toward River Road. He glanced down at the rolled rug on the consol between the seats, making sure Jim saw the thing. His natural curiosity would force him to open it soon enough.

"Would you shut this freezer hole?" Embry poked his thumb at the open window.

"You've got a switch."

Embry grinned at himself and closed the window. "What kind of emergency we got today, makes me choke down my second turkey sandwich? I was taking my time with that one. My old woman makes the best sandwiches. Uses sourdough shepherd bread smothered with mayo, slices of jack cheese and turkey, and fries it in butter."

Nason's mouth watered. He could taste it. He hadn't eaten all day. "You could have brought one for me."

"I asked her to make one for you but she flipped me off." He unzipped his coat and caressed his bulging tummy, deliberately punishing Nason. "My old woman can sure cook a turkey. Puts sliced leftovers on sourdough shepherd bread with lots of mayo and jack cheese. Man-oh-man."

"Embry, you look like the snake who swallowed the watermelon."

Embry grinned and looked closely at Nason. "You look all in."

"I was out on the highway all night. Had a bad one. Two dead."

"So, why'd you drag me out? Why ain't you over at Nancy's hugging thighs and pillows?"

Nason looked down at the rolled carpet again, prompting Embry to take a look.

Embry seemed too infatuated with his bloated belly, fondling the thing like a ripe peach.

Nason could hear the man think, planning on how to stuff some pumpkin pie in there. "How is it you stay so thin?"

Embry grinned.

Nason turned left onto the cleared pavement of River Road and looked in his rearview mirror. "No, not that!"

Carolyn Potter's Rover sped closer, only a quarter of a mile behind.

Embry asked, "What?"

"That Potter woman is right behind us."

"So?" Embry didn't have a clue.

"Listen, when we get to her barn, you put the chains on the rear tires and let me do all the talking."

"What are you *talking* about, chains?"

They passed the road to the upper meadow. Only the tips of a few fence posts showed above the snow, barely marking the edge of the road. The trail left by his truck the day before had been completely covered by fresh snow. "No, no."

"What?"

Nason turned up Potter's cleared cobblestone driveway, crossed the rise, and turned down toward the barn. Jake Pendleton's snowplow had cleared a wide turnaround. Nason said, "We don't have much time, so hurry it up." Nason parked in front of the barn and climbed out. Moving quickly, he reached up for the key and opened the barn door. He waved at Embry to get moving.

Embry grudgingly climbed out and looked back toward the house.

Carolyn Potter's Rover rolled down the driveway toward them.

Embry said, "Phil, what's going on?"

"Just put those chains on and keep your trap shut." Nason pointed to the big toolbox at the front of the truck bed.

Carolyn Potter stopped and climbed out of her Rover. "Just what do you think you're doing?" Even in a rage, she looked beautiful, those dark blue eyes, the way she moved, marching toward Nason.

Embry finally dug into Nason's toolbox. He wanted no part of this conversation.

With Nason thinking what to say, thinking this situation couldn't get any worse, their dog barked from their front porch and charged toward the barn. He didn't bother with the cleared part of the driveway. He bounded directly across the snow in the middle and rushed right at Nason.

Her young son ran right behind, following the lower edge of the cleared driveway.

Embry jumped into the back of the truck and backed against the open toolbox. He turned to look at the roof of the truck.

The dog lunged at Nason with his front paws, tongue out, just saying hello.

Nason rubbed the dog's large head and let it take his gloved hand, gnawing gently, still saying hello. Speaking to Carolyn, he said, "We hate to see you getting upset like this."

"Answer my question. How dare you enter my barn without my permission?"

His answer surprised him. "You told me yourself. There's a calf in there that doesn't belong to you." He'd just accused her of cattle rustling.

She didn't flinch. "So, what if there is? I brought it in to keep it from being hurt." She spread her arms in frustration and bit down against the cold. Speaking had to be a struggle, not wearing a warm coat. "Besides, it was on our property."

He looked inside the barn.

The calf was in the nearest stall.

He looked back into those blue eyes. "That calf belongs to Ralston. If I'd have gotten a warrant, I'd have to arrest you." *What a crock.*

"Arrest me?" Her shrill response brought Embry to his feet, back there putting on chains. He finally understood. Ralston's calf, the one they'd put out the previous day, was in her barn. He yanked the second set of chains from the toolbox and rushed to the other side of the truck.

The dog positioned himself between Nason and Carolyn, looking at whoever was speaking, trying to keep the peace.

She wasn't interested in peace. Only rage showed in her peepers. Her chattering teeth seemed out of place.

The boy stood at a respectable distance, taking it all in.

Nason entered the barn, no time to explain, took the small calf from the stall, and led it to the back of his truck. He didn't need the ramp.

Embry dropped the tailgate and climbed into the back.

Nason hoisted the calf into the back.

Embry pulled it forward and tied it to the hasp on the toolbox.

She had no interest in explanations. "I'm going to speak to my lawyer about this. Then, maybe we'll see what's what."

Nason said, "That is your right, madam." They were running out of time. He slammed the tailgate shut, left the barn door open, and climbed into his truck.

Embry sat in the passenger seat with his wild-eyed stare. "Gotta go, gotta go, gotta go."

Nason drove straight out through the unplowed snow in the center of the driveway and crunched onto cleared cobblestone, where the driveway narrowed, not caring about his tires. He turned right at River Road and right again, following the fence posts of what he knew to be the road to the upper meadow.

A little uphill, the tips of the fence posts vanished under snow, but the fence had caused a snowdrift ten feet to their left, easy to follow. With darkness closing around them, he turned on his headlights. The headlights reflected back into his face and he shut them off.

The upper meadow was just ahead. Snow couldn't cover that flat rock. He should be able to find that, even in this twilight. "Ah," steam rose beyond deep snow, the flat rock they used for this all-important ritual.

Squirming with concern, Embry said, "What happened?"

Now that Embry was looking, Nason poked a thumb at the rolled carpet between the seats. "Open that and take a look."

Embry lifted the rug onto his lap and cautiously unrolled it, like expecting to find a rattlesnake or something. "Holy . . . NO!" He rolled it back up and jammed it back between the seats. "What happened?"

"It tried getting into their house and their dog chewed it off."

Embry blinked and turned toward the rising steam, rocking back and forth like he could hasten their approach.

Nason parked and they both forced their doors open against still soft snow. One cold night would give it a hard crust. Nason dropped the tailgate and climbed into the bed.

The calf bellowed in fear. How could it know what was coming? Nason untied and led the calf to the tailgate.

Embry watched, not sure what to do.

"You can't lend a hand?" Nason jumped down, carried the calf to the ground, and led it around a deep drift onto the warmth of the rock.

Behind him, Embry shrugged and waved his hands in the air. He had no idea what to do.

Moron.

Those ever-present meadowlarks fluttered up and resettled into the brown grass at the edges.

Nason tied the calf to the iron ring and return to his truck.

Embry waited in the passenger seat. "So, let me get this straight. Are you saying what we need to raise up here is pit bulls?" They both laughed, until Nason put the truck into gear and plowed farther uphill.

"Ain't you leaving this rug here?"

"You know I can't do that. After last night, that thing might not even come here. It might head straight for their place or into the village, maybe even to your place."

Embry looked out at growing darkness. "We're not taking it up there, are we?"

Nason drove uphill, barely able to see the drift at the fence-line to his left. "No. I am. You can turn the truck around."

Lights from John Crow's house and light from the Perch helped Nason keep his bearing. He smiled, seeing Embry's face. "Be careful you don't get stuck in a bog, turning around. We don't want to be stranded out here tonight."

Embry squirmed in his seat, sounding pathetic. "Just leave it with the calf. He'll find it."

Plowing forward buried the front of Nason's truck with thin sheets of frozen snow, cracking as they piled up.

Just ahead, the waterfall shimmered in the moonlight. Nason said, "That's pretty enough." He stopped and put the truck into park. "You remember what happened ten years back, when J. J. chopped off his paw with an axe?"

"So what? I got a stone house, built by Willis his own self."

Nason tried to open his door but couldn't. "What about those who don't? You want the state police coming up to investigate, or maybe federal marshals? If it goes back to the Potter place, she's got family and people down below. There's bound to be an inquiry."

Embry clamped up, biting down on what Nason had just said, chewing it around in his mini-mind. He said, "You don't pay me enough for this."

"I didn't know I was paying you anything."

"See what I mean?" Embry smiled a little. "You're uninvited to Christmas dinner."

"Thanks. I'll tell Nancy. She'll be relieved."

Embry snickered.

Nason tried to push his door open again. The snow was too deep and the frozen crust was too hard. He rolled down his window and used the roof of his truck to pull himself out, sitting on snow, squirming to get clear. He leaned backward into freezing snow, broke the crust, and ice slid under his shirt collar. "Aye-yiyi!" It was cold.

"What's wrong now?"

Nason let go, crunched all the way into the stuff, and rolled over. He stood, sank knee deep, brushed himself off, reached back into the truck, and pointed. "Shut up and give me that."

"How long before you're back?" Embry climbed over to the driver's seat and handed Nason the rolled rug.

Nason said, "Hand me that flashlight."

Embry opened the center consol and handed him the flashlight. "How long?"

Nason didn't want to say that he didn't know. "The moon'll be up soon. Get this thing turned around." Moonglow already showed behind the mountain to the east.

Embry rolled the window halfway up. "You know what you can bite."

"Don't get into a bog."

"My bony butt." Embry rolled the window all the way up.

Nason wedged the rug under his left arm, turned on his flashlight, and plowed toward the waterfall as quickly as his tired legs allowed, lifting his knees to break the crust with his shins.

Ice made circling the pool and falls treacherous. Falling into the freezing water might be fatal.

He followed a small trail uphill as the top of the moon broke over the ridge behind him, making it easier to see. Maybe the trees under the Perch were tall enough to block the moonlight. Maybe that thing needed to see it. That thought provided Nason with a slender thread of hope.

He followed cut stone steps uphill through evergreen trees, winding his way onto a dome of granite near the giant rock called the Perch. Snow on the granite dome was deep and the crust was hard, but not hard enough to hold his weight. The sharp pain from using his shins to break ice felt like he might be bleeding.

One thing about cop flashlights, they were built strong. He turned it off and used it to break hardened snow as he went.

The full moon had already risen above the trees, lighting his way.

The solid slab of snow-covered granite rose steadily uphill toward the Perch.

The tall boulder was split down the center. He could see it clearly now, getting close enough. A stair had been built into the split. It led up to the timber and glass house built by Willis Donner, organic, beautiful.

"Dear God." Up in one of the many windows was a quickly growing shadow of something or someone.

"Ah!" The rolled carpet under his arm moved with power. *It's alive!* He unfurled the rug and let the hand fall onto the bottom stairstep.

"Oh, God!" Under the glow of the full moon, the hand changed, growing fur and long, blade like claws, growing larger. It moved again, trying to grab Nason's leg.

MOM WAS MADDER THAN Jason had ever seen her, not at Jason or Barnabas, but at the sheriff and Mr. Embry. Even angry, she still remembered to give Jason his pumpkin pie before sending him and Barnabas upstairs for the night.

He'd told her they were studying the Declaration of Independence in school and she told him to look it up on Wikipedia and to write a report. He didn't have time for that. There was too much going on. He'd find time to finish his report over the weekend. Right then, he needed to get out there and take care of things. Then Mom would feel better.

Barnabas followed him from the library into his bedroom, where he stopped at the door to pet his dog. "You need to stay here and you can't bark, okay?"

Barnabas licked Jason's nose. He understood.

Jason stepped into the upstairs hallway and closed his bedroom door. He hurried to the top of the stairs and listened.

She was on the phone in her office.

As quietly as possible, he hurried down the stairs and listened again.

She said, "How was the Bright Spot this year?" She was talking to Grandma. Grandma always had Thanksgiving at the Bright Spot on Sunset. Grandma never liked cooking, especially not big dinners.

If he stayed to the right, with her at her desk, she couldn't see him leave.

The heavy bar still sat on the floor, leaning into the corner. He never could have carried it down by himself, not without her hearing. He crossed the entry and grabbed his sheepskin coat, put it on, quietly opened the door a crack, and waited to see if she'd heard.

She was still talking to Grandma.

Jason stepped out, closed the door quietly, easy without the latch, hurried down the steps, and ran around the corner of the garage. It was really cold. He buttoned his coat all the way to the top and thrust his hands into his pockets.

The full moon made it easy to follow the trail up the slope, even through the trees. He followed their path from the day before.

Way up by the waterfall, headlights in deep snow pushed back and forth, maybe someone turning around, probably the sheriff and Mr. Embry. Why were those guys way up there?

Finding the flat rock was easy. He could see the steam from a hundred feet away.

The headlights moved straight toward him, with snow piled high on both sides. It was Sheriff Nason's truck.

Jason couldn't let them see him. He hurried onto the warmth of the rock and knelt behind the calf. He couldn't see the headlights from there, so they couldn't see him. A big pile of snow blocked his line-of-sight. He untied the calf, happy as anything to see Jason.

The birds took off and flew toward the full moon, maybe scared by the noise of the truck moving past, already moving downhill toward River Road. The sheriff and Jim Embry were yelling at each other. Unclear about what.

OLEN JACOBSEN BUTTONED the cuffs of his shirtsleeves, getting ready for their monthly meeting at the bank. A full moon that night made him feel only slightly less safe. The new house he'd built for Helfred hadn't been built by Willis but they lived in the village, a great distance from Potter's upper meadow.

That thing hadn't come this far up-valley for more than ten years, that horrible night it had taken their Gustov.

Back in the early days, Mary Lou and Jethro Potter had set up a community fund in case of emergencies like fires, flooding, damaging winter storms, and the like. It was kind of a private insurance company and everybody who was able paid into it. They'd set up a committee to inform the community on the status of the fund and to arbitrate any disputes that might arise. Their earlier monthly meetings had been held in Olen's store, and most of the local folks had attended. They all liked Helfred's coffee and cookies.

Ten years earlier, after that awful night, Helfred had insisted on this new house. She couldn't bare living in a place with so many memories of their only child, Gustov. Olen felt just the opposite. He enjoyed feeling Gustov's presence in the rooms above their store.

After Kidro built the new bank, the committee moved their meetings, making it easier for Bill Whatling to access bank files and records, if need be. He'd always been the unofficial chair of the committee anyway.

The monthly ritual had given additional purpose to the meetings. A couple of the ranchers had complained about losing a prime bull calf and the committee had passed a resolution to reimburse at fair market value.

Kidro Potter had voted against that resolution, even though calves were cheap. Such reimbursements were less than the fund's monthly income. Kidro had always been grudgingly spiteful. After the resolution was adopted, he'd stopped coming to the meetings. *Better that way.*

Only a handful of locals still attended the meetings, and Helfred wanted Olen to quit.

He couldn't do that. Their store was still the social center of the community. Their store, and the Rock Church. Olen saw himself at the center of their unusual society. If there was a committee, Olen Jacobsen needed to be a part of it. Maybe more so than Bill Whatling or Phil Nason.

He walked into the entry and pulled on his heavy coat. Buttoning up, he stepped into the kitchen doorway.

Helfred squeezed S and O shaped butter-cookie dough onto a baking sheet. She looked up, eyes drooping with worry. "I got a bad feeling tonight, like I won't see you again."

"Helfred, you say the same thing every month. You always got a bad feeling." From the look of it, her feeling may have been stronger that night.

She set her dough gun on the counter and wiped her hands on her apron, stepping closer to Olen. She looked more fearful than usual. "Why not stay home for once? It's cold out."

"Why don't you come with me? Bring your knitting. Bring cookies for the other fellas."

She glanced over her shoulder at the breadboard. She turned back with a sigh. "I guess not." She turned her cheek up and Olen kissed it.

He walked to the entry and opened the door. He didn't need to turn on the light. The glass vestibule was well-lit by the full moon.

The entry was on the south-facing side of the house, and uphill from the bank. He could see the whole valley from there, all but the Potter house beyond the tall trees at the bend in the river.

Somebody's snow-covered headlights pushed downhill from Potter's upper meadow.

Who can that be?

Maybe Phil.

Why would Phil Nason be up there at this time of night, under a full moon?

Something thumped the glass wall of the vestibule, like a pinecone blown by the wind. The snow-capped trees around their house showed no sign of wind. Something thumped the exterior glass again, and Olen looked up at the moon.

Birds circled overhead, some close to the house. He'd never seen them fly at night before, but this was a very bright night, the moon and all this snow. Maybe they always flew at night and he'd never noticed.

What? In winter?

He shook it off, opened the exterior door, and walked outside. "Aye-yoy!" He pulled his coat collar tight, started down their concrete steps, and slipped. He threw his arm out and grabbed a tree limb to stabilize himself. He'd cleaned the steps earlier that morning, but it had been a sunny day. Small puddles on the steps had frozen solid.

Day or night, he couldn't help admiring his store from the front of their house. Whatever Willis built was not only strong and secure, it was fun to look at, and fun to live in.

Olen followed the stair downhill to the covered sidewalk along the side of the bank, used the rear door, passed through a small vestibule, and entered the bank lobby.

"Here's Olen, now." Bill Whatling smiled, *hello*, sitting at his wife's desk.

Gilpin stood in front of the desk, giving Olen the evil eye. Who knows why?

Stan Ralston sat under the high, south facing windows, no need for bars up there.

Gilpin said, "Where's Nason?"

Olen said, "I saw his headlights coming down from Potter's upper meadow."

"You're both late," said Gilpin, maybe his reason for the evil eye. "I was getting ready to go up to your house and find you, so I can get paid."

"We need you to sign the release," said Whatling, sliding a sheet of paper across his desk toward Olen.

Olen stepped over and signed it. He didn't need to read it. He'd seen them before. He'd also seen Gilpin's evil-eyed sneer before. *Stupid slob.* If not for Gilpin, Kidro might still be alive. That thought made Olen smile, hard not to. He liked these new Potters better than he'd ever liked Kidro.

"Fine. Just put it into my account." Gilpin pushed his hat to the back of his head and turned toward the front door.

Ralston said, "Dang it, Bruce, why didn't you just stay to home?"

"And trust you bunch of crooks? Not me." Gilpin meant it. He didn't smile when he left.

JASON CLIMBED ONTO the stump at the front of the barn, just high enough for him to return the key. Everybody knew the niche was there, of course, so he didn't worry about somebody seeing him put the key back. What mattered was that the horses and the calf were safe inside, nice and warm. Why Stoner and Dandy wouldn't take apples seemed weird. Mr. Jacobsen had delivered fresh pippins, the kind they liked best. Something must have been bothering them that night.

Jason's pant legs had frozen stiff, having gotten wet when he'd walked to the upper meadow and back. His teeth chattered, even before he jumped off the stump, and they kept chattering all the way up the driveway toward the house. He stopped, and his teeth stopped chattering.

Something stood in the trees near the crest of the driveway, where it turned down toward River Road, something big and dark. It was looking at Jason. The eyes glowed bright red in the dark.

How could this be? That thing must have died. Mom even said so.

This must be a different one. It had all four legs, walking onto the crest of the driveway, so plain to see.

Jason hurried up the steps onto the porch.

Maybe if he didn't look at it, maybe if it didn't see his eyes, maybe it wouldn't see into his soul. Maybe it wouldn't know who he was. Maybe it wouldn't see him at all, he hoped. He prayed that John Crow had been right.

He pushed on the front door but it didn't budge.

Oh, no.

He turned to look.

That thing walked down the swept-cobblestone driveway toward him, making that same kind of scratching sound Barnabas made with his claws.

The red eyes looked angry, and Jason turned back to the door.

AFTER FINALLY GETTING off the phone with her mother, Carolyn had remembered that heavy bar and had lifted it into place, nice and secure for the night. She'd thought Willis would have come down to fix the Baldwin latch but he hadn't. It was still broken.

The weight of the door kept breezes from blowing it open but a strong wind might. If he didn't come down by the following day, she'd send John Crow to find out why. If Willis had gotten sick or injured, maybe she could help.

With the house secured for the night, she called Mr. Kirby to explain the goings on the night before. After she finished explaining, he said, "So, let me get this straight: That racket I heard last night was some kind of animal trying to get into your house, because you removed something it normally feeds on. Is that correct?" He didn't sound like he believed her.

"Something like that, yes." It sounded ridiculous, hearing him say it. She looked into the entry again, making sure that heavy bar across the door would protect them against the night. Why did she need to look at it again and again? A cold chill crossed her shoulders. *What if . . .*

No. She hadn't forgotten anything. She and Jason had already checked the basement entry from the garage. That bar hadn't been removed since they moved in. All of their windows were too high off the ground. Nothing could get in.

Still, she felt like something was terribly wrong?

Mr. Kirby said, "What? So, this wild animal leaves them alone if they give it a young calf?"

"Exactly. I wouldn't mind so much if they used somebody else's property."

Mr. Kirby said, "And, they say the previous owner gave them the right to use your property."

"Jason's grandfather. Exactly. They call it a trust deed. I'll email it to you. It's only one page."

"Look, I'm no lawyer, but I'll tell you what I know from experience. If something is encoded into a legally binding document, properly signed, notarized, and recorded, you're better off going into court to have it overturned than to try and take action on your own."

"What are you saying?"

Mr. Kirby said, "Again, I'm no lawyer, but if you hire a lawyer, it could take years to resolve. In the meantime, you need to let them continue to do whatever they've been doing. If you take action against a legal document and somebody gets hurt . . . Well, you know what I mean."

Instead of getting solid advice from her only sensible link to the real world, he'd made her feel defeated, even desperate. "Oh, Mr. Kirby, if you could see what happens to these poor baby cows. It's just awful."

"Hang on." He sounded sincerely eager to help. "Let me pull off the road and park."

She waited, mindlessly staring into the entry.

A minute later, he said, "What I don't understand is this . . . You still there?"

"Yes."

"Hi."

"Hi."

"Okay, what I don't understand is why doesn't this thing, or these things, why don't they just take what they want from the local herds?"

"I don't know. The sheriff ties them to this big flat rock where it never gets cold."

"What? The sheriff?"

"Yes."

"A place where it never gets cold?"

"It's geothermal radiation or something. It keeps the snow off and feels warm all around. We've got several hot springs around the valley. There are two that I know of, right here on my land. Anyway, maybe that's why it goes there, because it's warm. Good grief! That just sounds ridiculous."

"Yeah." His tone had changed, maybe no longer taking this seriously. "I need to get up there and take a look for myself."

"Could you? It really is beautiful here. Maybe you could talk to the sheriff while you're here." She decided to put aside her instinctive dislike for Mr. Kirby. He might be able to clear up this whole mess.

"Sure. How does Christmas sound? I need a break from this place, anyway." He sounded too eager, bringing back that feeling of something wet climbing up her leg. "But, listen, something else just occurred to me. You might be better off if you hire a professional hunter to track and kill this thing, or things. That way, you won't need to fool around with lawyers. I was just reading an article about the growing wolf population up there. The guy says you need to shoot, shovel, and shut up. I can't believe they're still protected by the EPA. Once they go endangered, they never come back."

A noise in the entry startled her.

Barnabas barked from up in Jason's room.

"Just a minute." She set the phone down and stood. The door was definitely secured.

A cold shiver rushed up her back.

She rounded her desk and hurrying into the entry.

Upstairs, Barnabas barked and clawed at Jason's bedroom door.

She heard it again, something outside the door. *Oh, God!* "Jason?"

"Mommy, Mommy." Jason knocked softly.

"Oh, God!" Carolyn lifted down the heavy bar, set it aside, and Jason rushed in.

"Hurry, Mommy." Jason slammed the door and helped lift the heavy bar into its stone cradles.

"What is it, honey?"

"It's another one. It's . . ."

"What do you mean, another one?"

"It has all four legs."

DRIVING HIS TRUCK BACK down River Road, Gilpin said, "Stupid committee." Ralston had been right. Gilpin could have stayed home. He could have told Whatling to make the deposit. "Nah." Calling them a bunch of crooks made the trip worthwhile.

Gilpin cranked up the volume, listening to the Grateful Dead sing *Truckin'* on CD, smiling at himself, proud to be a Gilpin, smarter than all those do-good hicks. He'd put one over for sure. Six weeks earlier, anticipating his need to put up another calf, he'd purchased a bull calf down in Bridgeport, an open range mix. He got it cheap. Nason had taken it in late October and the committee had just paid him for an Angus. "The morons." Good thing Nason hadn't been at the meeting.

Whatever happened to the open range calf was anybody's guess. John Crow and Willis Donner had probably eaten it already. Gilpin depressed the cigarette lighter and reached into his shirt pocket for a fat joint.

He'd harvested his crop back in late September and had taken all but five pounds down to his brother in Berkeley. His mountain grown buds had become a local favorite in the bay area, and why not? Pot was a crop he knew how to grow.

The lighter popped out and he pressed the glowing tip to the end of his hand rolled cigarette. He returned the lighter and sucked pungent smoke deep into his lungs. When the inevitable cough hit the back of his throat, he pinched his nose and pursed his lips, forcing the potent smoke into his sinuses and ear canals.

"Whoa." His vision whirled in a momentary stupor. He let off the gas until the dizziness passed and his vision cleared.

This straight stretch on River Road made a perfect black ribbon against the moonlit snow, piled high on both sides. A fuzzy, bluish glow rounded the curve down at the far end of the straight stretch, near his turnoff. It sped toward him.

A halo of sparks from the oncoming vehicle's underbelly fanned out in all directions.

"Nason? Wow." Gilpin took another toke.

Nason's tire chains caused a yellow halo of sparks against pavement. His snow-covered headlights created a bluish glow.

Space invaders crossed Gilpin's smoke inhibited brain. He laughed. "Shoot, Nason, the meeting wasn't that important." When they passed, a high-pitched hum of chains against pavement made Gilpin's teeth itch. He took another toke and looked in his mirror.

Yellow sparks and red taillights zoomed toward the village. The hum faded.

He slowed and turned onto the snow-covered gravel road leading to the bridge. He'd driven it a million times without chains. His truck nearly drove itself, following his own tracks from earlier. If the bridge looked too icy to drive across, he'd walk home and pick up his truck in the morning. He followed the wide curve in the road and rode slowly down the slight grade toward the bridge.

"What the . . ."

Something dark moved across the path of his headlights. Those stupid birds from up in Potter's meadow swarmed and fluttered over the near end of the bridge.

"What is that?"

Something big moved onto the bridge, something fast enough to dodge his headlights.

He accidentally dropped his joint between his legs and looked down to find it, frantically raking at the seat, not wanting to burn his tender nuggets. "Whew." He raked the smoldering joint to the floor and let it lay.

A huge swirl of those stupid birds blocked his headlights, more birds than he knew existed up there. They flapped and slammed into his windshield and attacked his side windows. "Ugh," he growled, trying to shout.

Past the birds, barely visible, something big and dark stood on the bridge, maybe a bear. It did not move, and the birds thinned. He saw it now. The eyes glowed bright red in his headlights.

Of the million thoughts and images flooding across his smoke clogged brain, one question stood out: Why hadn't he sold his worthless dump and moved down below, as had his brother.

He no longer cared about his daughter's free education, his meager herd of scrawny cattle, or his brainless wife. What did she know about good schools? *Stupid pothead.*

NASON FINALLY CAUGHT up with his breathing, feeling only slightly safer. Maybe he wouldn't break Embry's lame neck after all. Fool didn't even know how to put the truck into four-wheel drive, getting it stuck up there by the falls. At least he hadn't gotten stuck in the bog. That deep snowdrift had been bad enough.

Nason had reached his truck out of breath. All of his running, jumping, slipping, sliding, tumbling, and crashing into every tree and rock on his way down from the Perch, feeling that thing's claws at his back, being afraid even to look back, had exhausted him to his current, numb condition.

The snow had been so deep, where Embry had gotten stuck, that Nason needed to dig snow just to climb into the driver's side window.

Embry hadn't said a word, climbing over to the passenger side. Just as well he'd kept his mouth shut.

Look at him over there, having a conversation with himself, working it all out. *Fool.*

Nobody could work this out, including the vicar, including all the committees on this planet.

The buzz from the tire chains changed pitch, rounding the last curve on River Road, finally able to see the village. He let off the gas.

Christmas lights were up at Jacobsen's and over there at the Rock Church. Nice to see. Nason looked in the side mirror. Having slowed way down, the chains no longer sparked against the pavement. He knew he'd need new tires, probably new chains.

Embry said, "How can you expect me to turn this truck around? That ain't right."

"Why did you drive headfirst into that snowdrift, and then keep plowing? You mini-mind! You nearly got us both killed."

"It ain't right, you blaming me. That's all I'm saying. You said not to get into that bog and I didn't." Embry shifted in his seat and gazed out the window, talking low. "You see it up there by the falls?"

"Yeah, I saw it."

Embry turned to face Nason, tipping his head to one side, emphasizing his point. "He had all four legs."

"Yeah." Nason slowed, driving into the village.

Embry asked, "How can it grow another leg like that?"

"How should I know?" He pulled a U-turn and parked in front of the bank. "You saw what I took up there. It was a human hand." He slapped Embry's shoulder. "I need to get my mind off of that. I can't stop seeing that blood-soaked hand."

"See what I mean? That ain't right. None of it's right."

"Just shut up about it." Nason didn't want to tell Embry what it was when he got it up to the Perch, no longer human, alive and strong. He couldn't stop his brain from seeing it. If he even tried to explain it, Embry might pack up and leave. *They all might.*

Nason shut off his truck and both men got out. The high windows and full moon gave ample light to climb the steps and enter the front vestibule of the bank. "Don't mention that part. Don't say anything. Let me do all the talking."

"What part?"

"Just keep your trap shut." Nason pushed into the bank lobby.

Whatling, Ralston and Olen Jacobsen sat in their usual chairs. Their winter coats hung from the rack near the back door.

Nason and Embry took off and hung their coats with the others. Nason said, "Sorry we're late."

"That's okay." Whatling leaned back and laced his fingers behind his head, his official position. "We had a quorum and paid Gilpin, got him out of our hair."

Embry said, "Yeah, we passed him on our way in."

Nason glared at Embry but Embry wasn't looking. He needed to shut up.

Olen sat in front of Bell's desk, cleaning his fingernails with a pocket knife, like he wasn't interested in asking, "So, what kept you?"

Nason said, "We've got us a problem."

Embry coughed out a short, nervous laugh.

Don't get unwound. Everybody ignored Embry anyway.

Nason and Embry took their usual chairs under the windows and nodded their hellos.

Looking at his fingernails, blowing them off, Olen said, "Ja. We need to do something 'bout that Gilpin, by golly."

Embry laughed and shook his head. Everybody ignored him.

Nason said, "I'm not talking about Gilpin. I'm talking about the new Potter woman."

All but Embry leaned forward, totally interested.

Nason said, "She took the calf last night and put it into her barn."

"What?" Ralston jumped up and stepped closer to Nason.

"Yeah. It came down and tried to break into their house and their dog chewed off one of its front legs," He stopped. He hadn't intended to mention that. *I'm too tired for this.*

Whatling and Olen both stood. They joined Ralston, circling each other like vultures, all looking at Nason.

Feeling trapped, Nason stood and said, "She brought the leg to my office today. Me and Embry just got back from taking it up to the Perch. She owes me a new pair of tires and some snow chains."

Whatling wagged his fat head, obviously doubting that would happen. "How am I supposed to charge her for your tires? What happened?"

"I didn't have time to stop and take the chains off." *You idiot.* "Just take it out of her account." He leaned on Bell's desk and glared, making sure Whatling knew he meant it. "If she complains, tell her to come and talk to me about it."

Whatling looked down at his wife's desk, like he was reading a tally sheet. He finally sat and staired at his fat hands.

"What about my calf," asked Ralston, nearly standing on top of Nason's boots.

"We took it out of her barn on our way and left it in the upper meadow, like always." Nason pushed past Ralston and stood in the center of the room.

Whatling said, "So, what's the problem?" He folded his hands behind his neck and leaned back, officiating again.

"Didn't she come in to see you this afternoon?" Nason looked out the high windows at the full moon. A flock of birds circled in front of it. He shook off the strangeness and looked back at Whatling.

Whatling said, "Yes, she did. I gave her a copy of the trust deed. Don't worry, it'll hold up." He leaned his elbows on Bell's desk and shrugged, matter of fact.

"We've never had Potters standing outside this group," said Nason, pacing in front of Bell's desk. He'd thought about it all afternoon and they needed to understand. "If she gets a lawyer on this, there could be a lot of snooping around." The room grew still, everybody listening. "Kidro and Jethro knew the right politicians. They kept this business local."

"Someone's got to explain things," said Embry, standing and sauntering to the center of the room, as if he'd suddenly realized some profound truth, swaggering with confidence and self-induced brilliance.

Everybody waited.

"That's all." Embry jammed his hands into his pockets and looked out the high window at the moon, the birds. He whispered, "Would you look at those birds?"

Ignoring the birds, Ralston stepped in front of Embry and braced him with a stare. "Are you going to be the one to explain things?" Ralston chuckled and shook his head. "No, not you. Do you even know what brings that thing out?" He shook his head again and stared at poor Embry. "Well, do you?"

"The moon," said Embry, still gawking out the high window.

"Yeah?" Ralston glared angrily at Nason, frustrated with Embry. "Which month and in what year?" Ralston grabbed Embry's arm, making sure Embry understood the question. "That first night, years ago, when it attacked the Potter place, that was the first time in about six years, wasn't it?"

"Yeah." Nason stepped between Ralston and Embry, facing Ralston down. "A month later, it came out and took that first bull calf. So what?"

"It doesn't even do that every month." Ralston seemed frustrated, not angry.

"Let's all calm down," said Olen, trying to work through it. "Until Gilpin moved his calf that night, it hadn't come down for over a year." This old man knew more than he was saying, the look in his eye, the wry grin at Nason. He knew how to keep it to himself, too.

Ralston turned on Olen. "Is that what brought it down? How did it know the calf was gone? I mean, what brings it down?"

Nason chipped away at his still budding theory. "Kidro was talking about opening one of the mines." That got their attention.

"Okay," said Olen, putting up his hands, motioning the others to listen, taking a moment to collect his thoughts. "I'm going to say what we all know, deep down. This thing was put here by God or the devil, who knows, maybe some ancient Indian ghost put here to protect this place." He waited for a comment from somebody else that never came. They were all letting it sink in.

"We all got pretty good life here. Nobody ever gets sick. Nobody ever has a sick steer. Bea's chickens always lay good eggs and plenty of 'em. We never saw a dentist in our life."

"Okay, Olen." Whatling seemed open-minded for once. "So, what brings it out now?"

Olen had no answer.

Nason said, "We've got some new people in the valley. Who knows?" He looked questioningly at Olen, hoping for support. Nothing there, and Nason was suddenly very tired, with no food or rest in two long days.

"Ja, by golly." Olen grinned at Nason, sensing an opening to close their meeting and go home. "It's gonna be okay. I know it. I think these new Potters gonna be okay, by golly."

"Olen . . ." said Ralston, shrill with frustration. He had not been satisfied. "That night when it killed Kidro's wife and oldest boy, they'd cut off its paw with an axe and nailed it to a tree. Whatever happened to that paw?" He lowered his voice and stepped close to Olen. "Did you forget how it came back for Gus?" Ralston stepped back and dropped his head, sorry he'd said that. He watched the toe of his left boot sweep the floor.

Olen's voice shook. "How can I forget that awful night?"

Yeah. Nason flashed on images of Kidro, that rolled rug brought in by Carolyn Potter, and that bloody human hand.

A strange noise snapped him back. "Quiet," he whispered through a constricted throat. He looked out the high windows facing River Road, where swirling birds nearly blocked out the moon.

"What is it now," asked Whatling, tired of it all.

"Shush!" Nason held up his hand for silence, moving closer to the windows to listen. "There." A clicking noise from outside entered the bank.

Embry said, "Wind?"

Nason said, "No." The trees outside stood still, not a breath of wind.

The room hushed around him and everybody inched toward the high windows, all looking up. They all heard it, something walking on the pavement in front of the bank.

Whatling crept to the wall and turned off the overhead lights.

The others stood still, too frightened to move.

Nason wanted to look but his legs refused to move. He held his breath.

Ralston climbed onto a chair and stretched up to look.

"Son-of-a . . ." Ralston gripped the window ledge and climbed onto the arms of the chair, standing higher, able to see better. He whispered, "What is that?"

Olen and Embry climbed onto the two remaining chairs near the windows.

Nason and Whatling quietly moved chairs under the windows and joined them.

The creature passed under the bank windows, walking sideways on all fours like a large primate. Meadowlarks swirled around it, charging at the high windows and back, not hitting them.

"I don't know," whispered Whatling, no longer the officious banker. "Maybe it's a sasquatch or something. Look at those birds. Dear God, look at the size of it."

Ralston said, "I thought you said the dog chewed off its leg."

Nason said softly, "I told you, I took it up to the Perch."

Louder than he should, Embry said, "Maybe there's more than one."

It rounded the corner of the bank, not looking at them. The birds followed.

Embry said, "That's a sasquatch, sure enough."

Nason said, "Embry, how would you know a sasquatch from your old woman?"

"Bite my jumbo, Nason. That's a sasquatch."

"It walks like a baboon," said Whatling.

Nason whispered, "Will you shut up." He wanted to hear the thing walking along the sidewalk.

"No." Olen flew off of his chair and lunged toward the back door. He'd just realized where it was going.

Nason jumped down and grabbed him around the waist, pulling him back. He turned Olen and pushed him against the wall, pressing his hand tight to Olen's mouth.

Ralston quietly turned the wheel that secured the back door with the bank's four-bolt security lock.

Whatling quietly secured the front door and all five men stood in the dark, listening.

The creature clawed and raked the concrete steps at the side of the building. It wanted them to hear. It knew where they were.

HELFRED PULLED ANOTHER tray of butter cookies from the oven, slightly browned on top. *Gus's favorite.* He'd always said he could eat them for lunch and dinner. She set them on the counter, closed and turned off the oven, picked up an already cooled tray, and raked cookies into the big cookie jar for the store.

That time Gus had been invited to stay the knight with J. J.'s brother, he'd asked, could he take some butter cookies.

"Sure," she said out-loud, remembering. *Let me put some in a bag.*

The precious image, seeing him in her mind, brought tears to her eyes. She quickly swept them away. Under her breath, she said, "Getting close to Christmas." *Gus always ate too much at Christmas.* She raked the last tray of cookies into the jar and put the cookie sheets into the dishwasher.

She looked out the window at moonlit snow, the ice cycles hanging from her roof and nearby trees, the small, ice-covered stream that tumbled from the rocks behind their house, *so lovely.*

Curious. Birds swarmed through the trees, breaking off ice cycles, the ice cycles stabbing into crusting snow.

Her heart ached, her mind falling into a deep and dark memory. "What a terrible night that was."

She blocked those images for the thousandth time. She wanted to remember the good times, especially so close to Christmas, but her heart ached with the loss of her son. It seemed so recent.

The night he'd been born was a good night, *by golly.* The store and loft apartment had just been completed by Olen and Willis. She had loved the loft then. After the loss of Gustov, she could no longer climb the stairs.

She'd try to hold that good memory. She crossed her arms, holding her baby boy.

Those birds outside startled her, suddenly rushing at her kitchen window, flapping their wings into it, thumping into the glass with their yellow breasts, pecking and clawing like they were trying to get at her.

She backed away and a dark mood enveloped her, thinking of Willis, thinking of that wonderful day, of that awful night.

She turned toward the front of the house and looked down the hallway toward the front door. Someone was there. "Olen?" She walked halfway down the hall and stopped to listen.

She backed away from the sound of breaking glass, the sound when it fell onto the tile floor in the entry vestibule. Maybe a snow-heavy tree had fallen onto the house.

"What?" Something outside growled.

She gripped her breast against the pain of fear.

Out in the vestibule, glass crunched against tile. Something heavy had stepped inside.

Helfred's heart thumped loudly against her inner ear.

Stillness pressed upon her as their entry door silently splintered inward. No sound, but for the beating of her heart. Pieces of shattered wood slowly floated toward her, and there it stood.

Something big and dark filled their entry, standing on four legs. It slowly stood to full height on hind legs and looked down at her.

Those eyes. I know. . . "Gustov, is that you?" She smiled and extended both arms toward him.

Chapter Fifteen

What a mess. At 9:37 the following morning, Sheriff Phil Nason drove down River Road toward the Potter Ranch thinking about what to say, how to enlighten this new matriarch of their secluded community, and how to help her adjust.

He'd been two nights without sleep and his brain had bogged down like wet sand. Uncontrollable, aimless thoughts bumped into each other. His planning processes had flown out of focus. She needed to understand, and Phil had assumed the task.

The night before, they'd all remained in the bank until just before dawn. After that shrill, hyena sounding laugh, nobody dared make a sound, not even Olen. They all knew what it meant, that Helfred Jacobsen had been taken. They'd all been frozen in their collective fear. Even Nason.

At first light, moving in dazed semi-consciousness, Olen had walked across River Road to open his store.

Nason and Embry had agreed to clean things up. Olen didn't need to see what had happened to his wife. Big green flies had turned the scene into a surreal nightmare. *Very strange.* Flies were never around during the winter months.

Dr. Nancy accepted their stories about a rogue grizzly, *thank God*. That hadn't been difficult, with her being from down below. Nason had planted that seed when she'd first moved into the valley. Her coroner's report would reflect a rare, natural occurrence. That should satisfy the county medical examiner down in Sonora. They wouldn't ask any questions. Grizzlies were on the endangered species list.

Nason knew better, of course. What they'd all seen was no bear. Maybe it was the fabled Sasquatch. It had definitely looked like a primate, not a legendary werewolf.

He hadn't even found time to check into his office for messages. There were no unsightly cell towers in Potter Valley, so nobody owned a cellphone. They were a distinctly separate culture.

He turned onto Potter's cleared cobblestone driveway and drove over the crest, following the cleared path down to the barn, where the door stood partly open. He turned back up toward the house and their dog dashed down the driveway, bounding up and down at the side of his truck, looking at him through the window.

He parked in front of the entry steps, left the engine running, and climbed out.

The dog jumped up to greet him, cuffing his big front paws into Nason's chest, saying hello.

"Hello, Barnabas." Nason scrubbed the dog's muscular shoulders, surprised he'd remembered the dog's name. He put on his official hat and climbed the front steps, with the dog sniffing his boots, probably smelling Herlfred Jacobsen's blood. No matter how well he'd cleaned his boots, dogs would still smell the blood. He knocked on the door and it moved.

Yeah, that thing had tried to break in. It must have broken the lockset.

A chill crossed his shoulders, remembering the mess with Kidro, then earlier that morning with Helfred, hoping not to see that inside the Potter house. He knocked again, took off his hat, and waited.

The door swung open and Carolyn Potter's smile dropped to a thin, angry frown. "What do you want?" Her beautiful blue peepers pierced him to the heart; sure, secure, and angry.

Nason said, "We need to take a little ride into the village."

"What for?" She couldn't care less. She seemed finished with this whole community.

Nason's patience had been lost in three sleepless days. "There's something I need to show you. It won't take long."

"I'm working on an article for the magazine right now." She started to close the door.

Nason blocked it with his foot.

She yanked the door wide open and Nason braced for a slap in the face. It didn't come. He backed away and studied the inside of his official hat, using it as a cover for thoughts that didn't come; so tired. He put his hat on and looked back into her rage. "That'll have to wait. Sorry."

"How dare you tell me what to do?" She opened the door wide, ready to slam it into his boot.

He shifted and leaned into the door. "Please, don't force me to place you under arrest. Neither of us would like that."

Her rage turned to shock. "Arrest me? For what?"

He looked at her squarely, too tired to do anything else. "Ralston's calf is back inside your barn, isn't it?" Why hadn't he stopped to check?

She blinked and stepped back. "Why? Is that what this is about? Jason did that. I didn't even know until after . . ." She blinked twice and dropped her grip on the door.

He backed away and she stepped into the middle of the doorway, collecting her thoughts. "It didn't try to get in last night. It went away."

"Yes, I know. Come on, let's take a ride."

"Let me get my coat." When she turned inside, Nason looked for the dog. He'd evidently gone back to the barn. She returned with her coat, put it on, and followed Nason down the front steps. She said, "Jason's in the barn with John Crow."

"This won't take long. We'll be right back." He opened the passenger door and she climbed in.

Nason closed the door, walked around the truck, climbed in, tossed his official hat into the back seat, and drove toward the village. After riding most of the way in silence, nearing the village, she said, "Am I in some kind of trouble?"

"I don't know yet. I'm too tired to think clearly. I haven't slept in three days." He took the turn behind the emporium and parked in front of the clinic. He left his hat in the truck and led her up the steps into the front office. He didn't see his lady. "Nancy?"

"In here." She sat at her desk, her office door stood open, and Nason led Carolyn in.

Nancy worked at her computer. "Give me just a minute." She pecked at her desktop keyboard. After about a minute, she shut off the screen, stood, walked around her desk, and extended both hands to Carolyn. "Hello, Carolyn." She smiled that friendly-lady smile then cast a hard look at Nason. "I don't know why Phil insisted on bringing you in here." Her caustic tone sliced his soggy brain. "But, he's the sheriff." She pulled Carolyn into the small ward. Nason followed.

The small ward held two beds and a small lamp table between. Clean sheets had been spread over both beds, covering Helfred's separated remains.

Carolyn backed against the wall and planted her feet, obviously sensing something bad.

Nancy thrust both hands into the pockets of her white smock and positioned herself near the head of the first bed. "I've been here nearly five years and this is only the second time we've had an incident like this. The other was Kidro, your father-in-law."

She took one hand out of her pocket, grabbed the corner of a sheet, and walked down the length of the bed, exposing the headless shoulders and splintered sternum of Helfred Jacobsen. The body had been cleaned of blood. Her heart had been taken. Severed veins dangled over flattened lungs, with big maggots slithering around inside the chest cavity.

Nancy said, "I sprayed insecticide to kill the flies but maggots don't seem to be bothered. Sorry."

Carolyn gawked at the mangled corpse. She did not blink.

Nason gave Nancy the nod.

Nancy covered the body. "Bears are dangerous, as I'm sure you are aware. According to Phil and the others, this is a rogue grizzly, an extremely dangerous predator. Once they've tasted human flesh, they prefer it, so I've been told." Her angry eyes climbed all over Nason. Maybe her acceptance of a grizzly was fading.

Carolyn shook, her eyes rolled back, and her knees started to buckle.

Nancy reached through Carolyn's underarms and pressed her hands against the wall, keeping Carolyn from falling. "Are you alright?"

Carolyn looked at Nancy, took a deep breath, and nodded.

Nancy glared at Nason. "Was this really necessary?"

"Yes." Nason motioned toward the second bed.

Nancy reluctantly dragged the sheet off of Helfred's severed head. Helfred's half closed, glassy eyes stared at Nason. Two big, green flies crawled out of Helfred's half open mouth, another out of her nose.

Carolyn's legs buckled and down she went.

EARLIER THAT SAME MORNING, Willis Donner had awakened with his left hand restored. He knew not how. He had writhed in pain the whole previous day, not knowing how his left hand had been taken. He never knew what happened during those nights of the moon, always dealing with each day as it came. What else could he do?

His arm hurt and the bright red scar looked like his flesh had been torn, but his hand somehow worked. The hand had worked ten years earlier, but the red scar had indicated a clean cut above the wrist.

Who knows? Maybe, on the night before, he'd tangled with wolves or with a bear.

With the passage of time, the old scar had completely disappeared. This new scar might take longer.

What had that thing done over the last two nights?

God, don't let it be like ten years ago, when too many lives had ended. Mary Lou had died after that night, and J. J. had left the valley for good.

Willis knew that J. J. was dead. He didn't know how he knew, but he'd known for some time, possibly from the moment of J.J.'s death.

He subconsciously rubbed at his left arm where the bloody, chewed stump had been the day before. He could live with the pain, for however long it took. Not knowing what that thing had done was the worst of it. That, and not being able to do anything to stop it.

Still naked from the night before, he walked out the top opening of the Perch into bright sunlight and cold air. He took his usual bath in the hot spring and crossed solid rock to the slow-moving stream, where it left the pond before tumbling over the falls. He jumped into icy water and brusquely scrubbed his flesh, closing his pours. He climbed out, went inside, dried, and dressed. He didn't feel hungry.

He didn't want to go down that day, but the cattle needed feeding. He had responsibilities again, a real job like before Kidro, and he hoped to find a dead calf.

All Willis found in the upper meadow were meadowlarks nesting around the warmth of their rock, chirping their songs to Willis, the prettiest sound in nature. His heart sank at seeing the trail left by the boy, his dog, and the calf, leading through deep snow toward their house. He didn't want to go down there.

He cut across the tree lined ridge and followed the stream down to Kidro's feed barn. He loaded feed corn onto the truck and plowed the truck through snow. He filled feed bins along the stream and returned the truck to the feed barn.

Get it done. He looked uphill at the Potter house and started walking.

The front door to the house was closed and the barn door was open. John Crow was probably in there, a good sign. Willis knocked on the front door and waited. No response. He knocked louder and the door swung inward.

"Dear God." The latch had been broken. "Hello the house." He stepped inside, looked into her office, and looked up toward the second floor. "Anybody home?" Everything looked okay. He looked at the broken latch, mentally listing what parts and tools he needed to fix it. He stepped out and started back down the front steps.

The dog ran up the driveway and jumped into him, gnawing softly at his outstretched hand, happy to see him.

"Thank you, God."

The dog followed Willis down the driveway and into the barn, where both horses and the bull calf stood in stalls.

The boy and Crow were out in the corral, standing in knee deep snow. Crow twirled a lariat and tossed the lasso over a fence post, teaching the boy a time-consuming lesson.

Willis turned into the tack room and grabbed the double-edged axe. He ran his thumb across both blades. Both were sharp, the way he kept them. He grabbed a small box of Baldwin parts, a screwdriver, and a set of Allen wrenches. He set the axe over his shoulder and returned outside.

EXHAUSTED AND WEARY, Nason felt cramped in the small clinic with these two women. Nothing was so tiring as two women feeling sorry for themselves over events beyond their control, beyond even their reckoning. He didn't know if Carolyn Potter's pouting and moaning was seeking sympathy or if it was genuine remorse.

Either way, Nancy oozed sympathy all over her. Her condescending sneers in his direction finally did the trick.

Who needs this?

Neither of these women yet realized the benefits of living in this valley. Neither knew of this thing's indestructibility. Keeping them in the dark for as long as possible increased the probability that, in time, they would grow to understand what the rest of the people here already knew; that their lives were made richer by the shared experience of living in this special place, a place where they felt the presence of God, their shared Shangri La. As for the rest, who could explain that thing they had seen the previous night, that thing that had walked boldly up River Road and had taken Helfred Jacobsen.

It didn't matter whether these ladies understood. The Potter estate was passed down through male heirs. It was the beneficence of this young boy that was needed to keep this community whole. Nason hoped the boy wouldn't be as distant as his mother sometimes seemed to be. Her brain seemed to block out events that needed to be dealt with. She was lucky to be one of those women who could switch off.

He sometimes wished he could do that.

Enough. Nason's mind had been wandering, again. He needed to take this woman home and get some sleep.

He looked at Carolyn Potter's back, her head bent down, huddling with Nancy in her office, both of them shutting Nason out. They'd be there for a while.

He stood and said, "I'll be right back."

That seemed to please Nancy.

He left the clinic, crossed the street, and ducked into the sanctuary of his office. He'd grab some winks and let them walk across the street to get him.

The flashing light on his answering machine stopped him from sinking into the comfort of his chair. There were two messages. He pressed the button. The machine beeped, then, "Sheriff Nason? This is Sally Gilpin. Bruce never came home last night and we're worried. Did something happen? Can you call me?" The machine clicked and beeped. The electronic voice announced, "End of final message." Whoever had called the second time had not left a message.

Nason picked up the phone and dialed her number. The phone rang twice. "Hello?"

"Hi, Sally. This is Phil. Did Bruce get home yet?"

"No." She sounded worried and afraid. "What happened last night? He said he was just going to the committee meeting."

"We got there late. He was already gone. I'll check the road out to your place. Maybe he got stuck in the snow." *Stupid*. That was probably the source of her fear, that Bruce could have been stranded and had been frozen to death. Her long silence confirmed it.

"Sally?"

"Thank you, Phil." Her whining tone sounded like she was crying.

"I'm on my way." Nason hung up and cleared his answering machine.

By the time he crossed the road and re-entered the clinic, Carolyn and Nancy were standing, saying their goodbyes.

The Potter woman's bloodshot eyes reached inside him, asking could she please go home. She said, "What about Jason? Is he in some kind of trouble?" She stepped closer, slumping from fatigue. "Because, if he is, I'll swear it was me."

Nason cuffed the cobwebs in his brain, trying to grasp her meaning. "You?"

"I brought that calf into our barn. I'll swear to it on a stack of Bibles."

"Oh, so it was your son who took the calf?"

"No!" She stuck her chin out, daring him to take a poke. "I just told you."

"Don't worry." He suppressed a grin, wanting to laugh with relief. "We're not pressing charges." He wouldn't know how to proceed with any of that. "I needed for you to understand what can happen. We have a system up here that works. It's best if you stand back and let it be." He opened the door. "Come on, I'll take you home."

She offered a slight smile and he followed her out.

He drove the length of River Road in silence. They were both tired. When he turned up her driveway, she said, "Can I make you some coffee?" He took the loop by her barn, thinking how nice that would be. He stopped at the bottom of her front steps and she said, "You look tired. Coffee?"

"Thanks, but I'd better not. I have another call to make."

"Olen?"

"No." He left it there, not wanting her to worry about Gilpin.

She climbed out and he noticed a freshly cut silver spruce leaning against the entry door, probably cut by Willis.

How Ironic.

She stuck her head back into the truck and said, "If there's anything I can do . . ." She was asking about Olen.

"We'll let you know." Nason inched his truck forward and she closed the door. He drove back across the crest, down the curved driveway, and back onto River Road. He stopped in front of Gilpin's gravel road and shifted into four-wheel drive, no need for chains. Gilpin's tire tracks had already turned to slush.

He drove slowly toward the suspension bridge and scanned both sides of the road, looking for tire tracks. He rounded the last curve and drove down the grade toward the bridge.

"Oh, no."

The safety cable on the down river side of the bridge had been broken. He stopped a few feet from the bridge, set the brake, and placed his truck in neutral.

Under the trees near the river, the snow was deep in shady spots. The rest had turned to slush. He stepped out, closed the door, and walked onto the bridge. He grabbed the broken cable and leaned out to look below.

"No. Not again."

Thirty feet straight down, Gilpin's truck sat in four-foot-deep, fast-moving water. The top had been nearly torn off, maybe from the heavy, bridge-suspension cable. A large boulder kept the truck from moving downstream toward the steep waterfall, about a mile downriver, where the river cascaded down to Pickle Meadow.

Numb with exhaustion, he returned to his truck, took off his boots, and pulled on his hip waders. Tiny spots swirled in his eyes, from all the bright, white snow. His eyelids felt like they were lifting weights.

He took off his coat and pulled a sweatshirt from behind his backseat. He pulled on the sweatshirt and crossed the wader suspenders over his head, pulling the waders higher and making them more secure. He dug into his toolbox, found his repelling harness, and buckled it on. He grabbed his cotton rope and closed both doors. He left the engine running. The warmth from the heater might be needed later.

He returned to the broken rail, tied one end of the rope to a steel brace, and tossed the rest of the rope toward the far side of the boulder that held the truck in place. The rope played out downstream, way past Gilpin's half sunken truck.

Gilpin might have lost control and still be alive. He knew he should go for help, with Embry just across the road, but every second might make the difference between life and death. Hyperthermia was funny that way. Who it killed and who lived couldn't be predicted.

He stepped back and looped rope into his d-ring, two loops. No need to take chances.

"Lord." This operation was chancy.

He leaned backward over water, holding tight to the rope at his hip with his right hand. He held the rope high with his left hand to keep his upper body from flipping down, and released rope with his right hand.

Rope slid through the d-ring until he passed horizontal, and he pushed away from the bridge with both feet. His body swung in, his head neared the under structure of the bridge, and he released more rope. He tightened his grip, stopped sliding, and swung in the open space under the bridge. After three more drops, his feet reached the fast-moving water and turned his body, facing him downstream.

"Come on!" His shout echoed above the roar of rushing water, bouncing off the stone walls of the canyon. In his exhausted state, he hadn't planned well.

Gilpin's truck lay several feet to his left and he didn't have the strength to climb back up and reset the rope. He'd have to work his way through the current. He let out a little more rope and his feet found rocks in knee deep water. "Good enough." He eased out a little more rope, still on solid footing, and inched his way over slick rocks, keeping his grip on the rope with his right hand, struggling in the swift current, his left hand searched for something to grab. He reached the back of Gilpin's truck and grabbed the bed rail with both hands, working his way toward the cab.

The roof stuck straight up in the sky, ripped open from above the windshield. The passenger-door window was still above water. He grabbed the doorhandle and looked inside.

"Sweet Mary." Gilpin's decapitated body sat behind the steering wheel with his torso split open, just like all the others. Minnows swam in the still water of his chest cavity. His severed head floated in the space under the dash. His iced over eyes stared at Nason.

Nason shuddered, stepped back, and slipped. His legs churned, blindly searching for a foothold, and his waders filled with freezing water. The cold shock stopped his breathing and rope slid through the d-ring. He gritted his teeth against the cold and struggled against the current, desperately trying to grab rope. His full waders dragged like a parachute in high wind, pulling him downstream like a heavy anchor.

"A curse on all Gilpins, forever!"

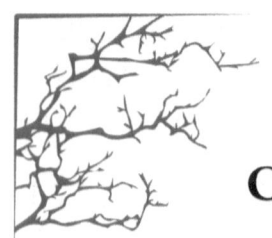

Chapter Sixteen

Memorial services were held at the Rock Church at 11:00 a.m., Tuesday. The school was closed that day and everyone in the valley came to show their respects, everyone except Willis Donner.

For the first time in his long relationship with Willis, Olen Jacobsen felt a black mass forming around his heart. On that Tuesday, Olen felt relief that Willis Donner had never attended church. After his son, Gustov, had been taken, Olen had not yet made the connection. He'd always thought it odd before, that this man would never enter into a building he'd built with his own two hands.

None of that mattered anymore. He never wanted to see Willis again. Seeing that thing on River Road and listening to Sheriff Nason talk about the Perch had dissolved the mystery of this valley.

Sheriff Nason attended the services wearing a red nose and watery eyes, sporting a nasty cold, a very rare thing in this valley. He'd nearly drowned in the river on Saturday morning. He'd climbed out of the river in the forest near the falls, far below Gilpin's bridge. He'd then walked all the way back to the Potter house through deep, ice crusted snow, and begged a ride to his truck from Carolyn. He'd lost his waders and sprained his back pretty bad, still bent sideways when he walked. Phil was a good neighbor to attend in such a condition.

John Crow stood in his usual place against the back wall, his slender frame much taller than the rest, showing his respect, maybe not for Helfred or Gilpin, but for Olen. Olen liked him for that.

Everybody came dressed in their traditional black, their Moon Sunday attire. A fitting thing to do. They'd often said that these costumes were to show their submission before God, but Olen thought it might be something else, maybe a fearful tribute to that thing. Whatever their reasons might have been before, these costumes were appropriate on that Tuesday morning.

Strange, how those meadowlarks only came to church on Moon Sunday's, all lined up along the roof ridge, with everybody inside dressed in black. He wondered if they were up there for this funeral. He'd take a look when they went outside, get his eyes up off the ground.

Vicar Twilby's words hummed in the background, mingling with Olen's memories of Helfred, all those happy moments before Gustov got taken. He could actually hear her contagious laugh, playing with Gus in his young boyhood.

Their first winter in this valley, they'd all watched Willis sketch out his early planning for the store. Was Willis who suggested naming it Jacobsen's Emporium.

Willis. The black mass around Olen's heart pushed Willis out, no stopping it.

Helfred's smile came into focus, remembering their early optimism, their passionate love for each other, their passionate love for this place. The rush of strong emotions sat him down, while everybody else remained standing.

For whatever reason, Carolyn Potter had insisted on paying for everything, the plot here in the church graveyard, the coffin, and such. Olen was grateful for that. Taking that burden off of him relieved his stress. He didn't need Potter's financial help, but the business of it would have been difficult to deal with. He and Helfred had been richly blessed. They'd built a solid financial base.

He felt grateful for these new Potters. He'd never liked Kidro.

Unlike Helfred, Olen had blamed Kidro for what had happened ten years earlier. J. J. had blamed him too, for the two of them being gone down to Reno that night, for Kidro's visit to the Mustang

Ranch, a whorehouse just south of Reno. He'd learned later that J. J. had remained in Kidro's truck, while Kidro went in to visit with the ladies. It was Kidro's fault for not being there to protect his wife and his older son, Ethan. If not for his going to Reno, Gustov might still be alive.

Now, after all these years, two more coffins rested up there on the altar, Helfred and Gilpin. This taking had not been Kidro's fault.

Willis.

The Gilpins had very little to start with. He hoped Sally and her daughter would stay. Maybe these new Potters could convince her. Maybe she'd be grateful. Her husband, Bruce, had never been grateful to anybody. He'd always been churlish, as had his father before him, as bad as Kidro.

Kidro had plenty and to spare, but he'd been just as boorish and niggardly as any Gilpin had ever been. He wouldn't have paid out one penny for any of this, not like these new Potters. They were more like Mary Lou. She could never give enough. This new Potter woman even offered two plots in their family cemetery. Olen and Sally Gilpin both felt better using the church cemetery. For Olen, it would be easier to visit Helfred, buried next to Gustov. Here, he could look out at them from their loft above the store.

Our loft. If only Helfred could have lived there after Gus got taken. She'd have been locked in there last Friday night. That thing could never have reached her. She was plenty strong enough to put up that oak bar and lift it back down by herself.

She'd still be alive, protected by what Willis had built.

"Amen", said the entire congregation, and Olen snapped back.

The poll bearers lined up around Bruce Gilpin's coffin first.

Jim Embry, skinny as can be, shoved Nason aside and took his place, referring to Nason's sprained back with a downward glance.

Together, he, Stan and Danny Ralston, Bill Whatling, John Crow, and Jake Pendleton lifted the heavy coffin, turned toward the front doors of the small church, and slowly marched out.

After they passed, Olen shuffled to the altar and ran his hand over the smooth, stainless-steel coffin of his wife. A hollowness in his chest forced him to lean on her with both hands, barely able to remain on his feet. He breathed deeply, blinked away tears, and studied the carved, polished brass corners and handles. Carolyn Potter had picked a beautiful and regal coffin. Helfred would have liked it.

"I'm sorry, Mr. Jacobsen." Young Jason Potter stood near the altar, looking up at Olen with true sadness behind his bright eyes, just like his poppa, *by golly*.

Standing next to him, his mother wiped tears from her eyes with a white handkerchief and tried to smile.

Unable to find words, not understanding why she and the boy had so connected with his loss, Olen simply nodded.

"I'll never do it again," said the boy.

Why you say that?

The precession of pallbearers returned from outside without John Crow.

Helfred had never liked John and had always made sure that everybody knew it. Olen had always liked John Crow, even then showing his respect.

The bearers surrounded the coffin, Olen took a grip, and they lifter her together. The walk out to the cemetery seemed too short. They set her on canvas straps above that deep hole in the ground, and they all stepped back.

The State of California required a waterproof vault covering the inside of the hole to protect the departed. Olen hated that. To Olen and his ways, ashes to ashes and dust to dust meant what it said. Here, in this modern world where the state could intrude anywhere and everywhere, the old way had been deemed unfit. Her bones might never find the natural dust of God's good earth.

Gustov's wooden coffin touched the earth around him. The earth could consume him and turn him back to dust. She'd be forever apart from that, apart from her Gustov forever, apart from Olen, when his time came.

Vicar Twilby tossed ashes onto both graves and looked at Olen. "At times like this, we must surely remind ourselves that God created the heavens and the earth; that He created all things that walk and crawl upon the earth, all things that fly, and everything that swims in the seas and waters. He created angels, and He created demons. Yes, that He even created Lucifer himself. We must ever remind ourselves, that all things serve God's purpose. Though we may not now understand why, our Lord and Savior promised us this understanding in the fullness of time."

The vicar reached out and took Olen's hand, Jason Potter took Olen's other hand, and the entire congregation joined hands to form a tight circle around the graves. Vicar said, "Lord, receive these two precious, beloved saints and keep them forever safe from any pain or harm. Bound together as we are, we deliver them forever into Thy loving embrace."

Everybody said, "Amen," and their hands separated.

Olen looked to the sky. She appeared up in those white clouds. He followed her stare down to the roof of the church, where meadowlarks had lined up on the ridge.

Maybe these birds came here for Willis, here to show his respect. *What a thought. How . . .* He closed his eyes and shook his head.

THE SERVICE AT THE small cemetery concluded and the villagers took turns consoling Olen before moving off in different directions. They all ignored the Gilpins and Carolyn's heart went out to them. They stood close to Sheriff Phil Nason and Dr. Nancy LaRosa, forlorn and alone. Even the sheriff ignored them, which was understandable in his condition. He probably wanted nothing more than for Nancy LaRosa to feed him some hot chicken soup and tuck him into bed.

Carolyn approached Sally. "Please, let us take you home."

The sheriff smiled and said, "Could you?"

Jason waited at their Rover with John Crow. John opened the back door and Jason helped little Sissy climb in. He positioned her in the middle, buckled her seatbelt, and stood aside for Sally to climb in.

John got into the back from the other side, Jason sat in front, and Carolyn started the Rover.

On their way down River Road, Carolyn said, "Sally, what are your plans?"

"I don't know. We wanted to go down and visit my parents in Oakland over Christmas, but now I don't even know how we can do that."

"What about insurance?" Carolyn turned off of River Road and drove down the grade toward the river.

"Bruce took care of all of that stuff. I think it's in a safety deposit box at your bank, but I don't know where the key is."

"I'll go in and speak with Mr. Whatling about it." Carolyn glanced in the rear-view mirror at the top of Sally Gilpin's head. "Would that be okay?"

Sally looked up. "Yes, ma'am. Thank you."

"I'll go in and see him tomorrow." They drove across the bridge and Carolyn saw the broken cable. It looked like it must be a pedestrian safety cable. The road up the other side of the river had deep ruts and exposed rocks, very slow going. When they rounded the curve and she saw the way the Gilpins lived, she placed a hand on Jason's arm, letting him know not to say anything. Whatever else happened at the bank tomorrow, she needed to find a way to help these people, maybe some kind of insurance trust or something. Gilpin's widow and daughter needed a decent home and a decent road to get there. They also needed transportation.

Carolyn stopped in front of their trailer and Jason jumped out to open the back door. Sally unbuckled Sissy and they both got out. Jason closed the back door and climbed back into the front, looking at Carolyn like he wanted to say something. She shook her head, rolled down her window, and said, "Sally?"

Sally stopped halfway up their broken-down steps and looked back.

"I'll call you tomorrow, after I visit the bank."

Sally smiled and nodded. "Thank you." She turned, led her daughter up the steps, and they went inside.

Crossing back over the bridge, Jason rolled his window down and leaned way out, probably trying to find Gilpin's truck.

Sitting in back, John said, "After the snow melts, his truck will be carried downriver and over the falls. They'll pull it out from Pickle Meadow."

Carolyn looked in the rearview mirror. "John, who can we call about repairing the bridge?"

"They used an engineer from down in Sonora. Your banker should know how to get him up here."

"Good. I'll see him tomorrow about that too." The gravel road from the bridge to River Road seemed well maintained, not like the Gilpin side of the river. "You think they can put some gravel down on the other side? Would that work?"

"You shouldn't just give stuff away, Mrs. Potter. In the end, people will hate you for it."

She knew he was right, but she still felt a need to help. Jason had interfered with the ritual. "How much would it take for you to work her place, you know, take care of her cattle and horses?"

John said, "I'll go over and take a look around tomorrow."

She turned onto River Road and drove toward home.

John said, "They got an extra horse over there. I might work the place awhile to pay for that."

Carolyn rounded the last curve, nearing the road to their upper meadow.

John said, "Right here's good."

She stopped in the middle of the road and John climbed out.

Jason leaned out his open window and said, "See you tomorrow after school?"

John nodded and smiled, put on his hat, and started up the snow-covered, gravel road toward the upper meadow, toward his home.

Carolyn drove up her driveway and over the rise. "Home. Dear Lord."

Jason smiled. "Huh."

The beauty of this place almost always took her breath away. She pressed the button on the garage door remote and drove slowly down the driveway, waited for the door to open all the way, and parked in the garage. Knowing this inside door to the house to be barred, she left the garage door open and they both walked toward the front steps. "Come on, let's go decorate the tree."

NOT KNOWING WHAT ELSE to do, following Helfred's burial, Olen opened his store.

Bell Whatling, Bea Ralston, and Maggie Pendleton had appointed themselves to keep him company. That bunch of clucking hens should just stay home and attend to their own.

They huddled near the cookie jar, sipping coffee and whispering their gossip. He needed to get busy but he couldn't tear his eyes away from their bobbing black bonnets. He wanted to shout for them to get out, wanted to hate them for being there, but he couldn't. They intended only good.

He dug under the counter and located Helfred's inventory book. He opened it on top of the counter and found a stack of delivery slips, billings, and her handwritten notes to place orders. How could she have managed to keep things in stock the way she kept her books?

Her young smiling face looked back from her notes, her happy face.

Can't do this right now.

He closed the book and slid it back under the counter.

Bell Whatling waddled up to the front of the counter, arms folded over her fat belly, holding up her huge, drooping breasts. Her sad voice sounded well-rehearsed. "Olen, me and the other girls were talking."

Irritated by her contrived sadness, Olen said, "Yes, Bell, I could see that you were."

The other ladies stood at a safe distance, both glowing with concern, allowing for Bell to explain things.

She propped her hands on her hips and leaned forward, determined. "Well, Olen, we're not going to stand still and let you suffer. No need to argue about it. Me and the girls have made up our minds." She leaned back and gave the others a confident nod.

Their tight-lipped smiles confirmed as much.

"We're going to help you around this place. We'll take turns and be here six days a week."

"You don't say." Olen stepped back and bumped the cash register.

"Now, Olen, that's what good neighbors do. They help out."

As if prompted by fate, the bell over the entry chimed and Willis walked in.

Bell's mouth dropped open, shocked at his brazen appearance. All three women turned their backs, shunning him.

Willis looked like he couldn't care less what these ladies thought of him. He showed no sign of regret. His smiling eyes fixed on Olen as if nothing had happened, boldly walking up to the counter.

The site of Willis filled Olen with an odd combination of rage, fear, and deep friendship, all strong emotions that are often hard to separate. They ganged up on his heart like a heavy anchor that pulled him down.

Olen knew what he wanted. A small package from the saddle and tack shop down in Carson City had been delivered, along with a heavy wooden box that had come from Germany a week earlier.

He poked a thumb toward the back. "I'll open the back door." His voice shook from way down, a place Olen had never before known. "I don't want you in my store, no more."

Olen thought he'd feel better having said this but he didn't. He felt worse.

Shock and tears welled in Willis's light blue eyes. His head and shoulders slumped. He turned and obediently walked back outside. The bell signaling his departure somehow had a distant ring.

The women huddled immediately and resumed their whispering, angry as a nest of hornets, too far away for Olen to translate their squawks.

Feeling only emptiness, Olen walked through the storeroom and lifted the heavy oak bar from the back door. When he opened the heavy oak door, Willis was waiting. His sad eyes searched Olen, thinking what to say, certainly having realized that Helfred had been taken.

How could he know, living way up there on the Perch? Olen stepped back and motioned toward the wooden box on the floor. The smaller, cardboard package rested on top. He turned away, unable to look at Willis.

Wood scraped briefly against the stone floor, Willis picking up the boxes, and he walked back out to the loading dock.

Tears clouded Olen's eyes and he closed the door, a door built by Willis. His knees gave out and he sat on the floor, weeping.

Willis hadn't known anything about what had happened. He had never known any of what had happened with each coming of the moon.

"THAT TREE LOOKS LIKE it was made for that corner." It was the most beautiful Christmas tree Carolyn Potter had ever seen.

"Huh." Jason had made a lot of suggestions along the way, earning the right to be proud.

The silver spruce filled a large hole in the corner of the living room, the corner nearest that big picture window and the wall that backed the kitchen. The way the roof timbers rose from the wall toward the fireplace gave the tree added vertical dimension.

"All it needs is this." She handed Jason a spun glass angel and lifted him toward the top of the tree. "Oh, you're getting heavy."

"Huh." Jason stretched high and positioned the glass angel over the top spur of the spruce. When they both knew the angel would stay, she lowered Jason and plugged in the lights.

The lights blinked on and they both stood back to admire their work. Jason said, "Do you think Grandma will come?"

"You want her to?" Carolyn actually hoped she might.

Chapter Seventeen

O ther folks had cleaned up the mess in Helfred's house above the bank. Gratefully, nobody had said a word to Olen. Phil Nason and Jim Embry had done the heavy lifting, moving Olen back into the loft above his store. Olen could never sleep in Helfred's house again. He could barely go there to pack his clothes and personals, feeling her presence in every corner.

Funny how life worked. After Gus got taken, Helfred had been unable to sleep in the loft, tossing and turning all night, every night, which was why they'd built her house across River Road, on the side of the mountain. *My Gosh.* After she got taken, Olen couldn't sleep in her house.

That dark cloud around his heart melted even more, remembering the way Willis had planned and built their store, paying special attention to their loft apartment, showing Olen how to chip and fit stone masonry, how to measure, cut, and tightly fit large, wooden beams. Even Helfred had appreciated Willis, maybe even loved him like a brother.

They'd put Helfred in the ground four days earlier, but Olen still smelled her freshly-baked cookies. He could see her smiling face, the way she looked at her Gustov, that special way she looked into Olen's eyes.

God, I loved her so . . .

"That should do it for me, Olen." Phil Nason walked out from the back of the store, near the stairs that went up to the loft. "Jim and his wife are up there putting the last of the kitchen stuff away."

"Thank you, Phil." Olen poured them each a cup of coffee and they sat at the table by the potbellied stove, a warm area where villagers usually gathered to share the latest local gossip, even talking about happenings down below and overseas.

Phil sipped coffee and shook his head. "I miss her coffee."

"Ya. She made good coffee, by golly."

"About your offer on the house. We don't feel right about it."

"Got to be more comfortable than that old house behind the jail." Olen didn't want to mention the doctor's quarters at the clinic.

Phil nodded and sipped coffee. "Your offer prompted me to speak with Nancy about tying the knot."

"Everybody knows 'bout you two anyway."

"Yeah, I know." He studied Olen for a minute, thinking what to say. "We don't feel right about the rent. We'd like to either buy the place or pay you something to live there."

"Ah." Olen looked into his coffee, slowly spinning the cup. "I don't want to sell her house. Not yet, anyway. You fix that vestibule and the front door, take good care of the place, you'll be doing us a big favor." *Still us.* It would always be 'us' for Olen. He knew that.

Phil sipped coffee.

Olen said, "You get your new tires put on?"

"Yeah. Danny put those on yesterday afternoon."

The bell over the front door jingled, Bea Ralston finally coming in.

Olen said, "Here she is now. Let's get started." He picked up the small wooden box that had come in the day before. He and Phil left their coffee cups on the table and stood. Olen nodded at Bea, shedding her winter coat.

Bea smiled, hung her coat, and walked behind the counter to pour herself a cup of coffee.

He and Phil grabbed their coats and went out through the back door.

Driving down River Road, Phil said, "How're the ladies working out?"

"Bell Whatling's got the bookkeeping all straightened up. She's good at that, working over at the bank and all. None of them makes good coffee. Kids like Bea's cookies okay."

"Yeah . . ." Phil looked at Olen. "Helfred can never be replaced by other women, no matter how many. She was one of a kind."

"Ya, she was." Olen swallowed and blinked, pushing past his emptiness. "Thank you, Phil."

"For what?"

"For taking me up to the Perch. It's a lot to ask."

Phil turned off River Road and drove up the gravel road toward Potters' upper meadow. Snow on the road had melted to slush in the bright morning sun.

Phil shifted into four-wheel drive and passed that flat, steaming rock. Meadowlarks fluttered up and down as they passed.

Much higher up, Phil's previously plowed path through deep snow ended. He turned into his earlier turnaround and parked. "Are you sure you don't want me to come?"

"No, Phil. I said some things a few days ago, right after the funeral. I need to talk to him 'bout that. This box coming in gives me an opportunity." He grabbed the small wooden box from between his legs, looking again at the German postmarks. "Thanks for waiting." He got out and followed Phil's plowed footpath through knee-deep snow toward the waterfall.

The tree sheltered trail up the slope had been recently traveled and was easy to follow, not so much snow under the trees. Since the other day in the store, when he realized the ignorance of Willis about events surrounding the full moon, he'd slowly peeled away bits and pieces of his anger and reached a place where he could forgive, maybe even pity. How could any man live with such a thing without knowing? How could he keep his sanity?

Willis's craftsmanship amazed Olen and changed the direction of his thoughts. The trail's chiseled and tightly fitted stone steps traversed up the steep slope through the evergreen forest and stunned Olen with it's wonder. Truly beautiful.

Olen thought how Willis might rather have this whole valley to himself, probably why he came here in the first place, to be alone with that thing, the brother he keeps locked in the closet.

Higher up, the trail cut close to the waterfall and icy mist stung Olen's face. Dripping icicles hung thick from trees and rocks. Filtered sunlight sparkled multiple rainbows of colors through glasslike crystals. He'd never seen such beauty.

The trail turned back through the forest for a short distance and Olen climbed onto a huge, snowcapped boulder that needed no steps. He followed Nason's path through waste deep snow to the base of the Perch, two giant, vertical boulders.

He stopped for a breather and turned to view the snow-covered valley below. River Road cut like a dark ribbon that stretched from the Potter ranch to the village.

From this place, he had a clear view of his store, of Helfred's house, the bank, the clinic, the Rock Church, and the few other snow-capped buildings they all referred to as the village.

Closer, just across the misty ravine and a little lower, John Crow's house stood like a half teepee stacked against the cliff. It's simplicity fit John Crow perfectly

He shifted the box to his other arm, turned, and looked up at the Perch, a sculpted structure of heavy timber, stone, and glass; a unique balance of solids and voids with intersecting roof planes. Standing directly under overlapping roof planes, Olen could only see part of Willis's house. The scale made him feel tiny.

The protected area under the high roof planes looked like a workshop. Carved chunks of wood had been partially covered with canvas. Tree stumps and gnarled roots had been neatly stacked with uniquely shaped rocks, and a few pieces of unfinished furniture looked like ongoing projects. A variety of hand tools made before electricity had been arranged with purpose, one task feeding into the next.

He stood at the base of a stone stairs between the two boulders and leaned back to look up. The stairs disappeared into a tight place under the roof, maybe 20 steps up.

Willis said, "Come on up, Olen." The closeness of his voice surrounded Olen. His heart thumped into his inner ear and he momentarily wavered. He caught himself and spun around. Willis was not there.

He took a deep breath, shifted the box, and started up the stairs. Near the top, he climbed onto a landing and turned right. After a few more steps, he entered a large, vaulted space with a solid stone floor. Cow, deer, and bear hides had been scattered around as rugs.

Willis sat in the center of the room near an open fire pit. White smoke drifted lazily toward a higher opening. The solid stone wall behind the open fire had been blackened from years of use. Pots and pans hung from an overhead beam. High above, glass panes had been fitted between overlapping roof planes, flooding the large chamber with plenty of light.

Willis ignored Olen, working on top of a large wooden table made from a split cedar log. The varnished tabletop highlighted the wood's natural shades of red and white. *Beautiful.*

Willis carefully fitted a silver and gold clock face onto a clock mechanism already mounted inside a highly polished slab of burled cedar stump. Polished brass chains, probably for winding the mechanism, had been fed through natural holes in the gnarled stump. The counterweights rested on the floor at Willis's feet.

Stacks of catalogues sat on a shelf behind Willis with a very old leatherbound Bible, well used from the look of it.

Olen finally said, "You sure got some beautiful spot here, Willis. Hope you don't mind me visiting."

Willis motioned for Olen to sit opposite and stretched out his hands, asking for the box. "It'll take me two trips to deliver this."

Olen gave him the wooden box and sat on a lamb's wool cushion, looking out different windows, viewing different parts of the valley, far below. If he moved around a little bit, he could see everything from there. *The Perch.*

He leaned forward to watch Willis work. "That's going to be a nice clock. For the boy?"

"For his mother." Willis carefully turned a machine screw into a steel post, a part of the brass-geared clock mechanism, securing the clock face. "For the house, really." He gave Olen a quick smile. "Found this cedar stump about twenty years back. Intended it for Mary Lou and Jethro. Then . . ." Willis shook his head, turning a second securing screw into another steel post. Bright red scars on his arm looked recent.

My God, how can that be.

Don't ask. Never ask that. Think of something . . . "You were saying 'bout this clock you been keeping all these years, that polished stump? Why do you bring it out now?"

Willis looked up at Olen, tired. "Kidro could never appreciate it." *Simple and honest.*

Olen smiled a little.

Willis reached into a wooden toolbox without looking and pulled out a flat pry bar, waving it absently toward Olen. "The boy's a lot like J. J." He picked up the smaller wooden box Olen had just delivered, slid the flat bar under the lid, and pried. Staples squeaked on their way out, prying it open, interrupting the stillness.

"You think he's got an eye for art, like his papa?" Olen had seen some framed pictures hanging in the entry of Potter's house, good for a little boy's work.

Willis set the lid aside and dug into the box. Popcorn foam dribbled onto the floor as he lifted a gold framed, beveled glass door with heavy, white-gold hinges.

"That's elegant, Willis."

Willis closely examined the glass face for flaws and glanced at Olen. "Yes, the boy has talent. Least ways, he observes things and draws pretty good sketches. I already framed ten of them. She's got his sketches hung in her office and bedroom, with three in the entry."

"Ya, I saw those, by golly, over on the plastered wall by her office door. One looks just like that big black horse. The boy drew those?" Olen knew he had.

Willis nodded the affirmative, using both hands to lower the glass door over the clock face, twitching it, testing it for fit. He set the glass door back into the box, stood, and stretched. He smiled, motioned for Olen to follow, and trotted up three chiseled steps to another flat area.

Olen joined him at the higher door opening near a stack of hides the size of a full-size bed. A new saddle had been stretched over a draw-down stand near the opening. "This is for the boy. I ordered silver trimming and a nameplate, along with a buckle for a belt he's making for his mother. That was the box that came up from Carson City."

"That's a nice saddle, by golly." Olen walked closer to the rear opening.

Steam rose from a nearby hot spring. Beyond that, a slow-moving stream ran down a naturally eroded gully and flowed into a pond above the waterfall.

Feeling the time was right, turning back to face Willis, he said, "Willis, 'bout what I said the other day . . ."

"I understand, Olen." Willis didn't want to talk about it either, the torment in his eyes. He said, "After all you've lost, who can blame you?" Willis stepped squarely in front of Olen, close. "You think the

Potter woman might buy materials for a new house? I mean, I'd like to do something for Gilpin's wife and daughter. I'll charge Sally a couple of steers, make her pay something."

"By golly, that's fine. I'd hate to see them leave."

"I reckon that pretty little girl might grow up here. She'd be the right age for the boy. You know, when the time comes." Willis looked out to his hot spring and beyond, obviously uncomfortable about this subject.

"I'd like to help. I'll talk to Jake Pendleton and the others 'bout all of us pitching in. She wouldn't need to do it all. The Potter woman, I mean. It could be a community thing." He remembered. "She's already talked to me 'bout this. She's working out an insurance thing with Whatling. She wants to make it look like Bruce actually provided for Sally and little Sissy."

Willis spun to face Olen, his blue eyes bright. "Good."

Olen hadn't seen Willis this animated since Mary Lou's passing, like he belonged to this community once again.

Willis said, "Jake's equipment would sure be a help."

Olen wanted to reach out and hug Willis, show him everything was okay. "You come into my store, anytime you want."

"You sure, Olen, after all that's been taken from you?"

"Not by you, Willis. Not by you." He looked into Willis and found bafflement. "I know that now. I think we all do."

A growing breeze flowed through from front to back, the lower opening to the upper, geothermal heat being replaced with fresh, cold air.

Out there, beyond the top of the nearby ridge, new storm clouds were building. The sunlight streamed through the west facing windows, flooding the room with bright daylight. The sun would soon hide behind the clouds.

More relaxed, getting philosophical, Olen said, "I keep trying to figure it out, me and some of the others, why we gonna . . . why we stay? I mean, we all got a small piece but . . ." The way Willis looked into Olen stopped him cold.

Willis said, "This place doesn't belong to any of us. Not to me. Not to you. Not even to the Potters. We belong to this place. All of us belong to this place." He looked out at the clouds building over the ridge. "You and Nason better go now. There's a storm coming."

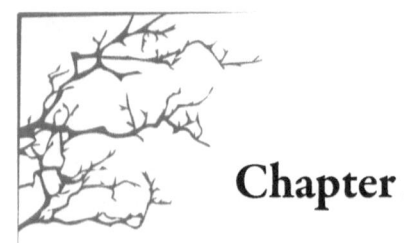

Chapter Eighteen

The only light in Ellen Winslow's living room came from her television, the old black and white version of *Miracle on 34th Street*. She'd seen it a million times and hadn't liked it since her distant childhood. The only thing dumber than watching it again was the stupid movie itself. She hated this stupid movie. People just shouldn't live like that. Mothers should never coddle their daughters. Daughters were selfish, just like this stupid little girl in this stupid movie, just like Ellen's own daughter, Carolyn *la-de-da* Potter.

Carolyn loved Jason just like this stupid mother in this stupid movie loved her little brat. Though Jason wasn't much of a brat yet, Carolyn's coddling would certainly make him one.

Ellen lit a cigarette, took two puffs, and set it in the ashtray with another lit cigarette that had burned down to the filter. She crushed the old butt into the heap of snubbed out smokes and took another puff from the newly lit cigarette.

Her telephone rang, probably some stupid salesperson from some stupid call center in the Philippines. It rang two more times before it bothered her enough to pick it up. "Hello."

"Hi, mom. Merry Christmas." *Great!* Her stupid, selfish daughter.

"How can I have a Merry Christmas without my grandson?"

"Well, that's why I called. We were hoping you could come up here. We have plenty of room."

"How can I? Isn't there snow on the roads?"

"Well, Tom Kirby will be coming up on the twenty third. I'm sure he'd be happy for the company."

"The twenty third? That's impossible. Our office party is on the twenty third."

"I thought you hated those."

"They expect me to answer the phones this year."

"Does that mean you won't be having any cocktails?"

"After what happened last year, they decided against the booze. They will allow us to bring our own beer and wine."

"What happened last year?"

"Oh, I didn't tell you?"

"Not that I can remember."

"Well," Ellen turned down the sound on her television, took a drag from her cigarette, and snubbed it out. "Kathy got up on Brian's desk and did a strip tease." She lit another cigarette.

"Oh, no." Carolyn laughed. "Isn't she in her fifties and a little overweight?"

"A little? She's Petunia Pig, waving her big, fat, cottage cheese butt at all the men."

"Oh, no." Carolyn laughed again. "That's so funny. I know you never told me before."

"I wouldn't tell you in front of my grandson."

"Oh, Mom." Carolyn whined her little sigh, the selfish . . . "So, how was your Thanksgiving?"

"I went down to the Bright Spot."

"How was it?"

"Not too many places are open on Thanksgiving. Not anymore. Besides, if their other customers don't complain, they look the other way when I smoke."

"Oh, Mom, I wish you'd give those things up."

"I will." She filled her lungs with smoke and let it drift out. ". . . one of these days."

"What did you have, the vegetable casserole?"

"They're not as good as they used to be. I think they hired a new chef. They used to put that graham cracker crust on top."

"Aren't you going to ask about our Thanksgiving?"

"What for?" Her daughter couldn't cook.

After a long pause, Carolyn said, "Here, Mom, Jason wants to say hello."

"Merry Christmas, Grandma."

"Merry Christmas, yourself." She couldn't help but smile, hearing his voice. "How was your Thanksgiving?"

"Awesome. Mom made a huge turkey with stuffing and everything. I got to kill it Wednesday night. I chopped off its head with a hatchet."

"What?"

"Willis and John Crow even came down."

"Are they some of your mom's new boyfriends?"

"Gosh, no. They're two of our neighbors. They help out around here, so they got invited. Willis cut us a really cool Christmas tree. It's a silver spruce. You should see it. We decorated it ourselves. Us and Barnabas."

"You still have that mutt? I thought a bear would have eaten him by now."

"Almost. That was a really scary night. Barnabas saved us. He chewed off one of its legs when it tried getting in."

"What? What kind of . . ."

"It's okay now, though. Willis already fixed the latch. It's a special Baldwin, because our door is three inches thick."

"What are you talking about? A bear?"

"They've got a system up here and me and Mom understand it now, so we don't interfere anymore. Not anymore."

"What?"

"Hi, Mom." Carolyn must have taken the phone away from Jason.

"What is he talking about? What's going on up there?" She sucked a long drag from her cigarette and let it drift out through her nostrils, waiting for her stupid, selfish daughter to manufacture an answer.

"It's difficult to explain. There's something going on up here, some kind of wild animals. They sometimes attack people, but don't worry about us. We're . . ."

"What?"

TOM KIRBY STARTED DOWN the north side of Lee Vining Summit a little after sunset. Wet spots in the road were turning to ice, getting tricky. The twilight made it difficult to see anything but this black ribbon of highway, snow piled high on both sides. A deep canyon on the left was visible between peaks of plowed snow.

He slowed a little, too easy to speed in his father's Bentley, and turned on the headlights.

How can she live up here? Why would anybody want to live in a frozen wasteland?

Bowl games were being played and he couldn't even get a signal on the dumb radio. The 18 speaker Bespoke Audio System was worthless up here. He had money on Ohio State, but that game wasn't until the following day. *No worries.* Ohio State could beat that spread in their sleep.

His father's Bentley was okay, but Kirby missed his Mercedes. His long streak of bad luck had to end. He'd already lost too much. His destiny was to be a winner.

That day, when Allison had ushered them into his office, Lester had been all business. Omar and Lummis had worn their angry faces, scaring the tar out of poor Allison.

Kirby had assured her that Lester was pitching a story idea. *What a crock.* Lester could never concoct a storyline.

Kirby had signed over the title to the Mercedes, given Lester the keys, and had politely ushered them to the elevator. That had put him back in Lester's good graces for the bowl games. Good luck was bound to follow.

He rounded a wide curve, cleared some trees, and drove downhill toward the lights of a small town. He crossed a low bridge where a sign read, "Bridgeport."

"Great." Kirby's eyes ached from driving in bright sunlight, reflecting off of white snow. He would stay the night.

He slowed and drove into the small town. Carolyn had told him to look on the left for the Sportsman's Inn. *There.* It looked every bit the quaint, two-story wooden building she'd described. "Okay." He turned across the narrow highway and parked in front.

Snow had been cleared to within a foot of the high boardwalk on what must have been a sunny day. Kirby stepped out of his father's Rolls and his foot slipped on a patch of ice. His elbow painfully slammed into the doorsill. He sat on the cold pavement for a few seconds, rubbing and testing his right elbow. Nothing had been broken.

He pushed up onto both feet, being careful where he stepped. He kept his left hand on the car, reached the back, and opened the trunk. He pulled out his suitcase, locked his car, climbed four wooden steps, and entered a small, warm lobby.

A pretty lady smiled at him from behind a wood paneled counter. Her ample breasts pushed her cowboy shirt to the max, buttons ready to pop. His eyes lingered. He couldn't help it.

"Welcome to the Sportsman's Inn." Her cheeks blushed red. Her teeth looked whiter than snow, smiling from behind her dark red lipstick. Her curly, strawberry blond hair flowed down to her shoulders. Her bright blue eyes speared into him, unflinching, surprisingly bold. He hadn't expected to find anything so juicy in a frozen wasteland.

He smiled and said, "I hope you have a room."

Her eyes held his. "This is the off season. We're loaded with empty rooms." She opened an old-fashioned registry and turned it toward him, no computer in sight.

He set his suitcase on the floor and signed in. "You take American Express?"

"I'm not supposed to." Her light blue eyes reached to the back of his skull. "For you, I'll make an exception." She spun the registry and read it. "Tom Kirby. I like that. I'm Mona." She offered to shake hands.

"Hi." He shook her hand and she held on, still looking into him. Her lips parted.

She finally let go and looked at the registry. "L. A. I knew it. Where's Fairfax?"

"On the west side. That's my office address. I'm here on business."

"Here in Bridgeport?" She turned and reached to the top of a mail-slot wall behind the desk. Her shirttail rose above her tight-fitting jeans, exposing her fine, white skin and a slender waist.

Kirby took a deep breath and watched.

She turned back and handed him the key. Her stare remained bold, even when blushing. She couldn't have known that the second button on her tight-fitting shirt had come undone. His eyes lingered. He couldn't help himself. She wasn't wearing a bra.

"Here in Bridgeport?"

"What?"

"Is your business here in Bridgeport?"

"Ah, yes. Uh, no." He stared at the fine white skin between her breasts before looking back into her light blue eyes. She liked being looked at. He said, "One of my authors lives up Sonora Pass. Is that nearby?"

"Right around the corner. The turnoff is nineteen miles north. You'll see the sign for the marine base."

"Marine base?"

"Mountain Warfare Training Center. It's three miles up Sonora Pass Highway."

He had to say it. He couldn't help it. "I never expected to find someone like you in a place like this. You're luscious. Do you have room service?"

"That depends." She blushed bright red but her eyes were still locked in. She leaned across the counter to look at his suitcase and her top button came undone, too fine. She said, "How heavy is it?"

He wanted to tell her that his handheld urine dispenser weighed ten pounds when fully loaded. "My suitcase? I can carry that."

"That's a relief." She stood back, realized she was unbuttoned, and turned away to correct the situation.

Kirby said, "I was hoping you could bring up a bottle of Canadian Club and some ice."

She turned back and smiled. "A pint, a fifth, or a quart?" No blush this time.

WELL AFTER DARK, WITH thin clouds spreading the glow of a three-quarter moon, Willis had plenty of light for deliveries. He'd finished making the clock and polishing the boy's new saddle with Christmas still two days off. He carried the saddle over one shoulder and the heavy wooden box under his other arm.

He walked wide of their house, keeping in the shadows, being careful not to be seen. He set the wooden box with the clock weights on the stump near the barn door and reached for the key. He opened the door, left the key in the lock, and carried the saddle inside.

The clerestory windows let in enough light for him to climb the ladder into the loft. He hid the saddle behind stacked bales of hay, climbed back down, stepped outside, and shouldered the wooden box. He returned to the loft and hid the box with the saddle. They'd never look there, not with Christmas two days off. He climbed down from the loft, locked the barn door, and returned the key to its niche.

Lights were still on inside the house so he stayed in the shadows. This far away, not even the dog could sense him. He'd bring the clock on Christmas Day, set it up before supper, and get back to the Perch before the moon. Hopefully, it would be a quiet Christmas. What a blessing that would be.

He stopped in the upper meadow and looked toward the village, toward Sonora Pass, toward the outside world. A cold chill rushed across his shoulders and down his back. He didn't know how or why, but he knew someone was coming, someone from far outside this world apart.

CHRISTMAS EVE MORNING found Tom Kirby exhausted. Moaning Mona had just left, not wanting anybody to know she'd spent the night. Her body had been finer than he'd ever seen. He found it hard to believe she'd still been a virgin, a first for Kirby. All of his previous ladies had been more experienced but none could compare. She must have been coached by somebody. He dozed off.

He woke at 9:15 a.m. with a bolt, already late. He got up, wrapped a towel around himself, and took two steps to the wall sink. After shaving and brushing his teeth, he hurried down the cold hallway to relieve himself and take a shower.

The Inn must have been a hundred years old, with no full bathrooms in the rooms. At least he had this communal bathroom to himself. While the plumbing and tile looked relatively new, the use of a common shower and toilet had long since vanished from all but the oldest and smallest hotels. This felt more like a bed and breakfast.

Kirby never wore anything but business suits so dressing casual meant no tie. He hurried downstairs, wanting to see her, but the entry desk and dining room were empty. He sat in a booth near the frosted picture window, where a quarter scale train and village had been set up around a nicely decorated Christmas tree. Luckily, the trains were not running and the deserted dining room was quiet.

An attractive, thirty something redhead pushed through a double-swinging, stainless-steel door and smiled, coming his way. "Good morning, Mr. Kirby. You need a menu?"

"I feel like steak and eggs. Can you do that?"

"Sunny side up or over." She didn't write anything down and Kirby hoped she could get it right. He never knew in hick towns like this.

"Basted." He hoped she knew what that meant.

"Whole wheat or rye?"

"Rye, not burned." Rye toast always came out burned or stale.

"Hash browns or house potatoes?"

"House, of course, and plenty of coffee."

"Juice?"

"Got any cranberry juice?"

"Sure thing." She scampered back into the kitchen with a butt that looked as tight as her little sister's. She could not possibly be Mona's mother.

Outside, across the highway, a shade went up from inside Doc' & Al's Sporting Goods. He still had some last-minute shopping to do.

"Here you go, Mr. Kirby." The waitress delivered juice, steaming coffee, and a full creamer.

Kirby sucked down the juice, cold and tasty. "Met your sister, Mona, last night when I checked in. What's your name?"

"Mona? She's my step-daughter. I'm Joanne. Welcome to the Sportsman's Inn." She smiled and bobbed her head toward the kitchen. "This time of year, I'm both cook and waitress." She backed toward the kitchen. "I work days. Mona works nights. We both work dinners." She turned away and disappeared into the kitchen.

The newly plastered dining room ceiling had only been half-painted, obviously a work in progress.

He spotted a stack of newspapers on a nearby table, got up, and found the sports section of the L. A. Times. He returned to his table, sipped coffee, and found the college basketball scores.

"What the . . ."

UCLA had already lost in a pre-conference basketball tournament. For the hundredth time, he knew he needed to quit gambling. It would be easy enough. Some guys had gambling addictions, but not Tom Kirby. He could quit any time he wanted. He'd just string together a few wins and slam the door, go out a winner. *It's my destiny.*

"Here you go." Joanne set a large platter in front of him, crowded with a thick New York steak, three eggs basted to perfection, and sliced potatoes fried with onions and green peppers. "Toast will be right up."

"Can I get some more juice?"

"Cranberry?"

He nodded and she hurried back toward the kitchen. He watched her tight backside disappear. He couldn't help it.

The steak cut tender and tasted smoked, pink inside, with just the right seasoning. The eggs tasted farm fresh. When she returned with juice and lightly browned rye toast, he said, "This looks like a good restaurant, for being so far out."

"You sound surprised." She smiled, sincere, not offended.

"What's your dinner menu like? I might come back tonight with a couple of guests."

"Folks seem to like us." Her brows shot up, remembering. "We have an unopened box of flash-frozen California lobster tails in the freezer."

"Umm." The medium-rare steak tasted delicious. "Do I need reservations?"

"How many?"

"Me, one of my authors, and her kid."

"I think we can handle that."

After breakfast, he ran upstairs, grabbed his overcoat, and hurried back down through the small lobby. Still no sign of Mona. He stepped out into the cold, pulled on his overcoat, and crossed the empty highway under a slate gray sky. He climbed onto the boardwalk and entered the sporting goods store, tripping a bell at the top of the door.

A few seconds later, a frail man in his seventies stepped from behind drawn black curtains in back. A little stooped at the shoulders, he stepped behind a glass-front counter with fishing reels, fishing tackle, and hunting knives. He looked across at Kirby. "Good morning. Merry Christmas." He stared at Kirby over the top of wire-rimmed reading glasses.

"It is, isn't it?" Something about a good night of sex always made Kirby friendly.

Three mountain bikes sat in front of the store. "Got any sales going on?"

"This time of year?" The old man walked from behind the counter and approached Kirby. "Everything's on sale. Take these mountain bikes, now. Summer time, this one sells for four-hundred-eighty-seven dollars and ninety-eight cents, plus tax." They all looked about the same, with one a little bigger.

"When did bikes get so expensive?"

The old guy grinned, pinching at his chin, standing firm. "You'd be surprised how many we sell. Kids get bored with fishing."

"How much at Christmas?"

The old man pulled off his glasses and polished them with his shirttail, thinking about it. He moved to one side of the bigger bike, propped his glasses back onto his nose, and knelt, pretending to closely examine the thing. "Let you have it for four-hundred flat, no tax." He didn't look up at Kirby, like he was saying goodbye to an old friend, the mountain bike.

"Come on! That's still too much." Kirby waited for him to stand and return his stare. When he didn't stand, Kirby said, "Listen, I need a good rifle and some special ammunition. Maybe we can work a package deal."

The old man stood and turned. His light green eyes searched Kirby's, like a reluctant Persian rug merchant. "You hunting bear, or wolf?"

Kirby crossed his arms and waited for an answer on a package deal.

"Both are protected, you know. I can't issue a hunting license."

"I've been planning to buy a good rifle. Why? Do you really care?"

"Deer went out of season after Thanksgiving." He cared.

"I'm not hunting deer."

The old man stepped back a little and eyed Kirby's clothes. "You shoot a bear up here, you might have some trouble."

"What about wolf. My friend owns a ranch. She's been having some problems with her cattle."

The wily old man pulled at the corners of his shirttail with both hands and strolled back to the glass-front counter. He turned and leaned back against his elbows, thinking about it. "I bought an M-1 carbine from a marine a few years back." His head bobbed toward the storefront window. "The owner of the Sportsman's Inn across the street. Marines don't use them anymore. He retired from the base at Pickle Meadow after the corps restocked with newer rifles. It's got no state registration, so I don't need to report the sale. Private sales are still legal. I don't know for how long. You understand?"

Kirby knew from serving at Pendleton, M-1s had been obsolete for years. "Does it still shoot?"

The old guy pushed off the counter and stepped forward with authority, closing the sale. "I've been a gunsmith for fifty-two years. For my money, that's the finest rifle ever made." He grinned a little. "Still shoot? You'd better believe it."

"Can you make some special bullets for it?"

The old guy looked out the window, crossed his arms, and leaned closer, like he was telling secrets. "I get up to Virginia City every year. They've got a Pioneer Day celebration. I just happen to have about a pound of pure silver in back." He leaned back on the counter, being conversational. "You're headed up Sonora Pass, are you?"

Kirby had no idea how this guy could have known that. He said, "Yes. Do you take plastic?"

"Master Card or Visa."

Kirby pulled out his wallet and opened it, ready to pull the card. "How about American Express? I'd like to charge this to my business."

"I'd have to call that in."

Kirby pulled the card from his wallet and handed it to the gunsmith.

The gunsmith took it behind the curtain in back. After a minute, he was talking on the phone.

Kirby couldn't quite hear his words. He leaned across the counter and held his breath. He still couldn't make the words out.

The phone hung up. The gunsmith returned and handed Kirby his card. "When I gave them the amount, they put me on hold. After a minute, they came back and approved it."

"We're in business, then. How much?"

"I figured two clips. That's all the silver I've got. That's sixteen bullets. Is that enough?"

"I hope so."

The old guy leaned on the counter and jotted numbers on a notepad. He'd already given the amount to American Express, adding them up now like he wasn't sure. Still looking at the pad, he said, "All together, that's eleven-hundred-eighty-seven dollars and sixty-two cents."

"Make it eleven hundred even and I'll pay for it now."

The old man lowered his head and stared up at Kirby for what seemed a full minute. "Eleven fifty and no warranties?"

"Can you put a red bow on the bike? It's for a kid."

"It's a boy's twenty-six inch. How old is he?"

"He can grow into it. It's the thought that counts. Right?"

"I can let you have a smaller one for the same price."

"If there's a problem, can he trade this one for a smaller one?"

"Sure, as long as he doesn't scratch it."

"Let's do it that way." The bigger bike had to be worth more.

"I'll see if I can find some ribbon in back. If not, I'm sure the wife has something over at the house. When do you want to pick it up?"

"Can I pick it up in the morning? I know it's Christmas Day but . . ."

"Sure. I'll be here at ten and wait for an hour. That work for you?"

KIRBY FOLLOWED THE highway nineteen miles north and took the Sonora Pass turn-off at 12:05 p.m. The marine base sign was bigger than the highway sign, making it impossible to miss. Another sign said the pass was closed. Carolyn already told him it was closed all winter and she'd have to have it cleared by their local plow. He hoped so.

Three miles up the pass a wooden sign on the right read, "Marine Corps Mountain Warfare Training Center." A hundred yards up a side road stood the guard shack. A little farther up, barely visible beyond a mountain of snow, he passed a group of snow-covered buildings. There was no sign of life in the cold and gray, but Kirby knew the marines were there. This was where John Potter's recon company had trained before shipping out for combat duty. These guys were known, throughout the corps, as badass marines.

At this elevation, low lying clouds sat like fog, bulging down in shafts, hugging rock outcroppings and pine trees. Shivers crossed Kirby's shoulders like ghosts crawling across his back.

"Be careful." The Rolls cruised up the speed grade without trying.

How can anybody live here?

He slowed and followed a wide curve to the left, where the narrow highway climbed steeply up the edge of a cliff, chiseled from solid granite. In places, he drove between cliffs on both sides, one uphill, and one downhill. The clouds thickened as the road climbed and he turned on his headlights.

"Oh, no." He'd forgotten to get gas. He looked at the gages, still not used to this car. It took a few seconds to find the fuel gage, less than a quarter tank.

He looked at a solid rock face in front of his car and instinctively swerved left. He looked over the downhill cliff to his left, nothing out there but air and treetops, and veered back to the right. Back on track, going slower, he decided to never look at these gages again, unless he was parked.

Thin sheets of water ran down and crossed the road everywhere, no doubt from melting snow. All would turn to ice if it got cold enough. *It will get cold.*

He passed the summit sign, where barren rocks stood tall on both sides of the road, like she'd said. Just ahead, the highway down to Sonora remained closed. He turned right and followed a wider road downhill for more than a mile before driving under a canopy of giant redwood trees. Their broad branches hung low with the weight of heavy snow. Icicles hung lower, some as long as five feet. He'd never seen anything so beautiful. *Well, maybe Mona.* He smiled, thinking about the night before.

He crossed a bridge over a canyon. The sound of raging water penetrated his sound-proof Rolls Bentley. The road took a wide turn to the right, entering a small alpine village that reminded him of Switzerland. Jacobsen's Emporium stood on the left side, like she'd said. He parked in front at 1:42 p.m.

He opened the door to cold air but left his overcoat in the car. He scrambled up the front steps and into the store, nice and warm inside. An old, wood-burning stove sat in the center of the large space. Several empty chairs had been arranged around the stove, an obvious place to meet.

Tightly aligned shelves stocked with canned goods, tissue paper, light bulbs, and other essentials crowded the ample floor space.

"Hello. Merry Christmas." A tall, slender old man in a long leather apron stood behind a glass-front deli counter at the back of the store, smiling at Kirby over a jar of cookies and several upside-down, white coffee mugs. "You must be that Kirby fella, from down below."

"Carolyn told me to stop here. She said you'd give me directions?"

"Ya, sure. She said you prob'ly need directions."

"I do. But first, do you know where I can get some gas?"

Chapter Nineteen

Jason had gotten together with Willis a few days after Thanksgiving, his first opportunity to speak with him alone. He'd needed advice on what to get his mom for Christmas. Willis knew about all kinds of stuff like that. Maybe John Crow, but Willis for sure.

Willis hadn't said anything, of course, *because he's Willis.* He nearly never said anything. He'd simply taken Jason into the tack room and shown him a paperback book on leather-craft. A faded book, well-worn from use. Later that same day, Jason had slipped into his mom's closet and borrowed a cotton belt that went with one of her summer dresses. She'd never miss it with so much snow on the ground.

Willis had provided a strap of thick leather the next day, and a catalogue of silver stuff for saddles, boots, and belts, with a lot of pages of men's and women's rings and bracelets and stuff, all made from silver. He'd helped Jason choose a belt buckle and matching tip for the other end.

Together, they'd sized the leather strap for her waist and for the buckle and tip. Both ends needed to be narrower for the buckle and tip to fit, but the center was wide, like a cowboy belt should be. That gave Jason plenty of room to imprint her name and decorative stuff.

Willis helped him stencil a pattern of flowers and leaves and stuff, and to choose the style of the letters for her name. All the patterns came from that well-worn book, making it easy to choose.

Willis got him started by stamping patterns into a different piece of leather, getting Jason familiar with the leather-craft tools hanging above the workbench.

By the time Jason started on the belt, his confidence soared. He knew she'd like it.

Willis brought the silver buckle and end tip down from the Perch a week later and helped Jason with the final fittings. It looked much cooler than the storebought stuff at the Emporium.

Mr. Jacobsen had delivered John Crow's present two days before Christmas, with some wrapping paper, ribbon, and tape. That gave Jason everything he needed. He finished and wrapped his present for Willis last. That was the only gift he wasn't sure about, whether or not Willis would like it. Who could sense what Willis liked or didn't like? *Because he's Willis.*

After feeding the horses on Christmas Eve Day, Jason collected his presents from different hiding places around the tack room. He snapped his fingers for Barnabas to follow, locked the barn, and turned toward the house.

A car he'd never before seen drove across the rise in the driveway and parked at the bottom of the steps. Mr. Kirby got out of the car and started up the front steps.

Barnabas lowered his head and charged, not sure who it was, and Jason snapped his fingers. The dog stopped and looked back, ears up, wondering why Jason had stopped him.

"He's a big poophead. You don't need to make friends with him."

The moron didn't even know Jason and Barnabas were climbing the steps behind him. He kept knocking on the door without looking back. He carried a small package under his arm, probably for Mom.

Jason held Barnabas and waited.

Mom opened the door and Mr. Kirby held up the package. "Merry Christmas."

When she took the package, the moron threw both arms around her and tried to kiss her. She used the package like a mask and squirmed free. She threw the moron her most angry look. When she saw Jason and Barnabas, she smiled. "Jason, look who's here."

Mr. Kirby turned and she backed into the house.

Jason and Barnabas pushed past them and hurried down into the living room. Jason looked back before pulling her present from under his coat.

They remained in the entry, talking softly, too far around the corner to hear, and Jason put her belt under the tree. He placed John and Willis's presents in front, making them easier to see.

Mom and the moron stepped down from the entry, both watching Jason. The moron said, "Come on, kid. I'm taking you two down to Bridgeport for dinner."

KIRBY KEPT HIS TRANSMISSION in low gear and took his time driving down to Pickle Meadow. He said, "Sonora Pass Highway? Ha!" This narrow thread of pavement was pure panic, a deep drop into the abyss on one side and a stone wall on the other. Heavy clouds pressing down to pavement reduced visibility to twenty yards. "How can you live up here? This isn't safe."

Carolyn said, "Our village snowplow laid down some salt. They spread salt on River Road, in the village, and on our driveway. It seems to work pretty well, so I asked him to spread plenty of it out here on the highway."

"Thanks. A little salt saves lives." Kirby didn't care how sarcastic he sounded.

The kid rode in the backseat, reading some book on his tablet or playing a video game, wearing earphones.

Carolyn said, "They had an awful accident up here about a month ago. A surprise storm came in and the highway was left open. They never had time to clear it. I don't think the state ever puts salt down up here. They just close the highway and we're snowed in for a couple of months."

"I don't know how you can live like this, snowed in every winter. Why not live in town during the winter?"

"Sonora?"

"No, no, no. I mean, L.A."

"We have responsibilities, like I said. Besides, we like the school here."

They rounded the wide curve at the bottom of the grade and Kirby pushed the gear lever into drive. He accelerated and reached the marine base in about two minutes. He said, "John never told me he grew up near this base. These guys are genuinely bad dudes. John took his mountain warfare training here, before they shipped out."

She said, "I didn't know that."

"Yeah. It was probably a walk-in-the-park for him."

They drove past the guard shack at the low end of the base and started down the grade toward 395, where large pine trees hugged both sides of the road. Plowed snow had been piled high against and between the trees.

They stopped at the intersection, Kirby glanced both ways, turned right, and gunned it toward Bridgeport. The Bentley sped down the black ribbon in a world of white.

Carolyn seemed not to appreciate Kirby's brilliant conversation. She sat quietly apart, looking out at nothing. The kid had fallen asleep in back.

Kirby had obsessed over a plan for her to open her present, gush with gratitude, and leap into his outspread arms. If he could slip it in, she'd marry him. Her conscience would demand it. She wasn't the type to sleep around. She was the marrying type. Best of all, her money could put Kirby back on top.

Mona smiled from the back of his memory.

Carolyn sat quietly, watching white zoom past, until they cruised into Bridgeport.

He couldn't help himself, plotting another brilliant conversation. He'd say, *You know, John was talking to my father about possibly investing in my company. It was just before my mother and father disappeared.*

Oh, she'd ask, not caring to look at Kirby, just being polite.

He'd say, *John didn't say anything to me, but father mentioned it before they left for Utah. I think it was at Felix's Restaurant, you know, after a Dodgers game.*

He knew it wouldn't work. By then, she'd be looking at non-scenery, not listening, not even looking at Kirby, exactly what she was doing right then.

Shortly before dark, he parked in front of the Sportsman's Inn and hurried around the car to open her door.

She'd already let herself out and was helping the kid out of the backseat.

Kirby closed the doors, locked the car, and followed them up the steps into the warmth of the inn.

Mona and Joanne stood behind the small desk watching them enter. Joanne smiled but Mona gasped and rushed into the kitchen. Joanne looked as bewildered as Kirby felt. He smiled and waved at Joanne. She cocked her head toward the kitchen, shrugged in that direction, and motioned for Kirby to find a table in the dining room.

Kirby led Carolyn and the kid into the empty dining room where the only light came from Christmas tree decorations.

Joanne turned on the overhead lights and dimmed them down until Kirby nodded, *good enough*. He guided Carolyn and the kid into a booth near the windows. Joanne came right behind with three menus.

Kirby said, "I don't need a menu. I'm having the cattleman's cut." He'd seen a framed photo of the prime rib platter on the wall in the entry.

Joanne grinned approvingly and looked at Carolyn.

Kirby looked at Carolyn. "They've got flash frozen lobster, or do you need a menu?"

"Lobster sounds wonderful."

Joanne smiled at the kid. "What about you, young man?"

The stillness shattered when a clatter of pots and pans erupted from the kitchen.

Joanne glared toward the kitchen and looked back at the kid.

The kid said, "Do you have any trout?"

"Flash frozen, but it's very good. My husband pulled it out of the reservoir." She poked her head toward the front door as if her restaurant sat on the edge of a lake.

"Okay." The kid didn't care where it came from.

"You want it pan fried or baked?"

"Pan fried in lots of butter."

"Of course." Joanne smiled at Kirby and asked the kid, "You want baked potato, au gratin, or wild rice?"

"What's awe . . ."

Kirby said, "You use real cheese?"

Joanne nodded and smiled.

"That sounds wonderful." Carolyn sounded hungry; a plus for Kirby.

"Make mine baked with heaps of sour cream and butter." Kirby's stomach had been grumbling all afternoon, nothing in it since breakfast.

Joanne laughed softly, a good waitress. She turned back to the kid. "How about you?"

"Bring him the au gratin," said Kirby. "It goes great with fish."

"I'll have wild rice," said the kid, being obnoxious, glaring at Kirby. He gave his mother a polite smile, slid from the booth, and went to the model train set near the window.

Good. Kirby could finally be alone with Carolyn. He looked at Joanne. "Are you open for cocktails?"

"Until 2:00 a.m."

"I'll have a C.C. on the rocks." He looked at Carolyn, hoping to get her a little high, maybe even drunk.

She said, "Water would be nice."

"What about the boy?"

Carolyn leaned toward Joanne. "Do you have V-8 juice?"

"Sure thing." Joanne folded her notepad into her apron. "Your drinks and salads will be right out." She scooted into the kitchen and a conversation started immediately. Kirby couldn't make out their words but it sounded like an argument.

Carolyn said, "Maybe we shouldn't have come on Christmas Eve."

"Nonsense." Kirby sank into her eyes, steady and gorgeous.

She looked away.

He said, "I talked to her about it this morning. She seemed eager for the business."

Joanne exited the kitchen and disappeared into the bar.

He said, "When we get back to your place, I have a surprise for you."

"Oh?" She sounded more cautious than curious.

"It's been in the works since before you left." What difference did it make that they hadn't put her stupid book together until after Thanksgiving? Considering how much Kirby Publications owed their printers, it was a miracle he'd gotten it published at all.

Joanne set a large tray on a nearby table and delivered their salads, throwing Kirby angry looks. She smiled at Carolyn and said, "We're all out of blue cheese. All we've got is ranch and this vinaigrette." She set the servers in the middle of the table then delivered their drinks.

After she returned to the kitchen, Kirby said, "I wonder what's gotten into her."

"Like I said, maybe we shouldn't have come."

"I told you, I set this up this morning. Besides, I'm looking forward to a good cut of beef."

Carolyn said, "We have plenty of beef. We're a cattle ranch." She sounded more confident since leaving L.A.

Kirby said, "I went on a cattle drive down in Texas. You know, like those *City Slickers* movies. The steaks were tough as my old sneakers." Kirby spooned ranch dressing onto his salad and took a bite.

Carolyn looked toward the kid and said, "Come on, honey."

The kid returned to the table and they both lowered their heads. Kirby stopped chewing.

After about 30 seconds, they raised their heads and the kid said, "Amen."

Carolyn spooned vinaigrette over her salad, took a bite, and smiled. The kid ate his without dressing.

Kirby said, "Kid, this ranch is terrific." The kid ignored him and Kirby sipped whiskey.

Carolyn said, "Willis Donner eats salads without dressing so Jason decided to give it a try."

The kid nodded and chewed lettuce, throwing another obnoxious look at Kirby.

"Who's Willis Donner?"

"He's one of our neighbors. He and John Crow help out around the place. I thought I told you." She ate more salad. She liked it.

"Willis and John have taken a hand in teaching us about the ranch. Jason likes them both." She left something unsaid, maybe because of the kid.

Kirby sipped whiskey, set it down, and chomped into more salad.

They finished their salads just as Joanne carried out three large dinner platters.

Kirby's prime rib stood an inch thick and his baked potato had been heaped with sour cream and freshly-cut, green onions.

Carolyn's lobster and the kid's trout looked equally spectacular.

Kirby cut into his prime rib and took a bite. "Mm. How did you cook this? It's delicious."

Joanne sneered at Kirby, smiled at Carolyn, and said, "We use all seven ribs, wrap it in rock salt, and leave it in the refer for at least a day before we cut it open along the bone and sprinkle in garlic powder. We let it stand for another day, then pepper the outside, cook it at five hundred degrees for an hour and a quarter, then turn off the oven and let it sit and cook slow for another hour. This was cooked last September and flash frozen. Still just as good, isn't it?" She smiled a little.

"It's fantastic." Kirby helped Carolyn de-shell her lobster, ignoring Joanne's icy stares. He asked, "Where do you get your beef?"

"This is prime Angus beef from the Potter Ranch, up the pass."

Kirby choked out a surprised laugh. "Well, Joanne, meet Carolyn Potter and her son, Jason."

Surprised, Joanne asked, "Are you from up Sonora Pass?"

Carolyn offered a shy smile and said, "We're really from Los Angeles. We inherited the ranch earlier this year. My husband was John Potter."

Joanne's friendly manner swarmed all over Carolyn and the kid. "For heaven's sake. We knew Kidro. He sold us our first order right after my husband bought this place. How'd you get hooked up with this . . ." she iced Kirby with a look, "gentleman?"

Wanting to push Joanne's face in, he said, "She's one of our best authors. Her husband was my chief editor and my best friend."

"Well, enjoy your meal." Joanne sneered at Kirby and scooted back into the kitchen.

Goodbye! He took a sip of whiskey and chewed into another piece of beef. It tasted like cardboard and his gut twisted with rage. He tipped up and drained his glass of whiskey. It didn't look like Joanne was coming back so Kirby got up. "Excuse me. I'll be right back." He took his empty glass to the double swinging kitchen door and knocked. There was no porthole window. He stepped back when Joanne pushed out to face him.

Mona stood in the middle of the large, commercial kitchen, red-eyed and puffed up from crying.

Joanne stepped out and let the door close behind her. "What now?"

"I'm dry." Kirby showed her his empty glass, ready for a fight.

She snatched the glass and strutted into the bar.

Kirby followed. "What's eating you two?"

She walked behind the bar but wouldn't look at him. Her voice shook. "Mister, if she were my little girl, I'd shoot you myself." Joanne set the empty glass in the bar sink and grabbed a clean one from the back shelf.

"What are you talking about?"

She put ice in the glass, poured Kirby a fresh whiskey, and set the glass on the bar. "A man your age aught to know better. You don't feed a little girl like that whiskey then take advantage. Now you bring your girlfriend around? You broke that little girl's heart."

"Stop it! Carolyn Potter is one of my authors. I told both of you we were coming in tonight. Besides, Mona brought the whiskey up to my room. She opened the bottle. She poured the drinks. I didn't feed her anything." Then it hit Kirby. "What do you mean, little girl?"

"That little girl turned sixteen the day after Thanksgiving. If I were you, I wouldn't be here when her daddy gets back." She tossed her head toward the back bar, toward a big framed picture of a marine staff sergeant holding up the head of a multi-tipped buck, probably the mountain warfare instructor the old man across the street had referred to.

"No, no." The whisper pressed through his suddenly very dry throat. The picture on the wall turned fuzzy and he braced both hands against the bar, struggling not to tumble onto the floor. He slid sideways onto a barstool and took several deep breaths. The dizziness passed and he looked back at the photo. "Your husband was a mountain warfare instructor?"

"You know my husband?"

"I bought his rifle from across the street. I'm a former marine myself. That's where I met John Potter." He thought about his next words. "Look, I thought she was much older. If I'd known . . ." Kirby had no desire to wrestle with this guy.

"Well, he'll be back tomorrow, Christmas Day. If I were you . . ."

IMPOSSIBLE. How could Mona be so young?

The lights of Bridgeport disappeared behind them as he rounded a curve, speeding toward Sonora Pass.

Carolyn turned off the makeup light and handed him a CD. He plugged it into the player, pumping out *Manheim Steamroller.*

Fine.

How could his luck turn this sour?

Carolyn sounded like she was speaking through a tin can with a string. "You barely touched your dinner."

"Excuse me?" He turned down the volume on Steamroller and turned up Sonora Pass Highway, speeding up the grade toward the marine base.

"I said, you hardly touched your dinner. Don't you like our beef?"

"Oh." He couldn't talk about it. He had no idea what to say about Mona. He didn't know what to think about Mona. *Oh, yeah.* "The beef was fine. I started thinking about something else, is all. You know how it goes."

He needed to get back on track, back to the reason he'd driven all the way up to this miserable freeze hole. "How was your lobster?"

"Wonderful. I guess the trout was good too. Jason ate his whole dinner."

"Yeah, that trout must have weighed two pounds. I probably would have had it stuffed and mounted, hang it over my desk at the office." He slowed, passing the base. Thick clouds dipped into the high beams of his headlights. He glanced back.

The kid had rolled into a ball, sleeping.

She asked, "Is something bothering you?"

"Nice of you to notice." He slowed for the wide curve at the top of Pickle Meadow and started up the steep grade toward the summit. "I've been under a lot of pressure lately."

"Oh?" She actually sounded interested.

"I've been doing some revamping at Kirby Publications and things have gotten a little overextended. It's only temporary, of course." Great. He'd finally planted that seed. It sounded okay, no need to push. Not yet.

"Revamping?"

Perfect. Unbelievable. "Yeah. We're starting a new line of books. I hired another editor to help out and I've reorganized the creative department. I even hired another printer." The magazine section still owed three issues to their last printer and the company bookkeeper, Esther Greenberg, had been asking questions about the money she'd put into the operations account; asking why these bills were not being paid.

He needed to fire that witch.

Carolyn asked, "Are you staying with children's books?"

"Yes. Of course. We're moving forward in three areas; fiction, poetry, and non-fiction. You know, how-to books for middle school." Kirby slowed to a crawl and turned on his fog lights, driving up the steep grade in dense fog on ice. He couldn't see past ten feet. "Thank you for salting the road."

"Our sheriff recommended it. I told him you were coming. They're all looking forward to meeting you."

Stupid, changing the subject like that. He got back on track. "I've been researching the young adult market, too. We need to expand or we start losing shelf space." *What a crock.*

"How many new authors have you published?"

Not good, letting her get ahead of him. "Listen, I need to concentrate on my driving." Like magic, the Rolls slumped off the shoulder and scraped against a rock. Kirby stopped, got out into frozen fog, walked around the car, and looked at the damage. He got back into the warm interior. "Not too bad." He put it into reverse and backed away slowly, grinding metal to get back onto pavement. He put it into low, drove slowly around a tight curve, and continued their slow climb under dense fog.

"What happened?" The kid was awake, leaning through the opening between the front seats.

Carolyn said, "Put your seatbelt on, honey."

The kid returned to the backseat and buckled up. "What happened?"

"Nothing." Kirby still couldn't see past ten feet, leaning forward, eyes sore from being wide open. "Just a little scrape."

The road levelled, nearing the summit. Those giant boulders rose into dense clouds on both sides of the road. He turned off the highway and followed the well paved road down through overhanging trees, much easier to see, light reflecting from dense fog in a tunnel of trees. They entered the village on properly cleared pavement, where the clouds formed a low canopy above River Road, a tunnel lit only by his headlights. Kirby put it into drive and stepped on the gas.

They reached the end of River Road quickly. The big boulders stacked across the road were easy to see. "It's hard to miss your place." He turned up Carolyn's driveway, rounded the curve, and crossed over the rise. He parked in front of her steps and got out, eager to help, eager to impress.

She'd already exited his car and was holding the rear door open for the kid.

He'd fallen asleep again.

She unbuckled the kid's seatbelt and picked him up. His head dropped onto her shoulder, still sleeping.

How could women be so strong, lugging kids around like sacks of potato chips?

Kirby closed the back door and followed them up the steps through their unlocked front door. He closed the door and watched her carry the kid upstairs.

Their stupid dog ignored Kirby, sniffing at Carolyn's feet, following them upstairs. Kirby asked, "Need any help?"

"No, thank you." She glanced down from the top of the stair. "Let me put him to bed and I'll come back down."

"Sure. Got anything to drink?"

"John's father kept a bottle in the office to your right. I think it's even your brand." She disappeared down the upstairs hallway.

Kirby stepped into her office and found the light switch. Lantern lenses fixed to a bull-horn chandelier gave the room a warm glow, *nice office*. Kirby found a bottle of Canadian Club and glass tumblers on a buffet cabinet behind the desk. Inside the cabinet was a small U-Line refrigerator. He filled the tumbler with ice, closed the refrigerator, closed the cabinet, and filled the glass with whiskey.

He sipped, strolled through another open doorway, and found the switch.

Rustic lamps on both sides of a king-size bed lit a large bedroom, finely detailed with coffers, wood paneling, and high windows. A stone fireplace on the back side of the living room wall had been properly loaded with logs and twigs, ready to light. The door to what looked like a large bathroom stood wide open.

"Mr. Kirby?" She sounded like she was coming downstairs.

"In here." He turned off the bedroom lights and stepped back into the office, just in time.

She walked into the opposite doorway and waited.

He said, "This is a really nice place. You should turn it into a lodge."

"I see you found the whiskey."

"Yes. Hope you don't mind me poking around."

"No. I was going to give you the tour, anyway."

"Ah, tour. That reminds me." He took her arm and led her across the entry, down the steps into the living room, and left her standing near the couch. "Sit down, please. I've got a surprise." He turned to the fireplace and found his package on the mantle, where she'd left it.

She stood in front of the couch, probably tired of sitting.

He switched on a table lamp, sat, and placed his drink on the coffee table. "Here." He patted the couch next to him. "Sit down and open this."

She obediently sat and he handed her the package. She knew it was a book, feeling around the edges.

Kirby grabbed his drink and waited.

She peeled the ribbon and Kirby slid closer, pressing his thigh against hers, nice and firm. The warmth of her nearness aroused him, inhaling that intoxicating aroma of lipstick and clean hair. She carefully peeled tape and unfolded the Christmas wrapping, looking at *Annie's Anxious Arrival*, her book about a little boy's anticipation of the coming birth of his little sister. It was actually pretty good for an author's first book. "It's always risky to publish debut authors." That was the only reason his father hadn't published it.

"Oh, Mr. Kirby." She held the book to her bosom and looked into his eyes. Tears welled in her dark blues.

His heart thumped in his ears, numbing his other senses. He knew he had to be cool, take it easy. "I thought you'd be happy." A lump formed in his throat. He slurped more whiskey.

She kept the book at her breast with one hand, grabbed the hem of her dress with the other, and bent down to dab her eyes. "Oh, Mr. Kirby, thank you." She looked at him, misty, smiling. "I can't think of a better Christmas present."

He slid his hand onto her thigh. "Well, Merry Christmas. And, please, call me Tom."

"Thank you, Tom." She softly pushed his hand away and looked at the book. "I just love the cover design."

"Some of the new people I hired. Yours is the first book in a new series. I'm submitting the cover design to Boston Bookbuilders and AIGA for awards consideration, and we're submitting to the Benjamin Franklin Awards for children's books. Since we're a small company, I'm submitting it to the American Booksellers' Book of the Year competition. I'm also submitting you for the Newberry Medal." He pressed his leg against hers and gulped the last of his whiskey. "Mind if I get a refill?"

"Here, I can get it." She stood and reached for the tumbler.

"I know where it is." He'd already told himself not to drink too much. He stood and stepped in front of her, brushing his stomach across her breasts, innocent enough.

She sat and fondled her book.

He said, "You look at your book." Feeling the moment, he nearly skipped across the wood plank floor and up the stone steps into the entry, eager to get back to her. He switched on the office light, rounded the desk, opened the refrigerator, and added more ice. He refilled the glass with whiskey, took a long drink, and filled it again. He recapped the bottle, closed the refrigerator, and stood in the doorway to her bedroom.

To himself, he said, "That's a big bed." He could see her sprawled on it, arms stretched out, inviting him to join her. If he could get her in there, she would be his. With her money . . . *I can only imagine.* He left the office light on and hurried back into the living room.

She still sat on the couch, slowly turning pages. He sat close to her, pressing thighs, pretending to read over her shoulder, breathing deeply of her intoxicating fragrance.

His brain swam in a dizzy, boozy pool, seeing blurry print and colorful illustrations. Her breasts were nice to look at, just a little cleavage showing, smooth skin slowly moving up and down with her breathing.

She said, "I had all but forgotten about this book. I love the illustrations. Oh, thank you." She closed the book and pressed it to her bosom, hugging it. She looked at him, warm and inviting.

That lump returned to his throat. He took a drink. "We're very excited about it." His voice cracked through the lump in his throat. His attention dropped to her breasts, swelling around both sides of the book. He wanted to touch her, touch every part of her. He looked back into those dark blue eyes. "I'm putting everything into the marketing campaign. I've already got you booked for two radio interviews."

"Oh, I don't . . ." Her face turned down with doubt.

"You can do those over the phone. I'll email you a list of talking points." He set his drink on the table and took the book, pretending to study the cover. "I've already lined up some billboard space in L.A., but I'm short of capital. That's why we're looking for an investor." He handed her the book and slid his arm around her shoulder, just being friendly, nothing for her to worry about.

She stayed close, staring down at the book, neither moving closer nor sliding away.

He reached across and cupped her face.

"Mr. Kirby, I . . ." She turned her face away.

He slowly pulled her back. "Please, call me Tom." He held her head in both hands and kissed her warm, soft mouth.

Her breathing quickened and her lips parted.

He pulled her closer and sucked her upper lip.

She pushed him back and turned away. "No, please."

He grabbed her shoulders, turned her back, and held her in place.

She dropped the book and balled her fists against his chest.

He kissed her again, harder.

Her breathing quickened and her lips parted. She wanted to be taken, like a cavewoman.

He couldn't stop, forcing her back onto the couch, pressing down on top of her, all his weight against her struggles, her gasps.

"No, please." She pushed at him but he was too strong. "Please, don't do this." She turned her head away and whined.

He sucked on her ear, hot against his lips. It tasted clean.

Her hips moved under him, trying to turn away. Her eyes turned back, staring into him with rage.

"What the . . ."

A low growl and hot breath pushed against the side of his face. He turned and stared into the hazel eyes of the kid's dog, growling louder, bumping Kirby's forehead with his nose. A warning.

"Nice dog." Kirby slowly sat up and she scooted off the couch. She stood, facing the fire, shaking and softly crying.

"No, no. I'm . . ." Kirby searched for words.

"You hurt my mommy." The kid appeared from nowhere, holding his dog.

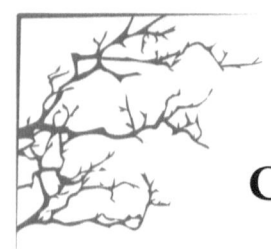

Chapter Twenty

"**Y**ou idiot!" Driving uphill, away from what they called the Village, Kirby slammed his palm against the steering wheel several times, stopping only because his hand hurt. He turned onto Sonora Pass Highway and drove toward Pickle Meadow.

That stupid kid and his stupid dog ruined everything. Another lousy minute and she'd have been moaning in ecstasy. *Just like moaning Mona.*

His car slid slightly, crossing a short stretch of ice, and Kirby remembered the road conditions, the low hanging clouds. He shifted into low gear.

"This road . . ." His high beam headlights reflected from low-hanging clouds, making it difficult to see the road in front of him. He couldn't see the edge of the road on the downhill side; might as well be at the edge of the world.

He hugged the uphill side of the road, with huge boulders and chiseled cliff so close he could reach out and touch them. If he happened to scrape a door or fender, so be it. At least he wouldn't drop off the edge of the world into the abyss.

His hands ached from his tight grip on the steering wheel and his eyes burned from being peeled wide open, staring into fog reflected light.

He wondered about the time but dared not take his eyes off the road to look at the dash clock. He'd left her house at around 10:30 or 11:00 p.m. It must still be before midnight.

He reached Pickle Meadow and drove under the canopy of clouds. He could see all the way to the end of his high beams. He shifted into drive and accelerated toward State Highway 395.

His dash clock read 11:42 p.m.

He turned left onto 395 at 11:53 p.m. and headed for the Nevada state line. The ribbon of black highway through Walker Canyon had too many curves, slipping and sliding on the best tires money could buy. He slowed to 55mph.

A truck coming in the opposite direction flashed his high beams up and down, nearly blinding Kirby. "You imbecile!"

After the truck passed, airhorn blaring, Kirby saw the sign, "Welcome to Nevada, Land of Unlimited Recreation."

"Oops." His high beams had been on since leaving Carolyn's house.

"Ahh," a sign on the right read, "Goldfield Casino at Topaz Lake." He slowed and turned right at Mark Twain Lane.

The street name caused Kirby to remember John Potter, how much he'd liked reading Mark Twain novels as a kid. *Small wonder.* Anybody growing up in this neighborhood had to have read Mark Twain. *Hicks, one and all.*

Kirby didn't miss that guy anymore. Having him killed was one of the smartest things he'd ever done. Potter had always been in Kirby's way. Carolyn's clinging memories of the guy were still in his way.

It didn't matter that John Potter had been the only man on earth to ever call Kirby a friend. Having friends was stupid. They only got in the way.

It was Potter's fault, anyway, "The idiot!" Anybody with half a brain would have had the contract notarized. Anybody with half a brain would have given a notarized copy to his wife before turning over that much cash.

That fool had always put too much trust in his fellow man.

Besides, he should never have gone behind his best friend's back to cut a deal with his best friend's father. "The idiot!"

That familiar knot formed in his stomach, his urge to get at some gaming tables. He'd change his bad luck to good and roll up some spending money. This had to be his time.

He slowed to a crawl, looking for casino lights. He only found snow-covered shacks and trailers on both sides of the narrow road. He pressed the gas a little, driving through a pine grove, thinking the casino must have burned down.

"Ahh!" A flashing neon arrow pointed right and he turned onto Goldfield Drive. He drove into a snow-covered parking lot and parked in front of a flat roofed, stucco building. It looked more like a rest home in Palm Desert than a casino.

The dark interior smelled of stale booze and tobacco. Giant Indians stood at the dimly lit bar, Paiutes for sure. He'd written an essay about them in high school, one of the Shoshone tribes. They were big in any average group of people, but they were enormous among Indians.

Tobacco smoke burned his eyes, still sore from being glued to the inside of his windshield. Their thick cigarette smoke formed halos around the lights over the gaming tables. His involuntary tears flushed and moistened his burning eyes. He wiped them away.

Most of the handful of Indians playing the tables looked drunk. Kirby liked those odds.

Delbert McClinton started singing, *Every Time I Roll the Dice,* one of a few songs Kirby actually liked, even over a tinny sound system.

A fat squaw got up on a small stage to dance her stuff. Her sloppy figure looked like she'd had six to ten kids. "Sit down, please." He didn't say it loud enough to get pounced on. One of these big boys might crush his lungs.

He shoved his way past the poorly lit bar, pulled out his emergency hundred-dollar bill, and sat at the only blackjack table in play. He nodded at the two other players. The woman must have weighed 300 pounds. Her cocktail dress fit so tight it pushed her boobs up under her fat, white-powdered chin.

The skinny guy with her wore a Pendleton shirt, classic plaid wool. He looked twice her age. He lit a cigarette and left it dangling from his thin, bluish lips. Smoke curled up into the guy's narrow slits, watching the deal.

The Paiute dealer wore slick black hair tied in a ponytail, well over 200 pounds of muscle. He stood at least six inches taller than Kirby.

"Give me some chips." Kirby slid his last hundred dollars onto the green velvet tabletop. *It's my time.*

KIRBY PARKED IN FRONT of the Sportsman's Inn at 3:07 a.m., exhausted. It hadn't taken long for him to lose his last century note and his credit cards were maxed. Even his American Express had to have reached its flexible limit. The sporting goods guy had trouble clearing it. He still had half a tank of gas, more than enough to get back up to her place.

He checked all of the hiding places in his empty wallet and slid it under the front seat. He'd tell her that he lost it when he got out to check the damage after driving into that stupid boulder. She'd have to loan him enough to get back to L.A. Hopefully, she'd invest in the company and give him a chance to get back on a winning streak. If not for that stupid kid, Kirby could have had it all. She'd been getting hot. *Stupid kid.*

Kirby shut off his car, got out, and slipped a little. He hung onto the door this time. He locked his car and went inside the warm lobby. Nobody worked at the desk. "Good." He didn't want to see anybody else that night.

He snuck upstairs and went straight to his room. When he opened the door, she was there. "What are you doing?" His quiet voice surprised him, considering his ugly mood. "Why didn't you tell me you were just a kid?"

Mona's face still glowed red from crying, sitting up in his bed. She'd pulled the sheet up to her collarbone but it didn't hide much. "I'm sorry for being such a baby. It's just that . . . she's so beautiful." Her mouth turned down and quivered. "I'm sorry."

"I told you before, she's one of my authors." He closed and locked the door. "That's all." He stared at her natural beauty. "You are gorgeous. You know that?"

She smiled slightly. Her lips parted.

Kirby slid out of his coat and let it fall to the floor.

LIGHT FOUND A WAY THROUGH the dried crust holding Kirby's eyelids shut. It scratched his eyeballs. Having been in this condition many times, he knew what to do. He sat up and pried one puffy eyelid open enough to see through the scum, a painful business. The rush of tears over his parched iris helped. He could see his watch, 10:23 a.m.

"No, no." He jumped up and throbbing pain nearly sat him back down. He swallowed hard to keep acid drenched booze from bubbling up and burning the back of his throat. He staggered to the wall sink and doused his face, hair, and neck with ice cold water.

His skull throbbed from whiskey and second-hand smoke. He whispered, "Stupid, slimy casino."

"Idiot!"

Hot water finally reached the sink and he used a washcloth to wash his chest and genitals. He dressed, packed, and rushed downstairs. He set his suitcase in front of the desk. Joanne still looked angry.

He asked, "Will you take a company check? I lost my wallet last night. I think the room was already paid on my American Express card." Kirby forced a sheepish smile.

Joanne sneered.

He glanced at his watch. 10:42 a.m.

She said, "We don't take American Express. Mona never should have offered to try."

"I guess I could wash some dishes," *you stupid hick.*

"Counting meals and drinks, your bill is three hundred and sixty-four dollars and twelve cents." She handed him a prepared bill. It didn't include the quart of Canadian Club whiskey from Mona.

"Okay. Fine." Kirby smiled politely and wrote a check for the exact amount, tore it from the checkbook, signed it, and slid it across the desk. He grabbed the receipt, picked up his suitcase, and headed out into a cold, gray morning. He opened his trunk, deposited the suitcase, and closed the trunk.

The Bentley started sluggish from the cold. He let it warm up for a full thirty seconds before backing across the empty highway and parking. His trunk faced Doc' and Al's Sporting Goods. He opened the trunk again, climbed the steps, and entered the store at 10:55 a.m.

The old man stood behind the counter wearing a heavy sheepskin coat. "Nearly gave up on you." He spun two sheets of paper toward Kirby. "Here's your bill of sale. I already signed both of them. If you can sign one . . ."

Kirby pulled his gold Cross pen and signed a copy.

The old guy looked over the top of his glasses at the signature then studied Kirby for a long second. More worried than joking, he said, "You look like a hard night in Reno."

Kirby didn't bother to answer. He turned to look at the mountain bike. As promised, the old man had added a red ribbon and bow. Kirby carried it out and carefully placed it into his trunk. He turned back and the old man handed him the rifle.

"I calibrated the sights. It shoots dead-on. Up to a hundred and eighty yards, there's no need to elevate. Silver bullets don't travel that good, anyway. They tend to tumble quicker. Wait till it's close enough to see its eyes."

Kirby placed the rifle against the back wall of the trunk and turned back for the ammo clips. The polished silver bullets had polished brass casings.

"These look fantastic."

"I did polish them, yes. Maybe they'll travel better."

"Thanks." Kirby jammed both full clips into the fabric storage pocket on the right side of the trunk and closed it.

No, no. A fourteen-wheeler rolled past the inn and turned down a snow-covered side street. Mona's daddy sat behind the wheel. No mistake.

Kirby turned toward the driver's side of his car.

The old man grabbed his arm. "One more thing." His stair felt cold, dead serious. "Silver won't flatten out on impact like lead. It'll travel straight through."

"That's okay. I'm a good shot. I'll shoot it in the head or base of the skull."

"Won't help, you know."

"What?"

"Silver bullets. That's just a superstitious myth."

"Then why did you make them up? Why didn't you say something?"

The old guy shrugged. "I guess I'm superstitious."

Chapter Twenty-One

Daylight didn't add much to Kirby's confidence, driving back up Sonora Pass Highway, "The devil's highway." Dense clouds still hung low over narrow strips of asphalt patches and repairs he'd somehow never before noticed. Knowing there would be no other traffic didn't help.

Crossing the summit and turning downhill toward her valley brought gratification. Relief, really. He put the Bentley into drive and accelerated down a well-paved and salted strip of road, feeling his muscles and nerves unwind.

He entered the small village and passed Carolyn's bank and the country store at 12:11 p.m. About a quarter of a mile down the road to her place, a pickup truck left the village and followed him. He slowed to turn up her driveway and looked back.

The pickup truck turned onto a snow-covered sideroad, two guys inside. A calf stood in the truck bed, maybe the problem she'd been complaining about. He smiled. *I'll take care of that.* After all, he was a Kirby, something he'd almost forgotten to be proud of.

He drove up her driveway, crossed the crest, and drove down the right side of her wide driveway toward her barn. He rounded the piled snow in the center and drove back up to the house. Parking in this direction, he could see anything that might approach from up in the direction of that sideroad. He shut off his father's car, got out, and walked around the rear toward the front steps.

What the . . . Red flowers poked through snow in front of her high porch. *Great!* He picked a stock and smelled it. "Phew." They smelled like skunk. He climbed the stone steps, tossed the flowers off the porch, and knocked on the door. "Phew." His fingers still stank.

The kid opened the door and frowned. *Just like his father.* He'd only once seen John's eyes that angry; their argument about the lost document in Kirby's bottom drawer. Kirby had taken two steps back and feigned ignorance.

The kid's dog pushed out onto the porch to sniff Kirby's legs and feet.

Kirby didn't move a muscle. "Merry Christmas, kid. Is your mother in?"

"Mom." The kid slammed the door in Kirby's face and left his dog outside.

The dog sniffed the hand that had picked the flowers, sneezed, and shook his head.

Kirby said, "You've got that right." The dog trotted down the front steps and lifted its leg on Kirby's back tire.

"Oh, man." For the first time, Kirby got a good look at the scrape on the right rear fender of the Bentley.

Carolyn opened the front door and smiled politely. Her normally gorgeous eyes did not smile.

"Merry Christmas. Am I forgiven?"

"Of course. Come in." She sounded as cold as dry ice.

The dog pushed past him and stood in the entry, staring up at Kirby.

Kirby walked past the dog and she closed the door. She said, "Have you eaten? You look awful." She sounded sure of herself, again. This place had definitely changed her.

"Awful?" Kirby slumped. "Thanks."

"Didn't you get any sleep last night?" She turned away and led him down into the living room.

"Not much. I still feel rotten about what happened last night." *Stupid kid.*

She didn't bother to respond or even look his way, walking toward the kitchen.

He said, "Listen, I noticed a truck turning off the main road. They had a calf in the back."

She glanced back and shrugged, not interested in that either.

They needed to talk about what had to be done. "Now might be a good time to have a talk with them."

She stopped in the middle of her kitchen and turned to face him, thinking about it. She stepped sideways, grabbed a nice sheepskin coat from the back of her kitchen door, and led Kirby back outside.

He put her into his car, walked around the back, got in, and drove back onto the village road. He parked in front of the turnoff, just in time.

The pickup truck rolled downhill toward them, following a well-traveled path through deep snow.

Kirby said, "Let me do the talking."

She said nothing.

The truck stopped near his father's car. Kirby Carolyn got out. Two men got out of the truck and walked slowly toward them. The bigger man wore a tan cowboy hat with a badge. The skinny man wore a weathered, black cowboy hat. Both wore sheepskin coats.

Kirby immediately regretted leaving his wool coat in the car.

"Merry Christmas, ma'am." The bigger man took off his sheriff's hat and smiled. He didn't look at Kirby, only at her. Both of them looked only at her. Who could blame them? She was a beautiful lady.

Kirby said, "Mrs. Potter has asked me to look into this matter. She's already emailed me your so-called irrevocable trust deed."

"Ma'am, there's a moon tonight." The sheriff wouldn't look at Kirby. "I thought we had all of this settled." He glanced at Kirby, not being respectful.

"Not by a long shot." Kirby stepped up to the sheriff, eye to eye.

The skinny guy took off his black hat and stepped toward Carolyn, not acknowledging Kirby's presence. "Remember, we got a special Christmas service this afternoon." They both put their hats back on, turned away, and climbed back into their truck.

Kirby would have loved slapping the skinny guy around but the sheriff was too big, the type that would slap back. "What are they doing? We're not finished here."

Carolyn pulled Kirby's arm toward his father's car. "Mr. Kirby, Jason and I both want to go to church today. We can talk about this later?"

Kirby turned and spread his arms. "What the heck, Carolyn? Why did we bother to come out here? Why did I drive all the way up here?"

"I thought we might talk them into moving this business someplace else, but I guess not. They're pretty set in their ways."

"So am I." He put her into his father's car.

KIRBY FELT BETTER AFTER eating a salad, waiting for her and the kid to dress for church. He rinsed his dish and put it into the dishwasher, went into the living room, and found them waiting in the entry. "What the . . ." They looked like Quakers, or Shakers, or Amish, or something of the kind. In her black dress and bonnet, and the kid's black suit and wide-brimmed hat, they both looked the kind.

Nobody spoke, driving back up to the village. Just before they reached the store, she said, "Turn right, here."

Kirby turned and saw the small chapel behind two giant redwood trees. "What a neat little church." He turned in and parked next to the sheriff's truck. A string of saddled horses had been tied to a rail fence in back. "This whole valley is a pretty nifty place. I'm beginning to understand why you're thinking about staying up here, especially after I kill that thing."

He got out and walked around his father's car, looking up at the high-pitched roof, where a flock of yellow breasted birds fluttered and perched. He shook his head in wonder, hard to believe in the cold of winter.

Carolyn climbed out before he got there and opened the back door for the kid.

He said, "Only problem is, there's nothing to do."

She didn't care.

The kid carried a leather-bound Bible to the front of the church and waited.

Kirby stepped around him. "Here, let me." Kirby opened the heavy, hand carved door and followed them inside.

The church had definitely been handcrafted, the pews, the hewn stone walls, the wood beams and inset glass. "Very nice."

They all looked like a bunch of Quakers, turning to watch them enter. They nodded and smiled at Carolyn and the kid, making Kirby feel like the stranger he was. He followed them to the front where their places had evidently been reserved.

Carolyn and the kid sat.

The sheriff and his skinny friend made room and Kirby sat. He'd never felt more out of place.

A gaunt, disheveled priest stood at the podium and said, "Now that we're all here, let us take a moment to welcome our visitor. I believe this is Mrs. Potter's lawyer from down below."

They all nodded. None smiled. Nobody ever smiled at lawyers. Kirby was happy not to be one.

The priest said, "Being the celebrated birthday of our Savior, we'll make this special meeting a short one, as is our custom. I know we all want to be safely inside our homes before the rise of the moon."

Strange. Tom Kirby instantly had no interest in what the priest had to say, making it a good time to look around.

A tall Indian stood in back, slender as a post, another Paiute. His weathered face made his age difficult to judge, staring at Kirby like a long-time acquaintance he couldn't quite place.

Other members of the small church stared at the priest, at their Bibles, back and forth, while the priest prattled on.

Carolyn and the kid shared their Bible, looking up and down like everybody else.

The priest's voice stabbed back into Kirby's hangover. "This is Lucifer's planet, his dwelling place, as stated in the Gospel of Mathew, during the Lord's temptation. His confederates lurk in the dark places but have no foothold unto righteousness. So, let us carry righteousness as a light to guide us into this night. Let God's light guide us unto good deeds toward one another. Let us carry that righteousness and light into the darkness like a gleaming torch." The priest scanned his congregation.

They all stood and Kirby climbed to his feet.

The priest said, "May God protect us all through this night, when the moon is full and bright."

Everybody said, "Amen," and started singing, *Silent Night, Holy Night.* It sounded nice, considering the absence of an organ or piano. They finished their Christmas carol and filed out through the main door and through a side door, not speaking to one another, not one Christmas greeting. They probably saw too much of each other.

The sheriff stopped at the entrance and looked down at Carolyn. She said, "Merry Christmas, Phil," nodded and smiled.

He smiled and put his hat on with a quick nod in Kirby's direction.

The others had cleared the parking lot before Kirby got the Bentley unlocked, watching the sheriff's truck turn right, away from the main road.

The horseback crowd moved away through the snow in all directions. Their black costumes against the white snow and gray sky creating a chilling sense of danger.

Leaving the parking lot, Carolyn pointed to a long, low building built of logs. "On a normal Sunday, they'd all be lined up next door to meet you. We always share potluck on moon Sunday's."

"Moon Sundays?"

"Not today. It's Christmas Day." She might actually believe he wanted to meet these hicks. "Everybody's anxious to get home. It's getting pretty late."

The kid said, "Stop the car."

Kirby stopped in the middle of the road.

"It's John Crow." The kid opened the back door and said, "Get in, John."

The tall Indian removed his hat, climbed into the back, and closed the door.

Carolyn said, "I'm sorry, John. I forgot all about you." She turned to Kirby. "This is John Crow, one of the men I told you about. Can we give him a ride? He was supposed to ride with us but I forgot. He's coming to Christmas Dinner."

"Sure. Of course." Kirby looked back. "You're Paiute, right? One with the Shoshone nation."

The Indian nodded, offering a slight smile.

Kirby smiled at Carolyn, having demonstrated his racial tolerance.

The ride back from the village was as quiet as the ride had been going in. When they reached Carolyn's house at 2:40 p.m., she said, "I need to get the roast into the oven."

Everybody but Kirby went into the house.

He took the mountain bike out of his trunk and carried it inside. *Great.* Everybody had gone into the kitchen. He crossed the living room and placed the bike in front of the Christmas tree where the kid would be sure to see it. His gift belonged in front of the other junk, no matter how nicely they'd been wrapped. This bike in front of the tree created a Christmas card image, something he might put on a future magazine cover.

He pulled out his I-Phone, viewed the angles, and took several shots. His final shot was his best smiling selfie, considering his hungover condition.

Somebody knocked on the front door behind him.

The kid and his dog ran out of the kitchen, charged across the living room, and bolted up the steps into the entry. Light flooded the entry and the kid said, "Willis! Merry Christmas!"

Kirby wanted to walk over and meet this Willis hick, but he didn't. He put his phone away and stayed planted in front of the tree.

"Merry Christmas, Jason." The hick spoke with a deep, full voice. "Here, this is for you."

"Oh, Willis, that's awesome."

The guy said, "I'll take it into the barn. Hello, Barnabas." The dog grumbled and moaned softly, obviously saying hello to a friend.

Carolyn stood in the kitchen doorway, wiping her hands on her apron, smiling toward the entry like a teenage girl on her first date.

No, no. That would not do.

The front door closed, nobody came down from the entry, and Carolyn turned back into the kitchen.

Who is this guy?

Kirby crossed to the entry but the kid and his dog had both gone outside. He turned into her office and fixed himself a tumbler of rye whiskey. He took a long pull and refilled his glass.

The front door opened and a weathered, muscular man stood in the doorway. He stared at Kirby, hard to judge his age. He carried a large slice of varnished tree trunk with some kind of mechanism mounted inside. It looked heavy.

Kirby had no intention to help this clod buster.

The kid and his dog followed the hick in and the kid closed the door.

Kirby pasted on his most polite smile, rounded her desk, and stood in the office doorway. "Merry Christmas." Kirby offered his right hand. "I'm Tom Kirby, Carolyn's publisher."

The guy stared at Kirby, not smiling, not nodding, and not saying hello.

Feeling stupid, Kirby withdrew his hand.

Both of this guy's arms were full of burled, varnished tree trunk. He couldn't shake hands if he wanted to.

Kirby felt completely out of his element. He wiped his sweaty hand on the back of his pants, watching the kid and his dog follow this hick down into the living room, without as much as a glance at Kirby. Kirby turned down the steps, wishing he'd stayed in L.A.

"Mom, look! Willis made you a clock."

"For the house, really." This hick, Willis, even spoke with a hick's accent. He looked uncomfortable around Carolyn.

Carolyn and the Indian stood near the fireplace, both admiring the slice of tree trunk. The hick set the heavy looking thing on the hearth and turned toward Kirby, a twitch of a smile, and extended his right hand. "Merry Christmas. Name's Willis Donner." His handshake felt stiff, not used to meeting people.

Kirby smiled, let go, and sipped whiskey.

Carolyn said, "Anyone else want a Christmas cocktail?"

Nobody else was interested in drinking.

She shot Kirby a wary glance.

He took another sip, trying to calm the bristling hair on the back of his neck. He'd never felt so out of place.

Willis went back outside with the kid, his dog, and the Indian.

Kirby followed at a distance and waited for the front door to close, before ducking back into her office to refill his drink. Fresh drink in hand, he strolled into the kitchen to watch Carolyn.

She placed a stack of dishes on a large kitchen table set into a large bay window with a nice view. He hadn't noticed her incredible kitchen when he'd wolfed down the salad. He said, "This is a really nice spot." He stood near the table and looked down across a meadow, some distance below the house. Feed bins had been positioned near a winding brook. Sleek, fat, black cattle ate from the bins. "What do you feed your beef," like he cared.

She set the table, keeping her distance. "It's a special corn feed. Olen Jacobsen has it delivered up from Sonora, once a week. All the local ranchers use it. Our Cattle buyers recommended it."

"Is that roast beef I smell in the oven?"

"Yes." She smiled politely, not with her eyes. "Sorry you don't like our beef."

"It's not your beef. I've got a lot on my mind. I started thinking last night and lost my appetite. Now, I'm starving. That salad probably saved my life." He said it playfully, desperate for her smile. It did not come.

She said, "It looked and smelled so good last night, I'm trying her recipe. I had to go online to find out how to apply the rock salt. It's only been on there since early this morning. I hope it comes out okay." She looked at the Regulator Clock on the wall, 4:03. "It's already time to turn off the oven." She crossed the kitchen and turned it off.

Someone had come back into the house, making noise in the living room. Kirby crossed to the kitchen doorway, sipped whiskey, and watched.

The hick climbed a wooden ladder with his large, gnarled slice of tree root propped on his shoulder. Maybe he'd fall and break his hick neck, turning awkwardly to hang the stupid thing.

Nope.

The hick hung it easily on a blackened bolt, nearly invisible in all that stonework.

"Made for each other," said Kirby. The gnarled stump fit into the pattern of the hewn stone as if the stonework had been done in preparation to receive it. The pattern radiated outward in all directions with the sawn stump at the center, and a clock at the center of that. Kirby admired it, a rare admission for Tom Kirby.

Willis said, "I had this redwood root when I built the house. I always planned to put it here for Mary Lou, the boy's great grandmother. Then she went back to the earth before I finished the clock."

Learning that this guy had built this house changed Kirby's mind about him. This was a definite craftsman, someone to worry about. He was that backwoods kind of man that some women find attractive.

Kirby wished he'd stayed in L.A.

Carolyn pushed past Kirby into the living room as Willis climbed down. They stood shoulder to shoulder looking up at the clock, ignoring Kirby. She said, "Oh, Willis, it's wonderful. Thank you."

Kirby sipped whiskey, nearly empty.

"Still need to get it running." Willis lurched toward the entry.

She said, "Where are Jason and John?"

"They're fitting Jason's new saddle to Stoner."

"New saddle?"

"Yes, ma'am." Willis stopped on the entry steps. "I made it up special. Figured he needed one of his own he could grow into."

Kirby wondered, was this hick a house builder, a clock maker, or a saddle smith? Or, was he just a backwoods scammer? How could Carolyn and the kid know if he was telling the truth, about anything?

Carolyn said, "Well, tell them to come and eat their salads. Dinner will be ready in less than an hour."

Willis nodded and went outside.

She pushed past Kirby like he wasn't there.

He said, "Did you see the Christmas present I got for your kid?"

She stopped in the doorway and looked, maybe not seeing it. "No." She wasn't being deliberately rude, just icy. She leaned around Kirby and found it. Her eyes brightened. "Oh, I didn't see you bring that in. That looks like a good one. I'm sure he'll love it." She smiled at Kirby for the first time that day, eyes and all.

He loved her bright eyes. "About last night. I didn't mean to . . . I mean . . ." He couldn't find the words because he hadn't actually done anything wrong. If not for her kid . . .

She said, "Let's forget about it. Okay?"

"I'd like that." He'd love it if she could forget. He followed her into the kitchen, sucking ice cubes from her glass tumbler. "There's something else. On the way back to Bridgeport, I had to make a pit stop, you know, dispense some fluids. Anyway, I lost my wallet. I've looked everywhere."

She looked at him, willing to listen.

"I don't have any way of getting back to L.A. Think you could loan me a couple of hundred bucks for gas?"

The others came back inside and the dog was already standing in the kitchen between Kirby and Carolyn.

She nodded and smiled, no problem about the money.

"Great. Thank you."

When the kid walked into the kitchen, she said, "Jason, look what Mr. Kirby brought you for Christmas."

The kid went to the kitchen doorway and looked toward the tree. "Cool. Thank you, Mr. Kirby."

Kirby strolled to the kitchen doorway, sucking ice, trying to be friends with her kid.

The kid only cared about what the hick was doing.

The guy set a wooden box on the hearth and eased past Kirby. His steely eyes cut straight through Kirby, without being unfriendly.

The hair on Kirby's neck stood up. Something about this guy brought back that feeling of danger. Kirby didn't like it.

The kid and the Indian followed the hick into the kitchen and into a room behind the kitchen door.

Kirby looked inside a large pantry, where all three stood at a large wash sink near a washing machine and dryer, all scrubbing their hands and arms with what looked like Lava soap.

Nobody used that soap anymore.

After they dried their hands and filed out, Kirby went in and washed his hands. It was Lava soap. He left his empty glass in the pantry and returned to the kitchen.

The others were already seated on the window benches. Carolyn sat nearest the kitchen counter and stove, all of them waiting for Kirby.

He sat in a wicker backed chair at the head of the table. When the others lowered their heads, Kirby followed their outdated custom. Carolyn and the kid each took one of Kirby's hands, like they actually believed in this nonsense.

Kirby felt even more out-of-place, if that was possible.

The kid said, "Thank you, Lord, for your wonderful blessings and you're your amazing grace. Protect and keep us safe at night, when the moon is full and bright. Bless this house and all who are in it. Bless this food, that it might nourish us. And bless us, that we might better serve Thee. In Jesus name we pray, Amen." The others said, "Amen."

Not me.

Being hungry for two days, Kirby picked up a bottle of ranch dressing and flooded his second salad.

The hick, the Indian, and the kid ate theirs without dressing.

"Excuse me." Carolyn went to the stove to stir a steaming pot of vegetables. She had not made a salad for herself.

"Not having any salad?" Kirby wondered if he might be eating hers.

She said, "I eat mine while I'm making everyone else's." Her smile looked warm and friendly. Maybe he still had a shot.

The others finished their salads, nodded at Kirby, and went back into the living room.

Kirby collected and set the empty salad plates in the sink, rinsed ranch dressing from his mouth, and touched shoulders with Carolyn.

She stepped away without a glance.

Kirby turned and followed the others back into the living room.

The hick stood high up on the ladder, pointing at a wooden box on the hearth like they all knew what he wanted.

The Indian grabbed one of three counterweights and handed it to the hick.

The hick hung it from the center chain and reached for another.

The Indian handed him the second weight and he connected it to the left-side chain. After hanging the third counterweight, the hick looked at the kid.

The kid looked at his Swiss Army watch, the birthday gift from Kirby, loose as a charm bracelet on the kid's wrist. "4:32."

The hick set the clock and gave the pendulum a shove. The tick-tock of the clock was barely perceptible, with an uneven pulse.

The Indian handed up a long, slender screwdriver like it had all been planned.

Willis turned screws at the top of the pendulum mechanism, adjusting the balance. A couple of turns with the screwdriver and the clock mechanism came into balance.

Willis closed the glass cover, handed the Indian the screwdriver, and climbed down.

"Oh, Willis," said Carolyn, standing near Kirby. "That's wonderful. Thank you. Come on, we just have time." She walked to the Christmas tree, pulled an envelope from between the limbs, and handed it to Kirby. Her smile looked genuine. "We didn't know what to get you so we bought you a vacation to Tahiti."

No, no. Tahiti had become too commercial, too yesterday, and too French. Kirby hated the place. "For two, I hope."

"Of course." She wasn't looking at him. "It's good for a year. We got you a booking at the Princess Resort. You need to call a month in advance." She smiled shyly at Kirby and pushed the kid toward the tree. "You do the rest, honey. Mommy needs to get dinner on the table."

Kirby folded the envelope into his pocket and followed her. He stopped in the kitchen doorway where he could look both ways, trying to keep this private. "Any chance of you joining me in Tahiti?"

She lifted the lid on the steaming pot and stirred vegetables, thinking about it before turning to face him. "You know I can't do that. I have too many responsibilities here." It sounded final.

"Thank you, Jason," said the hick, and Kirby turned back to the living room. The hick stood near the tree, looking at a piece of smooth, uncut bark. A fish painted on a piece of paper had been varnished onto the naturally smooth face. It looked nice. The hick looked down at the kid. "Painted this yourself, did you?"

"Huh," the kid's word for yes. He smiled, puffed up with pride. He handed a package to the Indian, treating him like family, all of them too close for Kirby's comfort zone.

"For me?" The Indian sounded surprised. "Looks like a book. How'd you know I can read?"

"We noticed how old and frayed yours was." The kid literally beamed, watching the Indian carefully remove tape and unfold the wrapper. He opened the box and showed Kirby and the hick a leather bound, New English Bible, Oxford Press. A nice edition with an embossed Celtic Cross.

The kid smiled at Kirby, the kind of insincere smile that tells someone to get stuffed. He brushed past on his way into the kitchen and delivered a small package to Carolyn.

Carolyn's mouth dropped, eyes wide. She dried her hands on her apron. "What's this?" She snatched the present and tore it open. She hesitated, looked into the box, then set the box on the kitchen counter and carefully lifted out a rolled strip of leather. She held a silver buckle and let the leather unwind.

Kirby said, "Very nice."

Carolyn smiled and held up a beautifully crafted cowboy belt. The tooling of her name and the floral pattern looked expensive.

Kirby looked down at the kid. "Where did you buy that?" He wanted one like it.

The kid spun around and said, "I made it. Me and Willis."

Carolyn rushed from the kitchen, ran through the living room, up the entry steps, and disappeared into the entry foyer.

For an awkward 5 minutes that seemed like 5 hours, Kirby and the hick exchanged icy stares.

Carolyn returned wearing a red silk blouse tucked into tight fitting blue jeans. Her new belt went nicely with a pair of slightly scuffed cowboy boots. "Dinner's ready." She led them all into the kitchen.

What is that? Kirby had discovered a new appreciation for horseback riding. Carolyn's figure looked as solid as any woman he'd ever known, including Mona.

The others slid onto the window benches and Kirby sat in his wicker backed chair at the head of the table.

Carolyn set a bowl of steaming greens on the table and smiled at Kirby, nodding toward the open oven. Kirby stood and she handed him two pot holders. He lifted the roasting pan with a heavy seven-rib roast from the oven and set it on top of the stove. She pushed him aside and stuck two large forks into the ends, using them to carry the roast from the pan to a large, silver, serving platter.

Her eyes smiled. "Can you do the honors?" Kirby obediently carried the roast to the table and set it in the cleared area in front of his chair. It looked burned to a crisp, charred black. She handed him a carving knife and matching fork.

Kirby said, "Wow!" The very sharp knife sliced off the crusted end with ease. Juices flowed from the pink meat inside. "Who wants the end cut?"

Nobody.

He let it fall off the fork onto the platter. He carved a half inch thick, medium rare slice and put it on Carolyn's plate. The way it worked, going around the table, he and the hick each wound up with a rib. Kirby couldn't have planned it better than that.

Willis cut off and passed his rib bone to the kid. They shared some kind of unspoken communication, like a father and son story in one of his children's magazines. Kirby had always questioned the authenticity of that type of communication. He and his father had never known anything like it.

The new clock in the living room chimed five times, a crisp and clear sounding bell. Very nice.

He sat and sliced a mouthful of prime beef, chewed it down, and smiled. "Carolyn, this is delicious. I never knew you could cook." He grabbed a baked potato, opened it, and knifed in a slab of butter. He added sour cream and chopped spring onions, salt and pepper, mixed it up, and took a bite. "Um, this is perfect." He ate like a bootcamp Marine. "I look forward to some mother and kid cooking articles." He raised a brow in her direction.

She smiled a little, more like a blush.

Outside the bay window, getting dark, a steady snowfall had begun. He said, "You guys need a ride home? It's getting dark and it's starting to snow."

"You can't give them a ride." The kid threw Kirby a condescending sneer. "They both live above the falls." He poked a thumb over his shoulder, pointing out the bay window.

Kirby couldn't see past ten feet out there, already snowing hard. Speaking to Carolyn, he said, "This is really a beautiful place. How's the fishing in summer?"

"Awesome," said the kid, eying Kirby's beef rib. He'd gnawed the hick's rib to the bone. He hadn't touched the thin slice Kirby had placed on his plate.

The rib was Kirby's favorite part. He reluctantly freed the meaty rib and said, "Trade you for that thin slice?" The kid held up his plate and Kirby made the switch.

"Thank you, Mr. Kirby." The kid grabbed an approving smile from Carolyn and chewed off a chunk.

Kirby waited for Carolyn's eye contact. "This valley's a great spot for a resort. You have plenty of room for a nice hotel. You know, skiing in the winter, trout fishing in the summer, maybe a little hunting in between. It's all private property, right?"

Emptiness filled the air and the table fell awkwardly silent. That feeling of danger returned. He again felt out of place but decided to go forward anyway.

Even the kid had stopped eating, giving Kirby his father's angry eye.

For the first time, Kirby missed John Potter.

Carolyn smiled shyly at the hick, not looking at Kirby. "Well, yes, Jason actually owns this ranch and everything else. The other ranchers and villagers own their properties, but Jason holds the timber and mineral rights for the whole valley."

The hick didn't know that Carolyn was looking at him. He sat quietly, staring down at his plate. He'd eaten almost none of it. He looked up, pinning Kirby's eyes. "What do you suppose might happen to this place?"

"This house?" Kirby's confidence grew. "It can stay as it is. Or, she could turn it into a lodge for special guests. She could find some very high paying visitors with a place like this."

"Willis isn't talking about our house," said the kid, still giving Kirby the angry eye. "He's talking about this whole valley."

Kirby said, "There's plenty of room right on this ranch. You could even keep your cattle. There's plenty of room. This place is too beautiful to keep to yourselves."

"You think a resort hotel won't change this place, all those people, all their trash, all their smoke spewing cars?" The hick's icy-blue stare raised the hairs on the back of Kirby's neck.

Kirby had never liked hicks, always stubbornly holding to their hick ways. He finally understood why John Potter had been so stubborn. He leaned into the hick's icy stare. Kirby said, "I was speaking with Mrs. Potter, not with you."

The hick didn't flinch.

Carolyn said, "Mr. Kirby," still looking at the hick. ". . . everyone in this house is free to speak their mind." She looked at Kirby, cold and resolute. "Everyone."

Kirby flinched back. "Ouch! Sorry, I just . . ." *Idiots.* He stuffed his face with baked potato.

"Willis is our friend," said the kid, looking at this stupid hick instead of Kirby. "He built this place. He has the right to say whatever he wants." He looked at the Indian. "So does John."

Looking at Kirby, smiling a little, Carolyn said, "So does Mr. Kirby." She smiled warmly at the kid. "Jason's the one you need to ask." She looked back at Kirby. "The family trust goes to the first-born male heir in perpetuity. This ranch, the bank, the mineral and timber rights, they all belong to Jason."

"Okay, okay. It was just a thought." The kid would never go for it.

The hick set his knife and fork down, his food barely touched, looking out the bay window at growing darkness and falling snow.

This discussion could wait until Kirby was alone with Carolyn.

The new clock chimed once; 5:30 p.m.

Willis said, "Getting late. Moon'll be up by ten. I'd better get going." He looked at Jason. "Be sure to bar both doors." He threw Kirby a brief, icy grin, slid from the booth, and stood, waiting for the Indian.

The Indian nodded, slid out, and stood.

Speaking to Carolyn, the hick said, "Mighty toothsome victuals, ma'am. Thank you for the invite. Good Christmas." He scrubbed the kid's head and smiled.

Toothsome? What an illiterate boob.

The Indian said, "Very fine supper, ma'am. Thank you."

Carolyn and the kid got up and they all went into the living room.

The dog woke from under the table and bumped past Kirby, following the others.

Kirby forked in his last piece of beef, stood, and followed them into the living room.

The others already stood in the entry.

Kirby walked across the room to where he could see and hear them.

The hick and the Indian pulled on their coats, the Indian put on his broad-brimmed black hat, and both men stepped outside.

The blast of cold air cleared Kirby's senses and his resentment toward this stupid, hick, clod buster grew. Changing this place into a money machine made nothing but good sense. It had too much to offer. It was perfect.

He wrapped his sport coat tight to his chest and climbed into the entry. Cold air from the open door chilled him to the bone. Her and her obnoxious kid could wave all the goodbyes they wanted, them and their stupid dog.

"Phew!" The odor of skunk jammed into his nostrils. "Those stinking flowers."

He turned into her office, got a fresh glass, some ice, opened a fresh bottle of rye, and filled the glass. He tossed back a swig and returned to the entry.

Carolyn and the kid came inside and closed the door.

Kirby shivered and smiled. "Thank you."

The kid glared at Kirby and said, "You ruined our Christmas dinner." He shoved past Kirby with his dog and Kirby could still smell those stinking flowers. The stench soured his stomach. He took another mouthful of rye whiskey and swallowed. It didn't help.

Carolyn gave Kirby an apologetic smile but she probably agreed with her little brat monster. "I don't like him talking like that. He should be more respectful."

Yeah.

She turned down into the living room where the kid looked at the bicycle like he wanted to kick it. She said, "Jason, stop that." She marched across the living room and spun him around. "You apologize to Mr. Kirby."

"No, I won't." The little monster's anger more than matched hers, staring at her like he wanted to kick her too.

She spun him around and swatted his bottom, instantly flexing her wrist in pain.

His dog didn't like it. He growled at her.

She said, "You shut up."

The dog growled again.

None of this was Kirby's fault and he needed to get back on track. "Carolyn, it's okay. He doesn't need to apologize to me. It's his Christmas and it's his house."

She said, "He's getting too big for his britches." She held both of the kid's shoulders at arm's length, staring into his anger. "Now, you apologize to Mr. Kirby. He should be allowed to speak freely in our home like everybody else, don't you think?"

The kid looked at his feet and leaned back against her grip, thinking about what she'd said. Without looking at Kirby, he said, "Okay. I'm sorry."

Her stupid little monster didn't mean it but Kirby needed to play the forgiving father. "That's alright, Jason. I apologize for any discomfort my comments might have caused." They both seemed to appreciate that one.

Kirby remembered. "There's something I've been meaning to do." He climbed into the entry, set his whiskey on the table, and went outside. Snow fell so thick he couldn't see past the glow of the porchlight.

Those stinking flowers were protected under the deep roof overhang and it was cold. He hurried down the steps, yanked up a bunch of flowers, and looked up.

Carolyn's hands covered her mouth and her forehead furrowed with disbelief.

He stretched up to let her smell the stinking things.

She coughed and spun away.

He said, "Exactly!" He yanked up more flowers but most broke off at the cold, hard ground, where the roots might survive. The stinking flowers might come back.

"What are you doing?" The kid yanked at Kirby's shoulder from the porch.

"These flowers stink." Kirby pushed a handful into the kid's face. "Here, take a whiff."

The kid wrinkled his nose and leaned back. "I don't care. Willis planted those."

"So what?" All of these stinking flowers had already been broken, yanked, and tossed into the driveway, where falling snow quickly covered them.

"I hate you." The kid kicked at Kirby, missed, and slammed past his mother into the house. His dog followed him up the stairs.

Good. Kirby could finally be alone with her.

"I don't know what's gotten into him." She crossed her arms and backed into the warmth of the open doorway.

"He's getting to that age where he needs a father." Kirby smiled. *Perfect.*

She watched him climb the front steps, hopefully thinking about it. Her new clock chimed once, 6:30 p.m., already totally dark. "You have a flashlight? It's time to get that calf into your barn."

"Maybe we should leave it alone. They have a system."

"System? Ha!" He shivered and climbed onto the porch, not a place for lengthy conversations. "Can you show me where it is?"

"It's already dark and it's cold. We'd better put on some heavier coats." They went inside and she closed the door. She led him through the living room, around the kitchen door, and into the pantry. She turned on the light, crossed her arms, and looked at Kirby.

Several sheepskin coats hung from pegs on a wall plaque near the washing machine.

Kirby turned to the sink and washed his stinking hands with Lava soap, dried them, and turned back.

She handed him one of the bigger coats.

He put it on, soft and warm. It smelled of leather.

She pulled on a smaller coat. "What time is it?"

"Your new clock just chimed." He looked at his watch, making sure. "It's 6:32. Why?"

"We still have plenty of time." She grabbed a flashlight from a nearby shelf and tested it before putting it into her coat pocket. "I'm not sure this is a good idea." She slowly led him back to the entry, thinking about it. "I don't want any trouble with the sheriff."

"He'll be fine after I kill it, whatever it is." Kirby opened the front door and pressed her shoulder.

"You'll be sorry." The kid stood at the top of the stairs with his dog.

Kirby couldn't see his face but he sounded angry. *Little monster.*

"I'm going to deal with this thing and keep you two safe."

"Mom?"

Stupid kid. Kirby pushed Carolyn outside and closed the door. "He'll be fine. You'll see."

She hesitated on the porch and looked back at the door.

For the first time, Kirby noticed the chiseled design. "That guy, Willis? He's a craftsman. I'll give him that much."

She nodded and smiled.

He pushed her again and she started down, leading him into falling, knee deep snow. She pulled out the flashlight, switched it on, and led him around the corner of the garage into the woods.

They traversed uphill through the forest, left turn and right. His legs and feet were already freezing wet.

The large, open space above the trees was covered by at least two feet of snow, wet and cold. They followed a path cut by Willis and the Indian for a short distance, then she turned and they plowed through deeper snow.

In the quiet, Kirby heard a waterfall, still at a distance. He couldn't see it.

Six inches of fresh snow had covered a hard, thin crust of ice that cut uncomfortably into Kirby's thighs like cold steel, painful in his thin trousers.

He wished he'd stayed in L.A.

Steam rose from a large, flat rock. The calf had been tied to a ring in the center. Falling snow melted on contact and birds nested around the edges. *Unbelievable.*

Kirby walked onto the rock and brushed ice off of his soaking-wet pants. "That feels good." The soles of his Bruno Magli shoes were thin enough to feel the heat. "Maybe we should sit down for a minute." *Warm our butts.*

"No." She held the flashlight on a heavy bronze ring.

Kirby knelt and untied the knot. "You have some hot springs up here? I think you already told me."

"Yes, we have several. There's a cabin built around one of them, way down there." She fanned the flashlight into falling snow and empty space, aiming somewhere past her house.

"Holy . . ." Birds swarmed up from around the rock and darted across the path of her flashlight, barely visible through falling snow. "That's creepy!"

"The birds? They're meadowlarks. They stay here all winter, near the warmth of this rock. They make beautiful music."

Kirby led the calf, following her, knowing more than ever that he was right. "Carolyn, I wish you'd think about doing something commercial with this place. It's gorgeous. Don't keep it to yourself."

She ignored him.

Following their tracks back down the trail wasn't as bad as coming up. By the time they walked onto her driveway, eight inches of additional snow had fallen, coming down even harder.

"It's up here." She climbed onto a stump near the barn door, reached into a niche, and pulled out a skeleton key. She jumped down, unlocked, and opened the out-swinging door. A deep, overhanging roof protected them from falling snow.

Kirby led the calf into the barn, much warmer than outside. A big, potbellied stove sat in the center.

She turned on a light and followed him in. "Put him in that open stall. I'll get him some straw and water."

When they got back into the house, she went upstairs to check on the kid. He drained his drink and ducked into her office for fresh ice and a double shot.

The living room fireplace had been loaded with logs, twigs, and kindling. A box of long stem, wooden matches sat on the mantle. He lit the fire.

The flames grew quickly and Kirby backed away from the heat. He sat on the couch, sipped whiskey, and looked at the book he'd published for her. Maybe this trip would work out yet. If he could kill the beast, he might earn her trust, her affection. He hoped.

"Oh, thank you." She turned down the short stairs from the entry and nodded toward the fireplace. "I was just coming to do that." She peeled her sheepskin coat and stuck out her hand, motioning for his coat.

He set his drink down, stood, and slipped out of the coat. She carried them into the kitchen and disappeared.

"I'll need that in another hour or two." He sat and sipped whiskey.

She came back with his coat and laid it across the hearth, open toward the heat.

He stared at her backside. Her whole body looked hard in those tight-fitting jeans, the perfect cowgirl.

She leaned toward the kitchen and looked at Kirby. "Want some desert? Olen brought us a cheesecake from the Cheesecake Factory." She kept her distance, wary of the couch, wary of him.

Yeah. He didn't want cheesecake right then. "So, tell me about this thing I'm going to kill."

Her eyes glazed over, maybe not wanting to think about it. "Cheesecake?"

What the heck? "Okay. A thin slice." Kirby stood and watched her tightly fitted backside return to the kitchen.

He set his drink on the table and hurried outside. He brushed snow from the top of the trunk, opened the driver's door easily, and pressed the trunk release button. The electric motor opened the trunk and he put the rifle and ammunition clips into the passenger side. Already shivering from the cold, he closed the passenger door, hurried to the back, closed the trunk, closed the driver's door, and hurried back inside.

He sat on the couch and watched her return with two plates of cheesecake. She set both plates on the coffee table and looked into him. "Want some coffee?"

"Sure. Why not?"

She returned to the kitchen and he drained his whiskey. He wasn't a cheesecake fan but this looked good, slumped over, moist.

He got up and stood in the kitchen doorway, watching her load a serving tray, two cups, spoons, sugar and cream, almost ready.

His stomach churned and he returned to the couch, not waiting anymore. The cheesecake had a smooth texture, very tasty.

She brought in their coffees and set the tray on the table.

He said, "This is excellent cheesecake."

"Cheesecake Factory is the best. Haven't you eaten it before?"

"No. I'm not a big dessert person." He took another bite.

She looked at him and tried to smile, just a twitch.

"What's up? Are you worried about me?"

She picked up her coffee and sat, not close enough. "Of course. This is a dangerous predator. It's already killed two people since we've been here, not to mention the baby cows."

He sipped coffee and stared at the fire. He took another bite of cheesecake and set it back on the table. "So, tell me more." He sipped coffee, a freshly ground blend of Mexican and Colombian beans. He knew his coffees.

She looked at him for a moment then looked away. "I was just wondering . . ." She set her coffee on the table and took a small bite of cheesecake. "Mm, that is good, isn't it?"

"You were wondering?"

She thought about it, then, "These people have been dealing with this problem for a long time. I'm sure they must have tried killing these things." She set her fork down and looked hard into him. "Maybe we should take that calf back up there while there's still time."

Kirby looked at his watch and not at that hick's stupid clock. "It's already nine thirty. He said the moon would be up by ten." The hick's clock chimed once. They probably still had time but that would ruin everything. He needed to kill this thing, mount its head on the wall next to that stupid clock, and show this stupid hick who's who.

"Oh, my." She nodded toward the picture window.

Those stupid birds had perched outside on the window ledge, probably getting away from the snow.

His recurring feeling of danger had become too familiar. He went into her office and poured himself another shot.

Chapter Twenty-Two

John Crow sat cross-legged on his Indian rug, nice and soft against the sand floor of his main room, nice and warm in front of his stone fireplace. He ran his fingers across the imprinted Celtic Cross of his new leather-bound Bible, preparing his spirit against the night. As was his practice, he placed the spline on the flat of his rug and let it fall open.

In the Book of Job, Chapter 33, John read Verse 15 aloud, "In dreams, in visions of the night, when deepest sleep falls upon men, while they sleep on their beds, God makes them listen, and his correction strikes them with terror."

"Amen." He closed his new Bible and set it aside.

The woman and the boy had now been exposed to this terror, a terror that struck deep into the hearts of men. Men and, yes, women. They had met the beast. Hopefully, the God of Heaven had already reminded them in dreams.

"God, let it be so." Hopefully, God would remind them again and again. Hopefully, they had both become a part of this place, this sacred valley of wonder.

Not the other, the one called Kirby. He sets himself apart. He follows nothing but those urgings that come from deep within us all, to throw your fists up to the heavens and shout, No!

This Kirby would never follow God's teaching. This man would always do what he wanted, with no regard for others.

Why?

Yes, maybe. For the first time in all the years, John Crow thought he recognized some meaning to it all.

Kidro Potter had been the same as this Kirby, defiant toward the power of this place. Kidro had always thought it belonged to him, but it never had. It belonged to something bigger than all of them, something stronger than John could ever grasp.

Only this one thing seemed clear. As the beast in the Book of Job had been allowed to bring disaster, so, too, was the beast in this valley.

Why would God allow this? Why had He allowed such pain to fall upon Job? John had never before understood the debate in the *Book of Job*. But, here in this place, he finally thought he might. This beast had the power to protect this valley of wonder, this physical evidence of the splendor of God's creation. This Shangri La.

Yes, maybe.

Yosemite had once been a sacred place to John's people. During the past century, Yosemite had suffered the slow death of the white man's civilization. The valley nearest Yosemite had also been sacred. The white man had dammed that sacred valley to create a reservoir and supply water for San Francisco. This sacred valley was all that remained of the once spectacular nature of the High Sierras. Only this sacred valley remained apart from the unintended evils of men.

People here lived long in years and in good health. Jethro and Mary Lou had both lived more than one hundred years, and Jethro had died before his time, in a freak accident caused by Kidro's carelessness.

John wondered how long Willis had lived.

Enough!

The hour was late, time to prepare. He opened his medicine bag and poured out his small stones, chips of bone, and smooth pieces of wood.

AT 10:44 P.M., KIRBY sat in his car with the engine running and the heater on high, trying to get warm. He looked at the half empty bottle of whiskey on the passenger seat, begging him to take a long pull.

He shook his head. "Stay sober, you idiot."

The interior of his father's car had not yet warmed. He hugged himself and rubbed his arms. "What the heck?"

Shaking from the cold, he spun off the cap, let it drop onto the passenger seat, and tilted up the bottle of Canadian Club rye whiskey. He barely let the bottle touch his shaking lips, keeping it clear of his chattering teeth, and poured cold whisky down his throat.

"Yikes!" He'd accidentally spilled cold whiskey on his shirt, trickling down his shivering chest. He yanked the bottle away and spilled whiskey into his crotch.

Even cold, the whiskey felt warmer than his freezing wet pants, socks, and shoes. He wiped his mouth with the back of his hand, recapped the bottle, and set it on the passenger seat next to his propped-up rifle. The butt sat on the floor.

The oak stalk had a nice polish from hand-rubbed linseed oil. It felt hot from the car heater.

"Idiot!"

He slipped off his wet Bruno Magli loafers and put them on the passenger side floor, under the heater outlet and next to the oak stalk of his M-1. He pushed the button and the electric motor and drove his seat all the way back. He lifted his wet pants and stocking feet as high under the dash as he could, close to the driver's side heater outlet, already getting warmer. He'd left the house only ten minutes earlier. With the Bentley heater, the large interior would get toasty, sooner than later.

He turned on the car radio and hit the scan button. The digital frequency numbers flashed through two rotations before stopping.

He opened the center consol and pulled out a CD. He didn't care which one. He pushed it into the slot.

S.O.B by Nathaniel Rateliff and the Night Sweats blasted and he turned it down.

Funny. Kirby knew that his father had had a wide range of tastes, but discovering that he'd liked Nathaniel Rateliff surprised him. He'd liked the Beatles and the Stones, of course, and he'd listened to classical in the office. He turned on the dome light and flipped through the selection. The remaining CDs were either classical or bluegrass. *Bluegrass? And these.* He'd thrown in two Manheim Steamroller albums to impress Carolyn. He turned off the light, closed the console, and settled into his seat.

By the time the Night Sweats hit their second cut, heavy snowfall had completely covered his windshield. The defroster couldn't keep up, not while heating the interior. He hit the wipers and swept it off. *Great.* He could watch falling snow.

One of those stupid birds landed on the hood and looked at him, renewing Kirby's sense of peril.

He tried to ignore the stupid bird but another bird landed next to it, both looking at him. Maybe they wanted to come in and sip whiskey.

"Ha, ha! Good luck with that." *Stupid birds.*

According to that hick's statement, the moon had to be up. He leaned forward to get a better look at the sky. Falling snow prevented seeing anything. *It's got to be up.*

He settled back in his seat and looked at the half empty bottle of whiskey.

"Not now."

"Ah." The car had warmed and his feet felt toasty. He switched all the heat to the windshield and watched the snow melt. The full-power defroster melted snow as quickly as it fell.

"What the . . ." Three more birds settled onto the hood, all five looking at him. His heartbeat quickened and his gut tightened.

Why . . . Maybe they were attracted to the heat from his engine.

The dash clock said 11:28 p.m. It was turning into another long night.

He settled back to get comfortable and his eyes grew heavy, nice and warm.

A bird smacked into his windshield and he bolted forward, wide awake. This one flapped its wings against the glass and pecked at it, rata-tat-tat. It reminded him of that movie, *The Birds,* by Hitchcock, the one he'd watched on TV when he was a kid.

Several more birds had arrived, too many to count, all looking at Kirby.

"What, you want to come in here and have a drink? Get stuffed and roasted."

His stomach twitched with intuitive fear. He looked at the bottle of whiskey.

"No, you idiot! Stay frosty." He needed to kill this thing, whatever it was. He could still win this woman. They'd stay up here during the summer. He'd go fishing with the kid. He'd have access to all that money and he could keep that little lady down in Bridgeport. Mona would make a perfect diversion.

More stupid birds pecked and slapped against his windshield and that sense of danger hammered his chest, coming on so fast.

He forced his thoughts back to Mona. He'd never in his life felt more secure than he'd been with her.

Of all the daddies in the world, why did hers have to be a Marine Corps mountain ops instructor. Those guys were hard-corps Marines. Hard to believe she was so young. Her ripe, firm body, and the way she hungered for his manhood felt more like a thirty-year-old professional.

She'd grow older but they'd still need to hide. Carolyn could never know about her. Mona could get on the pill. Kirby would make sure of that.

Kirby leaned across and found his shoes, dry and warm. He slipped them on and looked outside, all quiet except for the birds, by then too many to count. Most of them were looking at him, flapping or not.

Unexplainable fear tightened his stomach muscles. *Don't cramp.* He shouted, "Get off my car, you stupid birds." Bird poop could damage the finish.

The stupid birds didn't care.

From outside his conscious thoughts, guilt flooded into his mind. His actions toward Carolyn, his drinking, his gambling, his lack of control with Mona. Even after learning her age, he couldn't resist. A slower fear pushed his dread out of the way. For the first time, he admired John Potter's unwavering faith. The very reason Kirby had killed him? *Jealousy, I guess.*

Tears formed in his eyes. "Stop it!" He wiped away the tears and bit down, realizing he needed to clean up his life and plan for a better future. He needed for Carolyn to get on his magic bus. Her infusion of money would bring him back to where he belonged. One or two wins and he could quit for good. Going out a loser didn't compute. *Not my destiny.*

So what if her kid hated him? What did kids know?

Carolyn actually looked better up here than she did in L.A. She and the kid both looked super healthy. They had what he could only describe as an inner glow.

Images of Mona forced their way back in, so white, so tight. His handheld urine dispenser swelled with his heartbeat, getting ready for Mona. He took another sip of whiskey and let it grow. "So what?"

"No, no!" A whisper.

The birds had gone and the snow had stopped. He hadn't noticed when they'd left.

His heartbeat quickened, thumping in his ears.

"What the . . ."

Something moved in the forest above the rise of the driveway. He capped the bottle and set it on the passenger seat, straining forward to see. It might have been snow falling from a tree, bumped by a deer or a cow. *Something.*

"What is that?" Coming closer, something big bumped one of the trees and snow showered off the branches. No mistake that time. Another tree showered snow, coming closer.

Icy pain plunged through Kirby's stomach, a knotting pain that reached his spine with paralyzing fear. He forced his muscles to loosen. He couldn't afford to cramp.

Nathaniel Rateliff and the Night Sweats sang, *No Need to get Old* and Kirby ejected the CD.

Whatever was up in those trees was big, maybe a bear. "Yeah!" Carolyn had mentioned a bear.

"No." *Bears hibernate.*

Don't they?

"Idiot!" Why had he come up to this God forsaken place. He'd never even pretended to be a hero.

Yeah. He needed her money.

There it was again, something big moving through the snow, pushing smaller trees aside, steadily getting closer.

He looked at the whiskey bottle. "No." What good would that do?

He looked into the forest. Whatever was out there looked too big to be a wolf or a mountain lion.

"What am I doing here?"

He'd read how hard grizzlies were to kill, still more than a hundred yards away. Maybe he could get back into the house.

"You idiot." Kirby had told her not to open that door, no matter what.

A few minutes passed and he hadn't seen it again. Maybe it wasn't coming to her house. Maybe it was going someplace else. Maybe his luck had finally changed.

"No." *There it is.* It had stopped in the trees, still more than a hundred yards away. Maybe it was going down to the river.

"Moonlight fishing? You idiot. You nitwit!" He shut off his dash lights. The clock read 11:46.

Whatever was out there could see and smell the fumes rising from his exhaust. He turned off the ignition and sat in the dark, desperately hoping not to be seen. *Stupid.*

In the stillness, he could hear his heart beating.

"What is that?"

Coming out of the trees, a low form plowed slowly through deep snow, not toward the house. It plowed toward Kirby's car, still more than a hundred yards away. The large, dark form was impossible not to see, pushing through white snow.

Kirby checked the dome light switch, making sure the lights wouldn't come on when he opened his car door.

He pressed the handle, opened the door, and pushed it into deep snow, using his shoulder until the opening was wide enough. He stepped out into a foot of cold, wet snow and reached back inside for his rifle. He'd already made sure; it was loaded and ready to shoot. He slid his left arm over the top of the open door and pulled the rifle stalk into his right shoulder, taking aim.

"Wait." Maybe he could blind it. Maybe he could see it better. He leaned back into the car and switched on his headlights.

Idiot. His headlights reflected back into his eyes from high-piled snow. He shut off the headlights and his eyes readjusted to the dark.

That thing stood still, watching from seventy yards out.

Kirby rested his left arm on top of the open door and took aim, lots of time.

Glowing, red eyes stared back into his rifle sight. It stood upright on its hind legs, much taller than Kirby, and definitely not a bear.

Kirby's heart thumped inside his chest and pounded his inner ear. That ache that had speared his stomach and gripped his spine returned with paralyzing pain.

Remembering his Marine Corps training, he took a deep breath, relaxed, wiped sweat from over his eyes, and pulled the rifle tight to his right shoulder, forcing calm. "Easy does it," he whispered. He had plenty of time.

He aimed at the center of its torso, took another deep breath, and let it flow out slowly. He slowly squeezed the trigger with his whole hand. Nothing happened. He squeezed harder. Still nothing.

"Idiot!"

He quickly lowered the rifle, released the safety, and took careful aim again.

The creature stood tall, making itself an easy target.

Kirby slowly exhaled and squeezed with his whole hand. The rifle boomed with a flash of blinding light and kicked hard into his right shoulder.

"Ouch!" It had been a long time since he'd shot a rifle. The hot, ejected shell steamed and sank into fresh snow on the roof of his car.

The large animal fell backward into deep snow.

"Yes!" Kirby could barely hear his joyous shout above the ringing in his ears. He pushed through knee deep snow to the front of his car. The ringing in his ears eased and he coughed, a nervous laugh. *Victory*. His stress and fear had already become a distant memory.

"What the . . ." The exclamatory whisper hissed out from between his teeth.

That thing stood, looking at him with bright red eyes.

Soul-crushing fear nearly drove Kirby to his knees.

Those angry red eyes glared at Kirby, then it dropped onto all fours and plowed snow, rushing toward Kirby sideways, like a large ape or a giant baboon.

Kirby couldn't breathe, searching for words to ask God for help.

Get a grip.

He pressed the rifle firmly into his shoulder and aimed at that thing's huge head, breathed out slowly, plenty of time, and he yanked the trigger.

The rifle boomed, but the creature didn't waver, still charging sideways.

Stupid . . . Kirby sucked breath and aimed more carefully, squeezing steadily.

Boom, flash, ring, and the creature went down.

Kirby had aimed the first shot for its heart. The second must have missed. The third he'd aimed for the head. He lowered his rifle and stepped forward, with that thing only thirty yards away.

"No!"

It stood again, as huge as a Klondike bear.

"What are you?"

THE FIRST GUNSHOT HAD awakened Jason from a restless sleep.

Barnabas jumped from the bed and waited at the door.

Jason dressed quickly, and the second shot sounded.

Barnabas sniffed at the bottom of the bedroom door, growling and scraping, eager to get downstairs. Barnabas knew what that stupid poophead was doing out there, putting them all in danger.

Jason and his mom had already decided to let the sheriff take care of things. His mom should have never invited her know-it-all boss up here to ruin their Christmas. *He's going to ruin everything.*

Jason cracked open the bedroom door and a third shot rang out.

Barnabas tried to force his way through the crack in the door but Jason pressed his knee into his dog's nose. "No, Barnabas. You need to stay here."

Barnabas didn't like it, being such a good soldier and all, but those things were too big, and there were too many of them.

Jason squeezed out, closed his bedroom door, and rushed downstairs into the entry.

Much closer to the house, a fourth shot boomed.

Mom had her ear pressed to the barred front door.

Jason said, "I told him he'd be sorry, the stupid jerk."

Mom looked at him, worried, not angry. She didn't say anything.

"There's more than one and he can't kill them all. Some of them might get into the house. I told him not to . . ." Jason pressed his ear to the door and she held his back tight to her stomach.

A fifth shot rang out, a sixth. Their sound echoed through the forest.

"What are you?" Mr. Kirby sounded close and plenty scared, the big know-it-all.

Jason's fear choked his breathing.

Mom's mouth turned down and tears pooled in her eyes.

Barnabas barked and clawed from upstairs. He could smell those things and they didn't scare him at all. Nothing ever scared Barnabas.

Jason said, "You want Barnabas to come down?"

She didn't answer.

Another shot boomed, echoing through the forest, and Jason pushed away.

The poop-head pounded on the door.

Mom looked like she might do something really stupid.

"No, don't."

The pounding grew louder and Mr. Kirby shouted, "Carolyn, let me in."

She started lifting the bar.

Jason charged in and pulled the bar back down. "No, Mommy. Don't open it."

Tears flowed down her face.

Jason realized he was crying too.

Her lips moved, looking at Jason.

He couldn't hear her words. His heart pounded too loud.

She pushed Jason away, stood between him and the door, lifted the bar, and set it aside.

Jason rushed around her but couldn't stop her. "Don't, Mommy. Don't."

Barnabas barked from upstairs, telling her not to do it.

She turned the latch and opened the door.

The sudden blast of cold air stiffened Jason and he couldn't move.

A large creature climbed the front steps on all fours, something like Jason had never seen, not even at a zoo, not even on the internet. Its angry eyes glowed bright red, looking at Mr. Kirby, not at Jason or his mom. Blood oozed from two holes in its face.

Mr. Kirby backed into a corner of the porch where Jason couldn't see. Only his rifle barrel showed, pointing at the thing. The rifle boomed and bright light flashed from the barrel.

The creature flinched backward then leapt onto the porch, quick as a cat. It stood on its hind legs, much taller than Mr. Kirby, taller even than John Crow.

"Father, is that you?" Mr. Kirby didn't sound scared anymore. The rifle dropped to the porch and Mr. Kirby stepped over it, looking up into the creature's soft, blue eyes.

The creature looked down at Mr. Kirby, like they knew each other. The eyes quicky turned from blue to red, and the creature swiped with long, gleaming claws.

Mr. Kirby's head flew off, hit the open door with a thud, and dropped to the stone floor. His sad, fading eyes looked up at Jason. Dark blood oozed from his severed neck onto the stonework.

Jason's mom screamed in horror at the crunching sound, as the creature tore Mr. Kirby's chest apart. It lowered its head and ripped inside the chest with its teeth. It threw its head up and chewed something from inside the torn open chest. It turned slowly toward them and blood cascaded from its slack jaws.

"God, no!" Mom pushed, trying to close the door, but it wouldn't close.

Jason jumped in to help, pushing with all his might, but the door wouldn't close.

Mr. Kirby's severed head laid in the open doorway. His staring eyes had glazed over like ice.

The thing on the porch whaled into the night, a loud, shrieking, hyena kind of laugh that hurt Jason's ears.

Jason pressed against the door harder, trying to force Mr. Kirby's head out of the way.

A low growl came from outside.

Jason and his mom were violently thrown backward, flying across the living room, staring at each other for what seemed forever. Her eyes filled with of love, saying goodbye.

Jason landed on his shoulder and slid to a stop against the couch.

Mom slammed into the couch and sprawled onto the floor next to him, still looking at each other.

What did John Crow say? Jason remembered. He jumped to his feet and blocked his mom's head from turning, not letting her look, keeping his back toward the entry. "Don't look, Mommy. If you don't look into his eyes, he can't see you."

Jason wanted to look but didn't. He looked instead at the glass angel on top of the Christmas tree.

Behind him, claws scraped against the stone steps, climbing down into the living room.

Lord Jesus. Jason's voice didn't work, only his inside voice.

Barnabas howled and clawed from upstairs, their new clock chimed twelve times, and Jason found words. "Look at the glass angel, Mommy. Pray to Jesus to keep us safe."

A cold blast swept into the room from the open front door and Jason turned slowly, looking down at the floor, not daring to look into its eyes. It had gone.

Chapter Twenty-Three

It took Ellen Winslow until late January to finally convince herself to drive all the way up to her grandson's frozen wilderness. What that handsome, older man called River Road had snow piled high on both sides, but the pavement was smooth and dry.

That older man, what was his name? His coffee tasted good, waiting to get her car filled up. The cookies tasted okay, nothing to brag about. But that gentleman was certainly nice, refusing to let her pay. He was cute, too. She wondered if he was single.

Stupid thought.

She took one last drag and stuffed her cigarette into the ashtray, so full she could barely get it in there. She hoped it would go out, still smoldering a little. She rounded a curve and saw the dead-end that nice gentleman had described. The giant rocks were a quarter of a mile away.

She stopped in the middle of the road and wrestled with the ashtray, pulling it out. She opened her car door and emptied the ashtray onto the road.

"Oops." Her last cigarette was still burning. *Oh, well.*

She tapped the ashtray on the pavement, getting all of the tightly jammed butts out of the bottom. She closed her car door, put the ashtray back, pushed in the cigarette lighter, and dug into her purse for another cigarette.

"Not now!" A pickup truck was coming down the road behind her. She accelerated away from the scene of her crime, the lighter popped out, and she lit her cigarette. She reached the dead-end and turned into her grandson's driveway. There stood the big rock described by that handsome gentleman. "Potter Ranch" had been very professionally chiseled into the natural flat face on the giant boulder.

The driveway looked like real cobblestones, and in good condition, everything the way he'd described it. She drove over the crest and downhill toward the house, more beautiful than her daughter's descriptions. The cleared driveway circled down by a beautiful barn and back up to the house, where a parked car had been buried by snow. She parked in front of the snowbound car and opened her car door.

A faint sound of thunder mingled with the sound of rushing water, not too close. The thunder grew closer and louder, and a giant black horse rounded the corner of the garage at a full run.

Jason sat on the horse, leaning forward in the saddle.

Ellen pressed into the side of her car and the wind from their passing lifted her skirt.

Coming right behind, Carolyn rushed past on another horse, leaning forward, riding hard. Both horses ran through the open door and disappeared into the barn.

That filthy mutt charged around the corner, tongue hanging out the side of his face, and plowed into Ellen's legs, saying hello, jumping up with his dirty paws.

"Get away from me, you . . ."

Ellen brushed herself off and walked toward the barn, not knowing what else to do. A moment later, Carolyn exited the barn and hurried to meet her. Luckily, the mutt went into the barn to be with her grandson.

"Hi Mom. We're so glad you could make it." Carolyn took her arm and turned her back toward the house. "Jason will be up in a few minutes. He's helping John feed and curry the horses."

"John?"

"John Crow. He lives up near the waterfall." Carolyn pointed up the hill, in the direction from where they'd come with their horses. "John's been taking care of this ranch since Jason's granddad was a baby."

"Whose car is this?" She could see a little of the Bentley chrome on the front.

"That was Tom Kirby's car."

"Oh? Is he here, too?" Ellen hoped so. She opened her trunk, handed Carolyn Jason's Christmas present, pulled out her suitcase, and closed her trunk.

That question seemed to bother her daughter.

"Is he here?"

Carolyn didn't smile. "Yes, and no."

"Yes, and no?"

"He got himself tangled up with some local business and now he's buried behind the barn."

"What?"

"Yes. I called down to the office the day after Christmas." Carolyn led her into the house and Ellen dropped her suitcase on the floor, overwhelmed by the warmth and beauty of the place.

Carolyn closed the front door, set Jason's present on a table in the entry, picked up Ellen's suitcase, and led her upstairs. She said, "The office called me back a few hours later and said there was no will and that they found several irregularities with the way Tom was running the company. It seems I own some stock from an investment my husband made. They're drafting a proposal for me to consider buying a controlling interest in the company."

"What?" Ellen followed her daughter into a nice room at the top of the stairs, with a king-size bed.

"This room belonged to Jason's uncle. He died about ten years ago; not in here, of course." Carolyn set the suitcase on a bench at the foot of the bed and turned toward Ellen, expecting something.

Ellen allowed a brief hug, then Carolyn crossed the room and opened a curtain, where a set of French doors led to a small balcony. "If you need to smoke, please do it out here. The smell of smoke is hard to get rid of."

"What?"

That mutt came charging in, nibbling at Ellen's hand.

"Get away, you . . ."

"Let's go downstairs. Jason's back."

Ellen followed her daughter and the mutt downstairs, where Jason had already torn open his present. *Of course.* Her daughter had robbed her from seeing that.

"Thanks, Grandma." Jason set the telescope on the table and rushed to hug her.

"You're welcome. Merry Christmas." She stroked the back of his head. His hair had grown longer.

"Oh, Mom," said Carolyn. "That looks like an expensive one. You shouldn't have."

"I waited until after Christmas. It was on sale at a very good price." Speaking to Jason, she said, "There's a full moon tonight and not a cloud in the sky. Let's go set it up, so we can count craters on the moon."

Jason looked at Carolyn, thinking about it.

She seemed to have the same thought. Maybe they had some sick, private joke.

Finally, Jason said, "Not tonight, Grandma. I like it better when the moon's not all the way full."

THE END

Don't miss out!

Visit the website below and you can sign up to receive emails whenever Thomas Holladay publishes a new book. There's no charge and no obligation.

https://books2read.com/r/B-A-ZAQM-ZNMMB

BOOKS 2 READ

Connecting independent readers to independent writers.

Also by Thomas Holladay

The American Way
Deliberate Justice
Pursuit: The American Way

Standalone
Treasure
The Birthday Box
Meadowlarks
COMES THE CALL: For God and Country

Watch for more at www.thomas-holladay.com.

About the Author

Thomas Holladay writes from a Christian conservative world view, never preachy, never teach-me, always clean, almost never sweet. He creates riveting images through the senses of his vividly drawn characters to create fast-paced action, drama, and suspense that make his stories hard to put down. Read more at Thomas Holladay's site.

Read more at www.thomas-holladay.com.

www.ingramcontent.com/pod-product-compliance
Lightning Source LLC
Chambersburg PA
CBHW022206010726
47493CB00002B/442